"Liar! I saw him kissing you.

"He's in this ugly plot with you, is that it? Tell me the truth, for once, or I'll—"

"Do what?" she sobbed. *"Maul and abuse me, as your filthy cousin did? Go on then! I might know you're no better than he, to treat a lady so, when—"*

"Lady, is it?" He laughed harshly. *"Harlot, more like! A scheming baggage who seeks to steal that to which she has no right! A conniving . . . cheating . . ."* He had drawn her very close now, and the rageful words were uttered just a breath from her lips. They faded into silence. Desire came into his eyes. Farrar's lips closed over hers. . . .

LOVE ALTERS NOT

by Patricia Veryan

Book IV of
"The Golden Chronicles"

FAWCETT CREST • NEW YORK

A Fawcett Crest Book
Published by Ballantine Books
Copyright © 1987 by Patricia Veryan

Library of Congress Catalog Card Number: 87-16268

ISBN 0-449-21665-9

This edition published by arrangement with St. Martin's Press, Inc.

Manufactured in the United States of America

First Ballantine Books Edition: June 1989

For David

Love alters not with his brief hours and weeks,
But bears it out even to the edge of doom.

WILLIAM SHAKESPEARE
Sonnet 116

✆ Chapter 1 ✆

In the year of grace 1529, Muse Manor was an old house in the North Downs, some miles northwest of Basingstoke, its considerable charms embellished by two square miles of lush farmland, together with a Home Farm and a quaint village. Sir Isaac Cranford, having done remarkably well as a privateer, had married the lady previously denied him by reason of his lack of fortune, and had purchased the property for his country seat. His lady rewarded him with seven healthy children and, when the time came for him to go to his next, and it is to be hoped, heavenly abode, he did so secure in the knowledge that he left behind a firm foundation upon which his heirs could build a great dynasty.

Times, alas, were hard, and the dynasty did not materialize. Despite careful management, the fortune began to dwindle. The hunting box went in 1643, and in 1677, the great house in Town had to be sold. The Cranfords counted themselves fortunate to make the country house their permanent abode. And still prospects did not improve. Through the march of years, the fortune shrank and shrank and with it, acre by acre, the estate.

In 1733, John Cranford, the current head of the family, was driven to seek gainful employment. A loving husband and devoted father, it was his desire that his twin sons attend University, and his little daughter have a respectable dowry, that led him, with deep inner reluctance, to accept a promising post with the East India Company. Mr. Cranford was blessed with a fond and unselfish wife, Joanna, who refused to be parted from him. However, the terrible mortality rate among English children dwelling in India was well known to the Cranfords, so they

1

placed their offspring in the care of Joanna's unmarried sister, until the three should reach an age when it would be possible to send for them.

The parting of the little family was wrenching, but it was destined to be a much longer separation than any of them knew. Four months later word came that, having survived such dangers as a great storm in the Bay of Biscay and the desert journey across Egypt to Suez, the Cranfords had boarded another vessel bound for Calcutta. They never reached that fabled city. In the Hooghly River their ship fell victim to the terrible James and Mary Sandbank and was lost, leaving no survivors.

The Cranford children were devastated by their great loss, but that grief was succeeded by another threatened peril. Piers and Peregrine were twelve at the time, and their sister, Dimity, eight. The twins and the little girl were devoted to each other and dreaded that they might be separated. Their father, however, had done all in his power to provide for such a tragic contingency, with the result that by practicing strict economies they were able to continue to live together in the home they loved. The looming expenses for which poor John Cranford had been striving to provide were met in part by their great-uncle, General Lord Nugent Cranford who, moved by their bereavement, offered to pay for the boys' education. Their aunt, Miss Jane Guild, faithfully kept her trust through the years, managing in a bewildered but not unhappy state to cope with her two madcap nephews and the niece who, having grown up with her brothers and their friends, was an incorrigible tomboy.

Time works changes, however, and on a stormy August afternoon in 1746, the girl who stood in the entry hall of the old house would not by any stretch of the imagination have been judged a tomboy. At one and twenty, Dimity was a tall and shapely creature, with warm brown hair and long, slightly slanting hazel eyes. Despite her sad lack of a dowry, and although she was held by some to lack the gentle timidity a lady would welcome in her daughter-in-law, Dimity would have been wed long since, save for two stumbling blocks, the first being that she had yet to meet the man to whom she could give her heart, and the second that—with one exception—the twins had yet to meet a man they judged worthy of her.

Scanning her now, a slight frown in his blue eyes, Piers was

2

uneasy at the thought of leaving the Manor. Charles Stuart's short-lived attempt to wrest the throne from German George of Hanover had ended in bitter tragedy. Those Jacobites who had escaped the slaughter on Culloden Field were running for their lives, hunted to their deaths like animals. They were desperate men, poor devils, and rumour had it there was a fugitive in the vicinity. Dimity did not realize how desirable she was— especially in that simple cream gown with the wide skirts all ruched, or whatever the women called it, and the pale green ribands that threaded the lace at her generous bosom. Still, the servants were loyal, and it was foolish to worry. Even in his weakened condition, Perry would die sooner than—

"Piers," said Dimity, looking up into his handsome countenance anxiously, " 'Tis a dreadful day. Only listen to that wind. *Must* you go?"

He patted her hand. "An 'twas not important, you may believe I'd stay. But I promised old Baites I would discuss the sale of the river parcel with him tomorrow."

"I suppose," she said with a smothered sigh, "we have to sell?"

"Regrettably, yes. Unless I become a highly paid Ambassador to Versailles," he slanted an oblique glance at her, "or you choose to become Lady Glendenning." The immediate lowering of her lashes and the flood of colour to her smooth cheeks told their own story, and he went on lightly, "Never heed my teasing, m'dear. I know poor Tio is quite out of the running. Until you change your mind, at least." At this deliberate provocation her head came up indignantly, but before she could retaliate he glanced to the stairs and his expression became grave. "Mitten, you must see to it that Perry rests. No matter what he promises, he means to keep struggling with that stupid new foot, and—"

"He cannot struggle with it now, dear, because I've tucked it in the drawer, and since he's managed to strain the other ankle he will be quite laid by the heels for—" And she bit her lip, irritated by those inappropriate words.

A little over a year ago the twins had gone off together, full of patriotic zeal, to defend the realm against the Jacobites. During the Battle of Prestonpans, in a desperate attempt to keep deserters from driving a gun carriage from the field, Peregrine

3

had sprung in front of it, sabre drawn. The gun crew, convinced that to fight on was sure death, had not halted. At the very last instant, Peregrine had leapt for his life, but he'd stumbled over some obstacle and the heavy wheel had rolled over his right foot. The English force had suffered an ignominious defeat and fled for their lives. Disregarding his own peril, Piers had refused to join that frantic retreat and had searched through the carnage for his twin. He had found Peregrine close to death from shock and loss of blood, and carried him from the field. Only Piers' dogged determination had enabled them, two harrowing days later, to win to safety with their own people, and acquire the help of a surgeon. The foot was hopelessly crushed and, under cruelly adverse conditions, had been amputated. Piers had never told Dimity of his agonized conviction that Perry would not survive that crude surgery, much less live another week, but somehow the indomitable Peregrine *had* survived and although the thread of life had all too often been frail indeed, was still surviving.

Piers was not one to brood over past horrors, and thus was able to direct a twinkle at his sister and ask whimsically, "Slip of the tongue, love?"

"Sometimes," she shook her head ruefully, "it seems that everything I say is a reminder to him. How I can be so clumsy . . ."

"Nonsense. He's done splendidly these eleven months. You've done splendidly too, but as you start maudling over him, Perry will really comb you out."

"Yes, bless him. He's all pluck. But—when I think of how he has suffered! And that wretched Farrar—home, scot-free!"

Piers stiffened. "Not for long," he growled. "The man's an outcast, and God help him when he's hauled up before court-martial!"

"He should have been brought to book months ago! They've likely forgot all about it by this time."

"I doubt that. He's home on medical leave, merely. But even should he escape retribution, what kind of life has he? According to that Parker fellow who came to see us, not a club will admit him. No decent gentleman would so much as look his way, and he's cut everywhere he dares show his face. Egad! I'd sooner be old Perry doing the hop than Tony Farrar hale and

4

hearty any day!'' He took her by the shoulders. ''Enough of the yellow dog. With luck I shall be back from Town inside a week. All you've to do, Mitten, is keep Aunt Jane from driving my twin into the boughs. And be sure you do not accept half a dozen offers whilst I am gone!''

He gave her a brotherly buss on the forehead, and Dimity watched him clap the tricorne on his thick brown hair, now neatly powdered and tied back with a black riband. He turned at the foot of the steps, to wave to her, tall and well built, his white grin flashing, the wind blowing his cloak. Then he swung into the saddle of his rawboned bay horse, and went riding off through the blustery afternoon.

Closing the front door, Dimity walked across the hall to the stairs, wondering why she had such an oppressive sense of impending disaster. There was, however, no visible trace of her worries when she went into Peregrine's bedchamber.

Aunt Jane, wearing a particularly hideous shawl that she had knitted from a collection of odd scraps of wool, sat beside the bed reading aloud. She held the book very close to her nose, for Jane Guild was rather shortsighted, and her voice droned on in a singsong way that was devoid of expression. She was a plump, plain, good-natured woman, placid of disposition and having a complete lack of imagination that had stood her in good stead through some of the boys' more hair-raising adventures.

Peregrine, a finer-drawn replica of his brother, lay propped by several pillows, his curly brown hair rumpled and the blue eyes rebellious in the worn young face.

''. . . is the part of a wise man,'' read Jane Guild, her thoughts on the chicken that must go in the oven within another half-hour, ''to keep himself today for tomorrow, and not venture all his eggs in one basket.''

''Well, that settles it!'' exclaimed Peregrine, indignant. ''The fella's betwattled! Not a minute ago, Aunty, you was reading something about people getting scratched if they play with cats, and now the nincompoop's jibbering about eggs and baskets! What the deuce is he talking about?''

His aunt lowered the book and blinked at him. She loved all ''her children,'' as she called them, but if there was an especially soft spot in her heart, it was for this tall, intense boy, with his quicksilver changes of mood and fast-flaring temper, his

5

ready laugh and warm heart, and the unruly curls and fine-boned features that made him as handsome—almost—as had been his dear father. "Why, I am not quite sure, Perry," she confessed. "But I expect you should not refer to Mr. Cervantes as 'betwattled' for he has quite a reputation, you know. And speaking of eggs, I really must go and put the bird on. 'Tis Cook's day off, and with this weather blowing up she'll likely decide to stay at her daughter's in Hungerford and not come back until morning. Shall you be all right?"

She stood, shook out her voluminous skirts, and bent over to straighten his pillows and pat his pale cheek anxiously.

Quite aware of her devotion, Peregrine seized her by both ears and pulled her down to bestow a smacking kiss on the end of her nose. "Yes, thank you. Now take yourself out of a gentleman's bedchamber before all the boys know what a shameless jade you are!"

"I cannot think they would believe that of me," she said solemnly, resting the book on his middle while she carefully straightened her neat cap. "However, I will leave Mr. Cervantes here so that you may look up that bit about the cats. I must confess I don't even recall reading—Oh, here you are, Dimity. There now, your sister can find it for you, dearest." She wandered out, beaming at her niece, her plump countenance a little flushed as it always was when she was kissed.

Dimity walked over to the bed. Peregrine made a wry face at her. She took up the book and he said in low-voiced warning, "Do not dare!"

She chuckled and, drawing the chair closer, sat down. "Ungrateful wretch! How do you go on?"

"Jolly good. Where's my blasted new foot?"

"Put away where you cannot reach it! No, do not rail at me, Perry. The doctor said 'gently does it.' If you would give yourself time, 'twould not be so painful for—"

"Oh, fustian! Do I not get used to the stupid thing now, I'll never master it. Hand it over and let me try if I cannot—"

"I shall do no such thing! Yesterday you failed to adjust the straps properly, which is why you fell over and sprained your ankle!"

" 'Tis not sprained," he said defensively, but he was tired, and now to have his left ankle aching so miserably seemed confoundedly unjust.

Dimity saw the briefly defeated look and said swiftly, "I wish you will not make it difficult for me, dearest. Piers left strict instructions I was to take care of you." She sighed. "And you are such an impatient patient."

"Humdudgeon!" he snorted, at once firing up. " 'Tis nigh a year since Prestonpans, yet here I lie, meek as any lamb, allowing you all to bully me about and—and maudle over me, when I should be up and, er—" A guilty look crept into the angelic blue eyes. He was fully cognizant of how they had feared for his life when pneumonia had struck a month after the amputation, and again in May, when he had fallen on a wet London flagway. Their love and devotion had meant more to him than he would ever be able to express, and he added gruffly, "Not that I ain't grateful. I know what a curst nuisance I've been."

"Quite so. Monstrous selfish, too," she agreed, twinkling at him as she set the book aside. "But I am the one shall be blamed are you not fully recovered by the time Piers comes home. He will likely expect you to race him to The Teacup, as you and Tio used to do."

As she had hoped, he brightened. "Jove, but those were the days!" He sighed nostalgically and after a moment asked, "You, ah, have heard nought of Tio, I collect?"

It was a shade too nonchalant, and reinforced her own fears. "Not for a month and more," she answered. "I was sure he would come on your birthday, especially since he had promised to be here."

They exchanged sober glances.

Worried, Dimity asked, "Is it really true, Perry? He is Catholic, I know, but he always has been so fiercely patriotic, for all that he laughs at any show of it."

"Not all Catholics were for Charles Stuart, any more than all who fought for him were of that faith. Some simply disliked German George and felt Britain would be better served with a Scot on the throne."

Her unease deepened. "Good God! Do you say that Tio *was* out with Prince Charlie?"

Her brother, who knew very well that Horatio Clement Laindon, Viscount Glendenning, had borne arms against his sovereign, looked at her steadily through a brief silence.

She was appalled and said slowly, "Whatever would you have done had you faced him on the battlefield? Oh, how dreadful it all is! I am so very fond of Tio, but when I think of how cruelly you have suffered this past—"

"Oh, have done," he intervened, flushing. "I came off easy compared to some. You'll recall Aynsworth? He was with us up there y'know, and still carries a musket ball in his shoulder that they've tried to dig out many times without success and that properly gives him fits, I hear. If I was mauled, 'twas only because I was too clumsy to get my silly foot clear in time."

"True," she agreed, "but I was about to say that—in view of your vastly overrated exploits—"

He grinned. "Vixen!"

"—are you," she went on, "in favour of the Duke of Cumberland's methods for putting down the clans?"

The humour fled from his thin face, and his reply was so explicit that she clapped her hands over her ears. "Perry!"

He turned a smouldering gaze on her. "I'll say this, Mitten, if only half what I've heard is truth and I'd been up there to see it—been *ordered* to perpetrate such—" His fists clenched. "By God, but I would be damned first! And so would my brother!"

His voice had risen. She glanced to the door. "Have a care, love! I was sure you would feel so, but—if *you* do, certainly Tio must! Truly, I worry for him. He always has been so close to us, more another brother than a distant cousin. You do not suppose . . ." She hesitated, reluctant to put her thought into words.

He lifted himself to one elbow and looked at her narrowly. "*Have* you heard something of the maggot-wit?"

"No, but . . . the dragoons are beating the whole countryside, and I wondered—Perry, it is not—it could not be that—that Tio is the fugitive rebel they hunt down?"

"God forbid! And he is not, so never fret."

She caught her breath and half-whispered, "How do *you* know?"

Peregrine lay back again. "Never you mind, my girl," he said.

8

The storm, which had been drifting about all day, eased off during the evening, although it continued to rain with steady persistence. Dimity's slumbers were restless, and she awoke, heart pounding, from a nightmare in which she wore Scots plaid and Butcher Cumberland and a whole regiment of dragoons were chasing her, brandishing bayonetted muskets, their bloodthirsty howls drawing ever closer. She sighed with relief to find herself safely in the dear, familiar room, then jumped as a great gust of wind shook the house and sent rain lashing against the windows. Her mouth felt like parchment. She reached for the pitcher, but South, the rather irascible woman who served as abigail to both herself and Aunt Jane, had neglected to fill it. Grumbling, Dimity settled down again, reluctant to ring for South, who would undoubtedly clump down the stairs so loudly she'd wake Perry. It was no use, however; her throat was a desert, and at last she turned up the wick on her bedside lamp, slid her feet into cold slippers and, shivering, tied her dressing gown about her.

She lit a candle from the lamp, and went quietly into the hall. At once it became apparent that she need not have hesitated to ring for South. The wind was a gale, the rain hissed and rattled, and far off she heard the threatening growl of thunder. Even had the abigail complained all the way from the attic, she would scarce have been like to disturb Peregrine. But there was no point in calling her at this stage, and Dimity went downstairs, across the hall, and into the corridor beyond the dining room that led to the kitchen, and Cook's quarters.

Thunder rumbled as she opened the door. An unexpectedly cold gust of air blew out her candle, and she knew with terrifying certainty that she was not alone.

Her heart seemed to stop beating. She stood motionless in the pitchy darkness, longing to run, yet with her feet having seemingly taken root. Another gust blew the curtains over the pump and she could hear them flapping about. The window must stand wide! Gradually, she detected the sound of heavy breathing. Perhaps, if she fainted, he would not cut her throat. But she was too stiff with fear to faint. "Piers!" she screamed silently. But even had her vocal chords obeyed her will, Piers was now half-way to London.

By the glare of distant lightning, she saw the faint gleam of Cook's meat chopper. She made a grab for it as a muffled and incoherent mumbling apprised her of the fact that the intruder was definitely male, and probably intoxicated. She swung the chopper high, but almost dropped it with fright when a violent sneeze was roared from only a few paces distant. Somehow, the plebeian sound reassured her a little.

"Wh-Who's . . . th-there?" she quavered. There came a sound of shuffling movements and she added in a near shriek, "Stay back! I am armed!"

"M-Miss Dimity?"

The voice was vaguely familiar. At least he knew her. Still clutching the chopper, she said, "Yes. Who are you?"

"Samuels, miss. Lord Horatio's head groom."

Inexpressibly relieved, she gulped, "Oh! If you but *knew* how you startled me!" She put down the chopper and groped her way to the window. Raindrops sprinkled her face as she closed the casement. She called, "There's a tinder box on the mantel by the stove."

She heard him fumbling. He awoke a flame, and she crossed to re-light her candle and held it up, peering at him.

Samuels, a sturdy man in his late thirties, usually very neat of person, was barely recognizable. His hat was gone; his wig, a sodden mass, straggled untidily about his face; his clothing was soaked and muddy, and he shook violently, his teeth chattering as he eyed her in apparent anguish.

Fear knifed through her. "Dear, oh dear! Whatever is it? No—first, come and sit down, poor soul. I'll wake the servants and get you some dry clothing."

"No!" He croaked the word, swayed, and groped drunkenly for the table.

Dimity ran to pull out a chair and guide his sagging form into it.

"Your brother. Mr. Peregrine . . . Please, miss—call him."

"I cannot. He is ill." She started for the door, only to again be checked by his feeble demand that she not summon help.

"I must get back," he gasped, shivering. " 'Tis . . . If

I . . ." he broke into a racking spell of coughing, and sagged over the table, white and spent.

Dimity hurried to feel his forehead. It was hot and dry, although he shivered convulsively. Again, he mumbled a request for Peregrine, and she promised soothingly to call her brother if he did as she bade him. She managed to get him to his feet. He leaned on her heavily, and she guided him into Cook's room beyond the pantry. He unfastened his dripping cloak, then all but fell onto the bed. Dimity pulled off his boots, and at last had him under the covers.

Slightly winded, she knelt beside him. "Now," she said urgently, "tell me quickly, Samuels. Is it Lord Horatio?"

The groom moaned and muttered distractedly, but at last seemed to acknowledge his own helplessness. "Your brothers, miss," he said hoarsely. "They fought for the king . . ."

"They know Glendenning is in sympathy with the Jacobites," she put in, trying to control her impatience. "What has happened to his lordship?"

He bit his lip in an agony of indecision. "He'll have my ears for involving you . . . but . . . Gawd! I don't know what to do for the best."

Yearning to strangle him, she patted his hand kindly. "You have done your best. Have you been riding all night?"

"Waiting," he groaned. "His lordship went out to help a poor Jacobite gentleman who'd been hounded as far as Silchester and was too weak to keep on."

She felt chilled as her worst fears were realized. "When was this?"

"Two days since, Miss Dimity." He clutched at her wrist frantically. "He should've been home within *hours*! The troopers are thick throughout the Downland, and—Miss, I'm that *scared*!"

"This Jacobite he was to help," she said, holding his shaking hand tightly. "Is he of extreme importance? I think I never have heard of so determined an effort to take a rebel."

"He is—" he coughed again, then gasped out, "of *great* importance. And if they've took his lordship, his head will be on Temple Bar before—"

Her heart quailing to that terrible apprehension, she cried,

11

"Hush! Do not even think so terrible a thing! Now, tell me, did you go to Silchester?"

"Couldn't get nowhere near it! Troopers everywhere. Milord said if anything went wrong, he'd make for The Teacup. He thought your brother might help was he in dire straits. But—I've been waiting there since last night, with never a sight of him. I began to think perhaps he'd slipped past me and come here, and—and then I started to feel poorly, so . . ."

"So you came to us. Just as you should. Very well, I will wake my brother and he will send help to his lordship. Sleep now, and try not to worry." She smiled kindly, tucked the blankets closer around his chin, and went out, closing the door on his broken expressions of gratitude.

In the kitchen, she stood motionless. Horatio Glendenning was indeed more than a distant cousin to them all. A blithe, good-natured young man, he had seemed from boyhood to prefer their simple home to the vast estates to which he was heir. Her earliest memories included him: laughter, companionship, happy expeditions, growing up—and Tio. Dear Tio. . . . He was so much in love with her. And he was the man her brothers hoped she would marry. Certainly, such a union would solve all their financial woes. Only . . . it was childish of course, but she clung to a wistful longing to lose her heart to the man she would marry. The viscount was good-looking, brave, honourable, and deeply devoted, and she loved him as one loves an old and dear friend. Not as a husband. With equal certainty she knew that if any one of the Cranfords was in trouble, Glendenning would not hesitate for an instant to risk his life in their behalf. No less must be done for him.

She hurried into the hall only to hesitate again by the dining room door. Her first impulse had been to ask Peregrine to send some of the men out to search, but she saw now that it would not do. Perry was as reckless as he was brave. He would be out of bed if he had to crawl, strap on that wretched artificial foot and rush off, likely breaking his neck this time, rather than turning his ankle.

Distraught, she turned back toward the kitchen. But to go out to the coach-house, over which dwelt the grooms, seemed even less satisfactory. If she asked Sudbury, the head groom who also served as coachman, he would volunteer without an instant of

12

hesitation. So would young Peale, the under-groom; or Billy, the stableboy; or Peddars, their solitary footman. Only—Tio, bless him, was deep in Jacobite trouble, which was treason. And the penalty for aiding a traitor—especially a fugitive "of great importance"—was death in its most hideous form. One did not ask one's servants to take such dreadful risks.

And yet—what else was she to do? Unless . . .

The rain eased at about two o'clock, but although it no longer poured down, the fall was steady and, with the continuing flashes of brilliant lightning and the distant growling of thunder, gave every indication of becoming a torrent again at any moment. The sudden deep depression, known as The Teacup, was overgrown with trees and shrubs which afforded some shelter from the elements. Having tethered Odin to a tree, Dimity pulled her fur-lined hood and cloak tighter about her, and shivered. She had been able to gather some medical supplies and slip out of the house without difficulty. Her attempt to saddle and harness Odin had been less successful. She had chosen the big bay in case Tio needed a fast animal, but the horse, Perry's favourite, was a horrid creature and had rolled his eyes and pranced about in such a ridiculously ungodlike way that she had expected Sudbury to come down at any minute. Fortunately, she was tall and strong and, having grown up with two brothers who considered that any well-bred person must know how to care for his own horse, she was not inexperienced in such matters and had at last led the bay out to the mounting block without having roused the grooms.

Odin snorted and sidled nervously. Dimity patted his neck, peering about her. For a lady to ride alone at night was shocking. When her brothers learned of this episode, she would be in for a proper scold. But if she was able to help Tio they would be proud of her, no matter how they might grumble. On the other hand, if she was caught by the military . . . She shuddered. That did not bear thinking of.

A howling gust snatched the hood from her head. Thunder rumbled, but it seemed she had heard sharper sounds just before the peal. Had it been gunfire? Was that a shout? Or was her overwrought imagination at work and the sounds only some of

13

the many voices of the storm? It was silly to worry so. Tio was indestructible. She restored her hood, smiling faintly as she recalled some of the wild pranks the three young men had revelled in during their eventful school years.

A sudden thunder of hoofs. A dark shape rushing straight at her. Odin neighed and reared up in fright. The oncoming animal shied wildly. The rider hurtled from the saddle and lay unmoving, his horse galloping off into the darkness.

With a shocked cry, Dimity ran forward. She thought, ' 'Tis likely just a soldier . . .' But as she bent above that sprawled form the lightning revealed a hatless head, the drenched, unpowdered hair showing darkly red, and she knew she had found the man she sought.

"Tio," she cried frantically, dropping to her knees beside him. "Please, *please* do not be dead!"

"Wouldn't dream . . . of it," came the faint response. He stirred, but so feebly that her anxiety deepened.

"It's me," she said foolishly. "Tio dear, are you hurt?"

"Not badly." He sounded very tired. "Just a—musket ball, where 'twill do the least . . . damage."

Horrified, she demanded, "Where?"

"My . . . head."

She turned his head very gently and, her eyes having become accustomed to the darkness, saw that the left side of his face was all blood. She bit her lip, blinded by sudden tears. Then she scrambled up, ran to Odin and unbuckled the saddlebags. Thank God she had brought linen strips and a small flask of brandy. She flew back to Glendenning. He had not moved, and lay still and helpless in the mud, the rain falling lightly on him.

She had to call him twice before he answered. "I have brought brandy. Can you take some?"

"No time," he said faintly. "Must get on." He began to struggle to sit up. "Mustn't be . . . caught . . . ."

She propped him with all her young strength, but he sagged, his head rolling on her shoulder. "Can't," he groaned. "Dammitall! Perry, you shall have to . . . go, old fellow. Sorry. But— I'm done."

Her heart contracting, she thought, 'Oh, God! Is he dying?'

and said, chokingly, "Tio, I will bind your poor head, and we—"

Distant shouts were borne on the wind. Glendenning tensed. "They're—damned determined . . . lot," he gasped. "Perry, I—I carry the—the fourth stanza of that . . . blasted cypher. You must know all England's . . . searching for't. Found . . . courier just 'fore he . . . turned up his toes, poor chap. Gave me his—his damned message. You—you take it."

The shouts were nearer. Her blood beginning to run cold with terror of rope and axe, Dimity whispered, "Yes, yes. But we must get to the house. We can hide you if only—"

"No, I tell you!" One hand came up to clutch the edge of her cloak. "Dreadful to—ask, I know. Wouldn't put you in—in such a fix, but . . . life and death. Many deaths. Please . . . you—take it. For—for old times' sake, Perry . . ."

He was thrusting something at her and she felt the texture of parchment against her palm. His head rolled helplessly. His well-built, once powerful body was so limp. She sobbed, "Tio! My dear God! Tio—*where* am I to take it? To whom must I give it?"

As if with a tremendous effort he began to whisper something, and she bent closer, struggling to catch the words through the howl of the wind and the terrifyingly clear sounds of the riders.

"Decimus Green . . . All . . . Near Romsey. He'll know—" He shoved a purse at her. "You may need . . . this."

"Yes, dear. But—Tio, oh *please* wake up! Tio—*where*?"

His voice almost inaudible, he panted, "Fair . . . Decimus . . . All—all . . ." and he slumped and lay very still and heavy in her arms.

She knelt there, her head bowed over his unresponsive, so terribly marred face, and wept heartbrokenly.

"I tell you 'twas *this* way! In that last big flash I saw him head fer them trees!"

Another second or two and they would be found. If dear Tio was not dead, they would take him and hack off his arms and legs before a mindless mob, and—She shrank, sickened. Not Tio! They must not perpetrate their atrocities on this dear, gallant man! She let him slide as gently as she could, pushed the flask under one limp hand, and jumped up, tucking into her bodice the little scrap of parchment that was death. Running,

15

dashing tears away, she untied Odin, dragged herself into the saddle with a strength born of panic, and reined him around.

In the bright flash of lightning she saw that they were almost upon her. She rode out with no attempt at concealment.

Someone howled exultantly, *"There he goes!* After him, men!"

A musket barked, shatteringly. Half fainting with fright, Dimity rammed home her dainty spurs.

Odin was affronted. The master knew very well there was no cause to resort to such methods to get him to run. If this puny woman-thing on his back wanted speed, by hoof and hock he would show her! He gathered his mighty muscles and went like a black streak across the night, Dimity clinging desperately to the pommel with one hand, and the troopers following, firing occasionally when the lightning granted them a sight of the flying cloak and big horse of their valuable quarry.

❦ *Chapter 2* ❧

They were so close now that Dimity knew she would be shot at any moment, and the muscles of her back seemed to twist into knots as she crouched over Odin's mane, waiting for the bullet that would strike her down. From the snatches of conversation she'd overheard when her brothers and their friends spoke of the war, she knew it was a variable sensation: some men suffered a great shock, followed by a temporary numbness, and others apparently experienced immediate and overmastering pain. She thought she would prefer the former. At least then, one would know one had been hit, but there would be a space in which to prepare for the following anguish.

The wind buffeted her; the rain was driving hard, making it difficult to see even when the lurid lamp of the lightning lit the sky. Above the great bumping peals of thunder and the pound of hooves, she heard the occasional crack of gunfire, and each time gave a small cry and huddled lower. Odin swept like a juggernaut through the blackness. She wondered if he could see where he was treading, or if he was just running blind. And he should fall . . . The shot sounded farther away. She wrenched her head around and could no longer discern the darker pursuing shapes against the sky. 'Glory, glory!' she thought, and it came to her that the brutes had likely been chasing poor Tio all night, whereas Odin was fresh. Perhaps, after all, she had a chance of escape. And whatever else, she thought with a sudden leap of the heart, she had led them away from Tio. They believed they were still chasing him! Her elation faded. Was he dead, even at this moment? Lying there all alone, cold and slain, in The Teacup? She prayed for him, whether alive or dead, and reflected sadly that if he had to die he would probably just as soon it be there, where they had known such happy times together.

Ahead, suddenly, was a big fast-moving shape. It was the Portsmouth Machine, the raindrops gleaming like strung beads in the bright glow of its lamps. It would be the Oxford to Southampton coach, then, and running very late, probably delayed by the storm. Her mind began to race. If she could get to Short Shrift, where, she hoped, the Machine would stop to take on passengers, she might be able to buy a ticket, and even if the troopers came up with them, they'd be looking for a wounded man, not a girl. Hope lifting her spirits, she turned Odin in a wide easterly swing, not daring to risk being seen. Lightning betrayed her presence. She heard a shout, from the coachman probably, and prayed she had not been identified as a female.

They were past then, Odin maintaining his tireless stride, and Dimity peering desperately through the darkness, searching for the hamlet. At last, they reached the crossroad and the signpost pointing east to Basingstoke, southwest to Andover, south to Short Shrift and Winchester. Another mile and she would reach the hamlet. She glanced back again, but seeing no sign of pursuit, rode on, praying she would have time to stable Odin and buy a ticket before the dragoons arrived.

The hamlet loomed into view. A light glowed in one cottage window, and another shone brightly from the tavern on the single street where was the coaching office. Hoping that light meant the Machine would stop, she reined Odin to a trot and turned him off the lane. How on earth was she to stable him? Any ostler must be quite astonished to see a lady of Quality ride in alone at such an hour, and would certainly remember and describe her should the military make enquiries. She dismounted, sliding awkwardly from the saddle, her wet habit impeding her movements. The yard of The Spotted Cat was dimly illumined by the lantern that hung inside the open barn. Dimity bit her lip, knowing that each second she wasted might carry a terrible price.

"Buy a basket, lady? A nice warm shawl for your pretty hair? I read your palm for a groat . . . ?"

The young voice was tired and devoid of hope as it droned on. Dimity pulled her hood close and turned to the gypsy lad who stood there, a small cart beside him, the donkey between the shafts standing head down and apparently asleep. The boy

18

must, she thought, have come to meet the Portsmouth Machine at nine o'clock, and waited all these hours for it to arrive. Much chance he had of selling anything, poor creature.

"Buy a basket, lady?"

Come to think on it, she must have *something* to carry onto the coach, or she'd cut a pretty figure! She said in the gruffest voice of which she was capable, "I might. How much are they?"

For a moment the drawn face was blank with disbelief, then the soft dark eyes brightened. He said eagerly, "Five shillings. A florin. One and sixpence. A shilling for you, lady."

It was an odd accent, not foreign, but not quite English, and neither cultured nor common. Under other circumstances she would have been curious about him. As it was, she had no time for curiosity, and growled, "My husband awaits me in Winchester, and I've to stable my horse."

"I'll stable him," he offered, looking admiringly at Odin. "He's a fine big gry."

Dimity hesitated. She'd no wish for Peregrine to lose his favourite horse, but her situation was perilous in the extreme, for at any minute the dragoons might come galloping in.

"I'll take good care of him, mistress," the boy urged.

She opened Tio's fat purse and took out a crown. "Very well. Tell the ostler he is to be fed and rubbed down, and my husband will call for him tomorrow. I must go to the inn and buy a ticket for the coach. Bring me a receipt and a covered basket, and I will pay you your whole five shillings."

His eyes big as saucers, he fairly snatched the reins. "What name, lady?"

She dare not give her own, so borrowed one of Tio's. "Clement," she told him, and he nodded and led the big horse into the stableyard of the tavern.

Dimity hurried to the front door, wiping quickly at her wet face, and tucking her bedraggled curls under the hood.

The vestibule was draughty and dim. A long wooden bench beside the entrance was presently unoccupied. To the right, a corridor led off to what appeared to be the tap and a dismal coffee room, and to the left a shadowy flight of stairs rose to the upper floor. The coaching agent, waybills loosely clasped in one hand, snored in an armchair that had seen better days, and the tavernkeeper, perched on a stool behind the battered counter, eyed the sodden and dishevelled girl without approval. In response to her enquiry, he expressed the opinion that the Portsmouth Machine must have overturned, and if it ever did come, there likely wouldn't be no seats left. And what was more, he didn't hold with females travelling on their own. Especially the kind what had no luggage.

"I left my luggage outside," said Dimity, improvising desperately. "My mistress has been taken ill. We were on our way to join her husband, who has been visiting his father in Romsey, and I am sent to fetch him. I must get there quickly, for she is very sick and every minute counts!"

He was unconvinced, and questioned her so that she had to invent a farm, and the family who had been so kind as to allow her mistress to rent their best bedchamber, and to care for her until her husband arrived.

"Why didn't these 'ere folk send a man on the errand?" he asked suspiciously. "Blest if I ever heard of sending a young woman to—"

"All the men were commandeered by the military," she interposed. "There's a rebel been seen, and they're out hunting him."

His eyes gleamed with interest. "Wot? 'Tain't never the chap with the hundred guineas on his head?"

In his excitement his voice had risen, and the coaching agent woke up and blinked at them, stretching. "What's all the fuss?"

"Lady, here I am," called a low voice from the door.

"Outta' there!" snarled the tavernkeeper, reaching for a hefty cudgel.

The gypsy boy retreated. Dimity went out, hearing the tavernkeeper tell the agent about the Jacobite dog the troopers were hunting.

The gypsy waited at the corner of the building, basket in hand. "Your fine horse is nice and warm now," he said. "And I got you my best basket with a scarf to cover it, just like you wanted, lady."

"Oh dear," said Dimity. "That will never do."

The bright glow of hope faded from his eyes, but he did not protest, though his thin shoulders slumped despairingly. There was something about his wan face and humble manner that made her warm to him. She touched his sleeve and whispered, "What is your name?"

"Florian, lady."

"The problem is, Florian," she explained, looking worriedly at the basket, "that I thought it would be a proper lid. I should have some luggage if I am to get on the coach at this hour, but the basket is obviously empty, even with the scarf."

He regarded her solemnly for a moment, but if he wondered why she must appear to have luggage, he did not voice the question, but hurried to his cart, and rummaged about. He returned and showed her the basket stuffed with straw and some pieces of sacking, the scarf arranged over it so that it appeared well laden.

Dimity smiled and exchanged a crown piece for the basket. Florian grinned at her, knuckled his brow respectfully, and went off, clearly elated by his good fortune.

A great commotion arose now, and the Portsmouth Machine came with a flourish around the corner, the yard of tin sounding its strident summons. At once, all was industry and bustle. Ostlers, half asleep, came staggering out to change the teams. The coachman, muffled to the ears, and a heavy woollen shawl over his caped coat, clambered down from his lofty perch, damning everything and everybody. The guard, silent and glum, and looking like a drowned rat, swung down the far side. As if by magic, people appeared from every direction, clustering around the coach, all talking at once. Dimity's attempt to reach the coaching agent was frustrated, as he began to harangue the coachman. The coachman damned him quite explicitly, and Dimity drew back, waiting.

A shrill yelp made her jump. A small, fair boy, close behind her, was eyeing her resentfully. "You trod on my toe," he accused.

"Oh, I am sorry." Dimity glanced at the lady to whose skirts he clung. "I do apologize, ma'am. I hope I didn't hurt the little fellow."

"Well, you did," the boy proclaimed. "Very bad. I'spect my whole toe will turn black and drop off, an' then you'll be sorry."

Far from being alarmed by this dire prediction, the lady boxed his ear hard. "Hold your tongue, Master Sauce! And stop dragging my skirts sideways!" She turned to Dimity, disclosing a

21

dark, lovely face, framed by powdered ringlets and a stylish bonnet. She wore rather a lot of paint, thought Dimity, and her accent was a trifle affected, her voice loud and harsh. "Disgraceful," the lady continued. "Kept waiting for hours and hours, and not a decent meal to be had at this horrid inn. Never worry about the boy, ma'am. I am very sure you did not mean it, and he always is underfoot." She rolled her eyes heavenwards. "One way or another!"

Dimity saw tears glisten on the child's lashes, and a red mark was glowing on his cheek, but he blinked and his chin lifted defiantly. Touched, she said, "Oh no, truly it was not his fault, but my own. Such a fine boy. Your son, ma'am?"

"No, thank God! My sister's brat. And if you did but know the trouble I've been put to!" She tightened her lips. "Take off your hat and make us known to the lady. Have you no manners?"

The boy snatched off his hat and bowed jerkily. "I am Carlton, an' it please you, ma'am," he said, polite but fixing her with a steady and resentful stare. "This is my aunty, Mrs. Deene."

Shaking hands with Mrs. Deene, Dimity thought she had never seen so beautiful a little boy. Fair curls clustered about his well-shaped head, eyes of a deep green regarded her from under brows that already showed a firm line, and the delicately chiselled nose and cheekbones, the tender mouth, were saved from girlishness by that strong chin.

She put out her hand. "How do you do, Carlton? I am Miss Cr-Clement."

A glint came into the green gaze. He touched her fingers, but said nothing.

"*Ten minutes!*" roared the coachman. "Blast everything, we're so late now, ain't no use in rushing." He glared at the unfortunates making their groaning way from the coach. "Ten minutes! Hot chocolate and tea in the coffee room! Ten minutes!"

"Ten minutes, indeed!" protested Mrs. Deene, indignantly. "We have been delayed here for hours! Now we've to wait another ten minutes!"

"Ar, well you may be thankful as you was waiting in a cozy inn, 'stead of atop my coach, missus," snarled the coachman, shawl flapping wetly as he strode past her, bound for the tap, the passengers trooping inside after him.

"Insolent!" raged the beauty. "If ever I heard the like! He'd never dare address me so was I accompanied by a gentleman!"

A man wearing a frieze coat with a fur collar came stiffly from the coach, doffed his hat, and eyed her appraisingly. "I sympathize, ma'am. These Machines are an abomination, and the clods that tool them, a public disgrace. May I be of service?"

Dimity had seen the agent come in and she ran to try and buy a ticket. Three irate passengers claimed his attention before she could get in a word, and she was elbowed to the rear. She had never before ridden on a public conveyance, never been treated in so contemptuous a manner, never felt so alone and unprotected.

" 'Ere," bellowed an irate voice. "Wotcha igger-gnawing the lady fer, Bert? She been a'backin' and a'fillin' while you 'tended to everyone an' 'is bruvver! Give 'er a turn, mate, do!"

Dimity's champion, a robust middle-aged man with a London accent and the look of a prosperous farmer, beamed at her, and she gave him a grateful smile.

The coaching agent threw an irked look from the farmer to the lady who was so hidden in cloak and hood that he had no notion what she looked like. "Where bound?" he grunted.

"Romsey," she said, reaching for Tio's purse.

"Don't go to Romsey. Change at Winchester. Take it or leave it. I only got *that* place 'cause a passenger give up waiting at Abingdon. Make up y'r mind, miss."

Since a hatchet-faced woman was hurrying in the door with the look of a hopeful passenger, Dimity wasted not a second in paying what was undoubtedly an exorbitant price for her seat. "Miss D. Clement" was added laboriously to the waybill and, having thanked the farmer, she made her way out of the confusion surrounding the harassed agent.

Master Carlton was seated alone on the bench, looking very small and tired and forlorn. There was no sign of his aunt and Dimity supposed she must have gone into the coffee room. The bench was hard and the narrow bars along the back did not invite a long stay, but it was better than nothing. She sat beside the child, who eyed her without delight.

"Well," she said cheerfully, "we shall soon be off. I expect you like travelling in the Portsmouth Machine."

"I don't like it a bit," he responded bluntly. "It's crowded and smelly. I like riding better. An' they call them stagecoaches now."

"Oh dear, I keep forgetting. I wonder why they changed the name."

"Because this one fits better, 'course. It's a coach, and it goes in stages."

Despite the air of male superiority, his eyes were fixed yearningly on a pork pie the farmer had carried from the coffee room and was despatching while informing a frail-looking man that he'd been a merchant in the City all his days but was now a "gentleman farmer."

'So I was right,' thought Dimity, rather pleased with her perspicacity, and she asked, "Is your aunt gone in to buy you something to eat?"

He gave a derisive snort. "She went off with that man with the fur stuff on his coat."

Dimity's eyes widened. But perhaps the gentleman meant to help Mrs. Deene carry the food back. The coffee room looked smoky and none too clean. Probably, the lady would not wish to eat in there. She said, "I think I will try if I can get a cup of tea."

"Better not," he advised. "Jermyn said it's best not to drink nothing on a long journey."

Dimity's cheeks grew hot. The boy sensed he had said something improper and looked frightened. "Why is your face red? Did I do wrong?" and before she could reply, he pleaded with a glance to the coffee room, "Don't tell her. Please. Don't tell her."

"It was nothing, don't worry. Besides," she winked at him, "I have brothers." That won an easing of the scared expression and she went on, "But I really am hungry. Would you escort me, kind sir?"

He giggled, started up, then sat back hurriedly. "No, thank you."

"Oh, do come. In case your aunt forgets, I'll buy you a pasty, if—" She checked. He was squirming. "Carlton? What is it?"

24

"Nothing," he declared, but he was pale and looked even more scared.

Dimity reached over and grasped his left arm. "Oh—my goodness!"

The side of the bench had a curving iron armrest, secured to the seat by a bolt, on each side of which were several round holes. After the inexplicable fashion of small boys, Carlton had inserted his left index finger into one of the holes. "Good gracious!" exclaimed Dimity, low-voiced. "Can you not get it out?"

He admitted this, adding despairingly, "I've tried and tried. She'll be so cross! Don't tell her, will you?"

"Of course not, but she'll find out, you know. You cannot take this bench on the Por—stagecoach. Now never worry so. Let me see."

His small finger was quite trapped. Dimity said, "I shall put my basket on the seat, so no one will sit here. Wait just a moment." He gave her a look of stark tragedy, and she stood and wandered to stand near the farmer. She had noticed that the piece of paper holding his pork pie was excessively greasy, and he had discarded it and was wiping his mouth with a red handkerchief. Unobtrusively, Dimity scooped up the crumpled paper and hurried back to the child who seemed all pale face and great eyes. She sat down and proceeded to smear the grease over his finger. "Oh dear, you have made it bleed. Well, we shall bind it up as soon as we can. Try again. Gently, now."

He bit his lip but strove bravely and in only a short while had freed himself. He turned to Dimity with a beaming grin, and she clapped her hands. "Bravo! Now, let me tend your wound, sir." She took out the scrap of cambric and lace that served her as handkerchief and tied it carefully around the injured member. "That's better," she said with a smile. "Now there will be room for the rest of us in the coach."

He giggled and told her she was a "prime sport," and side by side, they started into the coffee room, only to hear the coachman bellow, "All aboard!"

With much loud complaining, the passengers came hurrying out, several clutching cakes or biscuits.

Carlton looked up at Dimity remorsefully. "Now you won't

be able to get anything. 'Cause of me. Are you tummy-ache hungry?''

"No," she said airily. "Are you?"

He sighed, but squared his shoulders. "No. I'm not, either."

His aunt appeared with the gentleman in the frieze coat. She carried nothing for the boy to eat, and Dimity, who seldom stood in judgement on others, thought her selfish for all her beauty.

Mrs. Deene glanced their way and hurriedly removed her hand from the arm of her escort. "Well, come along, Carlton. Do not dawdle or we won't get a good seat." She surveyed the farmer's bulk without enthusiasm and observed that as it was, they were like to be crowded.

Her prediction proved well justified. The interior of the coach was cramped, cold, and far from clean. The squabs had long since lost whatever plumpness they might once have had, and were lumpily uncomfortable; the space between the two seats was so small that Dimity's knees were constantly in collision with those of the farmer, who grinned at her appreciatively with each contact; and the basket held on the lap of the elderly lady smelled of strong cheese, mingling with the odour of the frieze coat which was damp and exuded an air of sheep.

Soon after the stagecoach lurched and jolted out of the yard of The Spotted Cat, the man in the frieze coat fell noisily asleep. The farmer, who was taking up far more than his share of the opposite seat, followed his example with even greater resonance, and a few minutes later, Carlton, crushed between the farmer and the old lady (who had very sharp elbows) dozed off also. With time to think, Dimity pictured her brother waking in a few hours and discovering that she had vanished. Samuels would be able to tell him what had happened, thank goodness. She could only pray that Perry would not insist upon going himself to find Tio, but would send one of the servants. Her heart sank as she came to the conclusion that he would not do so. He was bound to feel he *must* go himself.

"Captain, indeed," snorted Mrs. Deene. "A fine Captain *he* is! If he dares refuse to acknowledge the boy I shall tell him to his face that with *his* reputation he needs no more black marks against him!"

Dimity looked at her curiously. Whatever was the woman raving about?

" 'Twas downright shameful, the way he used my poor sister," continued Mrs. Deene. "I grant you the brothers *were* all but strangers, for they were orphaned very young and Walter was claimed by a hoity-toity uncle in Cornwall. Still, blood is thicker than water—eh, Miss Clement?"

"Yes, certainly. Do you refer to your late sister's husband, ma'am?"

"Who else would I refer to? The boy's father, did I not say it? His brother may deny us to his heart's content, but I've the marriage lines here in my reticule, so he'll catch cold at that!"

Shocked, Dimity said, "His brother's only child? Surely he never would do so unkind a thing. What would become of the boy?"

"Well you may ask! I have worked my fingers to the bone to support him since my poor dear sister went to her reward!" She threw a pious glance towards the heavens. "God rest her soul, she should have gone to Jamaica with her husband, but she was delicate and her doctor held it inadvisable, so Walter left her here."

"He must have arranged for her support, though," said Dimity, engrossed in this sad tale.

"Walter sent funds until my sister died of an internal disorder. For years afterwards I heard not a single word from him. A letter came at last; from his solicitor. He writ that Walter had died also, of one of the fevers that abound in those dreadful hot countries."

"How very tragic. Did he have no funds to leave his little son?"

"Ho, yes he did!" declared Mrs. Deene militantly. "And no one won't never convince me otherwise! A-er, acquaintance of his come home not six months ago, and told me as Walter had done well. 'Very plump in the pockets,' he said."

"Excellent! Then little Carlton will be provided for, and you properly reimbursed for all your years of selfless care and expense, ma'am."

Mrs. Deene shot a keen glance at the girl beside her. She never had obtained a clear sight of the face, but the voice was cultured and the pelisse, though a trifle worn, must have at one

27

time cost a pretty penny. "You would think so," she said grimly. "But all Walter's funds have been awarded to his brother, and that slippery Captain Sharp refuses to own the boy! Much good it may do the rogue!"

"Good heavens! How could anyone seek to deprive a little orphaned child? I never heard of such wickedness! Is this Captain Sharp poverty stricken, Mrs. Deene? Was he put on the parish when his own parents died?"

"Parish? Tush and a fiddlestick! Not that one! Lands on his feet always. Like a cat. He was sent to live with another uncle. Still lives at The Palfreys in the lap of luxury and will likely inherit now *their* son is dead." She broke off and muttered broodingly, "It'd not surprise me was the captain behind *that* ugly business, as well. Very convenient their son being killed, is what I say. *Very* convenient."

Her eyes as big as saucers, Dimity exclaimed, "You think he killed his own cousin? The son of his benefactor? Oh, surely, you cannot mean it! Why—he would have to be the fiend incarnate!"

"Quite true! And so I shall inform him does he not do right by us. And let me tell you, his carriage had best be waiting or the fur will fly. I do not never mean to pay for the hire of a coach to take me all the way to Romsey!"

Dimity's heart gave a jolt. "Romsey? Why that is where I am going! Oh, ma'am, if you are acquaint with the area, perhaps you can help me. I've to find a Mr. Decimus Green. I think he may be at the fair. Do you know aught of it? Or do you think your brother-in-law may?"

"I never heard of no such place. And from all I know of Anthony Farrar, the only fairs *he* knows of wear light skirts and—"

"*Anthony . . . Farrar?*" gasped Dimity. "B—but you said his name was Captain Sharp."

"Lud!" The woman gave an exasperated shrug. "An expression merely. Signifying a charlatan. How you could not know of it is beyond me. But—why do you seem so took aback?" She leaned nearer. "Do you know Farrar?"

Dimity said hotly, "To my sorrow, I know *of* him, ma'am! Because of his rank cowardice in battle my brother was crippled and has lost his foot!"

28

Mrs. Deene seemed less sympathetic than surprised that Dimity's brother should have served with Captain Farrar. "On second thought," she said bodingly, "it ain't so surprising. The country likely crawls with his victims. That man is beyond doubting, the most depraved—"

Whatever further aspersions she meant to cast on the character of the wicked captain, Dimity was not destined to discover. The stagecoach, which had been travelling at reckless speed, probably in an effort to make up for lost time, suddenly gave a violent jolt. Thrown forward, Dimity found herself lying on the farmer's chest. A terrible crash. A wild confusion of shouts and frenziedly neighing horses. Screams, fading . . . a loss of awareness . . .

The face hung in mid-air. A young man's face, the powdered hair severely tied back, the chin and nose strong, and the hard blue eyes reflecting a grudging sympathy. He said, his voice seeming to echo in her ears, ". . . coming around. She and the boy look the least hurt of the lot of 'em. How are you now, ma'am?"

Dimity noted with vague interest that a room was forming around him. It looked surprisingly like the vestibule of The Spotted Cat in Short Shrift. "Oh," she murmured. "Are we back again, then?"

The face retreated and she saw with a sudden clutch of fear that a red uniform went with it.

"I am Captain Jacob Holt, ma'am," he said, polite but chill. "Your papers, if you please."

Papers! Memory rushing back, she thought, 'My God! I have no papers!' and stared at him, horrified.

"I think this is hers, sir," said a trooper, offering a reticule. "It was round her wrist when we got her out."

The captain, groped in the reticule and brought forth a sheaf of papers. Glancing through them, he asked, "Are you Mrs. Catherine Deene?"

"I—cannot seem to . . . think . . ." murmured Dimity. "Pray—how is Carlton?"

The trooper, a kindly looking middle-aged man, who should, she thought, have made better arrangements than to have such an unpleasant officer, bent over her. "He'll be all right, never fear. Do you know who was the other young lady, marm?"

She gave a shocked gasp. "Who *was*? Oh, no—never say she is dead?"

"It would appear so, ma'am," said the captain. "If you can tell us of her identity we will notify her people."

"She said her name was Miss Clement," offered a childish voice. Carlton's angelic countenance hovered over Dimity. "Hello, Aunty. Poor Aunty. Are you hurting very bad? I am. I hurt my knee. We will be able to go on, won't we?"

Dimity stared at him. "Carlton . . . ?"

He bent to kiss her and whispered very softly, "She's killed. So I'll have you for my aunty instead, if you please."

✍ *Chapter 3* ✍

Shaken and bemused, Dimity was too grateful for the escape route Fate offered to deny her new identity, and with Carlton calling her his "dear Aunty" with every other breath, the captain asked no more questions.

It developed that the injured passengers had not, as Dimity thought, been conveyed back to The Spotted Cat, but had instead been taken to a small hedge tavern outside Winchester. The coachman had suffered a concussion; Carlton's aunt had been carried off to the apothecary in an apparently expired condition; the gentleman in the frieze coat was still unconscious; the old lady was in hysterics; and the farmer, his arm fractured, grimly silent. Dimity was ushered to the tavern's nicest bedchamber. Still incapable of rational thought, she was ministered to by the host's wife and her kindly maids and persuaded to drink a hot posset. Snuggling into a cozy bed, she fell fast asleep.

The sun was high when she awoke. She was still fuzzy-headed, but able to stand and walk about. The maids assisted with her toilette and helped her downstairs where Carlton joined her for a light breakfast. His swollen knee was bandaged but otherwise he seemed quite cheerful. Before she had entirely comprehended what was going on, Dimity found herself standing outside in the bright morning, her cloak around her, and a hackney carriage waiting.

A nervous, wispy little man introduced himself as the coaching agent, and said he had come over from Winchester. He apologized profusely for the inconvenience, and assured "Mrs. Deene" that people waiting for passengers from the wrecked stagecoach had been notified of the situation. She would be driven into Winchester where, if no one was waiting to receive her, the coachman would arrange transportation to her ultimate destination.

Dimity, very stiff and sore, was helped into the carriage and they set forth, the two horses stepping out briskly.

For a few minutes she was silent, striving to collect her scattered wits. At length, she turned to the child beside her. He gave her his angelic smile. Baffled, she said, "Never mind all that innocence, young man. Some explanations are in order. Why did you tell all those people I am your poor aunt? Are you not in the smallest grieved by her—her death?"

He regarded her owlishly. "She might not be dead."

"What?"

"That trooper who said she was, din't look as if he knew his business. You c'n tell if someone's dead by holding a mirror to their mouth. I saw Jermyn do it once, when—"

Horrified, Dimity cried, "My heavens! Then we must go back at once! Poor lady, she will be beside herself with worry for you."

"No she won't," he said unemotionally. "If she's not dead she's going to die. Prob'ly without waking up. 'Sides," he added, watching her thoughtfully, "if you go back, that captain will want your papers."

Staring at him, awed, Dimity asked, "How old are you, Carlton?"

"I'm almost seven. But I'm very bright. Jermyn said I was bright. He said—"

"Six . . ." she breathed. "Only six. And you can speak of your aunt's death without a vestige of sorrow."

His face crumpled suddenly. Great tears swam in his eyes and trickled down his cheeks.

'Poor little child,' thought Dimity. 'It was likely the shock, and now I've brought it home to him again.' She fumbled for her handkerchief.

Carlton held up his bandaged finger. "I've got it," he said, and dabbed the encompassed wound at his tears, then grinned up at her. "Was that better?"

She drew back with a shocked gasp. "I begin to think you are a very naughty boy!"

Sobering, he watched her. "If you send me back, I'll run away."

32

"Why? Mrs. Deene is your aunt."

"Aunts are horrid," he declared. "Don't you get any."

"I have five, and they are the very dearest creatures. Well—four are," she amended, Aunt Miriam's sour features drifting into her mind's eye.

"Do they box your ears an' twist your arms an' lock you up in dark cupboards all day if you do wrong?"

"Good heavens! Is that what your aunt did?"

He nodded.

"But—surely her husband would not allow—"

"She hasn't got one."

"Oh. Then you certainly should not be returned to her!" She bethought her of the laws of the land and retrenched, "That is to say—when we get this all sorted out, if your uncle will not have you, we'll try to find you a home with some of your other relations."

"Haven't got any." He saw pity come into the face he had decided would suit him for an always-aunt, and enquired, "Have you got lots 'n lots of relations?"

"Yes, I am very fortunate to have grandparents, and many aunts and uncles and cousins. But most of all, I have my brothers. They're twins and—" She paused, wondering how Piers and Peregrine were, and whether Tio was alive on this beautiful summer morning.

The boy was silent. Glancing up, she saw another tear trickling down his smooth cheek. He gave her an oblique look, then dragged a sleeve across his eyes.

She asked gently, "What is it, dear?"

"Nothing," he replied, his chin jutting. "I was jus'—jus' playing."

She took his hand. "I think you were not—that time."

He jerked his head away and looked out of the window. Dimity turned his chin and smiled into the veiled green eyes. "You can trust me," she said. "I won't tell."

He looked down, but, clinging tightly to her hand, muttered, "I jus' thought—how fine it must be to have relations. I never had no brothers or sisters, or no one. Jus' me." He swung his head up to glare at her fiercely. "An' that's jolly good, too. I—I know how to go on."

But his tender mouth trembled. Suddenly he was no longer a Machiavellian imp, but just a scared, lonely little boy.

Dimity pulled him into a hug and kissed his curls. "You have not 'just you' any more," she said. "You have me."

He sniffed and said a rather muffled, "Till we get to The Palfreys."

"Well, you'll have your uncle, then."

He drew back. "I don't want him! He doesn't want a nephew. She said he din't. And 'sides, if I get a uncle I want a real man. He's just a yellow coward!"

'Now, why did the wretched woman tell him about that business if she hoped Farrar would take him?' thought Dimity. "Well," she declared, "if Captain Farrar won't acknowledge you, I shall find a good home for you, Carlton. You have my word on it."

His eyes narrowed. "Man to man? Honest and true? No ratting?"

"Word of honour."

"An, you won't marry with some rich gent and forget me? You won't go away an' leave me? Never?"

"I cannot promise that much, I'm afraid. When Captain Farrar finds out I'm not really his sister-in-law, he may very well hand me over to the Watch!"

" 'Course he won't. He don't know what my aunty looks like. He never met her."

"Are you sure?" asked Dimity, hopefully. "Is there no one at The Palfreys who will know I'm an impostor?"

"What's that jawbreaker?"

"I mean, who will know I'm not who I say I am."

"Oh." He considered this. "I don't think so. Aunty Cathy wrote to him, but she never met him. She said they was all too hoity-toity to want anything to do with us. 'Sides, I shall tell him you are my aunty. Don't you never worry." He patted her hand manfully. "I'll take care of you!"

Smiling at him, Dimity had the uneasy feeling that to be taken care of by this strange little boy might be a mixed blessing.

Surprisingly, when they reached Winchester, the chariot from The Palfreys was waiting. Carlton scrambled onto the box, and Dimity was settled into the luxurious interior. A wooden-faced footman placed a fur rug over her knees and as the vehicle began to roll smoothly along the highway she leaned back against soft cushions of rich red plush. Within twenty minutes they had turned onto a private road and passed through wide iron gates. Everywhere she looked now were signs of prosperity; well-thinned woods, neatly scythed sweeps of lawn, charming landscapes.

And what on earth was she doing here? She sighed miserably. 'I have gone mad, is what it is,' she told herself. She had started out simply to help Tio. Now, she carried a scrap of parchment that spelled death most terrible for anyone possessing it; she had assumed another lady's identity and stolen her belongings; she intended to try and hoodwink a man of foul repute who might very well be murderously inclined towards her; she was likely to be accused of kidnapping a small (and decidedly dishonest) boy; and on top of all else, she had no doubt but that her poor brothers were nigh frantic with worry for her safety.

She sighed again. Her best hope, of course, was that Perry and Piers would find Tio and take care of him—if he wasn't dead, which God forbid! And then Tio would tell them about the paper he'd thought he was entrusting to Perry, and they would all come and get her out of this dreadful dilemma!

Rather belatedly, it occurred to her that the message itself might contain a clue to the whereabouts of Mr. Decimus Green, and she retrieved it, unfolded it carefully, and read:

4

> *All is quiet in the city.*
> *See the pigeons in the square,*
> *Indignant. Waiting for their corn or bread.*
> *Is it not strange, and dead?*
> *Enthralling to see the streets so bare.*
> *On mansion and hovel drifts snow, so white.*
> *One will bring food to the pigeons tonight.*

"What absolute nonsense!" she muttered. "How can this poem be so dangerous when it makes no sense at all?" But Tio had said something about a cypher. In that case, the meaning would be concealed. She stared down at it. Such a scrap of a thing to cause men to be hunted and tortured and killed. And women, mayhap. She shivered. But however reckless and improper the things she had done, they were justified; Tio had said many lives were at stake. She would not let him down! And if, in the process of delivering this message of death, she could also avenge herself on the evil Captain Anthony Farrar, why so much the better!

Having restored the parchment to her bodice, she glanced out of the window again. The drivepath was turning in a gradual easterly swing, and above some distant woods she could see chimneys and a high-peaked tower with a large weather vane atop it. Charmed, she turned to the left-hand window. Some distance ahead of them a rider was cantering down the steep slope of a hill. The horse he bestrode was a magnificent grey, but not too well broken to judge by its caperings. The rider swayed with lithe grace to the movements of his fiery steed, glancing back from time to time to where a golden spaniel followed, all ears and feet.

At the foot of the hill, the horse shied and launched into a gallop. The rider pulled him in sharply. The grey reared, forelegs flailing, then bucked furiously and for some seconds did all he might to unseat the man. The spaniel trotted up and sat down, watching pantingly. The grey made a bared-teeth grab for his owner's knee, and the heavy riding crop was brought down hard. The horse shook his head and stood quiet, but stamped at the ground as if to express some vestige of defiance.

From the box, Dimity heard Carlton scream, "Jolly good, sir!"

The rider looked their way and started the big horse to intercept them, and this time he obliged his mount, coming at the gallop. The carriage slowed and stopped. Dimity, quaking with nervousness, heard a deep voice raised in question, and the mumble of the coachman's reply. The rider, who had been temporarily out of her range of vision, came up to the open window and looked in.

He could not be Anthony Farrar, as she had first feared. Her brothers had unfailingly referred to him as a "miserable little worm," and this man was tall and well-built, with the lazy graceful carriage of the athlete. She eyed him uncertainly as he bent to look in at her.

She guessed him to be in his late twenties. He wore no hat, and his thick hair was powdered and tied back. The sun-bronzed, fine-boned face was enhanced by a pair of vivid green eyes wide set under heavy, brown eyebrows. The nose and chin warned of inflexibility; the mouth was generous and well shaped, but with

36

a haughty droop. He said with a sneer, "Mr. Deene allowed you to face it out alone, I take it."

Irritated by both look and manner, she said, "Then you should not, sir." The green eyes widened and the sardonic mouth relaxed slightly, and she went on, "I am a widow."

"Regrettable," he said, the ice returning full measure. "I'd prefer to have dealt with a *male* rascal."

He made no attempt to keep his voice low, and Dimity heard Carlton's wrathful squeak and the muffled rumble of a man's laugh. "Since I mean to deal only with Captain Farrar," she retorted disdainfully, "*your* preferences are not pertinent."

He drawled, "I have been remiss. Allow me to introduce myself. I *am* Anthony Farrar."

Dimity gave a gasp. "Miserable," certainly. But—"a little worm"? Piers and Perry must have been wits to let! Feeling decidedly hardly done by, she exclaimed an indignant, "Oh!"

Carlton's voice called, "Sir—are *you* my Uncle Anth'ny?"

Farrar had been about to speak, but at this he closed his mouth with a snap and glanced up at the box. "Most decidedly—*not*!" he declared unequivocally. And bending to the window again, added, "Take my advice, ma'am, and go home. There are no pullets for plucking here!"

"How fortunate," Dimity retaliated. "I had scarce expected an eagle, but to have to fleece a pullet would be extreme degrading."

He looked briefly surprised, then amused. Resting one hand against the side of the coach, he leaned nearer. "You're a pretty doxy, but—"

The grey, who had been behaving quite well, suddenly screamed and, head down and legs stiff, shot straight into the air and spun around twice. Farrar, caught off-balance and unprepared, was hurled from the saddle. He landed hard, as his mount thundered in the direction of the house.

Watching, astonished, Dimity waited for her antagonist to get up, but he continued to lie sprawled and motionless. She thought without great satisfaction, 'The horrid creature has broke his neck!' and wrenched at the door.

As she struggled to let down the steps, she heard a man shout a frantic, *"Captain!"* and then she was out and running to kneel beside Farrar.

The coachman flung himself down beside her. "My Gawd! My Gawd! Is he dead?"

With the experience gained from watching the twins somehow survive numerous brushes with an early grave, Dimity pressed her fingers below the strong jaw. "The heartbeat is steady. He is likely just stunned. Have you water anywhere on the coach?"

"Not water, ma'am." He turned to the carriage and shouted, "Jim! Fetch the brandy!"

The footman jumped down, pulling a flask from the pocket of his wide-skirted dark red coat.

The coachman glanced obliquely at Dimity. "Had a long wait last night," he grunted, by way of explanation. He slid an arm under his employer's shoulders. "I'll hold him up, ma'am. P'raps you can get some of this into him."

Farrar's powdered head rolled limply. Dimity thought that he looked dead, but she tilted the flask carefully. For a moment the amber liquor trickled from the sides of his mouth, Then he coughed, the long lashes blinked and the green eyes peered dazedly at her. He was perfectly white, but a smile of singular sweetness curved his lips.

He murmured faintly, "It's all right, dearest . . . only . . . ." Comprehension seemed to dawn. The words trailed off. He narrowed his eyes, frowningly, then reached up to thrust her hand away. "What . . . the deuce?"

"Polly had a tantrum, sir," offered the coachman.

"Like hell," snarled Farrar, and clambered to his feet, leaning on the coachman for a second and swaying unsteadily. He staggered towards the chariot, swearing under his breath, fury in every line of him. "You young . . . makebait! I'll break your damned neck!"

"Oh, no you will not!" Dimity ran to grip his arm.

A sudden sharp crack. A yell from the coachman. From the corner of her eye Dimity saw the open carriage door whipping at her. She was seized in an iron grip and thrown aside. Falling headlong, she gasped as something knocked the breath from her lungs, and, terrifyingly close, she heard the pound of hooves, the rattle of wheels, the creak of springs and leather.

"Hey!" roared the coachman, waving his arms madly and

sprinting in pursuit of his purloined vehicle, followed by the footman.

"Get off!" wheezed Dimity.

Dragging himself to all fours, Farrar knelt above her. His splendid riding coat was ripped at the shoulder; his hair, having escaped its riband, hung untidily about his face; mud smeared one cheek and blood from a small cut on his forehead crept down the other. "That *damnable* little bastard!" he gritted between his teeth. "I'll murder him!"

A distant corner of Dimity's mind registered the awareness that this cowardly yellow dog was extremely good to look at. He had, however, lost considerable of his consequence. In fact, the elegant lord of the manor was now a muddy mess. Suddenly, it seemed enormously funny. She tried to restrain herself, but failed utterly.

Looking down with incredulity at the girl beneath him, Farrar saw a pale oval face, delicate features, a pair of laughing hazel eyes that had a slight and very fetching slant to them, all set off by a mass of tumbled rich brown ringlets. "I trust," he snarled, coming painfully to his feet and helping her up, "you will find it funny when that imp of Satan runs my team into the bridge. The rains have caused the river to overflow and the ground is like a swamp there. Only let one wheel leave the drivepath and there'll be the devil to pay!"

Dimity's merriment died a sudden death. "Oh, heavens!" she exclaimed. "You—you mean that *Carlton* is driving?"

"Not with expertise," he snapped, starting away. "I assure you, madam, that if my horses are hurt, you and that little hellion will find yourselves clapped up for the next twenty years!"

Without waiting for a response, he ran off in pursuit of the disappearing carriage. Dimity followed, seething with rage. The man was beyond belief! Little Carlton had no more notion of how to handle that spirited team than would a sparrow. 'Twould be a miracle was he not killed, and all Farrar could think about was his horses! She halted as she heard a distant crash followed by an outburst of shouts. Her heart seemed to freeze. Farrar was running with a long, graceful stride.

She tried to run also, but her head, which had ached since the accident with the Portsmouth Machine, was pounding dreadfully, and she was stiff in every limb. She found herself thinking inconsequently that Piers would be glad of Farrar on the village cricket team and brought herself back to reality with a jerk. Piers would strangle him with his bare hands, is what he would do . . .

She heard hoofbeats, and turned to find that another horseman was riding toward her. He reined in the black mare, lifted the tricorne from his powdered head and watched her with concern in his fine grey eyes. He had a pleasant rather serious face and a kindly mouth, and she liked him at once.

"Ma'am?" he said tentatively. "Are you all right? I—Jupiter, but you're not!" The dark brows twitched into an anxious frown as he sprang from the saddle to take the hand she held out. "Whatever has happened? You are all mud!"

"An accident," she mumbled. "Captain Farrar went on ahead. The horses—er, ran away."

A look of awe came into his eyes. "*Tony* lost his team? Well, I'll be—" He broke off abruptly. "An I lift you, ma'am, can you ride?"

Dimity was feeling a little odd. "I think," she sighed, "it might be better was I to ride with you, sir."

He at once lifted her to the saddle, mounted up behind, and slipped a strong arm around her. They started off at a walk.

"You are very kind," said Dimity. "Thank you, Mr. . . ."

"Chandler. Gordon Chandler. And 'tis my very great pleasure, ma'am."

"My name is Mrs. Deene. Could you please go a little faster? My nephew was driving, you see, and he is only six."

Chandler whispered a startled expletive and brought the mare to an easy lope. In very short order they reached the curve in the drivepath beyond which chariot, coachman, and Captain had disappeared. Dimity blinked at the distant scene and uttered a moan. A small knot of people stood on a picturesque old wooden bridge; nearby, the wreck of the chariot hung crazily against what was left of the railing. As they drew nearer, she could see no sign of the child. Farrar and the coachman were inspecting the knees of a trembling horse, and the footman and three more men were gathered around another.

"Carlton . . ." whispered Dimity, appalled.

"Easy, ma'am," said Mr. Chandler. "Hey! Tony!"

Farrar turned his dirty, bloodied face and Chandler muttered, "Good God!"

"Where is my nephew?" called Dimity.

The response was so impolite that it was as well she had brothers.

Shocked, Chandler said brusquely, "You forget yourself, Farrar! The lady has—"

"Hah!"

"Is . . . is he—dead?" quavered Dimity.

One of the grooms offered, "I see a little boy run like a rabbit into the house, sir."

"Oh . . . thank God!" said Dimity.

"But *not* with a loud voice," snarled Farrar.

Chandler gave him a stern look and guided his mare around the carnage. They crossed the bridge in silence. Dimity felt drained and very weary, her headache seeming to worsen with every step the mare took. She did not realize she was drooping until Mr. Chandler's arm tightened around her. She leaned her head gratefully against his shoulder and was drowsing when a shout roused her.

The Palfreys was set in the lee of a gentle slope. It was a very large two-storey house built entirely of cream-coloured stone, with many big square-headed windows and a steeply gabled roof. There was an air of French Gothic about it, with its Norman tower, tall elaborate clusters of chimneys, and the gargoyles that were placed at intervals all along the north front above the ground floor. The west face had several smaller individually gabled windows under the eaves, indicating at least a partial third floor. Dimity, hazy but impressed, thought the house quite beautiful.

A stable boy came running as Chandler rode up, and simultaneously the front doors were swung wide. A tall, elegant butler, two footmen flanking him, walked onto the short terrace.

Chandler called, "Give a hand here, Leonard."

The butler gestured and the footmen hurried to oblige. "The lady has had a nasty accident," Chandler went on. "Easy now." He guided her down, then dismounted to slip an arm about her waist and support her up the three steps.

Carven into the lintel above the front doors the name of the house appeared above the likeness of two spirited horses, each brave with saddle, bridle, and tasselled trappings. Dimity peered up at the carving and when she lowered her eyes found herself in a wide, cool hall fragrant with the perfume of the great bowl of flowers on a side table.

"What have you done to my aunty?" Carlton's indignant tones shrilled through the vastness as he appeared at the top of four broad steps at the rear of the hall.

Farrar's deep voice growled, "Nothing to what I'm going to do to *you*—you despicable little varmint!"

Carlton squealed, and fled back the way he had come.

"Do not dare to strike him," cried Dimity, whirling on the enraged man as he made to step past her.

"*Strike* him? Strangle him, more like! Do you realize what he—"

Chandler interposed, "Mrs. Deene has suffered sufficient of a shock, Tony. There is no need—"

"Oho! Easy said when you're not one of the little bastard's victims!"

"Moderate your language!" gritted Chandler angrily. "There's a lady present!"

"I wish I may see one!"

"Then I invite your attention, Farrar!"

The female voice was deeply musical, but held a rim of ice. Dimity saw Farrar stiffen. Following his gaze, she saw the woman who had come to the top of the steps with Carlton peeping from behind her skirts. Auburn hair touched with silver and high-piled on her head made her seem very tall. She was generously formed and statuesque, and she wore a graceful negligee of striped blue and white silk with a long blue cape. Like some feudal queen, she stood there, surveying them all with proud hauteur.

"I cannot think it necessary," she continued, "that we terrify children in this house; whatever else we may have come to."

Farrar walked forward. "I think you do not comprehend, Lady Helen. The brat came damn near kil—"

One white hand lifted. "Pray make an effort to remember that you are no longer in the barracks room."

His jaw set, but he said in a milder tone, "My apologies, but—" one finger stabbed at Carlton, "a man don't hide behind a lady's skirts. Give it me!"

The boy took a half step and paused. "You wouldn't *really* . . . s-strangle me, sir?"

42

"Give . . . it . . . me!"

Lady Helen said coolly, "My nephew will not harm you, child."

Carlton trod awkwardly down the steps. Farrar advanced to meet him and, fearing for the boy's safety, Dimity advanced also.

Farrar held out his hand.

Carlton crept up and, shaking in every limb, deposited a slingshot in that large palm.

"Good heavens!" gasped Dimity. "Is *that* what caused the Captain's horse to bolt? He might have been killed!"

"And what a stroke of luck for you both," sneered Farrar.

Flushing, she said, "We came here to establish my nephew's claim, Captain. Not with intent to do murder."

He gave her a contemptuous glare, then jerked his head around to the boy, who had not retreated but stood as one awaiting imminent execution. "What in the *deuce* made you think you could drive my team? Do you realize you near killed two fine horses, wrecked an extreme costly coach, and smashed my bridge?"

"I d-din't mean to dr-drive it, sir," gulped Carlton. "I just w-wanted to see if I could crack the whip. Like the coachman d-did."

Farrar took another pace toward him. "You miserable little whelp," he said through his teeth, "I'll teach you—"

His hair wildly disarrayed, his vivid eyes narrowed and glittering with wrath, his face looking for all the world like the mask of a savage with its streaks of dirt and blood, he towered over the boy. Terrified, Carlton thought his end had come and, with a faint sob, fell in a swoon.

"Oh!" cried Dimity, kneeling by the small, pathetic figure. She glared up at the startled Farrar. "Evil, wicked brute! How *could* you frighten him so?"

"For Lord's sake, Tony," Chandler protested, hurrying to Dimity, "have done! The poor child is—"

"Is a vicious little monster who has wreaked more chaos in one hour than any—"

"There's no need to shout. Mrs. Deene has had enough to bear."

"If my tone of voice displeases, you are quite at liberty to leave, Chandler!"

"That will do," Lady Helen put in, frowning at her nephew. "Whether Mrs. Deene's claim is valid or not, and whatever accidental harm the boy may have done, we are not quite savages, I trust! Leonard—be so good as to carry the child to my quarters."

Farrar reddened. "Oh, I'll do it, ma'am," he muttered, and dropped to one knee.

"Thank you, but that will not be necessary. Leonard . . . ?"

His lips compressed, Farrar stood and stepped back, and the butler hurried to lift the child.

"You will please to accompany us, Mrs. Deene," said my lady in a gentle voice quite at odds with her former tone. "You have had a dreadful ordeal and are looking very tired. Gordie, would you be so kind as to help? We do not want two people collapsing due to our—brutality."

With a troubled look at Farrar's enigmatic countenance, Chandler helped Dimity to her feet.

It was absolutely ridiculous. The man was a murderer many times over; a foul-mouthed, foul-tempered brute of a man. But . . . Bound by her sense of fair play, she turned to face him. "Sir, everything you said was true. We are to blame for your injuries, your broken carriage, and the wreck of your bridge. I—I do not quite know how, but—I accept the responsibility. And—and Carlton will be punished."

Apparently not in the slightest appeased, he scanned her with eyes which seemed if anything more wrathful than ever. "Be assured of it, madam," he growled.

"You should not be up, Perry," exclaimed Jane Guild laying her book aside and looking distressed and rather pathetic in her rumpled nightcap, with two scrawny, mouse-coloured braids hanging down her shoulders.

Clad in a lurid purple dressing gown and leaning on a cane, Peregrine hobbled painfully into her bedchamber. "Where—is my sister, ma'am?" he panted.

She stared at him. "If not in her room, then out riding, I fancy. It certainly is a glorious morning. Why? If you need something, dear—"

"She is not in her room," he interrupted again. "And what's more, it looks as if she'd left in a proper rush. Garments tossed all over the place. Lamp still burning, and nigh red hot! Not like Mitten.''

A faint frown disturbed the serenity of Jane Guild's brow. "Good gracious, it most certainly is not!"

"Furthermore, I'd like to know why she was tearing up sheets.''

Incredulous, Miss Guild echoed, "Tearing up *sheets* . . . ?''

"Exactly so,'' he confirmed, trying not to wince as he shifted his weight from the artificial foot to the still painful left one. "Come and see. I don't like it. Don't like it at all!''

Miss Guild hurried out of bed and into her wrapper, then accompanied her tall nephew along the hall. Peregrine opened the door to Dimity's bedchamber and following his aunt inside, propped himself against the wall.

The bed had obviously been occupied. A dainty nightdress lay in a heap on the floor and a mutilated sheet was flung across the eiderdown, a pair of scissors had been left, open, on a nearby chair. Meeting Peregrine's grim stare, Miss Guild thought, 'Bandages?' and her heart began to flutter with fear. It fluttered even more as a series of piercing shrieks rent the silence.

"Jupiter!'' gasped Peregrine, and hobbled into the hall.

More shrieks rang out.

Miss Guild ran to the stairs, Peregrine making his awkward way after her. Halfway down, they both halted.

A small parade burst from the dining room. Mrs. Burrows, their cook-housekeeper, tall, fat, and unfailingly cheerful, led the way, still wearing cloak and bonnet, waving her arms and screeching at the top of her lungs. Behind her came South, the irascible abigail, and after her the buxom young housemaid, Tilly Thornton, both in full cry.

Peddars, the footman, who had been polishing the brass knocker on the front door, shot inside, his slightly protruding eyes huge in his pudgy face.

Johns, the sturdy individual who valeted the twins, rushed out of Piers' bedchamber with a pile of cravats in his hand, his square features pale with alarm.

"What a'God's name . . . ?'' shouted Peregrine, hanging over the rail.

Three distressed faces were raised to him.

"A strange man, sir!'' wailed South.

"Fast asleep, Mr. Perry-green!" sobbed Thornton, wringing her hands.

"In *my bed*!" the cook howled shatteringly.

Peregrine looked grimly to his man. "My pistol. Quickly!"

"Sir . . . it's only . . . me." The faint voice came from the man who walked unsteadily from the kitchen, unshaven and unkempt, wearing only a rumpled shirt and breeches.

"Samuels!" breathed Peregrine, his mind leaping to possible conclusions.

"Oh, poor soul," said kind-hearted Miss Guild.

"Sir—a word . . . private. Most—" Samuels began to cough, the seizure leaving him sagging exhaustedly against the wall. "Most . . . terrible urgent," he wheezed.

Sudbury, who had expressed deep disappointment that Miss Dimity should have hesitated one instant before asking his help, guided the small coach to the trees at the brink of The Teacup and reined to a halt. "Will I go and have a look, sir?" he asked in a hoarse whisper.

"Yes, if you please. But for Lord's sake try not to look so guilty about it!"

Sudbury jumped down and sauntered to the edge of the depression with such exaggerated nonchalance that Peregrine groaned his frustration. Beside him, Miss Guild said, "I do not know whether to pray they are here, or not. Perry—if Mitten took Odin as Sudbury says, might she not have given him to Tio?"

"Yes. Or ridden off with the silly gudgeon." He thought, 'But why hasn't she come home?' "Of all the beastly coils," he said. "And you should not be here, Aunty Jane. This is a desperate business."

"As if I would stay away with Tio and my dearest niece in peril!"

"You're a right one love." He gave her a squeeze. "Just the same, if there's searching to be done—"

Sudbury reappeared, running. Reaching the side of the coach, he gasped, "His lordship's down there, all right, Mr. Perry. Shot in the head."

Jane Guild gave a little whimper and pressed one hand to her mouth.

"Dead?" asked Peregrine, whitening.

"Or near it, sir. There ain't no sign of Miss Dimity, but—" his eyes fell. He said reluctantly, "Sorry I am to say it, but from the look of things there was one track going in from this side, but—a many horses going out—over there."

Cold with fear, Peregrine stared in the direction indicated. 'A many horses . . .' He thought, 'Troopers. Our Mitten led 'em off, else they'd have poor old Tio on the way to the Tower.'

Miss Guild began to weep softly. Peregrine slipped an arm about her. "We must get his lordship home. Can you manage, Sudbury? He's no featherweight."

"I can haul him, sir. Have to throw him over my shoulder, though. Thing is—how am I to get him into the house without we're seen?"

Miss Guild said, sniffing, "We cannot, I'm afraid. We will have to concoct some tale to pacify everyone." She dried her tears and, as Sudbury started off again, she put a hand on Peregrine's arm. "We must send for Piers, so that he can look for Mitten."

He flushed. "D'you fancy I mean to sit at home and wait? I only wish to God I knew where she might have headed! She should have come back by this time. Unless . . ." He paused, his thin face bleak.

Miss Guild pleaded, "Do not give up hope, dearest. She may not have been taken."

"I wish," he said heavily, "I could believe that. But what chance has a slip of a girl against a troop of seasoned fighting men?"

Jane Guild's heart was heavy with fear for her niece and with grief for gallant young Horatio Glendenning, but at this her small chin lifted and a spark came into her gentle eyes. She said, "They likely thought the same about Jeanne d'Arc!"

⌇ *Chapter 4* ⌇

With Gordon Chandler supporting her and Lady Helen Farrar leading the way, Dimity was ushered through a central music hall, at the far end of which was a graceful, free-standing, spiral staircase. She noticed vaguely that rooms opened off this long wide hall, but her head was aching so that she gained only a muddled impression of spaciousness, quiet good taste, and luxury. She paused at the foot of the staircase, peering upwards through a mellow golden glow.

Lady Helen murmured, "Poor creature, she is quite exhausted. Gordie dear, would you mind . . . ?"

Dimity was swept up and carried. After a confused interval, she found herself lying on a bed in a cool, quiet chamber, with the window curtains drawn. Lady Helen's face drifted over her. "Your luggage will be brought up and put in the boy's room," she said echoingly.

Something had been agitating at the back of Dimity's mind. She remembered now what it was and said feebly, "My reticule, ma'am? All my papers are in it."

Lady Helen had green eyes also. They must, thought Dimity, run in the family. A rather puzzled look came into those eyes. "Have no fear," said my lady. "I shall bring them in here for you."

"You won't let . . . him . . ."

"My nephew is not without—" A very brief check, then the serene voice resumed, "He will not go against my wishes, I assure you. Now why do you look so bewildered, child?"

"I—I cannot understand why you are so kind as to let me stay here, ma'am. Under the circumstances."

A strange little smile curved the sad mouth. "As you said, my dear—under the circumstances . . . Besides, if your ward is truly the son of Walter Farrar, my dear husband would have wished to see him fairly treated. Now—go to sleep."

Dimity was at the edge of exhaustion, but she retained sufficient of her wits to be aware that someone had removed her habit and her boots. She could feel the vital parchment tickling between her breasts, and dared not risk the possibility of the maids coming in and putting her into her nightdress while she was half asleep. She managed a smile and closed her eyes. The instant the door was softly closed and she was alone, she climbed from the bed and thrust the cypher as far under the mattress as she could reach.

Then, gratefully, she obeyed Lady Helen.

Gordon Chandler sprawled at his ease across the deep bay windowseat of the library, balanced a tankard on one drawn-up knee, and looked broodingly at immaculate flower gardens, rolling turf, and the curving sweep of the drivepath. Men were already repairing the railing of the quaint old wooden bridge, and the wreckage of the coach had been taken away.

Having bathed and changed clothes hurriedly, Anthony Farrar sat perched against a reference table, a small bandage taped to his forehead, wineglass in hand, regarding his friend with a scowl. "You don't believe me, I take it."

Chandler turned a troubled grey gaze to him. "Of course I do. Only—the boy *is* the spitting image of you when you were that age, Tony. The portrait of you that hangs in your aunt's bedchamber—"

"That *used* to hang there," interpolated Farrar cynically. Chandler looked aghast, and Farrar went on with a mirthless grin, "But he is not *my nephew*—thank the Good Lord! And—" he leaned forward, waving his glass for emphasis, "my brother did not at all resemble me! That's where they made their mistake. They took *me* for their model, instead of Walter!"

"He could very easily have inherited your looks, rather than those of his father, you know."

"Dammit, Gordie! Don't you see? I doubt that sly little harpy ever laid eyes upon Walter. Certainly, her sister was not married

49

to him! More likely this Mary Deene was his lady in keeping at some time, and when Madame Piety—"

"You mean the 'sly little harpy'?" interposed Chandler gravely.

"One and the same, my dear fellow, one and the same. And both steeped in avarice! As I was saying, when that consummate actress above-stairs learned of Walter's death and of the fortune he'd made in Jamaica, she began to write herself a colourful scenario wherein a secret marriage is followed by an equally secret birth, and now it's a case of—pay up or be blasted in the newspapers!"

Chandler was silent for a moment, and knowing his friend's way of considering carefully before he rushed into speech, Farrar waited. The comment, when it did come, was not what he had hoped for.

"Is Walter's fortune very large?"

"Ninety-eight thousand, approximately."

Chandler's brows went up and he gave a soft whistle.

"Precisely," sneered Farrar. "But no court is likely to judge that ha'porth of impudence to be Walter's son. I wish to heaven Helen had not permitted them to stay here." He scowled. "I'll have to find a way to get rid of 'em. Fast!"

Chandler pursed his lips. "One thing . . . Mrs. Deene don't quite fit the role you've writ for her. She seems to me a lady of Quality. Nor have I the feeling she would be an easy one to frighten. As for the boy, he's certainly been well bred up, and is full of spirit, by what I—"

"Spirit! That little monster! I tell you, Gordie, when I heard that whip crack and saw the carriage coming at us like any cannonball, I could have—No, damn you! Do not dare laugh!"

But Chandler did dare. Farrar's scowl eased to a grin and finally he broke into a reluctant chuckle.

"Do you know what I was thinking?" said Chandler, wiping his eyes. "I was remembering that time you and Quentin and I were down at Lac Brillant and he decided to climb the tower. You recollect?"

Farrar smiled nostalgically. "Jove, but I do. Your idiot of a brother fell."

"Yes, and you were balancing on a gargoyle and tried to catch him."

50

"Whereupon the curst gargoyle snapped off and we both went through your sire's brand new stained-glass window. Lord, but he was furious!"

"He was. But told me later that if you hadn't grabbed Quentin, he'd have been cold meat."

They looked steadily at one another. Farrar jerked to his feet, walked over to the fireplace and stared down into it. "Your ramshackle brother and his misplaced loyalty to Charles Stuart," he muttered. "How is the poor old fellow?"

Chandler brightened, as he always did when he spoke of his harum-scarum younger brother. " 'Tis what I came to tell you—he and Penny have hired a little place in the country, not far from Paris, and Quentin writes he is fully recovered and digging and hoeing—generally having a grand time."

"Praise be! Gordie, how did that trifle-top become involved in the Jacobite fiasco? He's no Catholic."

Chandler shrugged. "You know Quentin. Ever rushing in with no thought of consequences. But in fairness to him, I think he really admired Prince Charles. And he deplores the House of Hanover. A laudable opinion is one to judge them by Cumberland."

"Aye. That murderous whelp should have been smothered at birth!"

Chandler sprang up throwing a worried glance to the slightly open door. "For the love of God!"

"My people are loyal, never fear." The bitter grin twisted Farrar's mouth. "They'd have to be to stay with me."

"Few men are loyal when torment is brought to bear." Sitting down again, Chandler added cautiously, "And is time you ceased scourging yourself, old fellow."

"For what? The fact that my battery crumbled when I ran? The fact that because they also ran many good men died? Must I really cease scourging myself, Gordie?"

"What makes you think that had you not—I mean, had you stayed, you could have held them? They'd likely have deserted at all events. Your lieutenant must have tried."

"He did try. They ran over the poor lad with a gun carriage, I heard—God help him!"

Chandler bit his lip, but persisted, "When I came to see you in the hospital, you—" He checked. Farrar was staring blankly at him. "You don't recall my coming?"

51

The same slow travesty of a smile dawned. Farrar muttered, "My clever little *se defendendo* device. For example, I have absolutely no recollection of poor old Horry Rhodes going down, and yet I *know* he fell. What my mind cannot accept, you see, it blots out. You'd be surprised at how effectively it has protected me."

"You're too hard on yourself," said Chandler compassionately. "If the army believed you responsible, you'd have been held for court martial." A steady gaze was directed at him. Horrified, he leaned forward. "Good Lord! Tony—you've not been—I mean, they don't—You will not be—"

"Charged with desertion in the face of the enemy?" Farrar stared down at his boot and muttered expressionlessly, "I expected it. Long before this." He looked up, meeting Chandler's concerned regard enigmatically. "Two months ago, I received an official visit."

"Oh . . . my God!" whispered Chandler.

Farrar's attempt at nonchalance was not a great success. "I'm to hold myself ready."

'They'll shoot him,' thought Chandler, stunned. 'By God, they'll stand the poor devil against a wall and shoot him!'

The abigail's name was Rodgers. A dark woman, rather square of face and form, she had very pale, clear skin and was not unattractive, Dimity had decided, setting her age at about the mid to late thirties. She was rather devoid of personality, her voice seldom varying from a dull monotone, and she had a tendency to clear her throat from time to time, as though preparing her hearers for the coming observation. She did so now, remarking as she brushed out Dimity's hair that it was a nice morning, for a Monday, but rain had poured down in the night.

"Monday!" exclaimed Dimity. "I must have slept like a log!"

"Small—ahem—wonder, ma'am. My lady said she was s'prised you wasn't ready for burying after what you'd gone through. Are you feeling better?"

"Much better, I thank you. Er—my nephew . . . is he—?"

"With her la'ship. Took quite a liking to him, she has. And he sticks to her like glue." A spark of amusement brightened those dull dark eyes. "So scared of the master as he be, you cannot blame him hardly."

Dimity, who had already ascertained that the reticule, complete with Mrs. Deene's papers, was safely in the chest of drawers, agreed with this, and wondered how she was to make restitution for Carlton's disastrous mischief. Lost in thought, she paid little heed to what the abigail was about, but when the woman ceased her efforts and Dimity viewed the result, she was taken aback. Her brown locks were luxuriant, and Rodgers had styled them in a mass of ringlets with tendrils drifting beside her ears and tiny curls all across her brow. 'My heavens!' thought Dimity, 'Is too much!' and instinctively reached for the hairbrush.

The abigail had opened one of the two presses and now enquired, "Ahem—which gown would you wish to wear, ma'am?"

There was an odd note to the question. Dimity put down the hairbrush, and went over to inspect the garments that had been neatly put away while she slept.

Rodgers said, "This blue one is—er, pretty."

Dimity all but reeled. To say that Mrs. Deene's taste had been questionable would be a giant understatement. The colours were garish, the trims much too ornate, and the bodices so diminutive as to have been daring even when worn by a married lady. Aghast, she scanned the gown Rodgers had selected. It was overburdened with bows and frills, but at least the colour was not so offensive as that dreadful orange thing, or the lurid pink satin with the open lacing down the front of the strip that passed for a bodice. "Y—yes," she croaked. "That will do—nicely."

Her optimism was ill-founded. After the first attempt to fasten the buttons had failed, she clung to the bedpost, gasping, as Rodgers strove mightily with stay-laces. Poor Mrs. Deene had been an inch or two shorter, and rather on the thin side, whereas Dimity was tall and more generously endowed. She could almost breathe when Rodgers at last flung the skirts over, fastened the bodice in place, wrestled with the buttons, twitched and adjusted, then said, "Ahem," as she looked frowningly at the hem.

Following her gaze, Dimity saw more of her ankles than any gentleman had ever viewed unless a frolicsome wind granted them such a sight. It was all she could do not to moan aloud, but when she lifted her shocked eyes, she gave an involuntary yelp, and thought, 'Lord above! I had as well wear no bodice at all!' She raised a hand involuntarily to cover the voluptuous swell of her crushed breasts.

"Lawks!" whispered Rodgers under her breath. "Did—I beg your pardon, I'm sure, but—did you borrow it, Mrs. Deene?"

She could scarce claim to have borrowed *all* of them, and this one was the least offensive of the lot! "I fear . . . I have gained a—a few pounds," she said wretchedly.

"Ar. Well, let's find you some slippers. There was a nice blue silk pair here somewhere . . ."

The "nice blue silk pair" were strained to the limit when at last they were on Dimity's cringing feet. They were also covered with spangles and beads that sparkled so they must only attract attention to the dreadfully inadequate length of her skirts. 'If,' she thought cynically, 'the gentlemen are able to tear their eyes from my naked bosom!'

Staring, Rodgers uttered a faint "Ahem" and enquired if madam's abigail was coming.

For the first time, it dawned on Dimity that Mrs. Deene had been travelling with neither footman nor abigail. "Yes," she lied. "That is to say, she was with me but sprained her ankle, so I sent her home. My dresser will arrive in a day or two."

She saw by the slight lift of Rodgers' eyebrows that she had overdone it. Had the woman said a scornful "Dresser!" her disdain could scarcely have been more plainly expressed. The mirror revealed a creature who was at best vulgar, and at worst, a person of ill repute. 'I cannot go downstairs like this! I *cannot*!' thought Dimity in despair, and with a near sob of relief, remembered the scarf the gypsy boy had used to cover her basket. She had seen it yesterday morning, lying with the pile of luggage that had been salvaged from the wrecked stagecoach and, for no reason she could have told, had picked it up. She tottered to the chest and found the scarf, neatly folded, in the second drawer. "It's a touch chilly," she advised the staring abigail, draping the shawl about her shoulders. She opened the jewel box and, stifling a groan, selected the least offensive brooch and used it to pin the shawl in place. The brooch was small and

the clasp difficult and when at last she had it closed, Rodgers'
eyes were rounder than ever.

"But—ahem—but it's . . . *red and white*, ma'am!"

"Yes," said Dimity, who could have wept. "Lovely. Well—
off we go!"

Rodgers hurried to open the door. Dimity hobbled in her
wake and thought with a pang that she now had some slight idea
of what it must cost her beloved Perry to walk. "By the bye,"
she said, pausing in the hall. "When is the fair held?"

"It's been and gone, ma'am. Won't come back till next summer."

"Oh," said Dimity, hollowly. Tio had certainly said there
was a fair. Perhaps he'd not known the actual date of its arrival.

The abigail said with faint reproof, "Ahem—her la'ship's been
waiting and waiting, Mrs. Deene."

Meekly, Dimity followed her. She had noticed little of the
house on her arrival and was impressed now by the beauty of it.
The corridor they followed was wide, the ceiling high-vaulted,
the wainscoted walls topped by a magnificent carved frieze.
Dark wood floors gleamed with the patina of age and polish,
and were strewn with richly coloured rugs. Little chests and
tables held porcelain and crystal *objets d'art* and there were
several fine oil paintings. They passed five closed doors, Dimity's feet protesting every step of the way, and when they approached the spiral staircase, she saw that behind it, rising
majestically through both levels, was a splendid stained-glass
window. The corridor widened on the far side of the landing,
but the vaulted ceilings continued, a feature, she was later to
find, that obtained throughout The Palfreys, the most elaborate
examples being the beautifully carved lierne vaulting in both the
music hall and the chapel.

The prospect of another meeting with the irascible Farrar did
not enchant. Dimity asked, "Is the captain's suite in this wing?"

"On t'other side of the stairs, ma'am. This side is reserved
for her la'ship and her guests."

It would be interesting to know if Lady Farrar had always led
so separate an existence, or if the present arrangement had been
inspired by her infamous nephew's disgrace, but one could not,
of course, ask such a question.

Rodgers scratched on the second door from the landing. It

was swung open by an elegant footman wearing the dark red livery that Dimity vaguely remembered having seen yesterday. He gave a slight bow, but not before she had seen a look of shock come into his eyes.

He led the way through a charming little anteroom and opened the far door. "Mrs. Deene," he announced, and held the door a moment longer than was necessary, yearning to see Lady Helen's reaction to the glory of her guest. He was disappointed. My lady, wearing a pale mauve morning dress, her powdered hair stylishly arranged and adorned by a lacy violet cap, was seated at a desk in the pleasant parlour, reading a letter. She turned, smiling. For a split-second her smile was rather fixed, then she rose and came forward, holding out her hand. "Good morning, Mrs. Deene. I do hope you are better today."

Dimity dropped a curtsey. Before she could respond, however, a shout rang out, and Carlton came limping from an adjacent room, his curls neatly brushed, and his blue eyes alight. "Oooh—you *do* look nice, Aunty," he declared enthusiastically.

Aware that her face was scarlet, Dimity thanked him and bent to receive his kiss. "How is your poor knee?"

"Very good, thank you. Isn't this a fine place? Yestiday I went for a ride on a real pony. One of the grooms took me. And I watched my uncle fence with Mr. Chandler. Mr. Chandler won," he added scornfully.

Lady Helen said, "Captain Farrar was badly wounded, Carlton, and is still not quite himself."

"Yes, I know. My aunty told me. He was shot in the back 'cause he was running away like a rat. Aunty said he left all his men to be killed while he saved his own skin. Why did he do that, Lady He'n? A *man* wouldn't've done it."

Dimity scarcely knew where to look, and was horrified to see Lady Helen's serenity crumple into an expression of anguish.

A deep voice drawled, "I hope I do not interrupt a private discussion?"

'Oh—*no*!' thought Dimity, and wished the floor might open and swallow her.

With the sublime insensitivity of childhood, Carlton said an obliging, "I was just telling Lady He'n that my aunty said—"

"I heard." Farrar sauntered into the room, his gaze fixed on Lady Helen. "Sound familiar, ma'am?"

Glancing to him in abject misery, Dimity was slightly taken aback. Today he had not allowed his man to apply powder and she was surprised to find that his hair was very fair, in startling contrast to his tan. He wore a leathern riding coat and an openthroated white shirt. Knee boots and corded breeches completed his attire, and spurs jingled softly as he stepped past her. He made no acknowledgement of her presence, his entire attention on his aunt.

Lady Helen's response was slightly uneven. "Yes, the . . . boy has difficulty with my name. It reminded me—" but she broke off with a small, dismissing gesture, and did not finish the sentence.

Farrar nodded, turned his head, and enjoyed his first clear look at Dimity. His control was remarkable, but she saw the long fingers of his right hand stretch out for an instant. "Well," he remarked breathlessly, "you are looking ro—bust this morning, Mrs. Deene."

Oddly, his sarcasm was a relief. "You are too kind," Dimity murmured, dropping a graceful curtsey.

"Very true," he agreed, his fascinated gaze on her décolletage. "I expect you want to get—to it."

She stared at him.

The side of his mouth twitched. "One *presumes* you intend to produce your documentation," he drawled. "Before you leave us."

"Oh," she said, wondering if it was really possible that the papers had not already been thoroughly examined.

Misunderstanding her silence, Carlton put in helpfully, "They were in my aunt's reticule."

"I know, dear," she said absently.

Lady Helen directed a swift glance at her. "There is no hurry, Farrar," she said in her calm fashion. "Mrs. Deene is to breakfast with me, and since it will take some days to prove or disprove her—ah, claim, I think it only proper that she should stay here."

Dimity gave a gasp of astonishment.

No less incredulous, Farrar said, "You cannot be serious, Au—ma'am? These two are little better than—"

"How do *you* know what we are?" interpolated Dimity, frowning.

His gaze raked her up and down with such contempt that it was as much as she could do not to slap his arrogant face.

"If *that* is Walter's son," he sneered, jerking his head at the child, "I'll—"

My lady's hand dropped protectively to Carlton's shoulder as he backed against her skirts. "If we prove that he is not, he will be sent away, of course, but—"

"To prison," snapped Farrar, eyes narrow with wrath. "Together with his alleged—"

Lady Helen's voice rose. "But so long as there is the chance that he is Walter's son, he has as much right as—*any* of us, to live under this roof."

Farrar still faced her, but it seemed to Dimity that he had flinched slightly. Certainly, his gaze fell away. After a tense, hushed moment, the battle of wills was conceded. "As you wish," he growled. "On one condition."

"Which is?"

"That he come with me. Now. I waited out your aunt's recovery, my lad, but I've a few things to say to you."

Carlton turned white and began to tremble.

Dimity said, "If you mean to beat the child—"

He turned a blazing glare on her. "I've a Halifax gibbet in the dungeons," he sneered. "It seems the quickest way to get rid of the brat."

"Farrar!" exclaimed my lady, angrily.

Carlton stepped forward and stood with head thrown back as he watched the tall man's wrathful countenance. "All right, sir," he said. "You can gibbet me. I 'serve it for scaring your horses, but I din't mean it, you know. I only wanted to crack that whip." His eyes pleaded for understanding. "It did crack goodly, din't it?"

Remorseless, Farrar jabbed a finger at the door and followed as the child crept out.

Dimity turned to Lady Helen only to find her face averted and her head bowed. Distressed, she said, "Dear ma'am, I am so sorry. This is dreadful for you, and my naughty little nephew makes it worse. I will take him away at once. The—the captain would not really . . . ?"

My lady made a furtive movement with her handkerchief and managed a shaky smile. "I do apologize. It chances the child reminds me of—someone . . ." The words trailed off. Her green eyes, paler than her nephew's but remarkably handsome, had turned to the side. Dimity followed her gaze to the portrait of a young man that hung above the mantel. The artist had captured with lifelike realism the faintly bored smile, the gleaming curls of the dashing French peruke that tumbled attractively about a proud, aristocratic face. There was a look of Lady Helen there, although the fine eyes were deep blue, set off by high-arched brows. The features were regular, but Dimity thought them less finely chiselled than Farrar's, the chin not as firm, the mouth a touch too voluptuous. Still, there was no denying he was a very good-looking young man, and she asked, "Your son, ma'am?"

Lady Helen nodded. "My only child. Harding Bradwell Farrar. A rather wild boy, but—so very lovable."

"I've a brother who is rather wild, but I wouldn't change him for the world," said Dimity loyally. "How proud of him you must be." She saw at once the look of consternation and, too late, recalled what Mrs. Deene had said of Farrar's cousin.

Lady Helen sat in a brocaded wing chair and confirmed sadly, "He is dead, ma'am."

There was nothing to do but feign ignorance. Dimity sank to her knees beside the chair, expressed polite sympathy, and enquired as to whether it had been a long illness.

My lady's eyes hardened. "It was at Prestonpans. Harding and Anthony joined up together and were in the same Battery. Anthony was in command when—when Harding was killed."

So that was what Mrs. Deene had meant! Dimity thought, 'My God! What a tragedy!' and murmured numbly, "How perfectly ghastly for you." Lady Helen watched her with a puzzled expression, and she went on hastily, "I did not know. My sister had not mentioned it."

"But, of course. 'Twas my understanding she died some years ago."

'Oh Mitten, *do* be careful,' thought Dimity, aghast. "Yes. I'm being silly," she mumbled. "But—I was so shocked."

"I see. You have heard something of Farrar, I think?"

Dimity nodded.

"And you wonder, perhaps, if I hold him to blame for Harding's death?"

Yearning to be elsewhere, Dimity said, "Yes—No! Oh, dear! I-I really—"

"What would be your judgement, Mrs. Deene?"

What would be her judgement? She held Farrar to blame for Peregrine's injuries. Indirectly, of course. But—this . . . ! And why would Lady Helen ask such a question? She faltered, "I-I could not possibly answer. But—if you—That is to say . . . Oh, ma'am, however can you allow him to stay here? Could you not ask him to-to find other accommodations?"

Lady Helen stroked her hand absently. "He was such a dear little boy—who would have guessed . . . ?" She sighed. "But to answer your question, my dear, I cannot ask him to leave. You see, The Palfreys belongs to him."

"To *him*? But I had understood you took the captain in when he was a small child and his parents died."

"Quite true. But the property is entailed, do you see? Gilbert, my late husband, was the fifth baronet. He adored Anthony, and divided his fortune into three equal shares; one third to Harding, one third to me, and the final third to Anthony, each share to revert to the title-holder should the others die unmarried."

Harbouring the beginnings of a terrible suspicion, Dimity stared at her in silence.

My lady, inwardly intrigued by that obvious dismay, went on. "The title passed to Harding, of course, and would have gone next to Walter, since he was two years older than Anthony. As it is, title, estates, and two-thirds of the fortune have come to my only surviving nephew."

Dimity whispered, "Then—he is Captain Sir Anthony Farrar!"

"Unless your claim is proven, my dear."

"My . . . goodness!"

My lady bent nearer. "You surely have realized that—if Carlton is Walter's son, then the title would rightfully be his?"

"And," croaked Dimity, horror struck, "The Palfreys?"

"Yes. And the part of the fortune that is bound up in the entail, besides what came to Anthony upon my son's death."

'He will be ruined!' thought Dimity. 'Oh, how he must *yearn* to be rid of us!'

"But you scarce ate a morsel," said Lady Helen, walking downstairs beside Dimity, and watching the pale and troubled face with no little anxiety. "We can postpone this matter for a day or so and give you a chance to regain your strength."

Between her discomfort and the shock of learning that she had somehow been placed in the position of wresting a man's title and estates from him, whereby—if he was as base as everyone thought him—he had very good reason for murdering both her and little Carlton, Dimity had found it impossible to force more than one slice of toast down her reluctant throat. Not that she could have eaten more at all events, for her stays were so tight she knew her poor sides must be on the point of meeting in the middle of her stomach. To add to her misery, her feet felt raw, and she could barely endure to set one before the other. The sooner she was out of this perfectly dreadful mess, the better. She thought of the cypher under her mattress, and was so distressed that a faint moan escaped her.

Startled, my lady exclaimed, "No, really, I think we *must* call in our physician. Mr. Chandler will, I am sure, be willing to send him to us."

"Mr. Chandler is still here?" asked Dimity, clutching at straws.

"Yes. He and his brother Quentin and Anthony have been friends from school days."

"And your son, ma'am?"

"Well—no. Harding was not—He had his own friends."

They were halfway down the stairs at this point and, despite her misery, Dimity said admiringly, "Oh, what a *very* lovely house it is! See how the sunbeams come through the stained glass to light this painting. Isn't it pretty?"

"Quite one of my favourites," my lady agreed without expression. "Anthony did it."

Dimity lurched to a halt, staring her astonishment.

"He is quite a fine artist," said Lady Helen.

Dimity scanned the painting. It was a charming rural scene and although she knew little of art, she recognized a considerable degree of skill. The plaque on the lower edge of the elaborate frame read, "The Village Green."

Green. Memory triggered, she forgot to comment on the painting, and babbled, "That reminds me. An acquaintance of mine lives hereabouts, I think. Perhaps you know him, ma'am? A Mr. Green."

"Rafe? He was one my son's closest friends." My lady sighed and added regretfully, "But alas, he does not come here any more."

Dimity's hopes, which had soared, crashed down again. "No. This must be a different gentleman."

As they reached the ground floor, Carlton, face flushed and rigid, eyes glittering, stalked past with silent dignity and went limping up the stairs. The heavy riding crop still gripped in his hand, Farrar sauntered up the steps, crossed the music hall and stopped before them.

"Did you *dare* to whip that child?" cried Dimity, enraged.

He slanted a bored look at her. "I gave him ten of the best. And *daring* plays no part in it, madam. You claim the brat is my nephew. At present, happily, I am still the head of this house and thus have every right in the world to discipline him. Besides which," he brandished the crop before her outraged face, "had you one single grain of sense, you'd see that the boy wanted to be punished. Egad, but I'm almost driven to hope he *is* my nephew! Certainly, *you* would ruin him within another year or so! Already, he's almost completely out of hand."

Opening her mouth to denounce him, Dimity had a sudden mental picture of Peregrine or Piers, had Carlton done one tenth of what he'd perpetrated at The Palfreys. Seething, but bowing to the justness of his remarks, she closed her lips.

Gordon Chandler, his dark hair unpowdered today, hastened to join the little group. "Good morning, my lady, Mrs. Deene," he said with a polite bow.

Dimity swept him a curtsey. She rose to discover a glazed look in Mr. Chandler's grey eyes and Captain Sir Anthony's jaw at half mast. Uneasy, she said, "An I offended, sir . . ."

"No, no! Not at all, ma'am," replied Farrar, laughter dancing into his eyes. "I perceive you to be a woman of many—er, parts."

His gaze seemed incapable of moving from one such part.

With a gasp of fright, her hand flew to her bosom. Her curtsey had been a nice flourish, but a major error. The balky clasp of the ugly little brooch had parted. The scarf was hanging uselessly on her skirt. Instinctively, she grabbed for it. The brooch had fallen also, and the pin jabbed her finger spitefully. She gave a little jump of pain and shock. Another error. With unspeakable horror she felt something snap. She could breathe! And then, pop! pop! pop! pop! went the four buttons poor Rodgers had battled so hard to close.

In another second, her skirts would plunge.

There was really only one possible thing to do.

She fainted gracefully into Gordon Chandler's ready arms.

❦ *Chapter 5* ❧

Alarmed by her beloved master's distress, Shuffle stood with her front paws on his muscular thigh, her tucked-in tail quivering anxiously, adoration apparent in every inch of her golden body.

"It-it is quite . . . all right, old lady," gasped Farrar, mopping at his eyes with one hand and caressing her head with the other. He looked up from the hay bale in the barn that was serving him as a chair, and went on breathlessly, " 'Pon my oath, I've not laughed so much in months. No, really Gordie, however did you keep your countenance? Had I not departed—"

"Departed, is it?" His shoulders propped against a post, Chandler said, grinning, "Man, you ran like a rabbit!" And at once bit his lip, appalled by his faux pas.

Appearing not to notice that unfortunate choice of words, Farrar said, " 'Twas either run, or laugh in the doxy's face! What on earth compels women to persist in squeezing themselves into garments four sizes too small, and crippling their feet with shoes that make 'em look downright deformed? I'll wager Madam Deene's toes were curled halfway to her instep in those gaudy atrocities! And as for her quarter-deck! Heaven help us! I fancied we were going to have a bacchanalian revelation at any second! Jove, what a disappointment!" He lapsed into hilarity again. "And—and then," he wheezed, "to see you struggling upstairs with—the wench! Burn it if it wasn't like—like the climactic scene of . . . a poor farce! You, bearing the lightskirt up to your bed and . . . and staggering every step!"

"I was not staggering!" protested Chandler. "Though she's

no skin and bone wisp.'' He smiled reminiscently. ''All womanly curves and softness, rather.''

Farrar's mirth eased. ''Never say you've formed a *tendre* for the vixen? 'Ware, Gordie! I'd not want *that* one for my peculiar!''

''Which is as well, for I fancy you'd get your come-uppance did you suggest it.'' Sobering, Chandler murmured thoughtfully, ''She's no opera dancer, Tony.''

''She's not preparing for her presentation, either. Can you not picture her making her curtsey to the world?'' He chuckled. ''Come to think on it, she'd best not! Not in those gowns, or the world might see more than it bargained for!''

Chandler knit his brows. ''Yet the habit she had on yesterday was very well cut, did you notice? And although her hair was disarrayed by the time I saw her, it was not in that—er, unfortunate style she affected this morning. Her speech is cultured. And did you mark her hands?''

''Aye. Both of 'em. Deep in my purse!''

''No, I mean it. They are white, and quite lovely. Certainly well manicured. If she's ever scrubbed a floor or cooked a meal, I'll shave my head and wear a French peruke!''

Farrar stood, laughing at him. ''You *have* formed a *tendre* for her! Our chaste Gordon has at last—''

''Now blast your ears, Tony! If you're spoiling for a mill—!''

''Well, compared to Quentin, you *are* chaste.''

Chandler responded in French, the kennel language making Farrar chuckle again.

A groom led a fine mare from the barn, and as the two men started towards it, Farrar said with genuine regret, ''*Must* you go? It would be nice to chat of old times for a week or two.''

'Yes, I'm very sure it would,' thought Chandler, and said, ''I'll try to come up again before I go home. But I've business in Town I've already kept waiting too long.''

Farrar drew him to a halt. ''At Boudreaux House, perchance? Have a care, you clunch. Don't let Treve de Villars embroil you in his treasonable plottings.''

''Treve saved my brother's life. He may embroil me in whatsoever he wishes.'' But Chandler read concern in Farrar's eyes and gripped his arm, saying with a smile, ''Never worry so. I tread carefully.''

"You'd best tiptoe, old lad. The ground becomes a bog around those who aid rebels."

Chandler mounted up, and Farrar added more revealingly than he knew, "You will try to come back?"

"Aye." Chandler raised his gauntleted hand in farewell, then brought the mare to a canter. He did not look back. He knew that until he was out of sight Farrar would stand there, gazing after him.

For the sake of appearances, Dimity was obliged to remain in her bed for the balance of the day. Lady Helen came in several times and said it was perfectly understandable that she should be unnerved, and she must not think of getting up. If Dimity was unnerved, it was by the waste of precious time and by her inability even to try to cope with Mrs. Deene's wicked wardrobe. She asked about Carlton and was informed he was "with Farrar," that his care had been assigned to Cissie, who was very good with children, and that she was not to worry. She dozed and had a nightmare in which Farrar lured Carlton to a lonely copse and strangled him. Waking, shaken and not at all sure her dream had been so outlandish, she looked through periodicals, and fretted until evening. But even then she was forbidden to get out of bed. A tray was brought up and Rodgers sat beside her with the announcement that she had been instructed to remain until Mrs. Deene fell asleep.

To her great relief, Carlton stuck his head around the door, said he hoped she was feeling better, and before she could reply, gave a whoop and went galloping off. So Farrar had not murdered the boy. Yet.

Determined to wait out the abigail's vigilance, then get up and see what could be done about the gowns, Dimity lay down and feigned sleep. She was more affected by the series of disasters than she would have admitted, however, and between her aches and pains and her troubled thoughts, she fell fast asleep and did not waken until Rodgers brought in her hot chocolate the next morning.

She felt much better for her enforced rest and insisted she was eager to get up. Rodgers helped with her toilette, wrapped her in Mrs. Deene's lurid dressing gown, and ushered her along the hall to my lady's parlour. It appeared that Lady Helen had been called to see a sick tenant, and Dimity was not sorry to find she was to breakfast alone. Carlton was nowhere to be seen, and as soon as she had enjoyed tea, some delicious scones, and a slice of cold ham, she went back to her bedchamber.

She was delighted to find it empty, her bed neatly made, and the room tidied. She flew to the press and took down the blue gown. Sitting in the middle of the bed, she peered hopefully at the waistband. Someone had sewn the buttons back on, probably believing they had been torn off when she "fainted." She turned the great skirt inside out, and her hopes plummeted. The gown was cheap and poorly made, with small allowance in the seams. Even if she could enlarge the waist, it would not help much, for there was no turn-up at the hem of the skirt, the lower edges having been rolled. She thought despairingly, 'Besides, it must be a mile wide and would take *days* to sew!' Thanks to Tio, she had funds, but if she asked to be taken shopping and purchased more tasteful garments it would very likely raise suspicions about her identity. Nor dare she claim that her luggage had been mixed up, for it would take very little to send Farrar over to the Winchester coaching station, and if he started poking about, heaven only knew what it might lead to! Lady Helen had been kind; perhaps she could beg the loan of a fichu at least. The thought was scarcely born than it was discarded. Lady Helen was nobody's fool; she would know that the woman who had bought such gowns was not the type to cover what they were designed to display! She gave a small moan of frustration. There was *nothing* she could do! She would simply have to endure these dreadful clothes for a day or two, until she could find Mr. Green, pass on Tio's cypher, and go home!

The *cypher*!

She jumped from the bed, knelt beside it, and reached under the mattress. It was silly to be frightened because she did not at once find it. Groping blindly, she thought, 'Do not lose your wits, Mitten. It is, after all, quite small.' Two minutes later, she was tearing sheets, blankets and eiderdown from the great tester bed, and in another minute, had hauled the mattress to the floor. The cypher was gone! Stunned, she stood amidst the debris, biting at her knuckle. It *must* be here!

"Lawks!"

Dimity spun around. Rodgers stood in the open doorway, her face a study in amazement. "Ahem—whatever is wrong, ma'am?" she gasped. "Weren't it made up proper?"

"Did *you* make it up?"

Rodgers looked offended. "I am not a chambermaid, ma'am."

"Do you know which chambermaid was in here?"

"I—'spect it was Cissie." She said anxiously, "But, she's a good girl, ma'am. If you lay a complaint, she will lose her sittyation. I'll make it better for ye."

"No, no. Just send her up here. At once, if you please. And—the fewer people know, the better. I'd not wish to cause her trouble."

Rodgers flew, not taking the time to close the parlour door.

Dimity stared down at the debris for a moment, then knelt and began to pull the mattress aside so as to crawl under the bed.

"Good heavens!" Another startled onlooker had arrived. Wide-eyed, Lady Helen said, "I had thought to find you laid down upon your bed, Mrs. Deene. Not *under* it!"

Alone in the breakfast room, Farrar glanced up from the *London Gazette*, put down his coffee cup and sprang to his feet. "You are going to join me, ma'am?" he asked eagerly.

His aunt was dressed for luncheon in a charming dark blue muslin Watteau dress, the train sweeping gracefully behind her. A beautifully carved ivory cross on a golden chain hung about her throat, and her hair was powdered and swept into a high coiffure. "No, thank you," she answered. "But—pray do not let me interrupt your reading."

"I had much rather talk with you. Would you care to walk in the garden?" It was a question asked out of courtesy, and he was astounded when she agreed. He sent a lackey running for a shawl and when Lady Helen looked at him with arched brows, he said, "The breeze is rather chill, ma'am."

They set off when the shawl had been draped carefully about her shoulders. He knew better than to offer his arm, but he sensed that she was troubled, and walked beside her in silence, moderating his stride to her dainty steps, and whistling for Shuffle who ran to join them with much flapping of ears.

"It was nice to see Chandler," my lady said at length.

He was fairly certain that she did not wish to talk about Gordon, but answered politely, "Yes. He says he may come again before returning to Kent."

"How very good of him."

He flushed a little, but said nothing.

After a pause, Lady Helen came to the point. "Farrar, have you—er, noticed anything at all—odd . . . about Mrs. Deene?"

"Jupiter, ma'am, I've yet to notice anything *normal* about her! She is without doubt the most vulgar, brazen, mercenary little baggage I ever—"

"Not—little, exactly," she put in musingly.

Curious, he smiled down at her.

"Nor do I think—" She interrupted herself, "But that is no matter. What concerns me—" She shook her stately head and sighed.

Alarmed now, he took her arm. "Aunt Helen—what is it? An she disturbs you—" Her gaze was fixed on his detaining hand. His flush deepening, he released her arm. "Pray tell me what troubles you. I'll get rid of the jade do you but give me leave. She has no least shred of hope to win her claim, if that is what concerns you."

Her fine eyes lifted to his. She said dispassionately, "What happens to either this estate or the fortune concerns me very little, Farrar."

He stepped back with an odd, almost shrinking movement quite foreign to his normal manner and stood staring at the ground. She knew she had wounded him and experienced the usual helplessness because the need to strike at him did not alleviate her deeper pain. Stifling a sigh, she added, "I am afraid for that poor girl."

His bowed head lifted. Recovering himself, he echoed, "That—*poor*—girl? You cannot refer to our larcenous adventuress?"

"I cannot be pleased to hear you speak so disparagingly of a lady, sir."

"But—but, that—I mean Mrs. Deene—who wears no marriage ring, you'll have noted—is nothing but— Oh, now ma'am—you've *seen* what she is, for Lord's sake!"

"From what I have seen," she said slowly, "I begin to think that poor creature, she is—unbalanced!"

Farrar blinked. "She's shrewd as any vixen if you was to ask—Oh, very well, she is a charming victim of cruel fate, an that pleases you! May I ask what has brought you to the conclusion she is short of a sheet?"

"Not at all. She was fairly wallowing in them," she muttered, shaking her head.

"She—*what*?"

"When she fainted yesterday morning—"

"Pish! She no more fainted than I did! You likely heard that staylace snap just as I—"

"Farrar!"

He bowed his head to hide his quivering mouth and said a meek, "Your pardon, ma'am."

For a second my lady was silent, her sad eyes on the thick, crisply waving fair hair. Her hand went out as if to touch it, but was clenched and withdrawn. She went on hurriedly, "The maids told me she was feeling better this morning, but—I looked in on her just now, and—and she had torn the bed to shreds."

His startled gaze flashed to her. "Good God! Bed posts and all?"

Her eyes twinkled, but she said sternly, "I wish you will not be facetious. I am deadly serious. All the sheets and bedding were strewn about the room, and she was—playing with the mattress."

"Playing . . . with the mattress?" he echoed, awed. "By Jove, then she's off the road, all right! What did she say? Was she foaming at the mouth or anything?"

"No, thank heaven! But she behaved most odd. She claimed she had been trying to rest and had heard a—a cricket."

"What 'twixt mattress and boards? No, aunt—you hoax me!"

"An you put it together with those ridiculous clothes, and the way she faints all the time . . . Unless—" her expression cleared. "Of course! It must be the shock of the accidents she suffered! Why ever did I not take that into account? My apologies, Farrar, for having troubled you with it."

70

"I could wish you found more to trouble me with, ma'am. Could you spare the time to take luncheon with—"

"No, no. I'll leave you to your own—affairs." She started off, then turned so suddenly that she saw the wistfulness in his eyes. "By the bye, do you know of another gentleman named Green living hereabouts?"

He became very still. "No. Why?"

"Mrs. Deene had thought she might be acquainted with Rafe, but evidently her friend is another Mr. Green." She shrugged and walked on, saying, "It is of no importance."

For a moment Farrar stood motionless. Then, "Is it not, by God!" he whispered.

"The thing is, ma'am," said Cissie, twisting nervously at the hem of her apron and watching Dimity with frightened brown eyes, "the housekeeper said as you'd had such a drefful time, and the mattress had not been turned in a while, seeing as we get no company no more, so she said as we should turn it, so we did, Eth and me, and if I'd knowed you did not like a mattress turned—"

Dimity interrupted the flood. "It was most kind. Er, did you find anything underneath?"

"No, Mrs. Deene."

Rodgers put in defensively, "Ahem, and we've not never had no crickets in our beds since I been—"

"I did not mean a cricket. I said that to Lady Helen, but—" Dimity had no need to pretend a blush as she saw their intrigued expressions. She lowered her voice. "Surely, you found *something*, Cissie?"

"Nothing 'cept a scrap o' paper with some writings on. I can't read, but it was too little and crumpled up to be anything important, so I burnt it."

Dimity felt sick and uttered a strangled shriek. The two maids rushed to support her. Allowing herself to be lowered onto the bed, she whispered, "Are you—quite *sure* it—has been . . . burned?"

Much alarmed, Cissie gulped, "I'm that sorry, ma'am! I put it in the wastebasket, and one of the lackeys will have took 'em all to the rubbish heap by this time."

"Where . . . is that?"

Rodgers said, "It's round the back, on the far side of the house, ma'am. Down the hill. I'll go at once, if—"

"No!" cried Dimity. They were both staring. She sought desperately for an explanation. "That would—break the spell, you see."

"Cor," whispered Cissie. "Is it a writing from a witch, then?"

Dimity beckoned them nearer. "Promise you won't tell."

Two hearts were solemnly crossed; two promises given.

"If you tell a single soul," warned Dimity, "the spell will be broken, and—and the witch said whoever breaks it will suffer a—a terrible fate!"

They paled, and swore not to do so dreadful a thing.

"It is," said Dimity, improvising frantically, "a little piece of a love note. I have been a widow for some time, you know, and a gentleman has been—er, courting me, but he is very shy and every time I almost, ah—"

"Bring him up to scratch?" prompted Rodgers breathlessly.

"Er, yes. Every time, he becomes tongue-tied. So I went to a good witch I heard of, and she said if I would sleep with part of his love note under my mattress for three weeks, without once breaking the routine, he would offer next day."

"Lawks!" gasped Rodgers, eyes enormous. "And *you* went and burnt it, Cissie Simpkins! Do he live hereabouts, Mrs. Deene?"

"No." Struck by an idea, Dimity regrouped hurriedly. "Well, not very near. If I tell you his name, will you promise to keep it secret?"

Again their hearts were crossed.

"His name," Dimity imparted, "is Mr. Green. Do you know of him?"

They looked at each other.

Cissie, wiping away tears of fright, asked, "Does ye mean—Mr. *Rafe* Green, ma'am?"

Dimity stifled a sigh. "No. His name is not Rafe but—"

"That's true," said Rodgers. "But it's what everyone calls him, isn't it, ma'am? 'Cause he don't like his own name, I mean."

Cissie put in importantly, "So he uses his middle name, which is Ralph, only they all call him Rafe."

"Well, Mrs. Deene knows that, silly," said Rodgers, nudging her. "A lady certainly knows what her gentleman friend's name is!"

"I should hope so." Dimity's heart had given a great leap. She thought, 'I've found him! Praise heaven, one part of my wretched puzzle is solved!' Almost she asked for his direction, only at the last instant recalling she would also be expected to know the address of her "admirer." But that should present no problem. She would ask in the stables as soon as the opportunity arose.

The two maids stared at her radiant face and drew their own conclusions.

Rodgers said briskly, "Well, you'll want to run quick, Mrs. Deene. I fetched some tape up. I can sew it on your waistband if you like, so you can tie it closed. Might serve better than them buttons, and it won't show under the bodice."

In very short order, Dimity was hobbling down the back stairs. "Rafe Green," murmured Cissie, leaning against the bedroom door. *"Shy?"*

"And—tongue-tied," said Rodgers, and they both giggled.

"What if he comes here to pay her court?" said Cissie, with a suddenly scared look.

Rodgers folded her arms. "I'd give a month's wages to see it!"

"Not me!" Cissie shivered theatrically. "Lordy, Lor'! Not me, mate!"

The debris atop the ash pile looked huge, and although Dimity was inexpressibly relieved to find it had not yet been lit, it presented a daunting challenge with the mass of crumpled letters, newspapers, tree prunings, torn upholstery (which she recognized with a flutter of guilt as having been part of the doomed carriage), and all manner of crushed boxes and odds and ends. Cissie had said she'd put the invaluable cypher in a wastebasket. Dimity selected a sturdy branch from the prunings and used it to sift through the mass. She soon realized she dare not venture into the ashes wearing her stockings and the horrid slippers and, with a guilty glance around, took them off and placed them where she might quickly retrieve them if the lackey came to burn the rubbish. The sun rose in the sky and grew warmer; she knew that she might very well have been missed by now but, desperate, she sought on. If only the cypher was not so small! She saw then an empty hair powder box. That should be from the right area! The box was farther on the heap than she had yet ventured, and she trod cautiously in amongst the rubble. There it was! Lying half under a broken comb. She thought, 'How could I have been so *fortunate*?' and reached out, leaning perilously.

"Cinderella . . . ?"

The sardonic drawl was unmistakeable. Her heart jumping into her throat, Dimity tried to grab and turn at the same instant, and inevitably lost her balance. She fell, face down. Dry ash and bits of flotsam flew in all directions. So did her skirt. With a muffled sob of chagrin she snatched the cypher and thrust it in her bosom, then turned around.

The Craven was standing directly behind her. She fancied at first to see a certain wariness in his eyes, but there could be no doubt of the mirth which followed that expression. Without much success, she tried to look indifferent and poised.

Surveying a most unladylike creature in a filthy gown, a streak of soot between her breasts, her feet bare and black, her chin and eyebrows elevated despite the smutty face and the ashes adorning her hair, it was all Farrar could do to keep from howling with glee.

Shuffle darted forward, barking shrilly at the apparition.

Dimity said crossly, "Oh, be quiet, do!"

The dog sat down and looked at her, tail wriggling.

"You have made a remarkably rapid recovery," said Farrar, his voice none too steady.

"I come of sturdy stock," she declared, inwardly ready to sink.

His mouth quirked in a way she thought revolting. "So I—ah, see," he said, running mirthful eyes over her.

Dimity ground her teeth and glared at him.

"Perhaps," he went on, all innocence, "you would wish luncheon cooked and served out here in the—ah, fresh air? You are partial to spitted roast pig, perchance."

She began to assess the merits of cannibalism, and said regally, "Something of mine was accidentally thrown away. I was trying to find it."

He lifted his brows and reached out to her. Disdaining his aid, she put down one hand to brace herself. Unhappily, it landed in an empty (almost) tub of lard. She withdrew it with an "Ugh!" of disgust.

Momentarily overcome, Farrar was obliged to turn away. He wiped his brimming eyes and, regaining control, took a long stride, grasped her arm, and hauled her up. Dimity ignored the great show he made of wiping his hand on a snowy handkerchief, and Farrar ignored her rather ostentatious taking up of the sturdy branch with which she had poked at the ash pile. He kept well clear of her disastrous gown, picked up her shoes and slanted a hilarious glance at those bare black toes. "You could," he pointed out in a choked voice, "have sent a lackey to find it."

Treading daintily through the ashes, leaning on her branch, and with the precious cypher safe in her bodice, Dimity said loftily, "I do not delegate unpleasant tasks to servants."

"Hmmn. Well, it is nice that you found your—er, cherished possession, but—why is that particular one so valued, I wonder?"

She stared at him. All schoolboy innocence, he nodded to the stick she carried.

"Oh, for heaven's sake," she exclaimed. "You know perfectly well it was not this!"

"But—indeed ma'am, from the way you clung to it, I thought perhaps—"

"Very diverting," she said acidly. "Now, an you will be so good as to go away, I will put on my shoes and stockings."

"No, do you really think you should?"

Dimity transferred her glare from his smirk to her feet, and could have wept. She took refuge in disdain and walked on, employing her branch as a cane, and wondering miserably how she could possibly re-enter the house in such a condition, and what *ever* Lady Helen would think.

Carlton came charging from the direction of the house and stopped dead. His small face became one big scowl, and he flung himself at Farrar, fists flying. "What have you done to my poor aunty, you wicked beast?"

Shuffle jumped up, growling furiously.

Farrar said, "Shuffle—down!" and held the enraged child at bay by the simple expedient of placing one hand on his lowered head.

"No, Carlton!" cried Dimity. "Sir Anthony did nothing. I was—er, looking for something I had lost."

The boy lowered his fists and peered from the man's stern face to Dimity's dirty one. "Oh."

"You can do better than that," said Farrar.

Carlton sighed. "I 'pologize, sir."

"Accepted. Your aunt—er, fell and has become a trifle . . . dusty. Run up to the house and fetch a-ah—"

"Sheet," said Dimity mournfully.

He shot a sparkling glance at her. "A brush and comb. And—er, a shawl."

"Perhaps you could ask Lady Helen if I might borrow one," Dimity interjected.

The boy nodded and ran off.

"An I dare suggest it," Farrar drawled, "there is a more secluded spot along the stream where you could wash yourself." He indicated the north, and bowed politely.

Yearning to escape him, Dimity said she was sure she could find the spot, but he was not to be dismissed. "You will be quite safe with me," he assured her. "Especially since you have your branch."

She thought, 'And will not hesitate to use it, Captain Infamous!' but went with him helplessly, knowing she looked a perfect fright, and dreading lest they meet anyone.

He led her into the trees for a short distance until they came to a clearing ending in a shallow bank above a stream which gurgled merrily over its stony bed. Dimity tried not to see Farrar's quivering mouth as she told him with dignity that this would suit very well, and with a reluctant sigh he went away.

She laid her branch aside, sat at the edge of the bank and plunged her feet into the clear water, then withdrew them with a small scream.

At once, Farrar was at her side. "Another cricket, ma'am?" he enquired solicitously.

"A snake!" she lied, frowning at him and hiding her icy feet under her gown.

He clicked his tongue. "You would do well to present your case and leave my estate at once. Lord knows what may next befall you. By the bye, if you will tell me what you *did* lose, I'll send one of the gardeners to find it for you."

Perhaps a half-truth would be advisable, just in case the maids chattered. " 'Twas a letter. I had laid it on the dressing table and we think it must have slipped into the wastepaper basket."

"Ah. From your late husband, perhaps?"

Some people might judge his green eyes handsome, but she thought they held a horridly cynical leer. She snapped, "From my brother."

"Indeed? Now wherever did I gain the impression you had but the one sister?"

And why was it so difficult to remember that she was Mrs. Catherine Deene—*not* Miss Dimity Cranford? Her heart jumping with nervousness, she managed to shrug carelessly. "I cannot think."

"And may I know your brother's name, ma'am?"

"His name is Pe—" Lord, no! She dared not name Peregrine! "Peter."

Up went his eyebrows. "Pepito? What an unusual—"

"Peter!" she snarled. "I stammer sometimes."

"Do you? Well, that can scarce mar—" the sparkling eyes slid with much appreciation from her ash-littered and wildly disarranged hair to the dirty toe that peeped from beneath the sullied gown, "—such perfection," he finished with a sweet smile.

Dimity gritted her teeth but before she could give him a well-earned set-down, from somewhere nearby arose a furious uproar of throaty growls and deep, ferocious barking.

His smile banished, Farrar whispered, "Shuffle!" and was running.

The dogs must be very large, and they sounded horrifyingly maddened. Dimity snatched up her branch and followed.

Farrar sprinted across the clearing and into the wood. The clamour was appalling now, the yelps of a smaller dog adding to the din.

Shuffle tore through the trees and raced for her master, two gigantic mastiffs in hot and murderous pursuit. One of them sprang at the spaniel and she went down, whimpering piteously. Farrar ran up and kicked the brute away. The other, teeth bared, plunged at the cringing spaniel. Farrar flung out an arm to intercept it. Dimity screamed as the powerful jaws clamped onto his wrist. Her heart hammering, she flailed the branch at the dog who was growling and worrying horribly as Farrar fought to beat him away. The other mastiff hurled itself at her, and, terrified, she levelled her branch. The dog darted around her, however, and leapt at Farrar. Dimity swung the branch hard. The second mastiff gave a yelp and turned on her, but did not attack.

A piercing whistle sounded. The dog savaging Farrar let go and bounded off. The second mastiff, who had again started for him, halted as if it had been shot, but faced him still, the hair standing up all down its back, a rumble of menace sounding deep in its throat.

A horseman rode through the trees and reined up. "Damn your ears, Devil," he said in a high-pitched falsetto. "Come here at once, sir!"

He was a husky young exquisite, large of eyes, nose, and chin. The bay horse he bestrode was a beautiful animal, but so highly strung it was all he could do to control its prancing. He glanced at Farrar who stood, white and enraged, gripping his left arm. "Mauled you, did he, Anthony?" he sneered, his thick lips curving to an amused grin.

Farrar panted, "Had I a pistol in my pocket, you'd have a dead dog! And do I ever catch them on my lands again—"

"I've warned 'em against it," drawled the exquisite. "Alas, they seem to be attracted to something here. Dogs—stupid brutes—do love anything . . . rotten. Indeed, had not the lady screamed, I'd—" His attention had turned to Dimity, and he checked, staring at her. "Zounds, but who is—"

Farrar snatched her branch and slapped it at the nervous bay. A shrill whinny, a mad rear, and the horse bolted, the mastiffs following and the curses of the rider fading into silence.

Farrar's sleeve was torn and wet with blood. "Let me see," cried Dimity, running to him.

He avoided her and went to Shuffle, who lay whining softly.

"My God!" he whispered, kneeling to investigate the extent of her injuries. "They've hurt her!"

Dimity knelt beside him. His hands shook. "Let me," she said. He drew back and she explored gently, while Farrar caressed the frightened animal, an expression of stark terror on his white face. "I don't think it's too bad," said Dimity. "They tore her ear and her shoulder, but it's fright mostly. You got to her in time. How old is she, Sir Anthony?"

"Twelve," he answered hoarsely. Shuffle was licking his hand lovingly and he said, "I'll carry her to the house. Are you all right, ma'am?"

"Yes. But you must let me look at that arm."

He ignored her, gathering up the dog as if she were made of glass, and walking away. At the edge of the clearing, he halted and turned back. "Thank you," he said. "Whatever else, you're a brave woman. If you will stay here, I'll send the boy with the things you wanted."

Dimity came to her feet. "You're being very silly. That is bleeding much too fast. I hope you mean to bring an action against that revolting man!"

He stared at her for a minute. Then he carried Shuffle away.

"Well, I'm glad you wasn't really ill, and I c'n see my aunty's dresses wouldn't fit you. She was thin an' scrawny, 'n you're— nice an, not scrawny. I'd buy you lots of pretty dresses if I could." Carlton eyed Dimity's back appraisingly. "I got most of it off. Why were you sitting on the fire?"

She twisted her neck so as to peer over her shoulder at her gown. She felt shaken and confused and rather unsteadily repeated her tale of the lost letter.

"Oh." Carlton sat on the edge of the bank and looked down at the stream. "Who was that man with the dogs?"

"Somebody horrid." She sat beside him. "What did you do all day yesterday? They told me you were with Sir Anthony."

"Yes. He showed me a few things. This is a nice place."

She sighed, troubled. "How I *wish* my brothers would come!"

"Why? You got me. I won't never let him hurt you." He took her hand and grinned up at her engagingly.

Touched, she said, "You're a charming young man, Carlton Farrar. But you have been told that many times, I expect."

"Nobody never said it." He drew a deep breath. "Miss Clement—"

She glanced around uneasily. "Do not call me that!"

"All right, but I don't like calling you Aunty Cathy. Not when it's just you and me."

'Poor little mite,' she thought. 'He didn't have much affection for his aunt.' "My brothers call me a silly sort of name," she confided. "But you must be very careful not to let anyone else hear. It is Mitten."

He grinned. "That's pretty. *You're* pretty, Aunty Mitten. Do you think my Aunty Cathy was fibbing about Sir Uncle?"

"In what way?"

"Have you ever been bit by a dog?" He gave her a thoughtful look. "I have. It was just a little dog, but it hurt awful. That dog that bit Sir Uncle was big as a horse almost!"

Dimity shivered. "I know. I was very frightened when he put his arm right in front of the horrid brute. I am only glad you did not see it."

"I did. I was watching. I shinned up a tree in case those dogs came after me. I was scared. And I'm a brave boy. Jermyn said I am."

Combing her hair into some semblance of tidiness, she said, "I am very sure he was right. Who is Jermyn? You've spoken of him before, I think."

"He was one of the boys at the Home."

Astonished, she lowered the looking glass. "The—*Home*? But—were you put into a Foundling Home when your Mama died?"

"I 'spect so. They said I was 'on the Parish.' The other boys didn't like me. They said I talked like a nob and that I had pretty hair like a girl." His small jaw set. He said grimly, "I wouldn't talk like them, so they got me down and shaved all my hair off and they cut my head, too. A lot. There was buckets and buckets of bloody gore." His beguiling grin flashed at her again. "But I din't cry. Jermyn said that was brave."

"It most assuredly was," said Dimity, hugging him. She looked with regret at her slippers. "I suppose I must put those awful things on again."

Carlton picked them up for her and dropped them in the stream.

"Carlton!"

"Now you can say they fell in the river and go and buy some nicer ones."

She clapped her hands. "Splendid! You have saved my feet, my dear."

She finished her makeshift toilette and they started back to the house. Her thoughts busy, Dimity asked, "Carlton—was it very bad when Captain Farrar beat you with his riding crop?"

"He din't beat me. He give me ten of the best. With a switch he cut in the garden. It hurt, but I din't cry or nothing." His chin lifted proudly. "He said I was pluck to the backbone!"

"Oh."

He took her hand and jumped several steps. "Aunty Mitten, if a man's a coward, is he a coward all over? I mean—when Sir Uncle stuck his arm in front of that horse dog's great big teeth . . ."

Dimity frowned, troubled. "Yes, dear. I know what you mean."

❧ *Chapter 6* ❧

Dimity's attempt to avoid the eyes of the servants was foiled at every turn. Lackeys gawked at her in the side hall; footmen stared in the music hall, and when she crept, shoeless, up the stairs, she was sure she must have encountered every single maid in the great house. Slinking into her bedchamber, she found Rodgers sewing tapes onto the waistband of the orange gown that Dimity prayed she might never have to wear. At the sight of her, the abigail gave a squawk of horror. Relying on Farrar's discretion, Dimity explained that she had slipped on the wet bank and her slippers had fallen into the stream and been ruined. Rodgers was suitably sympathetic, but when Dimity said that she would be obliged to wear her habit, she was informed it had been sent out to be cleaned.

"Sent . . . *out* . . . ?" she gasped, paling.

"Ahem yes, ma'am. There's a woman in the village does our fancy cleaning and pressing. Her la'ship calls it lah blanchey divine, or something."

"La blanchisserie de fin," moaned Dimity, regarding the orange atrocity with despair. "I had hoped to change into my habit, but now I shall have to keep to my room, I collect. Certainly, I cannot wear a gown and—and my riding boots!"

Rodgers sympathized and went running to beg the loan of some slippers from milady's dresser. She returned with a pair of brown kid shoes that were not too hopeless a fit, Lady Helen's foot size being closer to Dimity's than that of Mrs. Deene. Adjusting the orange gown about Dimity's waist, Rodgers promised the riding habit would be available in time for madam to drive into Salisbury tomorrow, and with that Dimity had to be

82

content. She was able, at least, to supervise the dressing of her hair, but since the neckline of the gown was slightly less *décolleté* than that of the blue, she did not dare attempt to wear a scarf or borrow a fichu, and the afternoon had become too warm to justify a request for a shawl.

Lady Helen waited in her parlour and, upon hearing the tale of the ruined slippers, agreed at once that Mrs. Deene should be conveyed to Salisbury next day, if Farrar had no objection. In return, she asked that she be told what had happened in the woods this morning, "For I can tell that, as usual, the servants know more of what goes forward on this estate than do I!"

They were served a light and delicious meal, during which Dimity offered a considerably expurgated version of what had transpired. When she described the confrontation with the mastiffs, my lady was aghast. "But, how dreadful! I'd a word with Farrar just a few minutes ago. In fact, he said he would send for his solicitor so that we might meet this afternoon to discuss your claim." She frowned. "He looked rather pale, now that I think of it, but said nothing of the other business." She bit her lip and lapsed into a troubled silence.

"They seemed bitter enemies," said Dimity cautiously.

My lady nodded and murmured in an absent way, "He blames Anthony for—for Harding's death . . . They were so close . . . "

Dimity sipped her tea and wished she might soon be gone from this beautiful, tragic estate. Happily, none of it was her concern; still, she found herself saying, "Sir Anthony's arm looked ugly. It was rather brave, I thought. To try to protect his dog like that."

Lady Helen stared at her blankly, then appeared to return to the present.

"I only thank heaven that Shuffle was not seriously hurt. Farrar has taken a deal of abuse since Prestonpans, and has borne it well enough. But—if the dog were to be—Oh, it does not bear thinking of! He has a nasty temper at times. There's no saying what he might do!"

Dimity thought of Piers and how he had grieved when old Scamp died. She said, "One could scarce blame him for being enraged. It was a vicious attack, and he is very fond of her."

"Yes. She is all he has, you see."

Piers' words echoed in Dimity's ears again: "I'd sooner be

old Perry doing the hop, than Tony Farrar, hale and hearty . . .'' and she wondered if her brother had guessed how well justified were his words.

The solicitor was not expected for another hour, so she decided to find out how Shuffle was faring. As she went downstairs she was again struck by the beauty of the music hall. She paused to gaze admiringly at the high-vaulted ceiling, the graceful sweep of the long room bathed in the warm glow of sunlight from the stained-glass rear window. The sense that she was not alone caused her to turn suddenly, and she surprised a look of contempt on the face of a footman. 'He likely thinks I am admiring my new property,' she thought. Embarrassed, she enquired about the spaniel and he told her with wooden courtesy that the farrier had come and the master was with him in the stable block.

Outside, the breeze was lazy, the sky very blue, and the sunshine warm. Distantly, fine horses grazed or were being exercised in lush meadows. Closer at hand, the stable block was set amongst wide-spreading oaks some two hundred yards from the house. Grooms laboured industriously in well-kept loose boxes and a spacious barn. A boy came running and conducted Dimity to a neat tack room. Shuffle lay on the floor looking forlorn with a wide bandage about her shoulder and another around her head. Her tail quivered as Dimity entered, but she did not bark or stand.

A blistering flood of curses disturbed the quiet. Blinking in the sudden dimness, Dimity saw Farrar sitting on a long table, his bare left arm extended. A fat, red-faced man was engaged in pouring something over it while grinning broadly. She crept forward, saw the torn flesh, and gave a gasp of revulsion.

The farrier paused, staring at her uncertainly.

Farrar's head jerked around. He stood at once. "Do I keep you waiting, Mrs. Deene?'' His voice was as cool as it had previously been impassioned. "My apologies.''

"That is—dreadful,'' Dimity faltered. "You must see a surgeon at once!''

Amused, he said, "And that properly put you in your place, Jenkins. Oh, bind it up and have done, man! The lady is of a nervous turn of mind. The wonder is that she has not fainted at so gruesome a sight.''

Dimity frowned at him, but despite the teasing words he was pale and his face shone with sweat. The farrier took up some rough bandages. "Wait," she said, and went to inspect the wounds. Farrar held his arm rock steady and was silent, watching her. The flesh around the deep gashes was already bruising, and she guessed that by morning the arm would be black from wrist to elbow. She nerved herself and grasped his wrist.

He gave a startled gasp and pulled away.

Alarmed, the farrier said, "Easy, ma'am! That arm is so sore as Hades, whatever Sir Anthony do say."

"Those gashes should be stitched," she said, stepping back. "And there may well be a bone broke in the wrist. Only see how 'tis swelling."

"I'm not surprised," said Farrar, breathlessly indignant. "After your gentle touch, I'd not doubt—"

She interrupted with a serene, "Nonsense. But if you fear the surgeon, by all means let your farrier try for himself."

Eyeing his employer uneasily, the farrier reached out. "Like hell!" snorted Farrar, swinging his arm away. "Do as I tell you! Bind it up!"

Dimity shook her head, but she felt a little sick and turned to the door.

Farrar called, "I shall join you in only a few minutes, Mrs. Deene. Pray try not to faint again before then."

She swung around, vexed, but he was smiling at her, a twinkle in those long green eyes. For some idiotic reason, her cheeks grew hot. To conceal this embarrassment, she bent to stroke the spaniel, then went out, hearing the farrier say primly, "Now no more swearing, if you please, sir. Me ears is offended by bad language of a Tuesday."

Farrar laughed, but Dimity paused and stared worriedly at a swooping bird. Tuesday already, and she had fled the dragoons on Saturday night! If Tio was alive, her brothers would find her, she was very sure. If, on the other hand, the valiant Glendenning had died . . . She closed her eyes and sent another prayer winging heavenwards for his sake. But—if he *had* died without being able to tell them where she was, the twins must be frantic. She must not delay another minute. She would have to send off a letter. But—how? If she sent one with the maids, she could scarce specify that the bearer must be illiterate. And if anyone read the direction and relayed it to Sir Anthony, she was undone. Both Piers and Perry were known to him. He would put two and two together and likely turn her over at once to that unpleasant Captain Holt. She dare not risk that! Not with the deadly cypher still undelivered! She went into the house and walked slowly along the side hall. There was a way, of course. It would be risky, but it was the only thing she could think of . . .

She heard singing, and when she reached the music hall she found Lady Helen seated at the harpsichord, while Carlton knelt at her feet, gazing up at her in awe. She played well and her voice was sweet, but the key was minor and the words sad. Dimity was in time to hear the last two lines:

> *Make me to say, when all my griefs are gone,*
> *Happy the heart that sighed for such a one.*

'Oh dear!' thought Dimity, clapping her hands. "How well you play, ma'am."

Carlton turned eagerly. "Can you play, Mi—Aunty Cathy?"

Lady Helen glanced at him.

Dimity's heart gave a thud. Carlton flushed scarlet and looked frightened. She managed a laugh. "Because we are not so fortunate as to have such a beautiful instrument, you must not give up hope, Carlton. As a matter of fact, I can play, a little."

Lady Helen stood at once and begged that Mrs. Deene honour them. "It would be so nice to hear someone else again," she said. "My son used to play, but Anthony does not, although we would often sing together . . . long ago."

Dimity struck up a merry air. "In that case, let us sing now. If you do not know the words, Carlton, just sing 'la la la.' " Her voice was not remarkable, but she could hold a tune. Carlton joined in lustily, and very soon my lady's voice rang out sweet and true with the words of "It Was a Lover and His Lass." On the final chord, Dimity exclaimed, "Now, weren't we splendid!" and my lady laughed and said eagerly, "Yes, indeed we were! May we try it again?" They were halfway through when a pleasant baritone joined them. Dimity swung around on the bench, and the singing faded away.

Farrar stood at the top of the steps, staring as if he could not believe his eyes, but his was not the voice she'd heard. A newcomer was striding across the room; a tall, good-looking young man wearing a neat wig and a burgundy coat of velvet, the great cuffs heavy with gold lace. He flung his arms wide and with a joyous cry of welcome, Lady Helen ran into them, to be swept up and kissed heartily.

"Beautiful as ever," he declared, in an unusually rich speaking voice. "I vow, my best loved aunt, you grow younger each time I see you! And how glad I am that you have put off your blacks."

Lady Helen flushed guiltily. "It is not quite a year, I know, but Farrar worried I was—was becoming melancholy. It is wrong, but—"

"Not at all. He was right, for once." Despite the endorsement, there was contempt in that fine voice.

Lady Helen made haste to present her guests, and Mr. Phillip Ellsworth's wide-set blue eyes appraised Dimity with a faintly incredulous admiration, and lingered a moment too long upon her décolletage. She made him a slight curtsey, inclining her head in an effort to limit his view. He touched her hand to his lips with pretty gallantry and, holding it there, his eyes sparkling, declared her to be a most welcome addition to The Palfreys, adding, "For my poor aunt needs *something* to lift her spirits." Releasing her, he smiled down at Carlton, who had stood when my lady did and now made a stiff, shy bow.

"The *very* Young Pretender," murmured Ellsworth, flicking one of the boy's fair curls. "He is certainly the image of what Farrar once was, my lady."

It was innocent enough, yet in the very way he ignored his silent cousin, in the slight curl of the lip as he made the remark, Dimity read a calculated insult and wondered irritably why Farrar did not have the gumption to throw him out the window as Piers would likely have done.

The family solicitor arrived at that moment, bowed to Lady Helen, and remarked testily that he had driven up behind Ellsworth, and that if young people today had any manners they would use some patience instead of crowding their elders off the road.

Ellsworth caught Dimity's eye and made a wry face. He apologized to the frail but crochety looking old gentleman, but his elaborate periods were cut short. Mr. Norris, it would seem, had little time to waste on frivolities and would be grateful could they get to business at once.

He fixed Ellsworth with a piercing stare and barked, "In private!"

For a second Dimity thought to see resentment in Ellsworth's eyes, then he turned to Lady Helen and said that had she no objection, he would walk in the gardens while waiting for the meeting to end.

My lady clung to his arm and begged him not to rush away again, and he kissed her and sauntered out, almost colliding with Farrar, who stepped aside then led the way to a pleasant panelled study on the east side of the house, next to the library.

The old man of the law stamped over to the desk, set down his carpet bag, and adjusted his untidy scratch wig. When Lady Helen and Dimity were seated, he occupied the big leather chair while Farrar took up a position behind his aunt. Dimity thought he looked tired and rather worn but there was no sign of bandages and he gave not the least hint of discomfort.

Carlton whispered a plea to be excused. The old gentleman barked out a demand that he remain, and the boy crept over to stand very close to Farrar, this surprising Dimity and bringing a momentarily intrigued expression into the solicitor's faded brown eyes. Putting on a pair of scratched and dusty spectacles, Norris peered over them at Dimity. She met his gaze through a long pause, wondering what he intended to ask her, and grateful that she had looked through the papers and was fairly familiar with their contents. To her surprise, however, the first remark was directed to Farrar.

"I thought you said—" he barked.

"I did," interpolated Farrar hastily. "I may have been—I think I was mistaken."

"Natural enough." The shrewd gaze returned to Dimity. "You need not look at me as if I was your enemy, miss."

"Mrs.," she corrected demurely.

"You wear no ring. Don't look as if you ever wore one, moreover!"

She had already anticipated such a comment, and countered with the only excuse she could think of. "We were only married a year when he died, and my husband desired that I remarry."

"Generous of him. Why haven't you?" He sneered unpardonably, "Nobody asked you?"

My lady looked shocked, and even Farrar blinked, but Dimity guessed that this crusty old creature was trying to fluster her. The real Mrs. Deene, she thought, would be considerably flustered by such tactics. She sighed. "That is the whole trouble, sir. Lots of nobodies." She caught the veriest hint of a twinkle and added, "I expect too much, I fear. My grandpapa says they do not make men like they used to, and so far I have to agree with him."

Norris threw back his head and gave a cackle of mirth. "Very true, m'dear. Very true!" He recollected why he was here, cleared his throat, threw an apologetic look at Farrar, and went on briskly, "Well, I cannot fritter about like this. I do not mean to ask you a lot of questions, madam. If you're an impostor, as I suspect, you'd tell me a pack of lies at all events, and you've likely got the boy well primed." He shot a beady-eyed glance at Carlton. "Ain't that so, Master Shiver?"

"Yes," said Carlton, and clinging tightly to the skirt of Farrar's coat added, "An' I always shiver when I'm cross."

Again, the twinkle. "Do you! Then you may take yourself off and shiver somewhere else before your wrath unmans me! Your papers, if you please, ma'am."

Carlton gave Dimity a worried look and departed. Dimity extracted the sheaf of papers from Mrs. Deene's reticule and handed them to Farrar, who in turn passed them to Norris.

The solicitor waded through certificates of birth and baptism and marriage; a family tree, letters from Mr. Walter Farrar to Mrs. Walter Farrar, and a few letters to Miss Mary Arnold from Mr. Walter Farrar, dated prior to their marriage in 1735. Without warning, he rasped, "And how did you like Harrogate?"

Dimity had never been to Harrogate and racked her brain frantically for any scrap of information about that much maligned city. The shrewd brown eyes were fixed on her. "Well, madam, well? Says here your sister was wed there. I take it you attended her?"

She nodded and alleged that she had preferred High Harrogate to the Low Town. She was indebted to her maternal grandmama for the remark, that venerable dame having once journeyed thither to take the waters. It was all Dimity could remember, and she was relieved when her reply appeared to satisfy Mr. Norris, who addressed no further questions to her, and at length told Farrar that everything *looked* above board, "But," with a sinister scowl at Dimity, "that don't mean a fig. It will all have to be looked into, which will take some time."

Momentarily dismayed, Dimity reflected that it made no difference, for as soon as she could deliver that dreadful cypher, she would leave, and write Sir Anthony—That is to say, she would write Captain Farrar a letter explaining that she had no real knowledge of the matter, but that if Carlton did not prove to be the genuine heir and my lady did not keep him, she would like the boy sent to her at Muse Manor. The thought of home brought a nostalgic yearning . . .

"Are you gone off to sleep, ma'am?"

She jumped. They were all staring at her.

Norris snapped, "Your name *is* Mrs. Deene, I believe?"

"Y-yes," she stammered. "My apologies if my attention wandered. I was—er, wondering for how long I shall have to impose on Sir Anthony's hospitality."

The old gentleman gave a cynical snort. "You've an odd standard of values, madam! You worry about imposing on his hospitality for a few days, but don't wink an eye at dispossessing him of his rightful inheritance." Ignoring, but aware of, Dimity's painful blush, he gathered the papers together. "Do not forget what I told you, Farrar. I want those letters Walter writ you, and his birth certificate. Most of all, I want your mama's diary. Get 'em to me so soon as possible. Hear me?"

"Yes, sir. But I'll be dashed if I can see—"

"Have you the least notion of how much you pay me every year?"

Farrar gave a wry grin.

"Just so. And 'tis because I know how to go on in this sort of nasty business that I take so much of your money, my boy. I presume you are aware, Mrs. Deene, that you may very well wind up in prison for attempted fraud?"

It had been said without pause and with no change in tone. Dimity was startled, but managed to respond, "Oh, no. It does not apply, you see."

Norris glared at her. "Besides which," he went on, his attention returning to his client, "we can tell from letters whether they were writ with the left hand.'' He laid one finger alongside his hooked nose and shook his head as Farrar made as if to speak. Standing, he bowed to my lady, gave Dimity a curt nod and a searching look, then went with Farrar into the garden.

They walked together along the sunlit path, silent, until Farrar demanded, ''What was that business about the left hand?''

''An attempt to scare the gel—which, I might add, did not work. You gave me to expect a trollop, Tony. Are you gone daft?''

Beset by his own confusion, Farrar grunted, ''You saw the gown.''

''Fiddlesticks! She'd be a lady clad in three fig leaves!''

''I wish I may see it,'' said Farrar, amused. ''She's a shapely wench!''

''Hum. I fear she is also something shrewd. She gave me as good as I sent, did you mark it? One might think she don't give a farthing whether she wins or loses. You've a fight on your hands, m'boy. And what's worse, she don't strike me as the type to defraud a child out of a comfit—much less stoop to this kind of chicanery.''

''Then you're sure it *is* chicanery?''

''What I am sure of, and what can be proven in a court of law is another story. Why in the name of all that's holy d'you permit them to stay here?''

''I think Aunt Helen took a liking to the boy the instant she saw him. She insisted they stay. She has enjoyed these few days. She's lonely, you know.''

''Hum. Misses Harding, I shouldn't wonder. You should've put your foot down on this, though. Is the most lunatic arrangement I ever heard of.'' Farrar returning no answer, the solicitor slanted a sly glance at him, and said with a grin, ''You know what I'd do in your shoes? I'd marry the gel!''

He had spoken in jest and was surprised when Farrar gave a start, then laughed scornfully. ''What a fellow you are, Norrie! A fine surrender, to marry an adventuress only to silence her.''

The old gentleman pursed up his mouth and changed the subject. ''What's Ellsworth doing here?''

''Flattering Lady Helen. As ever.''

''And fairly slathering over Mrs. Deene. A careful gent, your cousin.''

The response was vulgar in the extreme. Norris cackled appreciatively. "I hear you've had more trouble with your neighbour's pets. Leonard said your arm is properly mauled. Not serious, is it, lad?"

Farrar clapped him on the back. "No. I thank you."

"We can take him to court. Only say the word."

"An I'd had a pistol within reach, we'd not have the need!" Farrar scowled. "Next time they stray onto my land, I swear I'll shoot the pair of 'em! You'd not believe the power of the brutes! They'd rip a man's throat out in a minute." He frowned thoughtfully. "And would likely have done so to me, had not Mrs. Deene come very bravely to my aid."

Norris stopped walking and eyed his companion in dismay. "Balks at murder, does she? Well, that's something to be said for the woman. But for God's sake, have a care! You've many enemies and you take too many chances. I'd be most damnably sorry to see anything happen to you."

Grateful, Farrar said, "You old curmudgeon, you're one of the few who'd not be delighted."

"No, I am serious, Tony. That pretty cousin of yours and his bosom bow would stop at nothing to—"

"Avenge Harding?" Farrar's expression darkened. "Perchance they think themselves justified."

"Balderdash! And you just keep in mind, my lad, that a large and enraged dog has as much strength as two men! Be sure you *do* carry that pistol!"

Dimity had gone in search of Carlton, and was returning without having located the child when Ellsworth appeared, strolling towards her through the gardens. The look in his eyes bade her to proceed with caution, but he was perfectly polite. He had a good deal of charm, and a ready wit so that her suspicions were lulled until she suddenly realized they were in the woods, and that his last three remarks had concerned her supposed brother-in-law. A warning bell sounded in her mind.

"Indeed yes," he drawled idly, taking her arm as he guided her down the slope towards the stream, "a fine musician was old Walter. If I know him, he had a full choir at his nuptials.

92

Must've been quite a ceremony in the cathedral. Wish I had been there.''

"I think you are mistaken, sir,'' she answered, her nerves tight. "Mary and Walter were married in a small church in Harrogate. If he was musical, I had no knowledge of it, nor did my sister ever mention such an accomplishment.''

"In which case, we are even,'' he said gaily, "for Walter never mentioned your sister, either.''

"Indeed?'' She opened her eyes at him. "Did you correspond with him, then? From what Sir Anthony said, I—''

He laughed. "Oh, but you must pay no attention to what that creature says.''

Dimity stiffened. "Sir, I must protest. Why it should be so I do not know, but Lady Helen and Sir Anthony have been exceeding kind to me. Indeed, it is incredible for I would think to have been thrown from the premises, instead of which I am treated as a guest.''

"I should think it more than incredible was so lovely a lady treated with anything less than the very greatest courtesy.''

It was charmingly said, and he was a charming young man, but Dimity experienced a surge of profound irritation and ignored the compliment. "Only consider the circumstances, Mr. Ellsworth. An I prove my claim, it will be a great loss to the family. To Sir Anthony, especially.''

"For my part, I can conceive of no more pleasant change than to have a beautiful lady at The Palfreys rather than the miserable worm who now lords it—''

Dimity frowned and stepped back, but Ellsworth paced even closer, smiling down at her. "You are displeased. Why? You are certainly aware he is a craven poltroon who—''

"You forget yourself, sir! Such remarks should be addressed to him. Not to me!''

"My, but here's a fiery defence the clod don't deserve. Make no doubt he knows my opinion of him. Did you not notice how he feared to come near me? My cousin and closest friend fell victim to his shameful cowardice. Although there may be more to that particular tragedy than we now know. You are our champion, Mrs. Deene! We welcome you with open arms!''

He moved closer, as though intending to demonstrate his words. Again attempting to step back, Dimity realized too late that she had retreated to the very edge of the bank. Her shoe slid downward. She gave a startled cry, but at once Ellsworth's arms closed around her and dragged her to safety.

"My heavens!" she gasped with a tremulous little laugh.

Still holding her, his hot blue eyes slid hungrily from her eyes to her mouth, to the shapeliness of the breasts crushed close against him. "How very lovely . . . you are . . ." he murmured.

"And warm," she said prosaically. "Pray grant me some air, sir." He made no attempt to relax his hold. "Poor girl. They tell me you faint readily, and faith, who could wonder at it! Are you all right?"

Mrs. Deene's gowns were becoming a major annoyance. "I shall be, when you have the goodness to release me, Mr. Ellsworth."

"You play your cards well," he said huskily, "but there's such a thing as carrying play-acting too far."

Dimity was very still. His handsome head bowed lower, then, abruptly, he released her. She wondered how much he knew and, frightened, turned from him and at once halted.

The omnipresent Shuffle at his side, Farrar stood at the top of the slope, watching them.

Ellsworth took Dimity's elbow and led her up the rough path, making an elaborate business of transferring himself to her right side as they approached Farrar. This time, his cousin did not move aside and Ellsworth murmured contemptuously, "It would be difficult to tell you, ma'am, which the captain does better. Run, or spy."

His enigmatic gaze on Dimity's embarrassed face, Farrar said, "You've a caller, Mrs. Deene. I am asked to escort you back to the house."

Ellsworth's grip on her elbow tightened. He began to guide her past. Farrar stepped squarely in front of them. "Do not test my patience too far, cousin."

Ellsworth's icy disdain slipped. "I wish to God I might!" he hissed. "For Harding's sake, nothing would give me greater pleasure than to slide my sword through your ribs!"

Dimity was a stranger to hatred, and the swift flare of ferocity between the two men appalled her. She moved back, watching them. Ellsworth's handsome features were distorted, the fingers of his right hand crooked as though he yearned to draw the sword that hung at his side.

Farrar was as cold as his cousin was inflamed. "Nor I be more willing to oblige," he drawled. "Unfortunately, to indulge myself with the joy of ridding the world of you would distress the Lady Helen."

"Shivering poltroon! You've no need to be inventing excuses! I'll provide you one!" Ellsworth lifted a clenched hand.

"No!" Dimity ran between them. "You cannot! Sir Anthony has no weapon and is disabled. His arm was badly savaged by a dog this morning."

"Had my cousin not been aware of that fact, ma'am," drawled Farrar, "he'd never dare be so bold, I promise you."

With a crude gutter oath, Ellsworth's hand blurred to his sword hilt. Farrar seized Dimity and fairly threw her aside. Steel glittered in the sunlight as Ellsworth leapt to the attack, his sword-point darting murderously for the unarmed man's throat.

Farrar's left arm whipped upward and knocked the blade aside. His right fist seemed to come up from his knees. Dimity heard the solid thwack of the impact. Ellsworth's blue eyes crossed. Slammed back, he landed heavily and lay in an ungainly sprawl. Shuffle ran to his side and barked madly into his still face.

Stepping over the fallen, Dimity reached for Farrar's hand. "Have you cut your arm?"

"Fortunately not. One benefit of a thick bandage." Both tone and eyes were cold. "Shall we adjourn, ma'am?" He proffered his right arm. Dimity rested her hand on it and, with not another thought for Mr. Ellsworth, allowed him to lead her towards the house. She felt triumphant, which was extreme unmaidenly, and wondered if the man beside her scorned her because she was not having a fit of the vapours, as a well-bred girl should under such circumstances. She glanced at him under her lashes. He looked bleak and forbidding, his lips set in a stern line, and she restrained the question she had been about to ask.

They were approaching the front steps when Carlton came racing around from the east side of the house. "Aunty Cathy! Aunty Cathy!" he panted. "Matter 'f life an' death!"

She halted, regarding him apprehensively.

"You terrify us," drawled Farrar. "Who died?"

Carlton grinned at him. "I need my 'lowance, please ma'am. Mos' desprit."

"Allowance . . . ?" echoed Dimity, taken aback.

"Certainly not," said Farrar. "When you go off to school, your aunt may perhaps agree to such an—investment. You shall have to wait, Master Carlton."

Rather to her own amazement, Dimity did not protest his autocratic interference, nor did Carlton seem surprised by it, although he wailed, "Two *years*? Sir—I cannot!"

"Child, you have no alternative. Unless you mean to earn it. That is another matter."

The boy perked up a little. "*Earn* it, sir? How?"

Farrar shrugged. "There must be many profitable opportunities for an enterprising young fellow. I know there were when I was your age. Try the kitchen—or see my head groom in the stables. Trade your services for what you want."

Carlton considered this, then started off at a gallop, only to come full circle and observe cheerfully, "Your hand is covered with blood and gore, Sir Uncle. Did you cut someone's gizzard out?"

Farrar whipped his left arm behind him. "No, you young ghoul. Begone!"

All knees and elbows, the boy sped away.

Dimity said, "So he did cut you after all! I cannot think why you must—"

"He did not cut me, ma'am." The chill in his eyes pronounced, he said, "The blow likely set it to bleeding again, is all."

She viewed him stormily. "If ever I saw such a disgusting display! My brothers would have—"

"*Brothers?*" His brows lifted. "I thought there was but one. Your family grows by the hour. Have a care, ma'am."

Dimity bit her lip. Before she could think of a suitable response, he went on, "Be that as it may, you are perfectly right. I should not have lost my temper with Ellsworth." His voice was bitter suddenly, his eyes dark and brooding.

"I did not mean to imply that *you* were disgusting, Sir Anthony! It was your cousin's actions I found unpardonable."

"Indeed? I'll own you surprise me." His mouth twisted into its most cynical smile. "When you were locked in that passionate embrace beside the stream, I rather gained the impression that you found him—er, more than pleasing.''

Infuriated, she said, ''And I find *you* more than obnoxious, Captain! Mr. Ellsworth forced his attentions on me, but did I think him the most 'pleasing' gentleman in Christendom, I must only cry shame for an attack on an unarmed man!''

He said thoughtfully, ''And you tried to stop him. That marks the second time you have come to my aid. I thank you, but in the light of such demonstrations of fair-mindedness, I can only be the more perplexed. You appear to dislike unsportsmanlike behaviour. Yet, by my standards, to plant the seeds of hatred and contempt in the mind of a child, 'gainst an uncle he has yet to meet, is no less unfair than Ellsworth's despicable conduct.'' He pressed a handkerchief to his left wrist, fixed Dimity with a grave stare, and waited.

Her mouth opened to voice a furious denial, then closed again. She was in the wretched position of being unable either to defend herself or to deny the justice of his remarks. Without a word, she walked past him and into the cool dimness of the house.

Humiliation died a sudden death. Between the shock of the fight and her vexation with Farrar, she had quite forgotten her reason for returning. Her ''caller'' stood and turned to face her as she mounted the steps to the music hall. He was young and powerfully built, his hair powdered and neatly styled. A tricorne was under one arm. And his coat was a bright scarlet.

Captain Jacob Holt bowed in perfunctory manner. ''I give you good day, Mrs. Deene. We have found you, at last.''

She felt very cold and, quite sure she was about to be arrested, managed somehow to keep walking and to extend her hand. Reaching for it, Holt checked and stood rigid, staring at her bosom. For an instant, Dimity was petrified by the fear that he knew the deadly fragment of parchment nestled in her bodice, then she realized it was the vulgarity of her gown that had astonished him.

Farrar, who had entered also, said, ''If you wish to—''

Returning his attention to Dimity, Holt gave her hand a brief shake. ''We are hoping you may be able to solve a puzzle for us, ma'am. Some of the other passengers—''

Dimity interrupted in turn, "I believe Sir Anthony addressed you, Captain Holt. You must not have heard him."

In a voice of ice Holt said, "I know of no such person, ma'am. I had as soon go to Winchester to conduct this interview. Indeed, I should take it kindly did you consent to accompany me. I mislike the—aroma in this house."

Dimity's nerves tightened. Farrar had just knocked one man down. Now, it would seem he must repeat the process. Unless he challenged. Certainly, no gentleman would take such an insult, least of all in his own home and in front of a lady.

She was mistaken. Farrar stared at Holt steadily, but as she watched, his eyes lowered. Neither looking up nor uttering a word, he walked past and continued to the stairs.

She stared after him, deeply shocked and baffled by his inconsistent behaviour.

"Ah," said Holt, with a thin smile, "the atmosphere improves. Will you sit here, Mrs. Deene? It is about the accident . . ."

Self-preservation demanded that she pull her wits together. Whatever happened, she must not go back to Winchester with Holt. If she met any of the other passengers face to face, she would certainly be unmasked as an impostor. She sat down and made an effort to appear calm. "You spoke of the other passengers, I believe?"

He drew another chair closer and occupied it. "There is some confusion regarding the injured lady."

Her heart began to play leapfrog. "Injured? You mean the poor lady still lives?"

"She is in some kind of deep swoon caused by a blow to the head. The surgeon is hopeful she will recover at any time." His eyes fixed on her face, he asked softly, "Does that disturb you, Mrs.—ah, Deene?"

'It terrifies me, you horrid creature,' thought Dimity, and answered, "Of course not. It is grand news, but what is the confusion about?"

"Only that—someone seemed to be under the impression the little boy was travelling with Miss Clement—the injured lady."

The palms of her hands were wet. She had to force herself not to shake. "It was an unpleasant journey from start to finish, and I quite understand the confusion. Perhaps you would wish to see my nephew . . . ?''

"Thank you, I should. May I?'' He stood and crossed to tug on the bell rope.

After a moment a lackey appeared and was sent off to find Carlton. He was only gone a short while but it seemed to Dimity an eternity, during which she responded somehow to the captain's small talk and prayed Carlton would not be trapped into betraying her. She felt a little sick when the lackey returned with the boy leaping boisterously beside him.

"Aunty Cathy, may I—'' Carlton began, then halted and stood mute, his gaze on the military magnificence.

The captain, who had remained standing, regarded the child sternly. "Come here, boy, and tell me the truth. Is this lady your aunt?''

Carlton marched to gaze up at Holt angelically. "I 'spect she must be 'less he 'dopted me for a nephew.'' He turned to Dimity. "Did you 'dopt me, Aunty?''

Marvelling at the little rascal, Dimity rose. "I certainly did not,'' she said truthfully. "But if the captain wishes to, he may!''

Holt smiled uncertainly, still staring at the boy, who giggled and went skipping off in the direction of the kitchens.

"If I can be of any further assistance, Captain,'' said Dimity, weak with relief, "you must not hesitate to call on me.''

He stood there looking at her in a considering way. Then he gave a short bow. "Thank you. I apologize for having troubled you. Good day, ma'am.'' He strode briskly down the steps and across the lower hall where a lackey waited to open the door.

Dimity wandered after him and stood on the terrace watching while a trooper came up leading his mount. When they had ridden out of sight, she walked slowly into the house and across the hall. She was, she realized, more than ever on borrowed time. She must find Mr. Rafe Green and deliver the cypher before poor Mrs. Deene recovered consciousness or Holt would be back, and next time with a troop, to carry her off to the Tower. She shivered, then it dawned on her that she was standing still and that Farrar stood at the top of the steps, eyeing her speculatively.

She stared at him in silence.

99

A dark flush appeared under his tan. "I suppose," he drawled, "you are thinking I just lived up—or down—to my reputation."

'Yes, indeed,' she thought, only to be reminded of the terrible risk he had taken for Shuffle, and how neatly he had disposed of his unpleasant cousin.

Watching her expressive face, he asked, "Am I such an enigma, ma'am?"

She walked slowly up the steps. "I think perhaps you are."

He bowed. "The discovery is mutual."

She thought, 'Oh, not another battle!' and said with a shrug, "I cannot guess why you would find me an enigma, sir."

"Can you not?" He started across the music hall beside her. "I might list a dozen reasons, but—just for an example, I had not realized the trouble you have with your ears. You are a little deaf, I think."

"I am no such thing!"

"No? And yet I called you by name this morning, and you did not respond, although I said 'Mrs. Deene' quite loudly."

He looked so bland, but he was watching her narrowly. Had he really called her, or was this just an attempt to trap her into a mistake? A series of loud thuds announced Carlton's unique method of travelling on one foot. "I was probably thinking of something else," said Dimity, keeping her eyes on the boy.

"And just now I said 'Mrs. Catherine,' " he murmured. "Twice."

"Ah. Well—you see, I am seldom called by that name. My brother—"

"Brothers," he corrected gravely.

"—call me . . . Mitten."

Carlton came up with them in time to hear that, and protested indignantly, "Ooh, Aunty! You said I was not to tell anyone that is your—"

"Yes, I know." Her back to the wall, Dimity still struggled gamely. "It is—er, a silly name, to be sure, but . . . well, I am used to it, you see."

They walked to the stairs, Carlton following, jumping in and out of the sections of the great stained-glass window that the sunlight painted on the floor.

Farrar mused, "Kitty, Kate, Cathy, would seem logical. But-Mitten . . . ?"

"Sir," she said firmly, "I do not care to be borrowing your aunt's things, and I certainly cannot wear riding boots with my gowns, so—"

"Oh, I don't know," he murmured, " 'twould enliven—"

"And so," she went on, cutting off such deliberate provocation, "I should like very much to go into Salisbury tomorrow and buy myself a pair of slippers. Your aunt said it might be possible."

"I make it a point never to contradict my aunt, can I avoid it. Besides, it chances, I have occasion to ride into Salisbury first thing in the morning. There are papers Norris wants, as you heard."

She came to a halt, regarding him uneasily. "I have no wish to impose on—"

" 'Twill be less of an imposition do you ride with me, rather than obliging me to call up coachman and carriage, Mrs. Mitten."

Why she should blush when he spoke her name she could not imagine, but she knew she was doing so and, flustered, said, "Yes. That is true, I fancy. And you could go about your business whilst I made my purchases, so—"

"Certainly not! I cannot have you wandering about, unescorted. Whatever would people think of you?"

Her blush deepened as his eyes slid to her bosom and remained there. She put up a hand, ostensibly to adjust the necklace she wore, but contrived to cover the attraction. Farrar shifted his gaze to the ceiling and went on, "I shall accompany you to an emporium where you may make your purchase. In return, perhaps you will come and hold my hand while the surgeon stitches up my arm."

Startled by the reminder, her eyes shot to his sleeve. "I see you changed your coat. Did your aunt bandage your arm for you?"

"My valet. He is a man of many talents."

"Had you cut it? Is that why you must see a surgeon?"

A slow and devastatingly attractive smile was levelled at her. "No. I thank you. But my man is in a fidget about it. Shall you mind if we ride? I prefer never to drive if the weather permits a gallop."

She managed to wrench her gaze from the smile that had also

crept into his eyes, and mumbled that she would be glad of a ride.

"Very good. Shall you require a pair of spurs, Mrs. Mitten?"

Again, to hear him speak her name was disturbing, and she wished she had not felt obliged to divulge it. She said rather sharply, "No. I have my own, thank you."

"So you have. I noticed them when you first arrived. I remember thinking how unusual it was for a lady to wear spurs . . . while riding in a stagecoach."

∞ *Chapter 7* ∞

Phillip Ellsworth did not reappear at The Palfreys, with the result that they sat down three to dinner in the beautifully scaled small dining room. The sun was setting, bathing the clouds with crimson, orange, and gold, laying its mellow light on lush meadows and darkling woods, and sending pink rays slanting through the tall windows. It seemed to Dimity that there was no room in the old house that was not a delight. She marvelled anew that, knowing she constituted such a threat to the owner, or that Carlton did, they were treated so civilly, but she suspected also that it might well be a trick, to lull her suspicions and catch her in a mistake that would disprove Carlton's claim. She dared not think there was a more sinister motive for their having been allowed to stay, but that melodramatic solution lingered at the edge of her mind. For all his cowardice, in some ways Farrar was a man to be feared. Whether he was capable of murdering a woman and child she could not quite decide, but his Parthian shot with regard to her spurs had frightened her. Clearly, he suspected something. 'I must,' she thought, 'be very, *very* careful!'

Lady Helen, wearing a dark brown velvet *robe volante*, was voicing her disappointment because Ellsworth had left. Irritated, Dimity frowned at Farrar, but his slight shake of the head was an unmistakable request for silence, and she said nothing. His aunt treated his few attempts at conversation with polite indifference, and talk languished. Driven by desperation, Dimity began to speak of music, whereupon my lady bloomed, her pale cheeks brightening and interest bringing a shine to her big eyes.

When the meal ended at last and they left Farrar to his port, Lady Helen led the way to the withdrawing room at the south end of the house. It was a large chamber, but warm and comfortable nonetheless. The butler carried in the tea tray and, in response to an enquiry from Dimity, informed her that Carlton was fast asleep in the pleasant room near her own that had been assigned to him.

Dimity murmured, "He must have been tired out. I fancied he would come in to say goodnight, but I've not seen him since Captain Holt left. It is good of you to let Cissie be his nurse, ma'am, but—"

"She's a very reliable girl, I assure you." Lady Helen began to pour the tea. "And although she had some difficulty finding him, I doubt he was too late to bed."

"I had no thought to criticize," said Dimity hastily. "Indeed, you are much too kind to us. Is only that I know he can be a handful. Where was he, ma'am?"

"With my nephew, I believe. He seems to have formed quite an attachment for Farrar."

"Oh."

"You are very fond of the boy," observed my lady, passing cup and saucer. "May I ask if you plan to remarry soon?"

Dimity stirred in milk and sugar and replied demurely that her brothers had not as yet approved any of her suitors. The thought of Tio brought the ache of worry and she went on quickly, "Dare I ask the same of you, ma'am?"

Shocked, Lady Helen arched her brows. "At my age, Mrs. Deene?"

"Why not? You are still young and very lovely and I fancy, no matter what you say, there have been many gentlemen paying you court."

My lady blushed and admitted that she did in fact have one or two admirers. "Before Prestonpans," she added quietly.

"But—surely, ma'am, they cannot hold you to blame for—er . . ."

"No. But I was in deep mourning. And now, they will not come here, and I cannot accept invitations."

She looked sad, and Dimity thought, 'How lonely she is, poor soul.' She said bracingly, "I would not suppose a quiet dinner party, or perhaps a recital, could be judged improper."

"Perhaps not. But to accept an invitation pointedly addressed to me alone, would make it seem as though I too were condemning my nephew."

After a rather pregnant pause, Dimity said, "I know I should not ask, but—my lady, are you *very* sure Sir Anthony did—as they say?"

Lady Helen stared at her teacup. "At the height of the battle, when it was clear their position was about to be overrun, Captain Farrar abandoned his men and ran to the rear. Had he not been shot, he might have fled the field." In a low, almost inaudible voice, she added, "If you—*knew* what I would give to think it a lie . . . But, alas—it is not."

It was a further reinforcement of what her brothers had said, but still she persisted, "He just does not seem that kind of man. Forgive me, but—have you discussed it at all?"

"Once. When he was first brought home he was still very ill of his wound, but in a little while I did ask him. He did not reply for quite a long time. Then he said just three words—'Guilty as charged.' My God!" She put a hand over her eyes for an instant. "We have never spoken of it since."

Farrar came in then. Dimity changed the subject hurriedly. A faint, cynical grin hovered about his mouth, and she knew he guessed they had been discussing him. He tried to persuade his aunt to play cards, but she refused, saying she intended to go early to bed. She rose only moments later, and having declined her nephew's offer of a short stroll in the gardens, said her goodnights.

Farrar walked into the hall to light their candles and, as my lady walked up the stairs, Dimity whispered, "Why did you not *tell* her, for goodness' sake? She should know what manner of man is Ellsworth!"

He looked at her enigmatically. "Good night, Mrs. Mitten."

She gave a little snort of impatience, accepted the candle he handed her, and went to her room feeling confused and irritable.

Rodgers looked surprised when she was told she would not be needed any more, but she went off gladly enough, and Dimity settled down at the graceful rosewood escritoire. There were several sheets of fine paper in the drawer, and the Standish contained ink and a nicely trimmed quill pen.

Having turned the pen in her hands for several minutes, staring blindly at the Standish, Dimity banished Anthony Farrar from her thoughts and started a letter to Peregrine. It was a difficult letter, and it was late by the time she had written and crossed her page. She read it over critically. There was nothing to interest the military in case it should fall into their hands. She had told him where she was and managed to convey something of her predicament without mentioning Tio or the cypher. It was a rather muddled epistle, but she found a lump of wax and sealed the sheet, hoping her brother would be able to understand this obscure cry for help. A few minutes later, her cloak wrapped about her, she was creeping across the stableyard.

A casual enquiry to Cissie had yielded the information that there was a Receiving Office in Palfrey Poplars, located in Pruitt's Sweets and Grocers' Shop. A few more enquiries of the stable boy had acquainted her with the fact that the village was just four miles to the west, and that all one had to do was follow the lane that joined the estate road about a mile beyond the bridge.

Dimity had succeeded in the really difficult task of saddling Odin before she left Muse Manor, and was confident she could manage the far more tractable black mare she had admired in Farrar's stables. She found the mare's stall with little difficulty, and led her into the barn. As soon as her eyes grew accustomed to the dimness, she was able to locate some fine saddles, several of which were for ladies. The mare was no problem. Much sooner than she had dared to hope, Dimity led her into the yard, where there was a mounting block, and a moment later she was riding along the rear drivepath and over the bridge.

Not until she was well clear of the house did she dare bring the mare to a canter. Once again, she was out alone at night, only this time she was in unfamiliar country, mounted on a borrowed horse, trying to find a village she had never seen. At least it was a still night, the moon riding high in a sky where only a few clouds drifted; the air was clean and sweet, and there was no wind. A far cry from the wild stormy night that had begun her adventure.

The lane joined the estate road, just as the boy had said, and the mare cantered along steadily through light and shadow, passing beneath great black trees, or between hedgerows fragrant with the wild roses that rioted there. But suddenly the road forked. Aghast, Dimity reined up. The boy had said nothing of a fork. She hesitated, torn by indecision, while the frisky mare danced impatiently. The left lane seemed to head more truly to the west so Dimity chose that fork, and to her relief chose correctly, for after much winding the lane broadened and a cluster of quiet cottages and the high Gothic tower of a church came into view.

Somewhere, a dog barked in a desultory way, but there was no other sign of life. Dimity walked the mare along the single street, scanning each building for a sign indicating a sweet shop or grocers'. She passed a cottage with a white card in the window and slipped hopefully from the saddle. The card imparted the information that the apothecary had gone to Salisbury and would not return until Wednesday sennight. Sighing, she walked on, leading the mare. At about this time it began to be borne in upon her that she was extremely tired. It had been a long, nerve-racking day, but the succession of events being so different from her usual pursuits had kept her alert. Now, exhaustion threatened to overwhelm her, and with all her heart she longed for the big tester bed at The Palfreys.

Ten minutes later, she stood forlornly at the point where she had started. The moon was sufficiently bright for her to have scanned every door and window but not one cottage had even faintly resembled a sweet shop or a Receiving Office. She was so tired she could have wept, and had to conjure up the memory of poor Tio's bloodied unconscious face before she could summon the energy to try once more.

She approached the second cottage only to halt, her heart leaping into her throat when the casement opened with an ear-splitting screech. A nightcapped head was stuck out. A cracked old voice piped, "Who be ye a'lookin' fer, marm?"

Grateful, she had the presence of mind to raise her voice to a disguising pitch before answering, "Pruitt's Sweet Shop and Grocers'."

"They do be closed," he cackled, and started to close the window.

"I know, but I've a letter I was hoping to slip under the door. It's very important."

The nightcap returned to view. "Why?"

Why. "It's about—ah, the accident to the stagecoach the other day."

"The what?"

"The Portsmouth Machine."

"Why did ye not say so first time? This here be a village as is set in its ways. We don't hold wi' new fangled names. There

107

bean't no need to go changing the name o' summat as has been called that name fer hunderds an' hunderds o' years. What about it?''

"Oh—well, one of the ladies on it was thought to be dying, but now they think she will recover, so I must send word to her family.''

"Why?''

What a difficult old gentleman! "Because they'll be worrying, of course. Sir, I am very tired. If you will just tell me—''

"'A' course ye're tired. Ye got no business capering about all alone in the middle o' the night. None of we people would 'low our females to do so mad a thing, and so I tellee! 'Sides which, it ain't proper manners t 'be waking honest folk at this hour and jawing their ears off.'' A scrawny arm was stuck through the lattice. "Give us yer writin'.''

Dimity hesitated. This cantankerous old creature might well forget all about her precious letter once he was safely back in bed. "Thank you kindly, sir,'' she called. "But I must find the Pruitts.''

Behind her, another casement screeched. Another nightcap appeared. "Give yer dratted writin' to un, fer pity's sake,'' cried a woman, irately.

A light glowed from the next cottage and the front door swung open. "Will ye please to be givin' himself the letter, me darlin','' yawned an Irish gentleman in a long nightshirt with a tattered tricorne on his bald head, "and let a body sleep.''

The window opposite was flung wide. A round-faced man roared, "Woman, he *is* Pruitt! Can ye not read the sign?''

All along the street candles were glowing and windows opening to the accompaniment of a babble of talk. Guiltily, Dimity hurried to thrust her letter into the frail, trembling hand. "What sign?'' she asked.

He leaned farther out of the window. "She can't see the sign,'' he screamed.

Shouts of mirth rang out. A woman called distantly, "What'd she say about the Portsmouth Machine?''

"Go back to bed, Millie. Does ye wake up Hezekiah, we'll not hear the end of't!''

Dimity dragged herself into the saddle. Starting off, she glanced back. Faintly, through the shadow cast by the moon, she saw that the entire side of the cottage was painted in huge letters, "PRUITT'S SWEET SHOPPE."

"Oh, dear!" she murmured, and touched her heels to the mare's side.

For quite some time she could hear them calling to each other. The last remark that reached her ears was an irate assessment of people who changed the names of vehicles as had been knowed as Portsmouth Machines fer a thousand years and more.

She was almost asleep when she approached The Palfreys, which may have accounted for the fact that she did not see the quiet dark shape that blocked the drivepath until she was almost upon him. He sat there, unmoving, like the figure of doom.

If it was the horrid Captain Holt, she thought, suddenly wide awake, she was as good as beheaded. If it was Anthony Farrar, she was likely about to be strangled. In a thin, quavering voice she called, "Who . . . is there?"

A moment of silence, then a laughing voice cried, "Ah, the dashing Mrs. Deene! Now here's a happy meeting!"

She drew a breath of relief. "Mr. Ellsworth! My goodness, but you startled me."

He walked his horse up, dismounted, and doffed his tricorne, his wig sleek and gleaming in the moonlight. "Faith, but you're a pretty creature," he said admiringly.

Wary, she asked, "Whatever are you doing here at this hour?"

"Oh, my friend's dogs are loose and I was afraid they might have come this way. Didn't want my dear aunt troubled by any more uproars." A few paces closer and he said softly, "You're out and about rather late yourself, lovely lady. Meeting the fellow who came calling this afternoon, perchance?"

It was quite obvious that he thought her a trollop. And who could blame him? But the moonlight revealed the dark bruise along his jaw, and the memory of his disgraceful conduct stiffened her back. "Captain Holt came to see me because—"

"So that's the way of it!" He laughed. "I'd the feeling you were not what you seemed. Spying, ma'am? I've heard the Intelligence people use females these days, but what would bring you to The Palfreys? I'd think the case against my craven cousin is clear enough."

It was ridiculous, but she had the feeling he was deadly serious. And perhaps it was better that he believe such nonsense than suspect the truth. "If I were truly working for the army, sir, I would scarce tell you so."

He stared at her thoughtfully. "Do you know what else I think . . . ?" He lunged at her, his arm whipped around her waist and she was torn from the saddle. She gave a squeak of shock, and fought wildly to free herself. He staggered for an instant, but his arms were steel. He bent low over her. "Egad, but you're a ripe plum, and all widows are willing, they say . . ."

"Not this one," gritted Dimity, pushing against him frenziedly.

He nibbled her earlobe, crushing her so close she could scarcely breathe. "Why pretend?" he said huskily, kissing his way down her throat. "You may not be a willing widow, but you're far from an innocent maid—come, yield to me, lovely one, and—"

He intercepted her tossing head; his mouth closed down hard over hers. She could smell ale, and she felt sickened and half smothered, and kept her lips clamped shut and unresponsive to his attempts to win her cooperation. His hand was busy at her bodice. He chuckled, "You're a cool one, but I warrant I can warm you up."

His handsome face, his purring voice, revolted her. Thrusting away that violating hand, she said fiercely, "I belong to another, Mr. Ellsworth."

He kissed her lightly. "A change is often beneficial, sweeting."

"And besides," she said, "I cannot admire anyone who would draw steel 'gainst an unarmed man."

He stiffened. An ugly light came into his eyes, and Dimity was afraid, but she managed to wrench free, and said steadily, "I've a grudge against Farrar myself, but I deplore your methods, Mr. Ellsworth."

"*My* methods!" He laughed jeeringly. "But yours are fair and aboveboard, eh? You little shrew! Oho, but I think you're one to be handled firmly!"

"I prefer not to be handled at all! I bid you good night, sir." She took up the mare's reins and walked swiftly towards the stableyard, her heart hammering, expecting at any second to hear him running up behind her, and resolved she would scream if he tried to force her again.

Instead, she heard a low chuckle, then he called, "Sleep

110

sound, little widow, but do not become too ambitious; 'twould be most unwise.''

Receding hoofbeats told her he was leaving. She gave a smothered sob and started to run, but her nerves threatened to give way, and she made herself walk steadily across the yard and into the silent barn. Farrar's big half-broken grey stallion woke up and eyed her suspiciously. Shaking, Dimity unsaddled the mare and rubbed her down with a handful of hay before leaving the stall and closing the gate softly behind her.

Exhausted, she slumped against it, closing her eyes, feeling as though she was being drawn deeper and deeper into a morass from which there would be no escape. She started to the house, so weary she could barely set one foot before the other. The rear door did not squeak when she opened it, and she slipped inside and crept to the stairs.

A sharp grating sound and a flame sprang to life. She gave a small, despairing cry. Anthony Farrar, clad only in shirt, breeches, and shoes, lit a candle and held it out to her. ''Would you wish me to escort you to your chamber, Mrs. Deene?'' he sneered. ''You must be ready for bed. One way or another.''

''I-I just went out for—a breath of air . . .'' she said feebly.

His smile unpleasant, he balanced the candlestick on the post at the foot of the stairs. ''I saw you. I wonder you've any breath left. I'll own I find Phillip Ellsworth's taste consistent.'' The deep eyes slid down her with a contempt that made her feel shamed and unclad. His hands shot out and clamped bruisingly on her arms. He grated savagely, ''What are you about, you scheming, lying little jade?''

Tears welled into her eyes, which maddened her, and she was so tired, that she ached with weariness. There was small hope of convincing him, but she said in a choked voice, ''I did not go to meet him. I—''

''Liar! I saw him kissing you. He's in this ugly plot with you, is that it? Tell me the truth, for once, or I'll—''

''Do what?'' she sobbed. ''Maul and abuse me, as your filthy cousin did? Go on, then! I might know you're no better than he, to treat a lady so, when—''

''Lady, is it?'' He laughed harshly. ''Harlot, more like! A scheming baggage who seeks to steal that to which she has no right! A conniving . . . cheating . . .'' He had drawn her very close now, and the rageful words were uttered just a breath from her lips. They faded into silence. Desire came into his eyes, and once again, Dimity knew she was going to be kissed by a man she scarcely knew. She had no will to resist. Only, of course, because she was so tired; there could be no other reason. Farrar's lips closed over hers. It was the oddest thing, but it was not at all abusive. His hands relaxed their grip and his arms slid about her, which seemed perfectly agreeable. It didn't matter that she could not breathe or that her ribs were being reduced to powder. She was warm and dreamy and content, save that her heart was beginning to beat its way through her crushed ribs. A fiercely intense wish that he not stop dizzied her. She swayed weakly when he raised his head and drew back.

He stared at her. The expression of contempt had quite vanished. He looked bewildered and oddly vulnerable.

Suddenly, Dimity was terrified. With a stifled sob, she snatched the candleholder and fled up the stairs. At the top, she peeped over the railing.

He was still standing there, gazing after her like a man bewitched.

Jane Guild heard the galloping hooves and sprang from the chair in the withdrawing room, her embroidery falling unheeded as she sped into the hall. Peddars sprinted past and flung open the front door, and Mrs. Burrows, her sleeves rolled up and her arms covered with flour, waddled from the kitchen hall and came puffingly to peer around the footman. The horseman raced around the curve of the drivepath to rein up with a flurry of pebbles and dirt clods. Miss Guild whispered, ''Thank God!'' and went out onto the steps.

Billy came running from the side yard and Piers Cranford tossed the reins to him and was up the steps in one long stride. With a muffled sob, Jane threw herself into his arms.

He said, ''Then there *is* something wrong!''

''Yes, yes. But how you knew . . .'' She smiled up at him wonderingly. ''Did you sense that Perry was in trouble?''

He kissed her and kept his arm about her as they walked into the house. ''Not bad trouble, I hope?''

He gave hat, whip, and gloves to Peddars, closed the withdrawing room door, and faced his aunt, his blue eyes anxious. "Everyone looks so strained. For the love of God, what—No, never mind. Let's go up to Perry, then you both can tell me at once."

Her hand on his arm restrained him. "He's not there, dearest. Oh, for mercy's sake do not be vexed. We have done as best we knew how. Only sit down and I will tell you what a dreadful fix we are in . . ."

Five minutes later, Piers sat very still and silent. Watching him nervously, Miss Guild finished, "So Sudbury and Peregrine have searched high and low these three days."

"My . . . God!" he whispered. "And—no sign?"

"Not a whisper of her. Perry went off again this morning. He is so tired, but—Oh, how glad I am that you have come! Poor Tio just lies there, and—and I really don't . . . know what to do."

Her voice cracked. Piers pulled himself together and crossed to lift her to her feet and give her a hug. "You've done splendidly. Let's go up and see him."

They entered the bedchamber quietly. Glendenning lay motionless and, save for his extreme pallor and the bandages about his untidy auburn head, might have been thought to be fast asleep. Samuels, who had been reading beside the bed, closed the book and sprang up as they entered, exclaiming fervently, "Thank Gawd you come, sir!"

Piers gripped his arm, then bent over his friend. "Poor old fellow. Has he said nothing at all since you found him?"

Miss Guild murmured sadly, "A few jumbled words at first, nothing understandable save for the name Green, but not even a movement since early yesterday morning."

"He looks very bad. Did the ball go through?"

"No, thank heaven! We thought at first it had, for there was so much blood, you know. But it was a deep score along the side of his head."

"You did not call a physician?"

"Dearest, we *dared* not!"

Piers drew up a chair for her, then leaned on it, staring miserably at Glendenning. "Damned idiot," he sighed. "If you were acting for Treve de Villars . . ." He swore under his breath. "My sister has led them off, all right, bless her brave heart. By Jupiter, but when we find her, I'll break her neck!"

A halting step was heard on the stairs, and the murmur of

voices. The door was thrown wide. Peregrine hobbled in, looking drawn and weary, but his blue eyes brightening when he saw his brother. "What brought you home?" he asked, wringing Piers' hand crushingly. "I'd not have thought Peale would have had time to find you."

"So you sent him, did you? No, he's likely searching Town for me, poor chap." Piers pushed him into the chair and leaned on the end of the bed. "For some inexplicable reason I'd the strong notion something was not well with you. Now I find it is nothing more than that you've let my sister rush herself into high treason, 'pon my word!" He saw Peregrine wince sharply, and cuffed his shoulder. "Dimwit! I know you'd no part in it. Mitten should be strangled, but I'll own I'm dashed proud of her!"

"And I. Though she must have tribes of woodworms between her ears to essay such a madcap trick!" Peregrine ran a hand across his eyes and muttered, "Had she not tried to protect me— No, don't eat me, I'll say no more on that suit, but—we've searched for miles around . . . My God! If—if she's—"

Piers said bracingly, "You great fool, if she were dead or arrested, we would have dragoons here! Lord knows whom she's inveigled into helping her, but I'll lay you odds we'll—". He stopped abruptly.

His lordship was moving restlessly.

Samuels fairly sprang to bend over the bed and murmur a gentle, "Master Tio?"

Glendenning opened his eyes and blinked at him painfully. In a very faint voice, he said, "That you . . . Sam? Piers! What— the deuce . . ."

"Tio," said Peregrine. "You makebait! Where the devil have you sent my sister?"

Glendenning made an effort to sit up and fell back, panting. "Did you—get it there safe?"

"Easy, old fellow." Piers shot an irked glance at Peregrine and held Lord Horatio's shoulders down.

Peregrine said in a calmer voice, "My memory is at fault. What was I to take? And where?"

His quiet words wrought even more havoc. His drawn face twisting with horror, his shadowed eyes dilating, the sick man struggled against Piers' restraining hands. "You *forget*?" he raved wildly. "Damn you! How—how can you forget? The *cy-*

pher, you dolt! The *cypher*! Did you—Did you—deliver . . ." He groaned, clutching his injured head.

Miss Guild pushed her disastrous nephews away and eased Glendenning back onto his pillows. "Of course he did. There, my dear, never be so distressed. Peregrine simply could not recollect the name of the man who . . . Oh dear, I'm afraid he's going off again."

His eyes closing, Glendenning whispered, "Glad . . . it's done. Does—my father . . . ?" And with a sigh, he sank from consciousness.

Piers muttered, "Well, at least he's alive. I suppose you have sent word to his illustrious—" He leapt from one invalid to the other. "Perry, old lad! What is it? Is that damnable foot—"

Peregrine straightened in the chair and lowered the hands that had covered his face. "The *cypher*!" he groaned. "Dear Lord, why did I not guess? You must be aware every dragoon in England is after it, and God knows how many bounty hunters!"

Piers exchanged a frightened look with his aunt, and it would have been hard to judge whose face was paler. He stammered, "I recall—some weeks back there was a flurry about a—a poem or some such nonsense, but—"

"Nonsense, is it?" Peregrine leaned forward. "Quentin Chandler is rumoured to have carried one of the stanzas, and got out of England by the skin of his teeth, and half dead! There is a reward of a hundred guineas for information leading to the arrest of any Jacobite found with the cypher on his person! Can you guess the ferocity with which the poor devil is hunted? And now . . . now my *sister* has it!"

Miss Guild wet suddenly dry lips. "Cypher? But—you said 'twas a poem."

"It is. In four separately despatched stanzas. Each is said to contain a clue to the whereabouts of the treasure Charles Stuart amassed to finance his Cause."

"If that foolish boy had a treasure," said Miss Guild, who had a soft spot in her heart for the handsome prince, "why ever did he not use it?"

"It could not be converted into cash in Scotland, so they tried to get it over to France."

"I wish them joy of that endeavour," Piers inserted grimly.

"The fleet prowls the waters 'twixt here and France, and I've heard a minnow cannot pass but what they search it!"

"Exactly so. Wherefore the treasure was diverted to England, the hope being to ship it from here, unsuspected. That plan failed also, for the Cause was lost 'fore ever the treasure could be put aboard ship."

"And—now?"

"The Jacobites mean to try and restore it to the original donors. Oh, never look so astonished, Aunt. Half the poor devils are starving and dispossessed for their sympathies. The return of their valuables would mean the difference between life or death to many."

Samuels put in dourly, "And the knowledge they'd contributed, an even surer death, to my way of thinking!"

The twins, who had forgotten he was present, stared at him.

Piers thought, 'The devil! Well, too late to be cautious now,' and said, "I still do not see. Why the cyphers?"

"Besides," said Jane Guild, "it seems to me far more dangerous to have sent out four messages instead of one."

Peregrine shrugged. "Had a single letter containing all the information fallen into the wrong hands, they'd have the whole. As it is, even if a courier is taken, the military or whoever gets him will have only one stanza, and without the other three, the chances of decoding are judged impossible."

Piers had been watching his brother narrowly. "You make-bait," he said, low and furious. "You—damned—stupid—*makebait*!"

Peregrine flushed scarlet and stared at the bedpost.

Miss Guild sighed. "I'd the same thought, Piers. He is involved."

"You were to meet Tio—is that it? How deep are you in this, twin?"

Peregrine said defensively, "I promised to help Tio only if he called on me. I know about the cypher because—a friend told me of it."

"De Villars!" snorted Piers. "I've warned you death stalks his shadow, but you must—"

"Oh, fiddle," said Peregrine, irritated. "Treve's a dashed good man."

"I'd be curst glad to have him at hand was I hunted, I grant

116

you, but to cultivate his friendship is to bring yourself under the eye of the military. 'Tis only a matter of time before he's arrested, you know that!''

"I'll own I like Trevelyan de Villars," Miss Guild interjected in her sensible way, "and I admire his courage. But that does not help us decide what to do now."

Piers looked miserably at Glendenning's motionless figure. "Tio is our only hope. God send he wakes soon."

Samuels asked, "Should we send word to the earl, Mr. Piers? He's a hard man and would fly into a proper pucker if he knew Master Horatio was involved in this business. But—he *is* his father."

"If we tell old Bowers-Malden, the fur will fly," muttered Peregrine dubiously. "He'll have Tio out of here in a wink, and we'll lose all chance to find out about Mitten."

"Is the earl likely to have missed his lordship, Samuels?" asked Piers.

"I doubt it, sir. They don't see eye to eye on most things. Lord Horatio has not met his father this month and more."

Piers nodded. "Then I fancy we're not being wholly ruthless in keeping the old boy in the dark another few days. Perry—do you stay here and hope Tio awakens in a rational state. I'm going down to Gloucestershire."

"Why must I stay? I'm not helpless, you know."

"No," grinned his brother. "Only hopeless! I'm going after Treve, you dolt! I fancy he's at his uncle's country seat. He's the only man might know Mitten's whereabouts."

Miss Guild sighed heavily. "Dear Mitten. I only pray her reputation is not quite ruined."

"You think some base villain would dare—" Peregrine's face darkened. "Now God help any filthy swine who lays a hand on her!"

∽ Chapter 8 ∽

Despite her weariness, Dimity had not slept well, waking once in the grip of a nightmare in which the two mastiffs were chasing her while she hobbled in Mrs. Deene's crippling slippers, and falling asleep again, only to wake once more and lie wide-eyed, reliving the moments in Anthony Farrar's arms.

She had not encountered him at breakfast for since they were to make an early start, a tray was brought to her room. Now, she slanted a look at the man riding beside her through the brilliance of the morning. She noted again that he rode very well, with a lazy, almost slouching grace that made him seem as one with the big grey. He looked stern and unyielding. She tried to picture him panicking in the face of a Scots charge. Her brothers had told her that the Scots were fierce and terrible fighters, but still she could not imagine anything causing this individual to panic and run. At once, she felt traitorous for harbouring such doubts. Perry and Piers despised Farrar, and they had *been* there. They had judged contemptible the man she now mentally defended; the man she had not only allowed to kiss her, but whom she was beginning—

"Guilty conscience, ma'am?" he drawled, not looking her way.

Her cheeks burned. "I should think *you* might be the one to harbour such sentiments," she answered. Then, realizing the double entendre, she added, "I mean—about last night."

He turned a sardonic gaze on her. "You are *sure* that is what you mean?"

She mumbled, "I—had never been kissed so . . . before."

"At least," his lip curled, "not for a full five minutes."

118

"I tell you Ellsworth *forced* himself on me. He was horrid! I did not willingly—" And she thought, 'Oh, heavens!' and was silent.

An iron hand was upon her reins. The horses came to a halt. It was very peaceful on the country lane with no other travellers in sight, the trees softly whispering overhead, and a lark singing gloriously somewhere. Farrar had not worn powder today, and the sunlight awoke a bright sheen on his fair hair and made his eyes an emerald glow in his bronzed face. Dimity concentrated on the lush slope of a nearby hill.

He demanded softly, "Do you say you *did* willingly kiss me?"

What nonsense. As if she would have done so disgraceful a thing! It would be to betray the brothers she loved and *that* she would never do! She drew a steadying breath. "How can you ask such a question? You know perfectly well that you seized me—like any bear!"

His grin mocked her. "How odd that I'd the distinct impression you enjoyed it."

"Odd, indeed!" But oh, *why* must her wretched heart flutter so? Frightened by her own reactions, she flared, "And quite at odds with both my moral standards and my reason for coming to The Palfreys."

The amusement faded from his eyes. Her words had hit hard. Stung, he retaliated with a contemptuous, "I'd have judged both to be deplorable." Predictably, she whirled on him in a flame, but he only shrugged, "Did you feel so violated, Madam Purity, I wonder you did not scream."

Why had it not occurred to her to scream? She had to grope for a response. "I wish I may see myself so distressing your aunt!"

"Aha," he jeered. "So next time I may count myself safe, eh?"

The knowledge that her feeble response had invited such vulgarity was no consolation. Outraged, she cried, "For shame! Whatever you think of me, I am a guest in your house, and—"

"You are a guest in my home, ma'am, only because my gentle aunt pities you!" He saw her flinch but seized her arm and grated, "Admit the truth. You're in this with my damnable cousin and his putrid friend!"

"No!" she gasped, striving in vain to break free.

His fingers tightened. "Then why did you creep out to cuddle with him? Having seen those passionate embraces, do you really expect me to believe that you are unacquainted with the creature?"

He was flushed beneath his tan, his eyes glittering with a rage disproportionate to the disgust he might have felt for a vulgar adventuress. Under normal circumstances Dimity, well equipped with common sense, might have noted such odd behaviour. Now, her own emotions rioting, she said, "Much I care what you believe! You were not slow to indulge *yourself* with some passionate embraces, when you'd done with peeping from behind curtains like any sneaking spy!"

"An I spied on you, 'twas because your behaviour had me offstride. Yes, I admit that fact. Hating me one minute, helping me the next; your actions saying you were my enemy, your eyes saying something very different. Oh, never deny it! When I kissed you last night, your lips were as hot as mine own! Why, madam? To buy me with your favours, perchance? You'll catch cold at that, and so I warn you!"

"Oh!" gasped Dimity. *"Oh!"* Her hand flew up. His intercepted it. "Contrary to your beliefs, Captain Farrar," she cried, "I am a very careful shopper and make it a practice never to buy a pig in a poke!"

The angry colour faded from his face, leaving him rather white. Releasing her, he said, "Oh, very good. You've a quick tongue, ma'am. You'll need it do you hope to oust me from my home."

Breathing hard and feeling vulgar and miserable, she took up the reins. "Your solicitor will doubtless inform you of my chances."

"Little fool," he muttered. "Did it not occur to you that you've given your only proofs into my hands? Were I as evil as you think me, I'd have instructed Norris to destroy them. Simple enough. Where would you be then with your scheming?"

She was stunned, but she must not let him see her dismay. It was quite possible that Carlton was an impostor, for his aunt did not seem quite respectable. But it was also possible that their claim was valid, and she must not be the one to ruin it for them. She was new to bitter quarrelling and felt increasingly weak and shaken, but managed a laugh. "La, but you take me for a ninny! My man of the law in London had all my documents copied and—and signed by a Notary Public long before I came here, I do promise you.''

Watching her, Farrar thought that if she really had a ''man of the law'' in London, *he* would have been the one to present her documents. But he did not confront her with that obvious fact. She was pale, and her hands trembled as she urged the mare to a trot, but however close they were, she did not give way to tears.

Touching his spurs lightly to the stallion's sides, Farrar's lips quirked wryly. She mounted a good fight, did the wicked widow!

An hour later, they were clattering over the bridge across the River Avon. The sun sparkled on the water, and the spire of the great cathedral rose proud and high against the azure skies. It was Dimity's first sight of Salisbury Cathedral and she forgot anger and the aggravating ache of hurt. ''Oh,'' she murmured. ''How beautiful! So tall and proud.''

''The tallest in all England,'' he agreed, as lost as she in admiration of the great building.

''It must be the most beautiful in the world.''

''No . . . in all honesty, there is a cathedral in Amiens I find even more beautiful.''

She glanced at him. His face held a dreaming look. ''Have you ever painted it?''

''Amiens? No, but—'' He started. ''I suppose Lady Helen told you that I dabble with oils.''

''I would say you do more than dabble, sir. I should very much like to see more of your work.'' He flushed scarlet and looked fixedly at his own hand on the reins. Amused, she thought, 'How shy he is about his talent.' But she had no wish to add to his embarrassment and said easily, ''I expect you have been much about the world. Is France your favourite country?''

''It is very lovely, certainly. Unhappily, much of my travelling was during a state of war which is not the best way to see a land. And at all events, to an Englishman there is only one favourite country, no? I fancy your brother—or is that plural? I forget— would agree.''

She gave him a level look. To her surprise he said with a boyish grin, ''I scored that time, eh ma'am?''

She rode on, hiding a smile and rather absurdly grateful for this truce. They passed under an ancient arch and along narrow cobbled streets where boys darted about hoping to earn a groat by holding horses, where muffin men cried their wares, apprentices polished latticed windows or swept thresholds, farmers and fine gentlemen rubbed elbows in the kennels, elegant coaches vied for space with great country wains and waggons, and everywhere was noise and confusion.

Lifting Dimity from the saddle, Farrar beckoned an eager street urchin and commissioned him to take the horses to the livery stable and see them watered and rubbed down. Then he offered Dimity his arm and led her along the busy street. "There is a popular emporium a little way—" He stopped, his face lighting up. "Hilary!" His hand went out. "Jove, but I've not seen you—"

The young officer, dashing in his military scarlet, came up with an answering grin. Then, consternation dawned in the fine face. He flushed darkly, dropped his outstretched hand, and deliberately turned on his heel and crossed the street. Farrar drew back with an odd, shrinking movement, then stood motionless. Several passersby stopped, gawking, and a youth giggled audibly. Dimity's emotions ran the gamut from shock, to horror, to a painful and overwhelming pity. Scarcely daring to look at Farrar, she saw his face dead white and a stricken helplessness in his eyes that, though swiftly banished, made her toes curl. She took his arm again and began to move on. She felt him start, then he was keeping pace with her. She ignored the mocking laughter that followed them, managed somehow to find her voice, and chattered about something, heaven knows what, until he began to offer polite monosyllabic answers and she recovered her wits sufficiently to urge that he let her shop whilst he went to his surgeon.

"I can scarce blame you for that, ma'am," he muttered.

She shot another glance at him. His eyes devoid of expression now, he said with his usual calm assurance, "But I could not permit you to go about unescorted."

Relieved by the return to normality, she argued, "Nor I permit you to suffer so. I know how gentlemen dislike to shop and I am no schoolroom miss, after all."

"I'll own that."

"Wretch!"

He smiled. "Still, it will not do."

"Why ever not? One might think I was not to be trusted!" She could have bitten her tongue the instant the words were said. It was the sort of flippant remark she might have thrown at her brothers without a second thought, but to have said it to Farrar in view of their unhappy relationship was absurd. She was not usually foolish, and realized her slip might well be attributed to the overwrought state of her nerves, but she was mortified and prayed he would overlook it.

For a moment he was silent. Then he drawled, "I wonder why I should not do so? You seek to dispossess me of my home, fortune, and estates and, perhaps more dastardly, are attempting to foist off on me an obnoxious little hellion for my nephew."

She may have brought that on herself, but she had tried to help him over some very rocky ground, and this was the thanks she got! Vexed and hurt, she attempted to jerk her hand away, but it was seized and held in a grip that she knew better than to fight.

"You charm my aunt," he went on in that low, grim voice, "even as you provoke and perplex me. You appear a wanton jade at one moment, a lady of Quality the next." They had come to the emporium, and he drew her to a halt and held her facing him in the curve of the bow window. "You came very bravely to my aid when I was confronted by savage dogs who would have reduced most ladies to hysterics and swooning. With shocking impropriety you crept out at night and I found you being made love to by that worthless cousin of—"

"He—"

Farrar put up a hand to stifle her indignant utterance, ignoring a large lady and two fat small girls who were staring at them through the emporium window. "You seek to poison a child's mind, by telling him the bitter truth about me, yet defend me to a justifiably irate captain of dragoon guards. You make it clear that I am the most repellent of men one minute, and in the next stand by me through—through a confrontation that must have been a most ghastly and shameful embarrassment for you."

The trio in the window had been augmented by a sales clerk who was markedly disapproving. Her cheeks very pink, Dimity asked, "Are you quite finished, sir?"

"Almost. Mrs. Deene—if you seek to confuse me—by God,

123

but you've succeeded! And I do not trust that which confuses me!''

"No," she said, "but you kiss it willingly enough!" And she put her nose in the air and swept into the bustling interior.

Farrar drew level with the fat lady and her two goggling children and, removing his tricorne, bowed deeply.

"Luvaduck!" gasped the fat lady, drawing her children closer.

"A commendable sentiment, ma'am," drawled Farrar, and followed Dimity.

She was inspecting a shelf of slippers. She took up a quite fashionable pair made of cream kid, with tortoiseshell buckles, high heels, and pointed toes. Farrar's hand closed over hers. She glanced up at him questioningly. His eyes grave, he shook his head. "Those will never do."

A shop assistant, a short, rather timid individual, had made his way to them and looked at the tall gentleman curiously. A nob, beyond all doubt, but why was he interfering? The young lady had made a wise choice.

Farrar selected a pair of scarlet satin slippers with very high Spanish heels and a quantity of jet beadwork set off by glittering paste buckles. "Now these," he murmured, "would look so well with that lovely blue gown."

Dimity had to bite her lip, but managed to preserve her countenance and with dignity tell the astonished clerk that she would like to try on the cream pair.

She was led to a curtained alcove at the far side of the emporium. Directing a scolding glance at Farrar, she saw him talking to a young woman with bright yellow curls who looked up at him with undisguised admiration. 'Shameless hussy,' thought Dimity in disgust, and told the assistant to kindly be quick with the fitting because her "brother" had an appointment with his doctor.

"A fine looking gentleman, if you'll forgive me saying so, miss," remarked the clerk, kneeling and removing her riding boots with discretion. "I trust he is not ill?"

Dimity stared at the top of his balding head. "Hallucinations," she said.

"Good gracious me! Does he suffer seizures, then?"

She wondered if the brassy-haired baggage was also managing to confuse the captain, and snapped, "Violent seizures. And one never knows when they may take him. The last time he was afflicted was during Holy Communion in the Cathedral. He fancied himself King Henry the Eighth, and stood up and commanded that the bishop and all the choir be taken out and burned at the stake." She gave a smug little smile, picturing such a scene, and then became aware that the kneeling clerk was staring at her, open-mouthed. Recovering herself, she added, "So you'd best hasten. He's not been feeling just the thing this morning."

The clerk's hands fairly flew. The shoes were judged a perfect fit. Dimity bent forward and whispered, "Have you any fichus?"

Replacing her boots, he nodded, his eyes very round.

"Could you please slip two of your best white ones, lace trimmed if possible, in with the shoes? Don't let my brother see, though. He does not approve."

"Of—of fichus?" he whispered.

She nodded solemnly. "Says they are works of the devil."

He gulped and shot from the alcove, clutching the shoes. Unwilling to miss ensuing developments, Dimity hurried in his wake.

The yellow-haired girl and Farrar were deep in discussion, apparently over the merits of a bolt of pink cloth. The assistant fairly tiptoed past, his apprehensive gaze glued to Farrar. Dimity came up and coughed slightly.

Farrar turned, raising a surprised eyebrow. "Can I believe it? Finished, so soon?"

The yellow-haired girl cast a glance of loathing at Dimity, who smiled sweetly at her and laid a hand on Farrar's sleeve. "I could not bear to think of you being bored," she cooed.

The yellow curls tossed and the girl flounced off.

Farrar's eyes narrowed. "What are you about now? I vow you look so saintly we could put a surplice on you and you might sing with the choirboys!"

The clerk dropped the parcel he had hurriedly assembled, and had to start all over again. Dimity vanished into her handkerchief. Farrar suddenly cried, "Hey!" and struck his riding crop smartly on the counter.

The unfortunate clerk leapt into the air with a yelp of fright.

"The lady purchased shoes only," cried Farrar, indignant. "What's all that other stuff you're slipping in there?"

Shaking in every limb, the clerk replied, "N-nothing, sir. Mi-mistake, do assure you. I'll—make all right . . ."

Under Farrar's stern gaze, he began to re-wrap the parcel.

Wiping tears from her eyes, Dimity asked a stifled, "Is there . . . some problem?"

"One might think you'd bought the whole store," grunted Farrar. "The gall of the fellow! And he's slow as treacle. They should light a fire under—Egad! Down it goes again!"

Dimity was obliged to "blow her nose" and was occupied by this endeavour until Farrar had paid for the shoes, accepted his change, and ushered her out of the store.

Repentant, she sighed, "Oh, dear. I must have dropped my handkerchief. No, do not bother to go back. I know just where I left it."

She made her way to the clerk, who was mopping his pale and sweating brow, and pressed a generous *douceur* into his shaking hand. "I do apologize," she murmured, bestowing her most winning smile on him. "You tried."

When she rejoined Farrar, he eyed her with marked suspicion. "Why have I the feeling there was more to that little transaction than I observed?"

"Probably because you were so entranced by some tinted curls that you suffered a lapse in your powers of observation," she said primly, and irritated him by vouchsafing no further information, but chuckling to herself as they proceeded to the solicitor's chambers.

Mr. Norris, it developed, was in court, but if they cared to wait, he should be back in about an hour for the luncheon recess. Farrar left the documents with the clerk and conducted Dimity outside again and along the flagway towards the High Street, where was his surgeon's establishment. This was a pleasant white-stuccoed and half-timbered house, the smells inside, when the porter admitted them, reminding Dimity of Peregrine's long ordeal.

Watching her covertly, Farrar saw the merriment in her eyes replaced by the sadness he had glimpsed there once or twice. The porter showed them to a tiny waiting room, and they sat side by side on a rubbed leather sofa.

Dimity said, "I apologize for teasing you. This will be nasty, I expect."

126

"I do not believe you were teasing me, madam. I think you were up to mischief again, and I'd give a deal to know what it was."

She hesitated a moment, then, with a dimple, told him.

His jaw dropped. He stared at her aghast. "Why—you little vixen! If ever I—" He was interrupted by a slim, rather untidy gentleman of late middle age, with a kind mouth and gentle brown eyes, who came from an inner room and called him. He went off, slanting a glance of indignation at Dimity, but with a grin lurking about his mouth.

The minutes drifted past. No one else came in and the time began to drag. Dimity had once watched their surgeon sew up a gash in Piers' arm when the twins' reenactment of the Siege of Acre had become too realistic, and the memory of that scene was beginning to worry her when the doctor wandered in again. He peered around the empty room myopically.

"Which one of you is with Sir Anthony?" he asked.

'Good heavens!' thought Dimity, and stood.

"Oh, dear. Did he not bring his man?"

"I'm afraid not. Is something wrong?"

"No, but—did you come by carriage, ma'am?"

"We rode." She glanced at the riding crop Farrar had left on the chair and wondered if the man was blind.

"Very unwise," he muttered, but apparently detecting her troubled look, gave a sudden huge smile and said with great jollity that there was nothing to worry about. "Might've been better had Tony had the sense to have brought a manservant and his carriage. Dog bites, y'know. Had to sear. Unpleasant business."

She winced. "Yes. I shall go and hire a carriage at—"

"Devil you will!" Farrar stood in the doorway, straightening the ruffles at his wrist and frowning at the physician. He was pale, but said steadily, "Roger, you old gloom-monger, what are you at now? The lady already holds a poor opinion of me without your adding to it by making me out too weak-kneed to bear your clumsy stitchery. I am perfectly fit."

Dr. Steel extracted a pair of bent spectacles from his waistcoat pocket, and affixed them to his nose. One lens drooped, and he tilted his head to accommodate that lapse, clapped a hand to his sliding wig, and surveyed his patient anxiously. "Yes, but you're not, you know," he sighed.

"Stuff!" Farrar cuffed him gently and strode past to take up his tricorne and whip. "If you are ready, ma'am?"

Dimity said, "I was hoping you would be longer. My feet are—"

He gripped her arm. "Mrs. Deene, do not add to your deceptions," he said, *sotto voce*, "I am a much-tried man."

"As well as a conceited one," she murmured as he rushed her through the door.

He maintained a brisk pace as they made their way along the bustling street, and rejected offers to buy a broom, to have his palm read, to have the pretty lady's palm read, to attend an auction of some prize pigs, or to eat two for the price of one at the new ordinary on the Winchester Road. They were almost to the livery stable when he was hailed by name and turned about, pushing Dimity rather roughly away from him, his jaw set, and the colour that had returned to his face, draining away again.

A tall, elegant gentleman, somewhere in the early thirties Dimity judged, stood leaning on an amber cane and fanning himself with his gold-laced tricorne. He had a strong, rather gaunt face with high cheekbones and a Roman nose. His complexion was dark, as were the thick brows that rose to sharp peaks over unusually beautiful grey eyes. The way in which he flourished his cane, and the excellence of his dark gold coat, primrose satin small clothes, and Mechlin lace cravat suggested the dandy; a suggestion the apprehensive Dimity thought belied by the determined jut of the chin and the firm mouth.

Sauntering over to them, the gentleman said in a deep, bored voice, "Anthony, my dear fellow, I rejoice to see you among the living." His admiring gaze, however, was fixed on Dimity.

"How odd it is, Treve," replied Farrar, "that I had thought you betrothed. Mrs.—er, Deene, may I present the Honourable Trevelyan de Villars? And caution you 'gainst placing too great a reliance on the adjective . . ."

Both amused and relieved, Dimity curtsied.

De Villars bowed with depth and grace, and murmured, "Is a courtesy title, dear boy. Not an adjective. And if you riposte by saying that in *my* case it is an adjective misused, I shall be obliged to restore you to your sick bed. Mrs. Erdene, I can only grieve that I am no longer at liberty to pursue so fair a—''

"Not *Erdene*, you great looby," interposed Farrar, grinning. "Mrs. *Deene*."

"But—dear dolt, you distinctly said—''

"He is not himself," Dimity interjected with a twinkle.

"What a relief," said de Villars wickedly. "Are we acquaint, dear lady? I would swear I have met you somewhere."

Her heart gave a jump. De Villars! Of course! Her brothers often spoke of the man. He was, in fact, a friend of Perry's, a friendship which she suspected did not enjoy Piers' endorsement. If he had detected the strong family likeness and mentioned it, she would be unmasked! Fortunately, before she was able to respond, Farrar groaned and clapped a hand to his brow. Dimity looked up at him anxiously.

"What a hoary old gambit!" he scoffed. "Really, Treve, one might expect better things of a fellow with your reputation."

"So dear Jacob Holt tells me."

The atmosphere became tense. Farrar said guardedly, "Yes? When?''

De Villars sighed. "Yesterday, I think. He fairly haunts me."

"You dashed idiot! Let be!''

Replacing his tricorne, De Villars murmured, "Soon, I hope. Have you seen our faithful Gordie of late?''

"Yes. He's off to Town, I believe."

"Ah. Boudreaux House, by any chance?''

Farrar nodded, watching him frowningly.

"Pity," said de Villars. "I'm not there. You look a trifle wrung out, dear lad. Some small indisposition?''

"Two large dogs," said Dimity.

De Villars' right eyebrow twitched upward. He rubbed the handle of his amber cane thoughtfully against his chin. "Not the puppies of Harding's grieving bosom bow?''

"The very same."

"I marvel you live. Were you present at this debacle, Mrs. Deene?''

"Yes, sir. And never have I been more terrified."

"Yet she managed to drive them off with a branch," said Farrar, looking down at Dimity with a faint smile.

"And was not slain? Remarkable. Tell me, ma'am, when you

129

wielded your branch at those misbegotten hounds, did they turn on you?"

"No, thank heaven. They had attacked Sir Anthony's spaniel, and when he tried to stop them, they mauled his arm badly."

"Yet," he mused, "when you intervened, they continued to concentrate on our Tony, eh?"

Dimity gave a little gasp. Farrar asked in a low voice, "Treve? What the devil do you suggest?"

"Merely that you use your head, dear boy. And do not go about without you carry at least one pistol. I suppose I must now trot in search of Chandler. Wretched nuisance. Farewell, ma'am, 'tis a joy to have made your acquaintance."

Watching him go, Dimity said curiously, "What an unusual man."

"Treve's a *rara avis*," he declared, with a rather troubled expression. "Well now, ma'am, I fancy you would like a cup of tea, at the least."

"Perhaps we could go to the new ordinary on the Winchester Road." He gave her a puzzled look, and she added demurely, "Two—for the price of one."

He chuckled. "I think we can do better than that."

He took her to a delightful old tavern where they sat on a rear terrace shaded by spreading oak trees, and enjoyed cold cider, some excellent pork pie, and sliced fruits. Farrar was quiet and it seemed to Dimity that his polite conversation about de Villars had little to do with his thoughts. He excused himself briefly at the end of the meal. She assumed it was for the customary reason and left the terrace herself. When she returned, there was no sign of him, but another gentleman was seated at a nearby table.

He was richly dressed and wore an elegant, flowing bag wig. He must be of great height, Dimity judged, and his girth was enormous. He leaned forward, drinking his soup noisily. It was not in her nature to judge by appearances, but she was conscious of a deep revulsion and thought that he resembled nothing so much as a huge toad. As she drew nearer, she detected the smell of the unwashed, and saw also, as one fat hand reached towards the basket of bread, that the ends of the fingernails were black. Had she not left her parcel on the table she would have been tempted, ridiculous as it seemed, to wait for Farrar's return.

Even so, she hesitated and glanced around, wishing he would come.

A chair scraped. She turned to find the new arrival standing, napkin in hand, watching her. His eyes were like black buttons in the pale flabbiness of his coarsely featured face, and they travelled up and down her with bold rudeness, an admiring smile beginning to curve the thick lips.

She thought, 'My heaven! He is a giant!' And indeed, he towered over her so that her urge to run away intensified.

He bowed with rather surprising flair. A deep voice rumbled, "Give you good day, ma'am."

That was polite enough. She was being silly, just because she'd had a rather taxing morning. Collecting herself, she responded with a nod and the faintest of smiles, and chose the farthest chair. Before she could touch it, he was pulling it out for her, standing much too close. Abruptly, her need to escape him was a near frenzy. She knew how to deal with impertinent admirers, but now her heart was pounding with a fear such as she had never before experienced and that robbed her of the words with which to depress this creature's pretensions.

His little eyes glittering, he moved even closer. She drew back instinctively, only to find herself trapped between him and the chairs around her.

Bending to her, he murmured with an incalculably suggestive leer, "Are all the men in this sorry world gone blind, to leave such a lovely lady all alone?"

"Not all, my lord."

Dimity would never have believed she could be so glad to hear that lazy drawl, but glancing up, she saw the big man's expression change to a malevolence that was appalling.

He stood very straight and without turning, sneered, "Well, well, so you have dared set foot off your own preserves, have you, Farrar?" He stared at Dimity with a very different look in his hard little eyes. "And this is yours, is it? What a pity, my dear, that you have such poor taste."

"Never blame the lady, my lord," said Farrar, one hand on the pillar that supported the terrace roof. "The error in judgement was mine. I was not aware that you patronized this house, you see."

That the big man had a violent temper became very evident.

131

The heavy features contorted and were darkened by a purplish flush. With a growled oath he swung around, one great paw flailing out. Farrar swayed aside with the smooth grace of the accomplished fencer, and a howl of rage and pain sounded as the savage blow landed full on the pillar.

Cradling his hurt, the big man roared, "Damn you to hell, Farrar! You've broke my hand!"

With swift precision Farrar had taken up Dimity's parcel, swept away the chairs that trapped her, and guided her towards the door. He glanced back and said over his shoulder, "No—have I? And here I'd fancied my day not very well spent!"

Chairs were sent crashing. Starting towards them vengefully, the big man checked, cursing and holding his hand painfully. "You miserable bastard!" he bellowed. "There'll come a day of reckoning, never doubt it, and you'll pay a hundred-fold for what you've done to me and my son!"

Farrar pushed Dimity through the door. He said scornfully, "You are ridiculous, as ever, my lord. I wonder you do not disgust yourself. You know perfectly well I cannot challenge an old man. If your son has the gumption, let him call me to account."

He closed the door swiftly on the resultant explosion of profanity and led Dimity across the coffee room and into the vestibule. The host was hurrying anxiously down the stairs. Farrar nodded to the terrace. "There's a poor fellow having a fit out there. You'd best summon a physician," he said, and opened the front door.

Dimity's hand trembled as she took his arm.

"Ecod, ma'am," he said softly, "your choice of admirers continues to deteriorate."

Angered, she snatched her hand away. "My *choice*? That horrid creature?"

He glanced covertly at her. "Dear me. And I had thought you old friends."

"Heaven forfend!" She shivered suddenly. "He made my skin creep!"

"Unfortunate, ma'am. He was obviously lost in admiration for you, and he is enormously powerful and . . . very rich."

"Were we not on a public thoroughfare," said Dimity between her small white teeth, "I would demand that you give me my new shoes!"

He said with bland solicitude, "Your feet pain you, ma'am?"

"Not at all. I merely have a nigh overwhelming desire to hit you with them!"

"Then I must indeed beg that you restrain such a desire. You have been sufficiently disgraced today, Mrs. Deene, but to raise your feet against me in public would—"

She had a mental picture of such a spectacle and her rich gurgle of laughter rang out. She caught a glimpse of a twinkle in his deep eyes and, her own alight with mirth, said, "No, be serious, do. Why does that horrible man hate you so? I vow I never saw such an expression in a gentleman's eyes."

For a moment Farrar continued to stare down at her merry face. "You still have not. Whatever one might call him, he is not a gentleman."

She looked at him curiously. "You called him my lord. Is—"

"Good God, ma'am! Disabuse your mind of the belief that a title qualifies its owner as a gentleman!"

"Well of course I do not think that! The most despicable of men may be a knight or—" She stopped abruptly.

He sneered, "Or—a baronet?"

She flirted her shoulder at him and said crossly, "Oh, you are hopeless!"

They did not speak again until they were mounted and riding through a landscape that was all blue, green, and gold perfection. Once the bridge was behind them Farrar left the busy highway and struck across country. The beauty of the afternoon banished Dimity's irritation and after a while she murmured, "You did not answer my question."

His lips quirked. "Jupiter, but you are fascinated by old Hibbard."

She refused the gauntlet and said in a very serious voice, "I would not have you think I have led a purely serene life, Sir Anthony. I have often been quite terrified. But I think I never knew such a depth of—of fear and revulsion. Oh, not because he is so physically unattractive—my grandpapa has a friend who is unbelievably ugly, yet with such a warm and gentle nature one never even notices his looks and he has more friends than any man I know. Yet—I think today I was more than frightened. I—seemed to sense . . ."

"Evil?"

She looked at him quickly. "Yes. Is he?"

"Very."

"And yet you antagonized him so!"

He shrugged. "The damage was done long and long ago." From the corner of his eye he saw her watching him, waiting, and could not restrain a chuckle. "Oh, very well, if you must have it. His son tried, when first we met, to patronize me, then to bully me, and then to buy my friendship. He has much of Hibbard in him and I—Lord, but I sound a priggish snob!"

"You did not want him for your friend."

He frowned. "I'd sooner cry friends with a scorpion! He apparently felt he had offered me the greatest honour and was infuriated when I avoided him. He never forgave me and when we were at University he spared no opportunity to make my life difficult."

Incredulous, she murmured, "And is that the only reason? Goodness! I'd thought perhaps some member of your family had run off with his wife, or stolen his fortune, perhaps."

He hesitated, and said reluctantly, "Well, there was another incident. Something that—er, happened at University. It was foul luck I should have been the one to see—At all events, it wasn't a matter to be avoided. When I was called in and questioned I had either to lie about a good man, or tell the truth about a bad one."

Dimity thought shrewdly, 'Somebody was cheating, I'll be bound!' "Then you had no choice," she said.

"His large lordship was of a different opinion. He had offered me a rather astonishing sum to keep still about the matter. When I refused—" his eyes became distant, "you'd not believe the venom . . . the threats."

"Good gracious! Do they fancy themselves above the law?"

"When it suits them—decidedly."

She was silent, thinking that it must have been hard to withstand so intimidating and powerful a man. "Sir Anthony," she exclaimed suddenly, "I must reimburse you, sir! You paid for my shoes."

"There is no great hurry, Mrs. Deene. I am not like to be

134

rendered destitute before we return to The Palfreys." He glanced at her and added a sardonic, "Am I?"

Why she ever lowered herself to sympathize with the impossible creature was beyond believing. She put her pretty nose in the air and disdained to respond.

Her nose abandoned its lofty tilt a few minutes later when she noticed that the countryside looked vaguely familiar. The Gothic church tower, for example, that loomed above the trees in the valley below them, was very like to the one she had glimpsed last night at Palfrey Poplars. Dismayed, she asked, "Are we not going ho—back to the house?"

"I've to make a quick call in the village. It should not take longer than five minutes."

She reined up. "I will wait for you here."

"No, do come. The village is called Palfrey Poplars and truly is a quaint and lovely old place."

It was as much as she could do to resist, but she dare not run the risk of being recognized, and thus said, "Yes. So I see. But an you do not object I shall wait under these trees."

The smile faded from his eyes to be replaced by one of his long enigmatic looks. He drawled, "How odd. I'd have thought you might wish to see some more of your nephew's future holdings."

She glared at him. He inclined his head and rode off without another word, his back ramrod stiff in contrast to his usual easy posture.

Slipping from the saddle, Dimity muttered maledictions upon Sir Anthony Farrar and his black moods and acid tongue. She glanced to the lovely old village and wondered if her letter had been put on the mail coach yet, and whether Tio still lived . . . Sighing, she tethered the mare to a low branch and the animal at once started to graze.

Farrar had reached the village. A small girl in a bright yellow dress ran out of a cottage, reaching up eagerly, and he bent to take her up in front of him. Dimity lost sight of him as he rode under the chestnut trees that edged the lane and her eyes drifted to the church. She was mildly surprised to find that it stood in ruins, looking to have been burned, a condition the darkness had concealed. The sun was hot and she retreated to the shade, found an obliging root, and sat down, contemplating the verdant scene with appreciative eyes. It was easily recognizable now as the village Farrar had depicted in his painting, and she envisioned him working at his easel, probably with the benefit of advice from that cantankerous old gentleman who had argued with her last night about the Portsmouth Machine. She smiled faintly. At least, the captain had the loyalty of his own people.

The birds twittered drowsily, and two butterflies danced among the leaves. A group of boys at the gawky age raced, laughing, up the slope and plunged into the copse of trees that ran along one side of the lane. How peaceful it was; how delightfully rural and innocent and unspoiled.

Her thoughts drifted back to Farrar. He had seemed to have himself well in hand until they'd met his military friend—or ex-friend. The mask had slipped then. The stricken look she had seen in his eyes haunted her. Rather hurriedly she thrust the memory away and concentrated on home and her family, only to be at once seized by guilt. No matter how she tried, she was not despising Farrar as she should. And it was not, she thought defensively, merely because he was an extremely attractive man. From the cradle she had been brought up to both expect and respect valour in a gentleman, to be repelled by a craven. Anthony Farrar made no least attempt to deny or explain away his cowardice, yet against all sense and every proper feeling, she found herself beset by a deepening sympathy with his personal tragedy; a resentment even, against those who (very rightly) judged and scorned him. She thought miserably, 'I must be a very weak and silly woman,' and gave a deep sigh.

Some ten minutes later, Farrar came into view again, the same small girl on his saddle bow. He set her down in front of Pruitt's Sweet Shoppe, and she made him a deep, wobbly curtsey. He doffed his tricorne and bowed to her, and she ran with a swirl of skirts into the shop.

Farrar started up the hill, holding the grey to a canter. Dimity waved, and saw the white gleam of his smile. Seconds later, the shouts rang out.

"Dirty coward!"

"Yah! Boo! Lily Liver Farrar!"

"Run, Sir Shivershakes!"

Sickened, Dimity thought, 'Oh, my God!' and scrambled to her feet.

Farrar came on steadily, with no indication that he heard those contemptuous howls. They increased in volume and became profane. Dirt clods and rocks flew through the air as he drew level with the copse. The stallion was struck and reared in fright. Farrar whirled the big horse about and sent him charging straight into that rain of missiles.

Dimity was already running to the mare. She used the root for a mounting block, gained the saddle, and started down the hill as Farrar emerged and came towards her at an easy canter. His hat was gone and there was a red mark on his cheek. His face was flushed, but he met her eyes steadily. She could not seem to find appropriate words and at last gulped, "They were just—children."

"Children with a good aim. How stupid I was to ask you to accompany me. You did well to refuse, ma'am."

She gave a gasp of rage. The man was insufferable! "You may be sure," she replied hotly, "that had I dreamed *that* would happen, nothing would have kept me from accompanying you!"

He gave her a brief, cynical glance.

A renewed outburst of shouts shattered the deep hush.

"Coward! Coward! Deserter!"

"Stinking murderer!"

Farrar's eyes flickered and his jaw set tight. Silent and grim, he started off.

Riding beside him, Dimity fairly seethed with fury. How *dare* he think she had been *afraid* to go with him? The beast deserved every bit of the day's unpleasantness. That fine looking young major had been more than justified in giving him the cut direct; the boys were perfectly right in their shouted abuse, their rain of stones. The twins would be in high gig when she told them about the shaming of Anthony Farrar, and she could only be delighted that she had been a witness to it all.

She clung with firm determination to those sentiments. For about a mile.

The Palfreys was wrapped in a sleepy hush when they rode into the stableyard. Dimity felt hot and sticky. Farrar, who had not spoken for the rest of the way home, looked haggard, and it occurred to her belatedly that he was probably in pain. At once, she felt wretched. With all that had transpired she'd completely forgotten his hurt. Small wonder if he'd been snappish and sarcastic, and she'd not so much as asked how he felt, or considered that he was a master at concealing his feelings. Contrite, she advised him that he would do well to go and lie down upon his bed.

"Such solicitude, ma'am," he drawled in his cynical way.

"I know. I'm a conundrum."

"A very charming one."

How different the tone. Astounded, she looked quickly at him, but he had turned from her and was watching Carlton, who raced up, curls rumpled, nankeens grass-stained, and Shuffle panting in hot pursuit, her ears flying.

"Did you bring it, sir? Did you?"

Farrar avoided Dimity's puzzled gaze and, taking a small package from his pocket, handed it down to the boy.

Carlton gave a shrill squeal and jumped up and down several times.

"Never mind all the fireworks," growled Farrar, dismounting rather wearily as a groom assisted Dimity from the saddle. "What d'you say?"

"Thank you, Sir Uncle! Thank you! What happened to your face?"

"Sunburn. I lost my hat. And do not call me 'uncle,' you finagling young reprobate."

Markedly undaunted, Carlton laughed, waved his package at Dimity and raced away.

Frowning, she said, "Captain, there is absolutely no need for you to—"

"You will pray excuse me, Mrs. Deene," he interrupted, bending to caress the ecstatic dog, "if I go and replace Shuffle's bandages. She's managed to tear them almost clear."

He beat a hurried retreat, leaving Dimity to walk into the house wishing most devoutly that she had never set eyes on The Palfreys.

Inside, all was cool and silent. A lackey came soft-footed to take her parcel, hat, and whip, and followed her upstairs with them. There was no sign of Lady Helen, who was probably, thought Dimity, laid down for an afternoon nap.

Once alone in her bedchamber, she unwrapped and admired

her new shoes, chuckling when she recalled the plight of the unfortunate clerk. She opened the clothes press and tried to make a choice between Mrs. Deene's surviving gowns, deciding eventually upon a jonquil satin not quite so lavishly endowed with frills, flounces, and bows as the rest, if equally sparing of bodice. Her habit was uncomfortably warm, and she decided to bathe and change early for dinner.

Rodgers soon answered the bell, but looked dubious when Dimity said that if convenient she would like to have a bath. Sir Anthony, it appeared, had just sent in a similar request, and it would take some time for sufficient water to be heated for a second bath. Dimity decided on a wash instead, and the abigail went off, returning a short time later with a tall copper ewer of hot water, and the news that Master Carlton begged admission.

The boy entered, clutching a crayon and a piece of paper, and asked, "How do you spell 'house,' please Aunty?"

Dimity told him and added, "Carlton, have you been pestering Sir Anthony for things?"

"I asked you for a 'lowance, an' he said no."

"Rightly so. But what was it that he bought for you today?"

"Oh. Jus' artist stuff." He gave her his dazzling smile. "I like to paint, like he does."

Dimity regarded him thoughtfully, and dismissed the interested abigail, then asked casually, "Have you seen him paint, then?"

"Lotsa' times," he said importantly.

She refrained from pointing out that this was only their fourth day at The Palfreys, perhaps because it seemed so much longer, and asked a few more questions, from which it developed that "Sir Uncle" had a studio on the other end of the hall, and that he had a lovely, painty old shirt that he wore, "an' he gets paint all *over* him when he does it!" which last fact she deduced to have been sufficient of a lure to capture the boy's wholehearted interest. "Is he working on a picture now?" she asked.

"He's jus' started a new one, but it doesn't look like much." He shifted from one foot to the other, and was apparently unable to restrain a small leap. "I 'spect your water's getting cold," he suggested helpfully.

Dimity had come to know that angelic look. "Carlton . . . ? What are you about?"

"I want to go and paint."

She smiled, sent him off, and began to unbutton her habit. Lady Helen had been right. He was indeed forming an attachment for his "Sir Uncle." The boy was a rascal, but had a very endearing way with him. 'What a pity,' she thought, 'if it is all bogus, and he is just another child being used by unscrupulous adults.'

✑ Chapter 9 ✑

Since Farrar had had the good sense to retire to his bedchamber, one could but hope, thought Dimity, going slowly downstairs, that he would rest at least until dinner time. At the foot of the stairs, a lackey carrying a pile of books stood aside, waiting respectfully for her to pass. She smiled at him and wandered across the tranquil music hall. That she should be so comfortably ensconced in the home of her enemy was a continuing amazement, but it did little to diminish her growing sense of depression. She seemed to be failing in every possible way. She had not even been able to see Mr. Green.

The butler approached, bowed, and ushered her to the breakfast parlour where a light luncheon had been set out and one cover laid.

"Oh, this is kind," she said. "But perhaps you should send something up to Sir Anthony."

His politely indifferent features seemed almost to threaten a smile. He said in an unexpectedly high-pitched voice, "A tray was sent to his room, ma'am. Does he come downstairs we can certainly put out another cover."

She allowed him to seat her, but said that she sincerely hoped Sir Anthony would not come down. "He has had an unpleasant time of it today, and—"

Leonard had picked up the teapot, and his hand jerked. His eyes, a pale blue, darted to her with undisguised apprehension. She guessed that Farrar would not wish her to mention his humiliations, and said quietly, "I meant because of his arm."

He finished pouring her tea without speaking, but his lips

were tight and as he replaced the teapot, he said in low-voiced anger, "Those dogs should be shot!"

"You are very attached to your employer," she murmured.

He looked at her steadily. "Very attached, Mrs. Deene."

"And you resent me. Naturally. But—am I mistaken, or have you pardoned me a little?"

She puzzled him. She did not, as he had told the housekeeper, "fit the mold." Just now, her smile was charming and her pretty hazel eyes very kind. Unbending slightly, he answered, "I am sure you must believe what you claim, ma'am. I don't understand it all, nor is it my place. But—I heard him laugh yesterday. It's the first time I've heard him laugh in—in an age . . . And my lady came down to dinner last evening. If you *knew* what that meant to the master."

Frowning, she asked, "Does he always dine alone, then?"

"From the day he was well enough to come downstairs, ma'am, no one has shared this table. Save for when Mr. Chandler comes to visit."

"But—but he has other friends, surely . . . ?"

He shook his head. "Mr. Chandler has been the soul of loyalty. I think many of the other gentlemen would have stuck by the master had he only denied the—er, charges. But . . ." he shrugged. "I suppose—you cannot really blame them, but—how he endures it I cannot think. Another man would travel, but no matter what they say, Sir Anthony is a courageous gentleman. He stays here and faces it." He sighed and added heavily, "He is the most solitary man I ever have seen."

Gathering her rather shaken sensibilities, Dimity said, "Well, at least, he has Shuffle."

The smile dawned then, quite transforming the gaunt features. "Yes. He has Shuffle, thank God! More tea, Mrs. Deene?"

He poured her a second cup and took himself discreetly away. It was peaceful and pleasant, but somehow the silence seemed oppressive now. Dimity found herself picturing Farrar eating in here all alone, day after day, night after night. She rose without finishing her tea and wandered into the fragrant gardens.

Lost in thought, she paced along the brick pathway until her troubled reflections were put to flight by the appearance of a large poster clumsily supported by two sticks stuck in the lawn. Intrigued, she approached this flimsy arrangement and read the

142

message that had been painted in oils, every word a different colour:

This way House 4 toor

A wavering arrow pointed to the east side of the mansion. With growing trepidation, she followed the instructions.

The hot water was relaxing, and Farrar leaned his head against the back of the hip bath and closed his eyes. 'Had I dreamed *that* would happen, nothing would have kept me from accompanying you.' How white and enraged she had looked. And how regal. She was a larcenous adventuress; a threat to all he held dear. It was utter folly to be thinking about her all the time. To even—Frowning, he tossed his head impatiently, but there was no point in denying her desirability; nor his attraction to her. She was the most brave, infuriating, beautiful, impossible, bewitching female he had ever met. What the *deuce* was it all about? God knows, he was not a fool, nor lacking experience with women. He'd had his share of *affaires de coeur* both in England and abroad. Even fancied himself in love a time or two. But never had he encountered the like of Mrs. Catherine Deene, with those long, slightly slanted hazel eyes that seemed always to hold a dance of mischief, and that yet could be so kind, so very tender and understanding. He reached to the chair nearby and with great care took up the small, stained square of lace-edged cambric that he had stolen from the boy. There was a beautifully embroidered letter "D" in one corner of the handkerchief, and if one sniffed very carefully, one could breathe the lingering essence of a sweet perfume. Carlton had said proudly that his kind aunt had bound a cut on his finger with "her own" handkerchief. Another little proof of the fallacy of it all! The "D" could stand for Deene, of course, but it was unlikely.

Ladies usually had the initial of their Christian name embroidered on their personal linen . . .

He jerked awake just in time to keep his left arm from sagging into the water. Steel had said he must keep the wounds dry for a day or two. He replaced the handkerchief on the chair and applied soap to sponge.

Did she really care for Green? Why would she have kept quiet, had that been the case?—unless theirs was a secret relationship. But if that were so, why mention it at all? Unless she'd been too dazed that first day to know what she was saying . . . Scowling, he began to apply the soapy sponge to his broad chest.

He heard the door click open and felt the draught of cooler air. This would be Jordan, coming back with the large bath towel that had for some stupid reason been denied him. The man had taken his time about it.

A clear childish voice announced, "An' this is my uncle's bedchamber. You c'n see it's a large an' very nicely 'pointed room. He painted that picture over the desk. He's a very good painter."

The sponge held motionless, Farrar sat frozen with shock.

"Wazzat?" piped a very young voice.

"Eh? Oh, it's a hip bath. An' you c'n see by the steam my uncle's 'bout to have a—" Carlton's bright face hove around the edge of the tub. "No," he corrected with his engaging grin, "he's not 'bout to—he *is* having a bath. This is my uncle, Sir Anth'ny Farrar and I'm his nephew Carlton Farrar."

Six boys, five small and one miniature, pressed in to view the exhibit.

His glazed eyes taking in this audience and the raucous kitten that struggled in his "nephew's" grasp, Farrar found his voice. "Carlton!" he roared. "What the *devil* do you mean by this?"

"You told me to use my 'magination." Shaken but defensive, Carlton advanced and held out his treasure. "I got traded a kitten for a tour of Palfrey. You said—" But at this point he caught sight of the scar on his uncle's shoulder and gave a gasp. He had never seen a gunshot wound before, much less the horror that could be wrought by a pistol fired at close range, and he was so unnerved that he dropped his prize. Onto Farrar's soapy chest.

The kitten was tiny, soft, and affectionate. It was also pos-

144

sessed of some very sharp claws. When it suddenly discovered itself sliding down a slippery surface towards what smelled horribly like water, it unsheathed those claws—purely for braking purposes. The captain gave another roar, and instinctively sprang to his feet.

Cissie, having just returned from her parents' farm, had not been advised that Sir Anthony was having a bath at such an unusual time of day. She heard the outraged roars, followed by the sudden appearance of a stream of little boys, who scattered, whooping, from Farrar's bedchamber. She was a warm-hearted girl and, afraid that Carlton had done something dreadful, she ran to investigate. On the threshold of the room, she halted, stared, emitted a piercing shriek, and fainted.

"Good . . . *God*!" howled Farrar.

"My *kitty*!" screeched Carlton.

Farrar scooped the wet and madly swimming little creature from the bath and grabbed for the small towel in the nick of time as Dimity, her fears of some contretemps verified by the uproar, charged to the rescue.

"Oh . . . my . . . !" she gasped feebly, halting in the doorway.

Holding the towel before the most vital area, Farrar, scarlet, raged, "Carlton, confound you, get your creature and your tour out of my bedchamber!"

Clutching his kitten, Carlton effected a fast retreat, taking with him the miniature tour member who still stood gaping at the nude in the tub.

Dimity's eyes had found the scar. In a desperate and ill-advised attempt to protect his chastity, Farrar swung around, thereby presenting her with a view of his broad back, slim waist, tapering flanks and long, muscular legs. She noted absently that the bullet had torn right through, but her attention was (disgracefully) fixed on his trim buttocks. She thought, 'My heaven, his body is beautiful!'

"What a'God's name are *you* doing in here, madam?" gritted Farrar, almost whipping his shield behind him until he realized the mirror would likely complete his exposure.

Dazed, she murmured foolishly, "I—did not pay you for my . . . shoes."

"Blast and dammitall! NOT NOW!"

145

A gasp behind her recalled Dimity to her senses. She whirled to find that Lady Helen, her jaw sagging, had joined the spectators. With considerably belated propriety, Dimity threw her hands over her eyes.

"I—thought you were murdering someone," said my lady faintly, also mentally approving her nephew's magnificent physique, but wincing at the ugly, puckered scar.

"You are only a *trifle* premature," snarled Farrar.

Cissie stirred, wailing.

"Will—*everyone*—have the goodness to—depart the public bath . . . ?" requested Farrar between his teeth.

Dimity peeped through her fingers at my lady, and together they bent to aid the sniffling maid from the premises, passing Farrar's goggle-eyed valet, who ran up, a large bathtowel over his arm.

Before they reached the stairs, Dimity was giggling. Lady Helen strove, but was soon joining in, and Cissie was unable to escape the contagion. The three women succumbed and laughed until they wept, and were obliged to sit together all three, wiping their eyes on Cissie's apron.

"But—how charming," drawled a well-modulated male voice.

They looked up as one, to behold a tall dark gentleman, impressive in black and silver, bowing from the foot of the stairs.

Cissie whispered, "Oh, *my*! And I thought Sir Anthony was handsome!"

Dimity thought, 'Good heavens! Pity the lady who gives her heart to this one!'

Lady Helen gasped, *"Mathieson!"* and ran down the stairs to fling herself into his ready arms. "After all these years!"

Laughing, he swung her off her feet, his jet eyes gleaming between thick, curling lashes. "Otton, my lady. Otton! Would you give my grandsire a palpitation?"

"Rascal," she said fondly. "How *lovely* to see you."

He looked, or so thought Dimity, mildly astonished. "Then I am received? I am more often thrown out than welcomed, you know."

She regarded him questioningly for a moment, then started as those fine eyes slipped past her. "Good gracious! My apol-

146

ogies—it was such a surprise. Mrs. Deene, I present Captain Roland—Otton. Roly, Mrs. Deene—er, stays with us."

A flash of white teeth. He bowed. Straightening, he took Dimity's hand, touched it to his lips, and, his eyes widening as they lingered on the diminutive bodice of her gown, murmured, "How excellently well I timed my visit."

"Do come and sit down," said Lady Helen, "and tell me that you can stay. Captain Otton and my nephew were at University together, Mrs. Deene, and later they both fought in the Austrian wars." She told a hovering footman to send refreshments to the withdrawing room, then led the way to that cool and spacious apartment. "You *can* stay, Roland?"

"My deepest thanks, but I must decline. I chanced to be in the neighborhood and somewhat out of temper, so—" a graceful gesture, the fascinating grin lighting the dark, aquiline features "—I came to renew acquaintance and recover my equilibrium. And what could be more soothing to a ruffled male than to discover you lovely ladies so merrily occupied?"

My lady directed an amused glance at Dimity's mischievous face. "Just a small household contretemps," she explained. "What was it that disturbed your temper, Roland?"

Leonard came in, followed by a footman carrying a well-laden tray. The butler's countenance was without expression, but, quick to sense the moods of others, Dimity thought that he did not approve of the new arrival.

"Oh, it is these confounded dragoons who flood the country-side," said Otton. "If I've been detained once twixt here and the mighty metropolis, I've been detained a dozen times." He accepted a glass of wine. "And thrice searched!"

"Dreadful!" said my lady, offering the plate of biscuits to Dimity. "One might suppose we lived in an armed camp. The Palfreys has been searched twice, and yet another troop came only this morning."

Very conscious of the parchment in her bodice, Dimity echoed, "This morning? Whatever did they want, ma'am?"

"Oh, it seems an unfortunate rebel gentleman is in the locality, and they are convinced some family hereabouts has given him sanctuary. As though any would dare do such a thing."

His black eyes alert behind their drooping lids, Otton was watching Mrs. Deene's suddenly white face and the hand that trembled as she nibbled her biscuit. "You would be surprised, my lady," he murmured, as the door closed behind the servants. "This area fairly swarms with sympathizers for the plaid and thistle. Indeed, I was given to understand the military have their quarry cornered, and do but bide their time before hauling him in, together with an even bigger fish." He thought, 'Aha!' as the girl's wide hazel eyes shot to him and, with the smile that he knew was hard for any female to resist, he added, "I'll own that for my part, any assistance I could render the poor devil would be willingly given."

It seemed to Dimity that those velvety dark eyes held a message. But if she erred, heads would roll, her own among them. She looked down and made no comment.

Lady Helen, however, darted a nervous glance to the door. "Let us not speak of such tragic events. Goodness knows, we've had enough of sorrow."

Otton put his glass on the low table, stood, and crossed to drop to one knee before her and take up her hand. "What an insensitive clod I become. I heard about Harding. My dear, I cannot tell you how sorry I am. He was a splendid fellow."

"Yes. He was. And you are very far from insensitive. Thank you, Roly. Now," she managed a bright smile, "we see so little company these days—pray tell me of the news from Town. How is the temper of the king? Are the ministers still fighting to take poor Sir Robert's place? Will there, do you think, be war with France?"

Laughing, he came to his feet and raised a pair of shapely white hands. "*Peccavi*, ma'am, I implore. I shall answer all your questions, but you must first satisfy one or two of mine."

'They are old friends,' thought Dimity, 'and will have much to discuss.' She begged to be excused, adding, "I must find Carlton, for he really has been very naughty." Escorted to the door by the dashing captain, she received a blinding smile from him and a grateful one from her hostess.

When she was gone, Otton returned to Lady Helen. "Tell me," he said, patting her hand, "how is Anthony?"

The smile vanished from her eyes. "Quite recovered. Physically, at least. But—I think he will never get over the shame of it, Roly."

"Poor fellow. Lord knows, we all make mistakes." He saw

her distress and changed the subject at once. "Now, what's this I hear about a fire? Did your lovely old village church burn down? Whatever do you do on Sundays? Stand in the rain?"

"Goodness, no. We go over to St. Michael's. It's not too far, and a nice young priest has taken over while Father Morehead is away. Such a fine looking boy. He preaches a sermon rather more—controversial than is entirely popular, alas, but he's a charming way with words, and *such* a lovely sense of fun."

"Which likely sets up even more backs." He said musingly, "Puts me in mind of a friend who also went into the clergy. Charles was a very simi—"

"Charles? Why, that is the name of our curate. Charles Albritton."

"The very same!" He drove a fist into his palm. "How famous! I shall have to hear him preach and tease, the rascal. Now, dear lady, one more question before I tell you all you wish of Town *on dits*. Am I wrong, or do I detect a hint of the ah—unexpected in the charming Mrs. Deene? An I speak out of turn you may tell me to put my curiosity in my pocket."

Lady Helen hesitated, but his handsome face was very attentive, his smile gentle, his long dark eyes so kind. She had always had a soft spot in her heart for him, and so she said confidingly, " 'Tis the most incredible development, Roland . . .''

"Incredible," agreed Jordan, shaking powder into Farrar's thick locks. "I would have come up at once, only I chanced to overhear something I thought might interest you, sir. All things being—er, equal."

"Well, all things were not equal in here," grumbled Farrar. "I was *never* more embarrassed! A whole herd of gawking females and staring children, and me standing in the altogether like some dripping damned museum exhibit! I fancy I shall have nightmares about it for years to come! How I'm to go down and face 'em all, I cannot think!"

His valet, managing with a strong effort not to grin, kept a discreet silence and after a fuming moment, Farrar grunted, "What's this you think will interest me? If 'tis too alarming you'd best not tell me, for my nerves are already tattered!"

Jordan considered Sir Anthony to have the steadiest nerves

149

he'd ever encountered, and he stifled a chuckle. "Why, it's about Mrs. Deene, sir. The most ridiculous thing. It seems the maids are terrified of her because she bought a spell from a witch."

Farrar, who had tensed at the mention of Dimity's name, now pulled up his downbent head and shoved his hair back, the better to view his man. "You been at the brandy, Jordan?"

"Sir, I assure you my first reaction was exactly the same, but the silly wenches are petrified. I overheard them whilst I was in the linen room getting your towel, and by what I can make out, Mrs. Deene put the fear of doom into them, saying that if they dare repeat her secret, the spell would be broke, and a dreadful fate would overtake them."

"Good God! What stuff!" And, contradictorily, "What kind of spell?"

"Why, it seems that Mrs. Deene purchased a love potion," explained Jordan, resuming his powdering.

"Did she now?" said Farrar, his eyes beginning to sparkle. "How does it work?"

"She has a note writ by her lover" (here, Farrar's eyes ceased to sparkle), "only the gentleman is reluctant to offer. So the witch told her, if she sleeps with the note under her mattress each night, she can bring him up to scratch."

"I see. So 'twas not a cricket."

"No, sir. She said she put that about because she didn't want folks to know the truth. But the *really* incredible thing, Sir Anthony, is that the gentleman for whom Mrs. Deene has such a *tendre*, is—" he grinned broadly, "is Mr. Rafe Green."

The powder box went flying. His eyes slits of wrath, his face pale save for two spots of colour high on his cheekbones, Farrar was out of the chair, his valet's cravat twisted in his hand. "You lie!" he grated savagely. "By the God that made you—you *lie!*"

Astonished, Dimity stared up into Roland Otton's laughing face. "I beg pardon, sir? I must have misunderstood."

Otton was already much too close for comfort, but he moved closer so that she was obliged to press back against the tree. "I said," he repeated, running a fingertip down the side of her cheek, "you are dealing from a fuzzed deck. How charmingly

150

you do employ the wide eyes and heaving bosom, m'dear. Especially," his hand strayed, "the latter."

Furious, Dimity smacked his fingers away and said through her teeth, "How *dare* you! Were my brothers here, you'd answer for—"

"Sweet little widow, who wears no marriage ring," he scolded, pressing his finger to her lips, "kiss it better. Come now, be generous. I am but trying to do you a kindness; you must not repay with cruel words and blows. After all, we are kindred souls, as it were."

His slumbrous eyes teased her; his hands were everywhere. But also, his words made her uneasy so that, restraining a clutch in the nick of time, she gasped, "What do you mean—kindred souls?"

His lips parted and he bent lower. "I can show you better than—"

"Stay back! An I tell Lady Helen you—"

"My lady has gone to change her dress. I am invited to dine, so you need not fear I shall vanish away, love."

"Fear, is it? I am more like to vanish you away with the nearest blunderbuss! What is this talk of—Oh! Stop at once!—of fuzzed decks and—"

"Heaving bosoms," he grinned, with a fast caress where appropriate. "Simply this, fairest, if you seek to pass off that brat as Farrar's nephew, you're fair and far out, because—"

"Good evening, Mrs. Deene."

The deep voice fairly splintered ice. Dimity tore free. Farrar stood nearby, Shuffle beside him, as usual. He had already dressed for dinner and was more elegant then she had ever seen him, in a splendid coat of dark green velvet, the great cuffs and pocket flaps embroidered in light green. His waistcoat was of gold brocade, his unmentionables palest green, and stockings with green fans adorned his well shaped legs. Not even the darkening bruise on his face could diminish his proud hauteur, and Dimity thought him magnificent.

"Hello, Tony." Otton put out his hand.

Ignoring it, Farrar drawled, "So you acknowledge me. You are more charitable than I, sir."

Otton's hand fell, but he said, unruffled, "Fustian. You forget we fought together in the Lowlands."

"I forget nothing. You are the one forgets." And as Otton watched him with eyes suddenly wary, he went on, "Quentin Chandler is a friend of mine."

"Ah-h . . ." Otton took up his quizzing glass and began to swing it gently on the long silver chain that hung about his neck. "You're right. I had forgot that attachment. Gordon has been this way, I take it."

"So here you all are." Lady Helen, who had changed into a graceful *robe volante* of dark rose silk, walked to the edge of the terrace, her rather uneasy gaze moving quickly from one man to the other. "Mrs. Deene, you will dine with me, of course. Roly, pray come upstairs and we can—"

"No, madam." Farrar's voice cut like a knife through her words.

She stared at him. "Roland dines with me this evening."

"My regrets, ma'am, but Captain Otton is not welcome here."

She gave a shocked exclamation. "He is *my* guest, Farrar," she pointed out, her cheeks flushing and her fine eyes bright with anger. "You will own 'tis seldom enough that I am given the pleasure of company."

Farrar said implacably, "I am aware. My deepest apologies to you, but Captain Otton cannot be welcomed into any house of mine."

Superb in her wrath, she drew herself up. "Come, Roland. I am sorrier than I can express that you should be subjected to such rudeness."

His eyes glinting with covert laughter, Otton stepped forward.

Farrar took one long stride and blocked his way.

"Tony," sighed Otton, shaking his handsome head ruefully. "Would you knock an old comrade down for accepting your lady aunt's kind invitation?"

" 'Twould give me the greatest pleasure."

Otton regarded that grim face thoughtfully. "Do you know, I really believe you would. And thus." He spread his slender hands in a faintly French gesture, turned to Lady Helen, and bowed low. "As always, your hospitality is a joy, ma'am, but—" he shrugged. "*Que faire?* I must depart lest I bring you more grief. *Adieu, mesdames.*"

Tearful and quivering with rage, Lady Helen said, "Roland—
I . . . I have *never* been so—"

He kissed her fingertips. "But you must not distress yourself
over so little a thing. Anthony has a good enough reason, for I
am the rogue he believes me, you know. No—you don't know.
But, believe it, dear ma'am, and do not scold him too harshly."

She smiled at him mistily.

"Otton," gritted Farrar, "you try my patience."

Otton chuckled and, swinging his quizzing glass, meandered
towards the stables. He called over his shoulder, "Have you had
Rump saddled for me, Tony?"

"I have."

"*Merci beaucoup*. Cheerio, old fellow."

"*Good-bye,*" said Farrar with finality.

Dimity, who had been frozen with embarrassment, slipped
towards the steps, but stopped as Lady Helen moved regally in
the same direction.

Farrar followed his aunt. "Ma'am, I beg you will forgive the
need for—"

She rounded on him, pale and furious. "There was *no* need!
No possible justification for you to cancel my invitation. Whatever Roland may have done, how dare *you* of all people—stand
in judgement on him?"

He halted, gazing up at her. "I know I have brought you
shame and—and disappointment, but—"

"Disappointment?" she echoed, and laughed rather hysteri-
cally, such a wealth of disgust in the sound that he winced.

Low-voiced he said, "What I did was—is past forgiveness, I
know. But, it was not done with cold and calculated cruelty, nor
for personal gain, and—"

Lost in fury, my lady interpolated, "Are you very sure of
that, Farrar?"

His tall figure jerked as though she had struck him. There was
a short, terrible silence, during which it seemed to the appalled
girl that her heartbeats must be audible. Then, Farrar gave a
strangled cry and reached out to grasp his aunt's arm.

"My God! You *cannot* think . . . You *could* not believe . . .
Dear Lord! How could you stay here, thinking I—"

Lady Helen pulled away. "I stayed only so as not to give the
gossips grist for their mills. But—now that you dare to dictate

whom I may or may not welcome here, I can stay no longer. I shall—''

"No!" His hand went out again as though to touch her, but was withdrawn when she jerked back. "I—beg of you. Do not go. You need not speak to me. I'll stay out of your sight as much as possible. But—*please* do not go.''

"You have left me no alternative. I shall leave so soon as I can complete other arrangements." She made her way with dignity up the steps but, despite herself, tears glistened on her cheeks.

For a moment, Farrar watched her retreating figure. Then, without a word or a glance to indicate that he was aware of Dimity's presence, he turned and walked away, Shuffle at once springing up and following. His head was bowed, his shoulders sagged, and he did not seem to notice when his feet left the path and stumbled through a flower bed.

He looked, Dimity thought, a broken man, whose last hope has been snatched away.

It was late and Roland Otton was tired when he guided his tall chestnut horse into the yard of the White Dragon posting house on the Salisbury Road. Having made provision for Rumpelstiltskin, he proceeded to the dining room and was doing justice to some tender roast beef and fried potatoes when a shadow fell across his plate. Without looking up, he invited, "By all means, cousin."

Captain Jacob Holt threw gloves and tricorne onto the opposite settle and sat down. "Well?"

"Not markedly."

Holt called for a tankard of ale. "I'd fancied you would wangle a dinner invitation, at the least."

"So I did. Farrar squashed it." Otton sighed. "Firmly."

"Lord! From what I've heard, one might suppose the fellow would be grateful did a *buzzman* offer to sit at his board." Otton looked aggrieved, and Holt chuckled. "My apologies. No simile intended."

"To an extent you're right, Jacob. Farrar *would*, I think, have accepted a pickpocket rather than myself. Fellow holds a grudge."

The devil-may-care look had vanished, and Holt regarded with curiosity a seldom-seen grimness. "Which disturbs you, I see. I wonder why. You know, Roly, I have always felt there was a deal more to that business with Quentin Chandler than I knew."

A pause, and then Otton answered slowly, "I've few friends, Jacob, but among 'em is a thoroughly decent fellow who calls me a rogue, but says he also names me friend because he knows me better than I do." His smile was brief and held a rueful quality that astounded his cousin. "I think I am a rogue. Certainly, I am a dedicated villain. But—I have never been so thoroughly the latter as in my dealings with Chandler. It—disturbs me sometimes."

Regarding the pensive countenance with interest, Holt prompted, "You fought him, I know—though you have never said where the duel took place. There is nothing despicable in fighting a traitor, and if that is all—"

"I wish it were." Otton gave an impatient shrug and said brightly, "I don't hold it against him that he proved the better swordsman, wherefore I lay abed for a month. He is safe away to France with—his love. It is over. Nothing I did would have changed the outcome."

The sleepy waiter carried over a tankard and yawned ostentatiously. Holt drank deep and ignored him. "Farrar's a pretty one to be criticizing others," he grunted, setting the tankard down and wiping his mouth fastidiously. "How much lower could a gentleman sink than to be a cowardly deserter?"

Almost, he thought his cousin flinched, but he decided he must have been mistaken when the merry light returned to the dark eyes. Otton said lightly, "I'm no longer considered a gentleman, thank heaven. And—to business. Jacob, I could catch no whiff of a concealed rebel, but—" he shook a slice of potato at the officer, "there is a luscious chit at The Palfreys calling herself Mrs. Deene."

"Yes. I'm aware." Holt's chilly blue gaze narrowed. "You think she uses a false identity?"

"As to that, I cannot say, but I'd venture a guess she is not what she seems. Her gown was—shall we say an open invitation? Yet when I attempted to avail myself of its—ah, bounty, I was balked and scolded as severely as though she was a perfect lady."

"Lord, Roly," said Holt contemptuously, "is there no woman whose bodice is safe from you?"

Otton leaned closer and returned so ribald a response that even his hardened cousin looked embarrassed. Chuckling, Otton pushed his plate away and reached for his tankard.

"At all events," said Holt, "I'd be glad of a shilling for every well-born lady who now finds herself reduced to a pinched style of living. These are hard times."

"Agreed. But most well-bred ladies who are so unfortunately circumstanced still somehow manage to retain an aura of gentility. And the gown our Mrs. Deene wore properly belongs on a trollop. Not only that—when I spoke of the Jacobites in a sympathetic way—"

Holt leaned back his head and gave a crow of laughter.

"I'll have you know, Jacob," said Otton, indignant, "that I am sympathetic to the poor devils! That merciless swine, the Duke of Cumberland—"

Holt jerked upright. "Quiet! You idiot! Would you lose your head?"

"I likely will at all events. Soon or late."

"Well, I'd as soon not accompany you! Do you say our beauty showed pleased when you indicated a kindness for the rebels?"

Otton nodded. "And gave me the most odd look—a sort of hopeful searching."

"Hmmnn. 'Tis little enough to go on, but when added to what I suspect . . . Do you mean to stay here?"

"For a few days. Even if nothing comes of my—our quest, the Widow Deene is a tasty morsel." He smiled dreamily. "I'm ready for a dalliance, Jacob. And I fancy the lady is ripe for it."

Holt's lip curled, and he stood. "You and your women!"

"They're all a joy, my dear coz. But not one worth more than a week, at most."

Chewing his lip, Holt scanned that lazy smile. His cousin was a disinherited, penniless rogue. A man without conscience or kindness, and with perhaps one friend to his name. A man whose own family would have none of him, and who was forbidden every great house in London. He should be crushed, shamed, and starving; a pitiful wreck whose best option in life was to creep into some dark corner and politely blow his brains out. And yet it sometimes occurred to Holt that, of the two of them,

Mathieson—or Otton as he called himself—derived the most enjoyment from life.

"One of these days, Roly," he said judicially, "you'll meet a maid you want to spend your whole life with. And is she a lady, she'll have none of you. I wonder what you'll do then?"

Laughing, Otton came to his feet and clapped a hand on Holt's broad shoulder. "Why, I shall but admire her the more for her impeccable judgement. But never tease yourself, dear boy. The lady does not exist for whom I would be willing to give up all others."

Holt grunted and they walked to the stairs together; cousins, yet as unlike as two men could be, save for one characteristic— a driving ambition that made each in his own way, completely ruthless.

❦ *Chapter 10* ❧

The tall case clock in the music hall struck three, and Leonard, who had dozed off in the chair just inside the front door, jumped so that he almost fell to the floor. He stood and stretched wearily.

From the third step Jordan advised, "He's not back yet."

Leonard walked closer. "How long have you been here?"

"Midnight." Jordan looked tired, but said staunchly, "Not that I'm worried, of course."

"No. Of course not. We probably should go to bed. He always tells me not to wait up."

They looked at each other, then Leonard returned to his chair and, again, silence held the room in the hollow of its hand.

When the clock struck the quarter, Jordan said, "Mr. Leonard. Did you . . . hear?"

"Yes."

"She's never even hinted at it before . . . as I recall."

"Sometimes, I've thought 'twould have been better if she had. But . . . at this particular time . . ."

They exchanged another long look through the gloom that was brightened only by the solitary candle on the table.

In a very quiet voice, Jordan said, "His new French pistol is missing."

Leonard closed his eyes and whispered something inaudible.

When the clock struck the half-hour, Jordan murmured, "At least, he has got Shuffle with him."

"Yes. He has got Shuffle."

At a quarter to four o'clock, Jordan stood, and stretched wearily.

Leonard said, "No. You stay here in case I don't find him." And he went up to the servants' quarters situated on the partial third floor to get his coat and hat.

Standing at her window, Dimity saw Leonard depart, holding a lantern high. Aeons earlier, a round-eyed and silent Rodgers had brought her a dinner tray. She had eaten half-heartedly, and the glass of wine had made her drowsy. When Rodgers returned to take the tray, she had told the abigail she would have no further need of her services, and at about nine o'clock she had fallen asleep in the armchair, waking stiff and uncomfortable when she heard Leonard's steps on the drivepath. She thought drearily that it was none of her affair. She had not brought this about. Captain Otton would have come even had she not been here, and the outcome would have been the same bitter quarrel between Farrar and the aunt he worshipped. But conscience whispered that his eyes this morning—yesterday morning—had held a very special light. And in the afternoon, he had found her with Roland Otton's hand in her bodice. Was it possible that had he not done so, his temper might not have escaped him? That he might not have challenged Lady Helen's right to entertain a man he despised?

Deeply troubled, she tidied her hair and then took up a candle. The hallway was dark and hushed. She tiptoed along it, as she had done once before, and went down the spiral stairs and through the Gothic archway that led into the chapel.

She sank into a rear pew and leaned back, letting the peace of this hallowed place soothe her soul. It was quiet and cold, and smelled of beeswax and brandy. *Brandy?* She sat up and lifted the candle, peering through the quiet sanctuary.

He was in the fourth pew, leaning forward, his head bowed onto the arms that were folded over the back of the pew before him. Shuffle, faithful as ever, lay with chin on paws in the aisle. The spaniel woke as the candlelight brightened the chapel and sprang up with a short, uncertain bark. Farrar's head lifted and he turned, blinking to the glow of the candle.

Dimity thought she had never beheld so haggard and hopeless a face. But even as she watched, the despair in the shadowed eyes changed to a blazing wrath. Her compassion changed to fear. She stood and ran to the aisle.

He passed her, moving very fast, and with a breathless shout flung himself to lean back against the door. "Slut . . ." he panted thickly. "Wha' the hell y' doin' bringin' y'dirty skirts into thish—thish holy . . . place?"

She thought, 'My God, he is drunk!' and said as steadily as she could, "Sir—I know how it must have looked, but I swear I never saw Captain Otton before today, and he—"

"Y'never saw *Roly*," he leered, his contorted face and glinting eyes terrifying her, "an y'din't know m' *cousin*! No decent woman'd 'low either of the—the dirty bastards 'thin armsh length. But—I f'get. You're *not* decent, are you, Mish's Deene? Took me fer a blind fool, d'intcha? Were r-right! Blinder 'n blind. D'you know . . ." he wagged a finger at her, "d'you know I almost—'N all th' time you were laughin' and ro-rompin' with Otton 'n Ellsworth. 'Tended y' din't know Rafe, neither. You *know* him, all right! Dirty, lyin' li'l harlot . . ."

He looked so wild, so maddened and Lord knows he had reason. She stretched out her hands appealingly. "Anthony—you *must* not use such language in—"

He seized her hands, laughing a racking, humourless laugh. "Y'know 'bout language, don'tcha?" He leaned to her, his eyes glinting and merciless. "Know 'bout lotsa other things, 'swell!"

Trying not to show how afraid she was, she said, "You must be very tired. You should—"

"Not too tired t' take a . . . whore . . . !" On the word, he sprang.

Dimity's shriek was muffled as he forced her head back, mumbling low-voiced accusations and profanities that fortunately were so blurred she could scarcely hear them and did not comprehend what he said. But she knew beyond doubting that she was about to be raped, and all kindness and understanding fled, swallowed up by an overmastering wrath. This was not the same man who had painted those pastoral scenes with such sensitivity; this was not the man whose eyes had been frantic with fear when Shuffle was hurt. This was a lusting brute, his intellect blurred by liquor, his civilized impulses wiped away. She was not desired with love but with savage anger, and no man was going to *force* her to his will! And so she fought him, retreating

160

herself to the primeval instinct for self-preservation: kicking, clawing, biting, and all the time gasping out words to try to break through the fog that brandy had wrapped around his mind, reminding him that he was in a house of God, that he was wrong in what he thought of her, resorting even to curses to try to shock him back to understanding as she half-sobbed, half-screamed that he would so bitterly regret this—that he was drunk.

"Yeh, I'm drunk," he admitted, gripping her chin in an iron hand. And despite her desperate struggles, his mouth found hers and violated it until her resistance ebbed away and she gave herself up to the bittersweetness of that brutal kiss. She was half-smothered when he lifted his head, but she saw the look in his eyes and with all her strength struck him across the face.

"Sir Anthony! Wake up! You—you're mad! *Don't!* Tony—please, please—*don't!*"

But he was past reason, past anything but hurting and disillusionment and the need to strike back at the girl who had precipitated it all, and whom he had, in spite of every vestige of common sense, begun to love. "You'll not lightly . . . cheat another," he growled, wrenching her close. His hands were steel, pawing her, shaming her, even while he kissed her throat and whatever he could reach with her fighting like a wild thing. She kicked out hard, and he growled and found her lips again, his hand sliding down and down . . .

With a surprised exclamation he flung her from him, and peered at the scrap of parchment he had found in his depredations. "Wha'sis?" He was unable to read, but saw enough to realize it was poetry. "Your stinkin' love note . . . !"

His diverted attention gave Dimity the chance she had prayed for. She picked up her skirts and fled. Farrar flung the parchment away and started after her. She had no choice but to run towards the altar, her heart in her throat, as she heard him reeling in pursuit.

And then he stumbled over Shuffle, and the dog yelped shrilly.

Farrar halted and stood swaying. With a groan of remorse he bent over the dog. "Poor ol' lady. Din't mean t'hurt you."

Dimity tiptoed around the far side of the pews to the rear of the chapel. She could hear him murmuring softly to the spaniel and so dared to search for the priceless cypher. Dawn was beginning to brighten the great rear window and by its glow she saw the

161

parchment at last, crumpled in the corner of a pew. She was kneeling to facilitate her search, and she snatched it up and restored it to her bosom. Farrar came stumbling along the aisle. Fighting not to breathe so hard, Dimity flung herself down and lay under the pew, holding her skirts as close as she could, and praying.

He went on past, the brandy bottle hanging from one hand. He did not even seem to be looking for her. Shuffle peeped under the pew and wagged her tail, then hurried to catch up with her god.

The rear door opened. Dimity felt the rush of colder air, then heard his steps receding. She put both hands over her face and wept, but choked the sobs back as she heard the crash of breaking glass outside. In another moment he was coming back. Her heart seemed to stop. She waited, scarcely daring to breathe, trembling violently, but he reeled past and returned seconds later to leave her again unmolested.

She lay still, her wide eyes fixed on the underside of the pew, but she did not see the neat web a small industrious spider had spun there. Her shocked mind could comprehend only Farrar's uncertain steps and the long deadly pistol now clasped in his hand.

Recovering her wits after a minute, she wriggled out from under the pew and ran to the rear door. The air was very chill with no breath of wind. The sky was dark grey, for the sun was not yet up, and she could not see very far. She strained her eyes, but there was no sign of movement. She went back into the house and climbed the stairs. The hall through Farrar's wing was deserted. She went back down a few stairs, peering into the dimness of the hushed music hall. Something moved. Her heart gave a flutter of relief. She sped down the spiral, but then, hearing muffled sobs, slowed her headlong pace. The shape on the sofa was too small, and a faint mew was half drowned by the sounds of grief.

"Carlton?" she said, bending over the child. "What is the matter?"

He looked even more angelic in his long nightshirt, the kitten on his lap, but the face he raised was tear-streaked. "I'll give her back," he gulped. "I—I din't think it would make him so cross. I don't want her." But despite that renunciation, his hand was caressing the tiny creature fiercely.

Dimity sat beside him. "Sir Anthony is not cross with you, dear," she began.

"Yes, he is! I tried to speak to him . . . jus' now. But he—he wouldn't even answer me. He—he jus' went off, like he wanted to—to murder someone. He'll prob'ly never come back. It's *my* fault!" He wept miserably, keeping his red-rimmed eyes fixed upon her. He was, as she had learned, a proud child, and it was some measure of his distress that he did not attempt to disguise it.

She pulled him into her arms and stroked his hair. "Carlton, it will be all right, dear. I'll go and find him. Come, you must to your bed."

He made no objection, picking up his kitten and allowing Dimity to lead him upstairs.

When she had tucked him into bed he blinked at her miserably through his tears. "You will bring him back, Aunty Mitten? Promise?"

She smiled. "I promise."

The hand over Peregrine's mouth was suffocating and he fought furiously to remove it until a familiar voice hissed an exasperated, "*Will* you be quiet, damn your eyes!"

Peregrine relaxed and, yawning away the vestiges of sleep, discerned his twin bending over the bed. "Piers? What's to do? It's the middle of the night!"

"Ten minutes past six. Tio's awake again. And raving."

Peregrine jerked up and flung back the covers. "Pass my foot, would you?"

Piers had already retrieved the required article and he dropped to one knee beside the bed.

Peregrine said, "Get away! I'll do it."

"Yes, and take till noon. I want to get after Mitten!"

Peregrine scowled at the top of his brother's tousled head. "Well, you're doing it all wrong, if you'd care to know. That strap comes up around my knee. Yes, that's bet—Easy! Do you want to cut off the circulation?"

"The idea is not without virtue," said Piers dryly, struggling with buckles. "How's that?"

Peregrine stood carefully and took a tentative step. "Jolly

good!'' He snatched up his dressing gown. ''Come on, don't dawdle about. What did Tio say?''

''Started yowling about his precious cypher, so I told him to sit on his temper until I'd fetched you.''

They went along the corridor with stealth, Piers studiedly not noticing the painful hobble and making no attempt to help, though his arms fairly ached to support his twin.

The best spare bedchamber was now a blaze of light, two candelabra adding their brightness to the bedside oil lamp. Horatio, Viscount Glendenning, was propped against the pillows. He looked thin and wan and pathetic with the bandage around his auburn head, but for the first time since they had carried him here, his eyes were clear and holding the light of reason.

Vastly relieved, Peregrine hid that emotion and instead, recoiled. ''Zounds, what a horrid sight!'' he exclaimed. ''A red gooseberry bush!''

Samuels, who had been plumping his employer's pillows, stepped back with a chuckle.

''Never mind that, peg leg,'' said his lordship, faint but irrepressible. ''You told me the—Sam, you'd best leave us.''

''Now, milord,'' argued the manservant. ''You know very well I'm up to your larks, and there's not no need to be protecting me.''

''True, my dear fellow,'' said Glendenning. ''Only, this is not a lark, you see. And the less you know of it, the better for your health. No—never argue. Off with you!''

Reluctantly, the groom left, closing the door softly behind him.

''Deuced good chap,'' said Glendenning. ''Still—Now, Perry, did I dream it, or did you tell me the cypher had been delivered?''

''You dreamed it,'' answered Peregrine baldly.

''Lord save us!'' gasped the viscount, jerking up from his pillows only to wince and add somewhat less vehemently, ''Do you say the cypher is still here?''

''No.'' Peregrine, who had been gingerly lowering himself onto the end of the bed, said, ''You gave it to Mitten, thinking she was me, you absolute dolt. And she went haring off with it, to lead the troopers away from you.''

Very white, Glendenning looked from one twin to the other and, finding those fine young faces unwontedly stern, he whispered, "Dear God! I must have been quite out of my senses! And—I've been lying here like a confounded effigy, so that you could do—nothing!"

"Nothing?" snorted Peregrine. "Devil fly away with you!"

"We've scoured the countryside for miles around," Piers said. " 'Tis as if the earth had swallowed her up. Where in the devil is she gone, Tio?"

Glendenning groaned, "God alone knows! No—do not murder me. I—I've a fuzzy sort of recollection of telling someone—I thought it was *you*, Perry!—to deliver it. But for the life of me, I don't know if I conveyed the complete destination. Kept sort of—drifting out, y'know."

Piers said, "I quite understand that you were in a devilish predicament—though if you would refrain from consorting with that ruffian Treve de Villars, you'd not run yourself into such a flyjar—but the fact is, things have gone too far for you to hold back now."

Distraught, the viscount threw a hand across his eyes. "To have plunged *Mitten* into this ghastly mess! How can you forgive me? No—I do not ask it, but—" Lowering his arm, he clutched frantically at the eiderdown. "You know—you must *know* how deep is my affection for your sister. 'Fore heaven, I would die sooner than—"

His voice was growing shrill. Piers moved to rest a soothing hand on his shoulder. "What a fellow you are," he said gently. "One would think we have not all three condemned Cumberland's butchery."

"Aye," Peregrine agreed, "and I told you I'd help any of the poor devils did the chance afford, so do not be talking like any mangel-wurzel. You do but waste time."

My lord flushed, and apologized meekly.

Piers regarded his flamboyant twin in astonishment. "Accepted, of course, Tio. But now you really must tell us where to search for Mitten."

"I wish to heaven I knew how much I'd told her. I do recollect saying the cypher was to be delivered to Decimus Green, and—"

From somewhere close by, Samuels' voice rose in ire. ". . . cannot go in there! Lord Glendenning is a sick—"

There was the sound of a brief scuffle, then the door was flung open. A tall, broad-shouldered, very good-looking young officer stalked inside. "Gentlemen," said he, with a click of his heels, "I am under orders to search these premises and all within."

"You may search my without," said Peregrine, always irritated by pompousness, "but be damned if you're going to search my within!"

A sergeant, overhearing as he entered the room, grinned.

Unamused, the captain nodded to Glendenning. "Start with this individual."

The sergeant hurried up with a tablet and pencil. "Name?"

"Well, of course," drawled his lordship.

The captain stepped closer to the bed and said silkily, "You will be wise, sir, to cooperate."

"I am cooperating," declared the viscount, injured. "Fellow asked a question. I answered. Politely."

The twins glanced at each other, eyes full of laughter.

Smothering another grin, the sergeant asked, "*What* name, sir?"

"Horatio."

"Ho-ray-sho," muttered the sergeant, writing laboriously.

"Clement."

"Horayshow Cle-ment. Thankee, sir, I—"

"Laindon."

The sergeant took up his pencil again. "Lane—done," he muttered.

"Now then, Mr. Laindon," began the captain.

"My name is Glendenning," said his lordship, sweetly.

Peregrine, convulsed, allowed a snort to escape him.

The captain's fine features darkened. "I fancy you think you're being very funny."

"Personally," said the viscount, "I find it hilarious, but my sire appears to like it, else why would he have chose such a revolting mouthful of—"

The sergeant, who had experienced a thought, said, "Your father wouldn't be the Earl of Bowers-Malden, would he, milord?"

Glendenning considered this. "Well, he was the last time we met—but I suppose one cannot be sure. Things change so these—"

"Why are you here, my lord?" demanded the captain. "And what happened to your head? Simple answers if you please. I

166

do not care to waste my time with schoolboy frivolity. Especially with a Catholic.''

Interested, Peregrine enquired, ''Should you care for some schoolboy frivolity with two Protestants, sir?''

A cold glare was directed at him. ''I think it might be a deal more worthwhile were I to arrest the three of you on a charge of obstructing the king's justice. Your answer if you please, my lord. At once!''

''Let me see,'' mused Glendenning. ''How can I simplify it? Ah! I came here to visit my friends. And I hurt my head when they threw me down the stairs.''

''Threw you—down the stairs . . . ?'' echoed the sergeant, staring.

''Only thing to do,'' said Peregrine gravely. ''He complained about our cook, so—''

''Let's have those bandages off,'' snapped the captain, out of patience.

''What?'' cried Peregrine, astounded.

All traces of humour vanished from Piers' eyes. ''That will be just about enough!''

''Our opinions differ,'' sneered the captain. ''You've had your games with me. Now we shall see who holds the stronger hand. Sergeant!''

The sergeant set aside tablet and pencil and moved forward uneasily.

''By God, but you'll do no such thing!'' cried Peregrine. ''Glendenning's a peer! You do not dare—''

''Rank enjoys no privilege in a treasonable matter, Mr. Cranford. A traitor was cornered near this house. He escaped and has not been seen since. However, he was wounded, and it is not beyond the bounds of possibility that the troopers were drawn off by a friend. Smartly does it, Sergeant, and—'' the beautifully shaped lips curved into a benign smile, ''—should you contemplate interfering, gentlemen, I've a full troop well trained in how to deal with—''

''My friends will not interfere,'' said Glendenning, all icy hauteur. ''Sergeant, you have my sympathy. Get it done.''

The sergeant proceeded with marked reluctance. Pale with wrath, the twins watched. The sergeant eased the last layer of lint away and flinched. Glendenning swore softly.

"You started it to bleed again, you dolt!" raged Piers. "Captain, his lordship and my brother engaged in some simple horseplay, and Lord Glendenning fell down the stairs and gashed his head open on that brass-bound trunk in the hall. We've had quite a time with him, and if you cause him to suffer a relapse, the earl will take it up with your C.O.!"

The captain snapped, "Be sure there is no message hidden in the bandages, Sergeant."

Piers was an easy-going young man of even temperament, but he could be daunting when he was angered, and he was angered now. "My brother and I both served with His Majesty's forces in Scotland. Your manners, sir, are not only boorish in the extreme, but completely unwarranted. I demand to know your name."

The officer bowed slightly. "It is Lambert. Brooks Lambert." His gaze flickered over Piers' civilian attire. He sneered, "Out of uniform, are you, Cranford?"

"Out of the army. Which is neither your concern, nor indicative of treason, I believe. You have evidently been poorly instructed. I take leave to tell you that to attempt to intimidate an injured gentleman is not conduct befitting an officer."

"I really am not very frightened, dear old boy," murmured Glendenning, holding the bandage to his head.

"An emotion we share," said Lambert. "I want each of these men stripped and searched, Sergeant." His lip curled. "Especially, his Catholic lordship."

Sputtering with wrath, Peregrine started forward, only to stumble. His face twisted painfully, and he caught himself by the simple expedient of clinging to the captain's magnificence.

"Are you foxed, or what is it, Mr. Cranford?" Lambert wrenched free and as Peregrine staggered, he snarled, "Make an effort to control your feet, sir!"

"It ain't easy," gasped Peregrine. "Belike you could do better with one of these damned things," and he sat on the bed and took off his artificial foot.

Appalled by any infirmity, Lambert stared, turned pale, and fled the room.

His contempt suddenly very apparent, the sergeant watched the door close, then turned to the three friends who, after an astonished silence, lapsed into scornful laughter. "Come along now, gents," he said, grinning. "Orders is orders."

Piers asked, "Sergeant, were I to give you my word of honour that none of us conceals anything of a treasonable nature, would you accept it?"

The sergeant scanned the aristocratic young face and steady blue eyes. "Aye, I would that, sir." He leaned against the bedpost and folded his arms. "But—" he jerked his head to the door. "You'll 'ave to make believe I treated you 'arsh-like. Fer my sake."

Glendenning said wearily, "An ugly customer, is he, Sergeant?"

The sergeant hesitated, but there was that about these three that warmed his heart. "Very ugly, milord," he whispered. "Very ugly hindeed."

The sun was high when Anthony Farrar awoke. His first sensations were of extreme cold and a pounding headache. Groaning, he tried to turn over and a twig dug into his cheek. He opened his eyes to a bright blur that formed into trees and bracken and Shuffle lying beside him, eyes fixed on his face. He started to remember then, and sat up, propping his shoulders against the tree trunk, swearing softly, and holding his head on. Shuffle clambered onto his lap and began to lick his face, and he smiled and stroked her and told her he was all right. She wandered off and he leaned his head back and closed his eyes, letting memory have its way with him.

Mrs. Deene and Otton. The bitter confrontation with Helen. His hopeless retreat into brandy. Stupid and stupider! And something else . . . something more a dream than reality. Had he really mauled the trollop in the family chapel . . . ? He put a hand over his throbbing eyes. Lord, but he went from folly to folly! If he had raped the woman in a house of God, he was worse than Otton. His efforts to remember only made his head ache more viciously, and he lowered his hand and looked about for Shuffle.

He saw bright orange silk, a naughty expanse of very trim ankles, and a pair of hauntingly familiar cream kid high-heeled shoes. He quailed and clapped his hand over his eyes again.

Dimity relaxed her grip on the knife in her pocket that she had taken from the Armour Hall in case she was obliged to defend herself. She stepped nearer. "I brought water. If you want it."

If he wanted it! His throat was a desert. He stretched out his hand blindly, and she put a flask into it. He drank thirstily, replaced the stopper and, very cautiously, turned his head to look up at her. She stood a short distance away, quietly composed. How any woman could look so heavenly in that hideous gown was past understanding. He saw the cold contempt in her face then, and closing his eyes again, bowed his head. "Did—did I . . . harm you?" he faltered.

"No. You would have, I think. But you stepped on Shuffle and forgot about me."

He dragged himself up and clung to the tree trunk until the woods stopped spinning. He should go to her, but he wasn't sure he could walk without making an ass of himself, so he steadied himself against the tree and with his head still downbent said as clearly as he could manage, "I—There is nothing I can say that—that will . . . that could—I mean, I am very, very sorry."

She was silent, watching that untidy fair head. She could feel the bruises he had put on her, but it was hard to hold anger when honesty compelled her to admit that her actions must at the very least have baffled him; that he could scarce be blamed did he judge her a loose woman who plotted against him. And so her voice had lost some of its edge when she asked at length, "Did you read the poem?"

He looked at her fully, remorse in his darkly shadowed eyes. "Poem?"

'Thank heaven,' she thought. 'He didn't read it!' "I know, Captain," she said, "that whatever I am—or whatever I do, is of very little importance to you. But—I would like it very much if you would try to believe that I never met Roland Otton before last evening."

He was remembering more now, and he turned away from her. "It is none of my affair."

"True. But it is very much mine. I know that my presence at The Palfreys is a threat to your—er, birthright. But—on my honour, I had no intent to hurt you. Or to distress Lady Helen." And even as she spoke the words, she knew they were useless, for how could he help but scorn such a declaration under the circumstances?

170

He stared dully at a ladybird busied about some small task in a cleft of the bark and shrugged. "It doesn't matter."

The weary apathy, so at odds with his usual vitality, frightened her. She trod nearer. "May I ask you something?"

He sighed, and said in wry understatement, "I seem to have a slight headache. The fruits of my overindulgence."

Dimity came quite close, found a suitable root, and settled herself on it.

Farrar eased his way down, and stretched out his long legs.

"Why," she asked, "did you not tell her?"

At once, his thick lashes were lowered. He pulled up a weed and began to inspect it. "Tell her—what?"

"What you said about Quentin Chandler. I gather that Captain Otton harmed him in some way. Did they fight a duel?"

He gave a faint, mirthless smile. "They did, as a matter of fact. But that's not what I hold against him."

"It is something very bad?"

"Yes."

"What?" He frowned but did not answer, and she leaned closer and said intensely, "Sir Anthony, this is the fifth day I have been here, and I am not blind. You love her very deeply. If you told her the truth, perhaps she would have a chance to understand, but—"

He made a small gesture of finality. "No. I cannot speak of it in honour." His lip curled. "I have a little left, you see."

"You have a great deal."

His head turned against the tree and he looked steadily at her. "What a very bewildering creature you are. I wish I could understand you." He shrugged. "But it makes no difference. This has been coming for a long time. It was inevitable, I suppose. I just . . ." his voice cracked and he turned away. "I just hoped she wouldn't believe . . . *that*. But—it doesn't matter now."

Dimity gripped her hands and shifted her attack. "How old were you when you came here?"

"Five."

"Will you tell me about it?"

He hesitated, wondering why she wanted to know. But his brain was still clouded with the fumes of the brandy, and his head ached, and if he talked, he didn't have to think. "Walter was seven," he began, haltingly. "He was to go off to school

171

the following autumn. In early spring our parents were killed. A ridiculous accident—my father had insisted on taking the reins of his new coach, and he rushed the horses over icy roads. The coach overturned. Went into the river. It wasn't a great shock to us. Neither of us had known them very well. I believe my father spoke to me occasionally. Mama was always off to a soi-rée, or a musicale, or some such thing. We were sent to live with my uncle.'' He stared broodingly at his weed.

"But you did not stay together. Was your uncle not in good financial colour?''

He smiled faintly. "He is the Earl of Elsingham.''

"My heavens! Then could he not have kept you together?''

"Certainly. Only he had no use for me. Nor I for him, for that matter. He was not unkind, do not mistake. It was just—he was exactly like my own papa. He ignored us. Walter didn't mind. He thought the castle splendid, as it is you know. Our governess was bored with everything except the first footman who was a very grand fellow. There was so much I wanted to know. To do. Most of all, I suppose, I wanted to be *with* someone. Someone who talked. Or who would listen. And who would read to me.''

Dimity thought of her own wonderfully full and merry child-hood and, perhaps for the first time, knew how richly she had been blessed. She thought, 'How perfectly dreadful!' and prompted quietly, "So you asked to come here?''

"No. The Farrars came down to visit. Sir Gilbert was the best kind of man and he and I were friends at once. I thought Helen the most exquisite lady I'd ever seen. She was so beautiful. She still is, of course, but—in those days . . .''

"I can imagine. And she was kind to you?''

"She was an angel. They had a boy of their own—Harding. They thought I would be a companion for him, but—well, he was older and went away to school. Then my uncle's health began to fail. I remember how worried Helen was, but somehow she found time for me. We walked every day, and she taught me so much. She has a great eye for beauty. She would point out the reflection of sunset in a puddle, or the dappling of shade along a lane; the sheen on a dragonfly's wings. She opened a whole world of wonder to me. She read to me—night after night. And we talked, and talked, and talked.'' His eyes had softened as he spoke, and his smile was very tender. "I used to think of her as—my Madonna."

Dimity thought, 'You still do.' "And your cousin? Harding?"

There was the smallest pause, then he said, "He was a good fellow, but we had very little in common. Harding was two years ahead of me at school. I never saw him. When we came home for the Long Vacation or at Christmas, he had his friends, and I had mine. My uncle had died by the time I went to University. When I came down, Harding felt—" He checked, his lips tightening. "I bought a pair of colours."

"Because you longed for army life? Or to leave the field clear for him?"

He turned his head toward her. She asked gravely, "Was he terribly jealous?" He looked away, frowning, and after a minute she prompted again, "Lady Helen said you both joined together."

"That was later. I sold out in '43. I had a feeling something was wrong at home. I was right." For a minute he looked very grim. "My aunt is a sensible lady, but she has no head for business. Harding was hopeless at finance. It took quite a time to get things straightened around."

She asked shrewdly, "Did he resent that you were able to do so?"

"No, of course not. He was glad, in fact, that—" He hesitated, then went on rather lamely, "that I was home."

She smiled. "Rather than being the dashing soldier, off at the wars?"

Again, the muscle in his jaw rippled, but he said nothing.

"So when the Uprising started you went back into uniform and he joined also. Why? Trouble at home?"

He smiled faintly, then muttered, half to himself, "To an extent he always had wanted to be in uniform. I warned him it was a hard life, but—he laughed at me, and said I was trying to keep him out of the fun, and that it would be pretty much a shout and a flourish and the Scots would run." His smile very cynical, he said, "As it turned out, in that particular battle, the Scots shouted and—*we* . . ." he bit his lip, but finished doggedly, "ran."

"Was he a good officer?"

A sudden twinkle brightened the brooding green eyes. "You have made me talk much too much, Mrs. Deene. Perhaps *you* will answer some questions now. For instance, what your real—''

The question was never to be finished. The quiet was rent by a terrible and familiar outburst: Savage, deep-throated barks; an anguished yelping.

Farrar was racing into the woods, pistol in hand, even as Dimity scrambled to her feet.

She followed, holding up her skirts and running as fast as she was able, her high heels sinking into the thick carpet of fallen leaves and twigs and mosses. She heard a shout and blood-chilling worrying snarls. She was very close now, but found her way blocked by a deep declivity and had to make a detour around it. The sounds had ceased; all sounds had ceased, and her heart shrank within her. Had those two savage animals killed him? Was she about to come upon a ghastly scene . . . ?

The shot fractured the sudden hush and brought a chorus of cries and flutterings from frightened birds. Terror-stricken, stumbling, out of breath, Dimity came at last to a little glade, and she halted, mute with horror.

There was no sign of the mastiffs. Farrar was kneeling, the pistol in his hand still sending blue wreaths of smoke curling upward. As she stood there, frozen, he bowed lower. For a hideous moment she thought he had shot himself. Then, she caught a glimpse of the small broken shape before him; a little golden tail that would wag no more. And with a sob, she ran forward.

Still on his knees, he lifted his head, his face working and tears bright on his cheeks. ''Do you want to see?'' he asked hoarsely. ''Do you want to see? Look, then! Look!''

Dimity allowed herself one quick glance, and spun away, her hands over her eyes. Somehow, she managed to say in a thready, far-away voice she scarcely recognized, ''Come home. I'll send one of the grooms.''

''Like . . . hell! If I—if I hadn't been . . . babbling to you . . . she'd not have wandered off. Poor little Shuffle. My poor little Shuffle . . .'' Racked with grief, he averted his face.

Her own tears falling fast, Dimity quavered, ''Sir Anthony . . . do not—''

''Go!'' he shouted, rounding on her. ''Take your lies and your scheming and—go! Damn you! Get out of my sight!''

174

She fled.

In a little while, she heard her name called, and the butler, his face white and drawn with fear, ran towards her. "I—heard a shot," he panted, coming up with her. "The—the master . . . ?"

She pointed towards the glade. "Stay with him, Leonard. No matter—what he says. Please. stay with him."

How it could possibly be so, Dimity could not understand, but when she went into the house the case clock was striking half past five. She walked wearily into the music hall and started up the stairs, but glancing towards the lower steps, saw someone huddled there. She crossed the big room quickly. Farrar's valet was awkwardly asleep on the second step. She woke him and told him quietly what had happened. He stared at her, aghast, then ran across the hall and sprinted up the spiral staircase. Dimity went over to the wing chair beside the fireplace and sank into it. She fell asleep at once, and awoke reluctantly when a rough hand shook her.

It was broad daylight, and Farrar bent over her. He had shaved and changed into riding dress. He was pale, his face set and harsh, but he had regained control.

"Anthony," she murmured, her hand going out to him.

He stepped back. "It is my understanding, madam," he said in a voice of ice, "that you wish to pay a call on Mr. Rafe Green."

So the maids had chattered despite her dire warnings. Her heart sank. How he must despise her! "Yes," she whispered helplessly.

"Come, then."

She stood. The jonquil gown looked as though several horses had rolled on it. She knew her hair must be a fright, and she had not washed, nor dusted her face with powder for hours and hours. "I will only be a moment," she said. "What time is it?"

"Eight. And I cannot wait a moment."

"Nor I pay a call at this hour! Looking like this!"

His mouth curved into an unpleasant smile. "Make up your mind, ma'am. 'Tis now or never."

He meant to be rid of her. Heavy-hearted, she followed him

to the side hall, aware that awed servants watched and whispered, and wondering if she was to be allowed to see Mr. Green and then be handed over to the military. If that was the case she would have no recourse but to throw herself on Sir Anthony's mercy and tell him the truth of it all. "I *must* change into my riding habit, sir," she said, feeling like a doomed prisoner being taken to her execution.

"No need. The trap is waiting," he said relentlessly, and opened the door.

A groom sat in the trap, reins in hand. Another man clung to the head of Farrar's grey stallion and threw a desperate glance at his employer.

"Fresh, is he?" enquired Farrar, handing Dimity into the trap.

"As a—bloomin' daisy, sir," gasped the groom.

Farrar swung into the saddle and took the reins. "Stand clear!" he called, and the man leapt away. The grey shot into the air and bucked, startling the well-mannered roan between the shafts of the trap. Farrar pulled the rambunctious stallion down with an iron hand. "Drive Mrs. Deene to the Hall, Younce," he called, and was off at a plunging gallop.

Dimity did not see him again as they drove through the brightening morning. The trap followed the estate road for a while, then turned northward. The groom looked miserable, and Dimity, busied with her own sad thoughts, was silent. At least the cypher was safely in her bosom. She would give it to Mr. Green as soon as she ascertained that he was the proper recipient. Then, she would return to The Palfreys and tell Sir Anthony of her part in this horrible business. She would not dare speak of the cypher, of course, but certainly she should be able to invent some plausible tale to account for her need to impersonate the real Mrs. Deene. Perhaps, when he understood that she had been helpless, he would not be so contemptuous of her. If only she could make him listen . . . He was obsessed just now with his loss. Poor little Shuffle . . . She sighed, and wondered if Anthony would kill the man who owned those mastiffs.

❧ *Chapter 11* ❧

Dimity had hoped Farrar would accompany her, if only to ensure that she gain admittance to Mr. Decimus Green's home. That kindness having been denied, she realized that she would present more than a figure of fun to Mr. Green; very likely he would judge her as fast as she was unkempt. Her best hope was that he was not of the same stamp as Ellsworth and Roland Otton, who had both obviously decided she was a wanton and behaved accordingly. With luck, Mr. Green would turn out to be a gentleman who, however repulsed by her appearance and by the want of manners that sent her to his door unescorted at this hour, would not abuse her.

The drive took a little over half an hour. The morning was mild, but the sun had not yet warmed the air and, with no shawl to cover her bare arms and shoulders, Dimity was shivering by the time they reached the lodge gate. The gatekeeper came out in response to Younce's hail, shrugging into his coat, and with eyes becoming very wide when they beheld Dimity. The young female was most certainly not dressed for driving, besides which he considered Farrar's groom a poor substitute for a chaperone. He opened the gate, however, after exchanging some witticisms with the groom, and stared derisively as Dimity was driven past.

They followed an ill-kept drivepath that wound through sadly neglected grounds. It was some minutes before the house came into view; a sprawling grey stone edifice rather too blessed with architectural extravagances in the Italian style to suit Dimity's taste, but quite well maintained, which must be no mean task in view of its great size. Her heart sank when she thought of facing the butler who would likely open the door and at once deny his master to such a poorly bred female. She was grateful when they pulled up before the massive front steps and Younce tossed the reins to a goggle-eyed stableboy, jumped down to help her dismount, then walked close behind her up the steps.

They passed between two stone lions who turned their lofty noses and wide empty eyes upon the simple trap as though disdaining anything less than a coach of State. Dimity began to wish she had approached via the tradesman's entrance, but she was reminded suddenly of the occasion on which she and her brothers had been invited for the first time to Glendenning Abbey. Perry had said nervously that he was terrified of Tio's illustrious sire and Tio had laughed and told him that if ever he was afraid of a man, he must picture him clad only in his underclothes. Fortified, she waited as the groom tugged on the bell chain.

After a moment the door was opened to reveal an inscrutable and elegant individual who, with increasing horror, surveyed her from head to toe. The dark brows lifted, and the door swung an inch or two closer to being shut as he enquired in frigid accents, "Are you perhaps lost, madam?"

"If this is Mr. Green's residence, I am not," she said, managing to sound cool. "I am quite aware that I present an unfortunate appearance, but there has been an accident. I bring a most urgent message to your employer. Please announce me to him at once."

Her unruffled manner and quiet, cultured voice, were points in her favour apparently, because after a brief hesitation she was admitted to a great marble hall. A part of her mind registered the fact that it was cold and smelled damp, but then she was dealing with the butler's inevitable question by admitting that she had neither reticule nor card case with her, but that she was Mrs. Catherine Deene.

She fully expected to be denied, but although he looked most shocked, he eventually pursed up his lips and took himself off. He had a long way to go, for she heard his footsteps echoing into the distance. She waited, shivering, and uncomfortably aware that an upstairs maid who peeped at her from a railed balcony that ran along the far end of the hall, had evidently beckoned a friend, for stifled giggles could be heard. She was relieved when the butler trod his stately way back to her, and announced that Mr. Green was about to depart for an early ride, but could spare her a few minutes. The elevation of his nose clearly implied that this was a regrettable lapse, but he conducted her across the hall, along a dim, echoing corridor, and into a beautifully appointed study, at which point he gave her the barest of nods and left her alone.

Dimity glanced around curiously at well-stocked bookshelves, a large desk, and a reference table that had an unused appearance. There was a particularly fine print above the fireplace, showing a Saxon settlement with huts and arable lands and animal pens clearly and neatly laid out. She was studying this when a highpitched voice behind her said rather irritably, "Well, ma'am? What—"

She spun around and recoiled with a shocked gasp. The tall young gentleman who faced her, impeccable in a dark blue riding coat and corded breeches, was the owner of the mastiffs.

An incredulous smile dawned on his face. "Well, well. We meet again!"

She said numbly, "*You*—are Mr. Rafe Green?"

"*Assurement*, my delectable creature . . ." Clearly captivated by the enchantments of her bodice, he advanced with a glint in his rather protuberant eyes that she did not at all care for. Stunned, she thought, 'Oh—Lord! No wonder Anthony was so furious with me! He must have thought I knew this horrid creature that day in the clearing!' Green was bearing down on her. He reminded her of someone, but she could not think who it was. She retreated quickly, stammering, "And—and you are familiar with—the fair, sir?"

He checked, puzzled. "Good Gad, I should hope so! You are *in* it, Mrs. Deene. This is Fayre Hall."

Then there could be no further room for doubt although that this could be the man she was to entrust with the life-and-death cypher was incomprehensible. And how ridiculous that she should feel so. Because Tio was such an honourable man did not ensure that every Jacobite sympathizer would be well-bred. Nor did the fact that this man had been responsible for killing Shuffle make him an ineligible recipient of the cypher.

Nonetheless, she said, "Mr. Green—how could you have done so dreadful a thing? How *could* you have sent your dogs to attack that poor little spaniel?"

"I most certainly did not do so, dear lady." He put up his

179

glass and surveyed her through it, the magnified eye alight with sly amusement. "I am fond of animals."

Appalled, she stammered, "Then—then you meant to kill *Farrar*! My God!"

The frown returned to his petulant face. "You would find it very difficult to prove such a thing! For my part, ma'am, I think it incredible that so—er, peerless a creature as yourself should protest the matter. You're busily intent upon defrauding him yourself, by what Ellsworth tells me!" His eyes narrowed. "Is your message to do with that business? Are you come at this ungodly hour and in that—er, costume because dear Anthony has—er, tossed you out upon your delicious derrière?" He strolled nearer.

His smile held the element of lust she was beginning to recognize. She retreated once more. She had obviously misunderstood when she'd thought Tio said "fair" and "all"; he must have been trying to say Fayre Hall. Certainly, it was near Romsey, and this creature *was* Mr. Green. But she felt intuitively that something was not right, and so said in desperation, "Are you expecting a message, sir? A—very special message, perhaps?"

He paused, looking at her narrowly. "Curse me, but I am! Though I'll own you are not the person I'd thought would deliver it! 'Tis an extreme—delicate matter."

"And highly dangerous, Mr. Green."

He nodded and lowered his voice. "You're a cool one, I'll admit. Have you it about you?"

Her hand slipped instinctively to her bodice.

Green laughed softly and sprang, seizing her in a crushing embrace. "No, but you must give *me* the pleasure of collecting it, ma'am."

Dimity had often heard her grandfather remark that clothes make the man. During the course of this nightmare adventure she had learned beyond all doubting that the adage also applied to females. Struggling furiously, she made a mental vow that for so long as she lived she would never again wear a plunging neckline.

A voice of ice cut across her squeals of indignation. *"Green!"*

Dimity's heart seemed to stop beating, and she felt the man who held her give a sort of jolt before he released her and spun around.

Anthony Farrar stood just inside the open window to the garden. His head was slightly lowered, his unblinking stare fixed with deadly menace on Green, every inch of his tall figure poised for violent action.

Green whispered his name and made a mad dash for the desk and the pistol that lay there.

As fast as he moved, Farrar was faster. His face contorted with the lust for vengeance, he launched himself across the room, catching Green at the knees and bringing him crashing down. Farrar rolled, smooth and catlike and was on his feet while Green still sprawled. Frantic, Green kicked out and Farrar reeled back. Scrambling up, Green made another wild dive for the desk, but Farrar was after him. One hand caught Green by the shoulder and wrenched him around, the other came up explosively to connect under his chin and send him hurtling across the desk and to the floor beyond it. Farrar vaulted lightly over the desk, but Green was not one to fight fair. Blood streaking from the side of his mouth, he was on his knees, bringing up the pistol which had gone down with him, his thumb pulling back the hammer, a murderous triumph in his eyes. Farrar made a lightning snatch for the pistol and wrenched it aside. Green's left fist swung with the strength of desperation and landed hard beside Farrar's ear, staggering him. Farrar's left arm was considerably weakened, and it was all he could do for a minute to hang onto Green's wrist with both hands and keep the pistol pointing away from him.

Getting his second wind, Green snatched up the heavy marble Standish and flailed it at the point where throat and shoulder meet, and Farrar, unable to breathe for an instant, saw stars. He hunched his shoulders up and hung on dazedly through a rain of blows. Driven to his knees, he lost his hold on Green's wrist. With a triumphant shout, Green whipped the pistol around, but the mists were clearing from Farrar's mind. He lurched up and with all his strength rammed his head into Green's midriff. Green said an explosive *"Ooosh!"* and doubled over. He clung to Farrar and both men went down. Farrar landed on top and caught Green by the throat.

"You filthy . . . slug," he panted, tightening his grip. "You didn't have the backbone . . . to come after me yourself. You trained those hounds to do your . . . dirty work! If you blamed me for—for Harding's death, why didn't you—call me out like . . . a man?''

Consciousness fading, his eyes starting from his head, Green abandoned the fruitless attempt to dislodge Farrar's merciless hold. He managed to grasp the fallen Standish and with all his remaining strength swung it upward. It struck home just below Farrar's left elbow and his arm became useless, the pain sickening him.

Sobbing for breath, Green snatched up the pistol and brought the muzzle into line with Farrar's heart.

Dimity screamed at the top of her lungs, and Green's hand jerked. Farrar flung himself sideways. The explosion was deafening, but the ball smashed harmlessly into the wall.

Green howled curses and fled weavingly. Farrar staggered in relentless pursuit. Green reached the bell pull and tugged it desperately, a split second before Farrar's knotted fist connected solidly with his jaw. He went down and lay sprawled and moaning, his arms flapping about helplessly. Farrar advised his victim in acid if breathless terms of his deplorable ancestry. "My little . . . spaniel,'' he finished unsteadily, "was worth . . . *ten* of you, you unutterable worm!'' Having said which, he stepped onto the middle of Green's waistcoat and proceeded to wipe his boots with great deliberation on that already ravaged garment while Green shrieked and gasped out obscenities.

The butler and three footmen sprinted in.

Dimity screamed, *"Tony!"*

Farrar was slowed and he turned too late. The footmen grabbed him by the arms and dragged him from the writhing and bloody creature that was their master.

"Kill . . . him!'' sobbed Green, clutching his stomach. "Set the . . . dogs . . . on the—stinking—swine!''

The servants eyed each other uneasily.

Struggling to free himself, Farrar panted, "Do your own dirty work, for once! Send your seconds to me and I'll oblige . . . the world by blowing your slimy head off.''

- The butler contemplated his employer's gobbling hysteria and took matters into his own hands. Snatching up the pistol, he brought the butt down hard on the back of Farrar's head.

Dimity gave a sob of horror as Farrar slumped and hung loosely in the grip of the footmen.

"Take him out to his horse,'' the butler growled, "and get him off our land." Green being so obliging as to faint at this point, he added, "Best be quick about it, or we'll have the master forcing us to throw him to those damned great hounds. And that's murder, and you know who'd swing on Tyburn for it!"

The two men nodded sombrely and dragged Farrar's limp body out. The butler and the remaining footman started to lift Green.

Recovering from the shock that had held her motionless, Dimity hurried to bend over the battered Green with every appearance of deep concern. "Is—is he . . . dead?"

"Not quite, ma'am." The butler directed a sly wink at his underling. "But I'd say he got the worst of it."

"Sir Anthony done the master up tidy," agreed the footman cheerfully.

Green opened his eyes and blinked at Dimity without recognition.

She touched his cheek caressingly. "Poor Rafe," she cooed, and bent lower to kiss him as she slipped her other hand into his coat pocket.

"Wh—what.. . ?" he groaned.

"It's in your coat pocket," she whispered, her lips at his ear.

The butler rolled disgusted eyes at the footman. "Best stand clear now, if you please, ma'am."

She watched them carry Green from the room. Then, with the feeling that a great weight had been lifted from her shoulders, she turned to the window, only to stop and stare at a miniature which had fallen from the desk. She snatched it up. The artist had tried, but there could be no mistaking that fleshy face and cruel little eyes. Nor could there be any doubt about the resemblance. Rafe's eyes were different, but there was the same large nose and chin, the coarseness to the features, the thick lips. "My lord" was Lord Hibbard Green, and his son was the man Farrar had caught cheating at school. "Farrar!" she thought, and throwing down the miniature, ran to the window, clambered through it and, picking up her skirts, ran to the trap into which Farrar had been thrown.

Green's servants were starting back to the house and they eyed Dimity curiously as she came up. "Get him away as fast as may be," one of them called over his shoulder. "If the master wakes up, he'll set the dogs loose for certain!"

Younce muttered something under his breath and assisted Dimity into the trap.

Farrar was sprawled unconscious on the narrow seat. Frightened, she touched his still face and asked, "Is he badly hurt, do you think?"

"He's not going to snuff it, ma'am. He's come through worse. But we must get him out of this. I'll ride his horse, if you can manage to drive." He propped Farrar against the seatback making room for Dimity.

She took up the reins. "I can manage, but this will never do. He'll fall out. Try if you can lay him across my knees."

Younce struggled until Farrar lay face down as she suggested. "Got himself properly whipped," he muttered glumly.

"From behind," said Dimity with vehemence. "And you should only see Mr. Green!" He checked and looked at her, his eyes brightening. "Is this all right, ma'am? I'm afraid your gown—"

"Never mind about my gown. That's much better. Now hurry! Hurry!"

He jumped from the trap and went over to the solemn-eyed stableboy who was with difficulty holding the big grey. Dimity slapped the reins on the back of the roan and the animal started off at a trot. Seconds later, a shout rang out, and the stallion shot past, Younce clinging to his back and sending a startled look at her before he was borne from view. She urged the roan to greater speed and followed. The trap jolted along, and Farrar's head slid helplessly. She put her arm across him to keep him from falling and prayed they would get safely back to The Palfreys before Green sent his dogs after them.

She judged that ten minutes had passed, and she was beginning to be really afraid that Farrar was seriously injured, when she heard a smothered moan and then he clutched her knee, dragged himself up a little, and peered at her in bewilderment. A contusion was darkening along the right side of his jaw, the cut above his eye had broken open and bled profusely, and the side of his mouth was lacerated, adding its mite to his gory countenance.

Appalled, she said, "Oh, you do look dreadful! I am very sorry, but I did not dare stop and try to help you. Is there a stream where you can wash?"

His hand was still on her knee. He stared down at it and said feebly, "You did help me. The Lord only knows . . . why." He snatched his hand away then, and gave her an aghast look, a faint tinge of colour staining his white face. "Good God! Your—your pardon! I—"

She said calmly, "Don't be silly."

He blinked at her. "I cannot think how you got me away, but—" He broke off, frowning, then asked in a firmer voice, "Where are you taking me, ma'am?"

"Home, I hope. Why? Am I going the wrong way?"

With an obvious effort, he pulled himself upright. "Not—if you wish to go to Fordingbridge. Give me the reins."

She hesitated, but he seemed capable, for all there was a frown between his brows and he was so pale. She handed him the reins. "I may have taken the wrong turn at the crossroads. There was no sign and I've a dreadful sense of direction. Your groom was carried off by your great Polly." She checked and asked inconsequently, "Why do you call him that?"

"I don't." He turned the roan off the road, swore under his breath as the trap bounced, and added, "His name's *Poli,* which is French . . . and means—"

Dimity smiled. "He did not look very *refined* when he went charging off with your poor servant hanging on for dear life!"

Farrar drew rein in the shade of some trees at the foot of a broad hill. He stared at Dimity for a moment, then climbed from the trap. "There's a stream—" he began in a fading voice, and swayed, clutching dizzily at the tall wheel.

Dimity scrambled down and tethered the roan to a shrub. Farrar was trudging off erratically. She followed and took his arm. He stopped and looked blearily down at her. "Be damned if I can make you out," he muttered.

"I know. And I can tell you the truth now. Oh dear, you *are* feeling poorly! Can you manage if you lean on me?"

He managed, but when they reached the stream, he sat down abruptly on the bank and closed his eyes, looking so close to swooning that she abandoned formality and ransacked his pockets until she found his large handkerchief. She dipped it in the stream. When she turned back with icy water dripping from the linen, Farrar's head was bowed into his hands. She pulled his shoulders back and began gently to bathe his face. The cold water restored him, and in a short while he opened his eyes and said faintly, "If you could be so good as to wet it again, I'll put it on this cricket ball on the back of my skull."

She rinsed out the handkerchief and folded it into a square. Farrar's head was downbent again. She untied the black velvet riband, spread the fair hair and found the large lump. Thanks to the thickness of his hair, the skin was unbroken but it was already starting to bruise. With caution, she laid the handkerchief over the injury.

Farrar gave a groaning sigh and reached up to hold it in place. "Thank you. Though why you should help me instead of staying with . . . your lover, I—"

"Oh, he is only one of many," she said, kneeling beside him and watching his battered face with compassion.

He tilted his head back, looking at her, his eyes narrowed painfully.

"Poor soul," she said. "I know you must feel dreadfully. I remember when one of my brothers was struck on the head by a falling tree branch, and it hurt so badly he was sick."

"I echo his feelings," he said threadily, "but perhaps I may refrain from being sick if you will relate the next chapter."

Dimity settled herself more comfortably, unable to blame him for the dry scepticism in his tone.

"Oh, Gad," he exclaimed, then, "I've bled all over your gown. My apologies."

She glanced down. "It is not my gown."

"Ahh . . ." breathed Farrar.

"Nor am I Catherine Deene," she went on. "And Carlton is not my nephew." He watched her steadily and she reached up to dab her handkerchief at the cut on his brow. "A dear friend had asked me to deliver a message of great importance. He was—taken ill, you see, and could not deliver it himself. His . . . enemies were determined to prevent me from completing my task, and I was very afraid they would find me." She paused uneasily. It did not sound nearly as convincing as when she'd rehearsed it on the way here. She peeped at Farrar and met a sardonic grin, so hurried on, "When the accident happened—"

"Which one? My life—since you came into it—seems to have been one long accident!"

"I know." She gave him a repentant look. "I am truly sorry. I

186

mean the accident when the Portsmouth Machine turned over. I was stunned, and when I woke up they had mistaken me for Mrs. Deene because her reticule had become draped over my arm.''

'''So you let them keep on thinking it, for fear your—er, friend's enemies—or is it your enemy's friends? . . . would find you.''

''Yes. And because I had no papers with me.''

''Thus, you were glad to hide at The Palfreys. But—are you not anxious to complete your mission?''

''I have. Today.''

He stared at her. ''Do you mean that your message was for that creature I just—argued with?''

''Yes. But I had never met him, you see, and I'd no idea he was the son of that horrible man we met in Salisbury. He is—no?''

''Yes. Rafe's father is Lord Hibbard Green. And your—er, message is safely delivered?''

''At last! I am free. I don't have to pretend any more!''

''Egad—what a melodrama!'' He frowned. ''Then—where is the real Mrs. Deene?''

''Recovering, I'm afraid—Oh dear! I don't mean that exactly, but she will probably be coming to claim Carlton at any hour. She lies at a hedge tavern near Winchester where we were carried after the wreck.''

''I see. Then—you cannot know whether Carlton is, or is not, my legal nephew?''

''No. He is a very dear little boy, though, do you not think?''

''Very dear! As witness my broken coach and shattered bridge—to say nothing of his confounded House Tour!''

Dimity chuckled. ''Yes—and the paints you bought him, and the time you have spent trying to teach him how to go on. You likely thought I did not notice.''

Farrar was experiencing the inevitable reaction from his debauched night and violent morning. His head pounded savagely, and his arm felt even worse than it had yesterday. He knew a grim sense of satisfaction because he had in some small measure punished Green for his beloved Shuffle's death, but that loss was still too terrible a thing to be faced, and he escaped it by allowing another realization to please him. If what she said was truth this time, this beautiful and courageous girl was not engaged in trying to defraud him, and may well have had a reason for some of the outrageous things she had done; certainly for those disgraceful gowns. With the startled awareness that he had been staring at her, he said, "Your pardon—what did you say?"

"I said," Dimity replied, her cheeks rather pink because of the look in his eyes, "that Mrs. Deene is rather a—formidable lady, I would think."

"Is she, indeed? It would be interesting to know if that is the reason why that young rapscallion did not remain with her."

"As a matter of fact, he was most willing to leave her and told me he would as soon have me for an aunt instead."

"So would I," said Farrar, foolishly. Then, colouring up he added, "By the way, ma'am, may I ask—what is your real name?"

Her real name . . . Oh, dear! "It is Dimity—Clement."

"Aha! Now I understand the 'Mitten'! And—is it—*Miss* Mitten?"

"Yes," she said, miserable suddenly because she must still lie to him about her true identity, and even more miserable because if he learned her real name he would know how her brothers despised him—how she *should* despise him. She stood and took his arm. "Now, come. I must get you home."

Farrar leaned on her heavily as they returned to the trap. It was a battle to climb in, and when it was accomplished he sat in a strange sort of daze. He was not too dazed, however, to be enchanted by the glimpse of her lovely ankles as she clambered up beside him and took the reins. He leaned his head against the back of the seat and gazed dreamily at her.

"Miss Mitten," he murmured.

Dimity turned to him, a kindness in her face that made his heart leap. He knew he was a prize fool. It seemed that on at least half the occasions when he'd seen her, some rake had been exploring her bosom. She had lied to him from the beginning. There was no reason to believe that this time she had told him the truth—that she was not, in fact, a quick-witted mercenary adventuress. Yet, how sweet the rich curve of her lips; how dainty the shadow of the thick lashes on her delicate cheekbones; how enchanting the slant to those liquid hazel eyes.

"Yes?" she answered. It was so very difficult to keep in mind that this man was a coward, responsible for the loss of many lives and for her beloved Perry's maiming, and even believed by some to have deliberately engineered his own cousin's death. 'It is a filthy lie!' she thought fiercely. But then she was frowning because for a soldier to panic and run from the battlefield, deserting his comrades, was a dark and shameful thing, but for an officer to surrender to fear, to abandon his men to their fate while he fled to protect his own skin—that was vile; a deed beneath contempt. And she wished she did not like him so very much.

Thus the thoughts of two young people sitting in a trap in the peaceful quiet of a summer morning, while the breeze played softly among the tall grasses, the warm sunlight bathed them with its golden rays, and the roan horse began to graze once more.

"Miss Mitten," said Farrar again, a husky note to his voice now. He dragged himself up and slid an arm around her shoulders. "Do not . . . drive up to the front," he said, one finger tracing the lovely curve of her ear.

"As you . . . wish . . ." she answered, shivering.

He was tilting her head towards him. His eyes were a tender caress, his lips were coming ever nearer. She closed her eyes and swayed to him, and was kissed gently, then less gently, and then with a passion that left her breathless. She drew back, flushed and guiltily happy, and touched his mouth, her fingers feather-light. "You'll hurt yourself."

"But what a delicious hurting," he whispered, kissing her fingers. "Mitten . . ." He was very tired, and let his head droop onto the dimpled shoulder once more.

"Yes—Anthony?"

"Don't tell Lady Helen . . . your real reason for—for coming to The Palfreys."

She frowned a little. Her real reason . . . "Why?"

He closed his eyes contentedly, his reply so low that she had to bend to hear it. "I do not want you . . . to leave us."

She smiled and took up the reins again.

As it turned out, she had no choice in the manner of their return. Younce had spread the word of the battle at Fayre Hall, and as the trap approached the drivepath some half dozen grooms, footmen, and the captain's valet galloped to surround them.

Jordan, anguished, said, "Oh ma'am, we have been so very worried. If you will stop, I'll wipe the master's poor face."

"No," said Dimity.

"But—he's all blood! If Lady Helen—"

She gave him a steady look, then started the roan once more. The men formed an escort on either side, Jordan faintly smiling.

That their coming had been observed was evidenced by the fact that the front door flew open as they drove up. The change in motion woke Farrar, and he sat up straight as Carlton, closely followed by Lady Helen and Leonard, ran onto the front steps. "Oh—blast!" groaned Farrar.

Carlton advanced in a series of leaps, his eyes blazing with excitement. "Did you strangle the life out of him, sir?" he shrieked. "You look drefful so I 'spect he's dead and wallowing in his gore! I hope you stamped on his horrid face!"

"You bloodthirsty little fiend." Farrar's eyes flashed to his aunt, who stood pale and motionless, her hands pressed to her throat. He said, "I'm quite all right, ma'am," and started to climb out of the trap. The Palfreys tilted crazily when his feet hit the ground, and Leonard darted to fling an arm around him.

Dimity called, "It's his head. He beat Mr. Green fairly, but they struck him down with a pistol butt!"

A growl went up from the men. Lady Helen reached out as Farrar was aided up the steps, but then stood aside.

Jordan assisted Dimity from the trap, and Carlton, racing back from having escorted Farrar into the music hall, grasped her hand. "Are you badly hurt, Aunty? You're all over gore!"

"I know, but it's not mine." She drew level with my lady and said, "Your nephew was superb, ma'am."

Jordan ran past and followed Leonard and Farrar to the spiral staircase.

Lady Helen said, "I heard—Leonard told me—about the poor little dog."

"It's the wickedest thing I ever heard of," said Carlton. "I hope Sir Uncle cut his throat! I hope he pulled his heart out and fed it to the toads!" And he went leaping off in pursuit of the returning warrior.

"I am absolutely appalled," said my lady. "If Rafe holds Anthony to blame for my son's death, he should have challenged him honestly, not set his dogs on that dear little animal! It is disgraceful! Disgraceful!"

"No, ma'am," Dimity said coolly. "It is attempted murder."

Lady Helen gave a gasp.

"Mr. Green had trained his mastiffs to attack Sir Anthony," Dimity went on. "I suppose poor Shuffle, being so constantly at his side, and being caressed by him, carried the scent those dogs had been made to hate."

"Oh! How *frightful*! And—and now, there must be a duel . . . of course."

Dimity nodded, and wondered if it was possible that next time Mr. Green would fight fair. She doubted it.

Not the man to raise a fuss over an injury, Farrar refused the services of his doctor. Between lack of sleep and the severe blow to his head, however, he was obliged to bow to the proprietory bullying of his valet and take to his bed.

Also exhausted, Dimity was aghast to find herself trembling, weak in the knees, and tearful. Lady Helen, who had accompanied her to her bedchamber, took charge. Dimity was bathed and tucked into bed with a warming pan at her feet. The chef was required to send up a brandy posset, and when she had drunk this concoction, the window draperies and bedcurtains were drawn and she was told to go to sleep and assured that no one would disturb her.

The door closed, and she snuggled deeper in the blankets and started to say her prayers . . .

Disturbed by something, despite my lady's promise, she opened her eyes.

Carlton, kitten in hand, peeped at her through the bedcurtains.

"Hello, Carlton," she said, yawning.

He looked solemn. "Aren't you ever going to wake up?"

She stretched. "What time is it?"

He pulled back the curtains and sunlight flooded the room. "I think it's ten o'clock nearly," he said, peering doubtfully at the little gold and silver clock on her bedside table.

He was wrong, of course. It had been later than that when she fell asleep, surely? She took up the clock and sat up with a rush. "Good heavens! Is it still Thursday?"

" 'Course not. It was Thursday yesterday." He asked apprehensively, "Are you cross? They said I must not come in."

191

"I am cross because I have slept such an age. I must get up now, so run along."

He looked doleful. "Why do grown-ups always say 'run along now' just when you don't want to run along? But if you *want* to run along, you are made to sit still?"

"I know. Life is full of horrid things like that," she told him, smiling. But he looked so troubled that she relented, and patted the bed invitingly.

Relief dawned in his small face, and he scrambled up beside her and watched his kitten declare war on the eiderdown. It was a pretty little tabby with a white chin, a snowy cravat, and a white tip to its miniature tail.

"What do you call him?" she asked.

"Swimmer. Only Leonard says he's a her."

She chuckled, her eyes tender as her thoughts turned to Farrar standing roaring in that hip bath.

Carlton said, "Why is your face red?"

"I must be sleepy still. What—er, did you want to talk about?"

His expression became sombre. "You're not really my aunty."

"No."

"If she comes here, you'll go away."

Would she go away? Had she any choice?

Having waited hopefully but received no reply, the boy went on in a miserable little voice, "And if they find out I'm not really Sir Uncle's nephew—"

Her attention shot to him. "Aren't you?"

He shrugged. "I dunno. She says I am. But—if I'm not, they'll put me back in the Foundling Home, 'cause she won't want me."

"If ever I heard such twaddle! You are her sister's only child!" The boy looked glum, and she went on bracingly, "Besides, if your aunt does not—er, find she can take you, we shall try if we can bring you to live with us—my brothers and me."

He said a dispirited, "Thank you. But—I'd like to stay with him."

She stroked his curls. "With Sir Anthony?"

He nodded. "He's like me. He's got no one, and he's very sad 'cause of Shuffle. I know how he feels, 'cause I never really had someone till I traded for Swimmer. Now I've got her, at least.''

Dimity blinked rather rapidly. "Sir Anthony has his aunt, and—''

"She 'spises him. I heard the lackey say so. They had an awful fight 'bout it.''

"Good gracious me! The menservants fought about Sir Anthony?''

He nodded. "The second footman and a lackey named Billings. Billings liked Mr. Harding, and he said Sir Uncle killed him dead.''

"That's not true!'' she declared angrily.

"Jordan was ready to scrag him, I 'spect. He said he'd tell Mr. Leonard and Billings would lose his salvation, an' have to find another place, and the chef chased him with his chopper, an' everyone was screaming!'' He had brightened at the memory of this lovely scene. "It was great fun.''

"Yes, I fancy it was. But it was also disloyal. If a man works for Sir Anthony, he should be loyal to him. It is very bad to take a man's pay and speak badly of—Oh! Look at your raving beast!''

Swimmer had found her way underneath the eiderdown and was rushing madly about, a small hurtling lump that suddenly became a curled up, pedalling fury.

Carlton threw back the eiderdown, retrieved his pet, and bore her off, close cuddled in his neck.

Dimity rang for Rodgers, who came in agog with excitement over the death of Shuffle and the fight at Fayre Hall. "I know he's your friend, ma'am, "she said, brushing out Dimity's hair. "Ahem—but, if you was to ask me, Mr. Green got a little taste of what he's been asking for ever since they brought the master home. I wish I'd a groat for every nasty snide remark he's made to her la'ship. Him and Mr. Ellsworth both, never letting her forget what the master done, and Sir Anthony keeping his tongue 'twixt his teeth, for her sake. Fair idolizes her la'ship, he does. James Hinkley says as they'll go out now, certain sure. And if Sir Anthony is killed, *then* her la'ship will be sorry!''

Farrar slept as one dead, and awoke with a persistent headache, an assortment of unpleasant reminders of his battle with

Rafe Green, and memories of the journey back to The Palfreys that brought alternate extremes of joy and despair. He let Jordan maudle over him and rendered the man ecstatic by quietly admitting to the truth of a rumour, apparently started by "Mrs. Deene," that he had cleaned his boots on Green's waistcoat.

In no mood for breakfast, he made his way to his studio. This spacious room, located at the end of the hall in his private wing, was well equipped with easels, benches, stacked past efforts, and several canvasses in various stages of completion. He looked sombrely at one of these, then went with reluctance to another portrait. He was not a master, but his work was very good and the painting of his lost friend was so lifelike that he could scarcely endure to look at it. He refused, however, to put the canvas where he would not have to be reminded. Shuffle was too dear to be banished. He sat back against a bench, folded his arms, and communed in silence.

Aunt Helen had presented him with the tiny puppy for his seventeenth birthday. There had been partings, of course, through which he'd been told the dog was subdued, as one waiting. Whenever he'd returned home, she had been wild with joy, and they'd been inseparable. His eventual disgrace had left him very alone, and through this long, dark year, Shuffle had been his only solace—an unwavering friend. He knew that many people would say "She was only a dog," but to him she had been ineffably more: a beloved companion whose loss left a gaping hole in his life and a bruise on his spirit that would not soon heal. The most difficult thing to accept was that she had died not from age or illness, but because of a man's hatred for him. Looking at her faithful eyes, he suffered the pain of knowing she would never gaze at him so again; that he must become accustomed to walking without the immediate click of her nails following; that when he sat in his favourite chair in the evening, her cold nose would not push into his hand, her warm little self would not be curled at his feet. Perhaps, there was a heaven for dogs who had given as much love, loyalty, and solace as had Shuffle. He prayed there was . . .

He had not realized how low his head had sunk until a stealthy sound caused him to look up. Carlton was watching him, a sympathy in his young face that brought a grateful smile to Farrar's lips. Not a little embarrassed, he started to say something light, but the set of the boy's chin told him that this was not a light moment, so he was still. From the corner of his eye he saw that someone else stood in the open doorway, but he did not shift his attention from the child.

Carlton came forward, Swimmer clutched to him. "Uncle Sir Anth'ny," he said rather hoarsely, "I don't care what they say 'bout you. I think you're the—the bravest man what ever was. I know a cat's not—not much use. Not like a dog, I mean. But—here—" He thrust the kitten at the man who had come to his feet and regarded him gravely. "You have her. I—got nothing else to—to . . ." His control broke. Farrar took the squirming kitten, and with a muffled sob, Carlton fled.

Dimity found it necessary to resort to her handkerchief. When she lifted her eyes, Farrar was holding Swimmer up and inspecting her.

He said with a wry smile, "I've already had one baptism of fire from you, little lass. Now it would seem I must provide for you."

Dimity walked to him. "Have you the remotest idea of what he just gave you?"

He put the kitten on the bench behind him and reached for her hand. "I think you refer to the poor widow in the Bible."

She nodded. "He gave you his—two mites. All he had. I think you will never receive a richer gift, Sir Anthony."

There was a pink blush on her cheeks, a soft glow in her eyes that he had seen once before. He pressed her fingers to his lips. "I begin to think," he said softly, "that I may have—"

Quick footsteps sounded in the hall. Leonard appeared in the doorway, looking worried. "A gentleman has called on a matter of—of urgent business, sir."

✑ *Chapter 12* ✐

Farrar had a fair idea of the "matter of business" his caller had come to discuss. He told Leonard to show the gentleman to his study and, having excused himself to Dimity, repaired to that chamber. He was glancing blindly at some estimates for the restoration of the old church in Palfrey Poplars, and nerving himself to receive the dread visitor, when Leonard opened the door.

"Mr. Roland Otton, sir."

It went to show, thought Farrar bitterly, where cowardice led one; if he'd had the gumption to ask the name of his "caller," he might have spared himself some very unpleasant moments of anticipation. Throwing down the estimate, he sprang to his feet.

Roland Otton, impressive as always and clad in a dark brown velvet riding coat, buckskin breeches, and knee boots, strolled into the room, a faintly insolent grin playing about his lips.

"I warned you," grated Farrar, starting around the desk.

Otton lifted a languid hand. "I am here in a matter of honour, Tony."

"Much you know of—"

"Alas, we both are rather—ah, tattered in that regard, *n'est-ce-pas*? No, you really cannot throw me out, my dear fellow. I represent our admirable Rafe."

Fists clenched and eyes glittering with wrath, Farrar checked. "Dear me, you *do* look dreadful," said Otton clicking his tongue.

"Whereas your friend Green is unmarked, no doubt."

"Acquit me of that! Rafe is not my friend. And as to his appearance, egad 'tis enough to make a man vomit!"

"But you mean to second him?"

"Unhappily, yes." Otton sighed regretfully, but his black eyes gleamed with mischief. "I would have acted for you, dear boy, but you'd have none of me and does one stay under a man's roof, one cannot very well refuse . . ."

Farrar stared. "Do you say that you are acting for him only because you are his guest?"

"Well, I don't *know* the fella! I must say it's very disobliging of you to put me in such a fix."

"Put you . . . What in the devil are you talking about?"

"Merely that had you been more hospitable I'd not have had to finagle my way into Fayre Hall, and thus—"

With an effort recollecting his loathing for this scoundrel, Farrar snapped, "When does he wish to meet?" and returned to his chair.

Otton perched on the corner of the desk. "Only give me the names of your seconds." He inspected a fingernail and murmured mildly, "You—er, can muster one or two, I presume?"

"Assuredly," said Farrar, wondering if Leonard would second him. "When?"

"Tomorrow morning. He's very cross with you, Tony."

"Pistols?"

"I said he was cross—not stupid. He knows your reputation. Swords."

'Damn!' thought Farrar.

Otton read the bleak look correctly. "Yes, I hear he's very good with a rapier. But you did challenge, you know. Loudly."

Standing, Farrar nodded. "Where?"

"In the meadow by Black Spinney. At seven."

"Agreed. Good-bye."

Otton straightened, bowed in his graceful, mocking way and started out, then paused. "You will send your people to the Hall? Green has asked Ellsworth and me."

"A motley crew," sneered Farrar. "You had best warn your principal, Ro—Mathieson, that if his dogs come in sight, my seconds are instructed to shoot at once."

"Shoot his *dogs*?" For once Otton looked shocked. "Jove! But perhaps I do not take your meaning?"

So he did not know about the mastiffs. Gratified for some obscure reason, Farrar said a clipped, "Green will. Good day to you."

Dimity hurried across the terrace and down the steps. There was no sign of Carlton, but because she knew how much Swimmer had meant to him, she was anxious to find him, and she followed the drivepath until it curved up to the old bridge. The breeze was stiff, hurrying clouds across the pale sky and whipping the treetops into swirling pirouettes. She had chosen the green gown this morning. It was a sickly colour, but the maids had been unable to remove all the stains the ashpile had left on the blue, nor the bloodstains from the jonquil dress, and she would die before she'd wear that absolutely disgusting bright pink atrocity with the open lacings to the waist! The skirts of the green gown were as voluminous as the bodice was scanty, and she struggled to hold them down as she trod up the bridge. Carlton was not to be seen, and although she called his name several times, he did not appear.

She wandered down the slope towards the river, wondering when her brothers would arrive. If her letter had reached them, they would be here at any moment. Sighing, she turned and was swept into two strong arms.

"Let me go at once!" she cried furiously, pushing against Roland Otton's broad chest.

"Now, sweeting," he protested, laughing down at her. "Never say you did not put on that—er, delightful dress and trip down here to meet me. Confess, bewitching wanton, that—"

"You have no right—" she snarled.

Brazenly, one long finger traced the hollow between her breasts. "When a lady flaunts her charms so—enticingly," he said with a chuckle, "what is a poor man to think?"

It was true! Bother the horrid creature, it was true! Enraged by both her sense of sportsmanship and her inability to escape this wretched imposture, she tore free, putting a shielding hand over the area that so enticed him.

"Ah, no! Pray do not hide so lovely a sight," he pleaded, trying to move her hand away.

"Well, well," drawled a gentle, cultured voice. "What a surprise, Roland."

Otton jerked as though he had been shot. All affectation was wiped from his face, and he was suddenly chalk white, his dark eyes wide with shock. He was, she thought, even more attractive without the mantle of cynicism. He spun around then, so fast that his sword slapped hard against her hoops. The word he spoke was so softly uttered that she could not be sure what it was, but it sounded like, "Muffin . . .'"

Following his gaze she saw a magnificent personage standing a short distance up the slope, quizzing glass in one hand and a long, gold-handled cane in the other. He wore a superb purple brocade coat, the front openings and pocket flaps richly embroidered with silver thread. His waistcoat was quilted lilac satin and satin unmentionables of the same shade looked as though the word "crease" was unknown to them; his stockings were of white with a lilac lattice up one side, and upon his feet were high-heeled shoes with amethysts gleaming from the buckles. His countenance was thin and haughty, with a hooked nose, pale blue eyes, and stern mouth. His chin was long and his forehead high. A slender gentleman, somewhere past sixty, she guessed, he was neither brawny nor tall, yet it appeared to her that he towered over the young man who stared at him in such speechless surprise. And sprawling at his side, head lazily propped on an immaculate shoe, was a large dog of dubious parentage and nondescript lines who snored softly into the amethyst encrusted buckle.

"Your . . . Grace," gulped Otton.

"How charming in you to remember me." The duke allowed the quizzing glass to fall to the end of its silver chain and extended his hand.

Otton stared at that slim hand as if he could not believe his eyes, then lifted his gaze to search the bland countenance. In a marked departure from his usual supple ease of movement, he approached the newcomer cautiously, dropped to one knee, but again hesitated, glancing up into the inscrutable eyes before gingerly touching the thin fingers to his lips.

"Perhaps," drawled the gentleman, smiling at Dimity, "you will be so kind as to introduce me to this lady."

Otton returned to take Dimity's hand and lead her forward.

"Sir, it is my honour to present Mrs. Catherine Deene. Ma'am, his Grace the Duke of Marbury."

The duke removed the tricorne from his elegant pigeon-wing wig and offered a low bow.

Dimity swept into a curtsey, wishing with all her heart that she wore her riding habit.

The duke bent over her hand. His brows lifted slightly as his glance encountered her bosom and when he straightened he said with a twinkle, "My *very* great pleasure, ma'am. I trust this regrettable—er, person was not annoying you."

"He appears to have understood that I had come here to meet him, your Grace."

"Whereas, of course, you had not." Marbury sighed and shook his head chidingly. "I wonder why it is, Roland, that on the few occasions you cross my path, you either have a sword in your hand or a lovely woman in your clutches."

"Very few occasions, sir," said Otton, flushing but steadier.

It was the first time he had recovered himself sufficiently to speak in a normal voice. The effect upon the dog was extraordinary. He writhed convulsively, sprang up, and flung himself at Otton, barking wildly. Laughing and staggering back, Otton fended him off, jerking his head away from the flailing pink tongue and telling him firmly, "Beast! Down! Blast your ears! Down, sir!"

A brief frown disturbed the duke's serenity, then he was saying whimsically, "Do you know, my dear, I can never understand why he does that. It goes to show that dogs are not nearly the shrewd judges of character they are held up to be."

The waters here were murky, she thought, and she enquired evasively, "Are you a friend to Captain Farrar, sir?"

"Let us say that I am extreme fond of Lady Helen," he replied, just as evasively. "Now I wonder why you are here, Roland. What—or whom—do you hunt this time?"

Beast sat at Otton's feet, tongue lolling as he panted up at the dark young man. Fondling the head that was neither Alsatian nor Mastiff, but something of both, Otton murmured, "I wonder you can ask, sir, having seen this lovely lady."

"Do you?" His Grace bestowed a thoughtful glance on Dimity. "You must not underestimate me because I am in my dotage, dear boy."

"I think I am not so unwise, your Grace."

"Nor I so foolish as to imagine you pursue Mrs. Deene. Among the things you lack, Roland, is obtuseness. Not only is this delightful creature a lady of Quality, but, knowing her brothers, I suspect any pursuit of her would inevitably lead you into a pair of duels." He had noted Dimity's start, but went on urbanely, "While I do not mistake you for a craven, I suspect you do not hazard your life—save for gold."

"*Vraiment*, but you know me better than I thought, your Grace."

"To the contrary, I know you not at all. It was my misfortune to know your sire, however. And—your mama." He lifted one hand; an unhurried gesture that yet effectively stopped the response that Otton, his eyes flashing, had been about to utter. "Good afternoon, Farrar."

Striding up, grim-faced, Farrar bowed. "Welcome, your Grace. I regret I am unable to extend that greeting to your—to Otton."

"It is quite all right, my dear boy," said the duke expansively. "Reluctant as I may be, I do not deny the relationship. However, in view of—forgive—your own unhappy predicament, I would have thought, er . . . You and Roland *did* serve together—no?"

"In the Low Countries, sir."

"And were at one time—close friends?"

"Times change, your Grace."

"Oh, indeed. But—pray forgive my curiosity—what brought about the change in this particular instance?"

Farrar hesitated.

Otton said defiantly, "Farrar objects because I was among those who—interrogated a traitor with whom he cries friends."

"Ah . . ." The duke smiled gently at the scowling Farrar. "It is not wise, Anthony, to befriend traitors. I am convinced," he amended, musingly, "we cannot refer to the interrogation of poor Quentin Chandler . . . But of course not." He made an apologetic gesture. "Even Roland would not stoop to the savageries perpetrated on that boy, much less participate in such brutality."

Otton was silent, looking down, one hand nervously fondling the dog's ear.

"Beast!" snapped Marbury, his tone making Dimity jump,

"Heel!" In rather startled fashion, the dog at once returned to his master.

No less startled, Dimity saw that the duke's mild eyes had taken on the aspect of Polar ice, the stare he levelled at his grandson causing the breath to catch in her throat.

"I will have your answer, sir, an you please."

Very pale, Otton said hoarsely, "In—in time of war, your Grace—"

Like a knife of steel, the duke's voice cut through the stammered words. " 'Twas not done by reason of patriotism, for you lack a single iota of so worthy a sentiment! I'd heard rumours you were involved in tormenting Chandler, but would not believe you could sink to such a depth of depravity!" The impassioned denunciation ceased. Marbury drew a breath and with a faint smile murmured, "Faith, but I'll own you have outdone yourself."

Otton's shoulders straightened. "Had you expected anything else?" he drawled with his normal veiled insolence.

"You are right," smiled Marbury. "I forget myself. One must always keep in mind the adage of the—ah, silk purse and the sow's ear . . . You may leave us, Roland. As rapidly as may be."

Otton jerked a bow and, looking neither to right nor left, retreated with an unwontedly rapid stride toward the stables. Marbury bent and patted Beast, whereupon that exhausted animal slid slowly down his leg to sprawl on his shoe again.

Dimity turned a scared glance to Farrar. He lifted his brows and said a silent, "Phew!"

"I am desolate," said Marbury, standing erect and regarding Dimity wistfully. "I allowed vexation to abrogate manners. I upset you, I fear, and most humbly crave your pardon, dear lady."

He was all gentle humility once more, but she was not deceived. She had seen steel and knew that a man would do well to tread very lightly around this complex individual. But she was not a man, and the sight of the trickle of moisture on his temple touched her heart. She said kindly, "I think he has many good qualities, your Grace. Perhaps he regrets—whatever it was that he did. Perhaps he is not quite as—as base as he seems."

His answering smile was like a warm embrace. He said softly, "Few of us are quite what we seem, are we, Mrs. . . . Deene?"

She blushed guiltily. He extended his arm. Taking it, she walked beside him towards the house, Farrar following.

"It is most kind in you to have made such a generous observation." Marbury directed a glance over his shoulder. "Never hide back there, Anthony. You know very well I shall have to be told about your face. By the way, where is Shuffle? I do not—" He broke off. "I have said something gauche, I perceive. You may leave us, my boy. I wish to hoard this beautiful young creature to myself for a little while."

Farrar bowed, threw an uneasy look at Dimity, and strode off.

The duke led the way to the bench under an old beech tree that dappled a lacy shade beside the drive. "Farrar is angry with me," he said, taking out his handkerchief and spreading it on the wooden bench before allowing Dimity to occupy it. "But I am consumed with curiosity and beg your indulgence of a lonely old man who leads a very dull life." He sat beside her, and went on, "Advancing years have not led, in my case, to a diminution of selfishness, and thus, before I burden you with the plethora of questions that come to mind, I beg you will explain your kindness in behalf of my deplorable grandson. I had somehow formed the opinion you were an unwilling—ah, captive."

"Yes. And also, most curious, sir. Forgive, but—are you *really* his grandsire? You do not look—"

"I know." He patted her hand. "He is revoltingly handsome. How perverse of Nature to indulge evil with beauty, while someone as pure and noble as myself—"

She laughed. "Out upon you, sir! I did not mean that, which you know perfectly well! 'Tis just—well, Otton must be at least—nine and twenty . . . ?"

"I suppose," he said with a twinkle, "that did I tell you he is an elderly sixteen, you'd not believe?"

"I would try," she answered, amused. "But—heaven help the world if 'twere truth!"

He sighed. "You have a point. So I must confess—I was wed very young, and my lamentable son was seduced by Roland's mother when he was barely eighteen." She looked at him uncertainly, but his face was bland and unreadable, and he went on, "But we do not speak of the fascinations of Marbury, but of Roland Fairleigh Mathieson, who calls himself," he shuddered, "Otton."

"Yes, and your Grace had asked why I spoke kindly of him." She paused, considering. "I think I do not understand it myself. Certainly, if he is as cruel as you implied . . . Yet—there is something rather likeable about him. Perhaps it is just that he does not pretend to be other than what he is. Then again," she added musingly, "one cannot always judge a man by his reputation. Only look—" She broke off, startled by the realization that she was speaking her thoughts aloud.

Marbury, who had been watching her intently, murmured, "I have seen *you* look at Farrar, which is more to the point. Ah, how prettily you blush." He took her hand, his pale eyes that had been so piercing and terrible when he questioned his grandson, now very kind.

"When I came here," she said ruefully, "I hated him. Indeed, it would be wrong not to despise such a man." She searched his face. "No?"

"Because of Peregrine? How is the dear lad? Now you really must not regard me so fearfully, child. I am not a witch or a warlock—simply a man with an eye for family traits. Your brothers share with you the Cranford contradictions of a tender mouth and a stubborn chin. Besides which, long before you were born, I knew your lovely mother, God rest her. I have absolutely no right to ask, but shall, of course; why did you come here, if you hated Farrar? And why—dare I be so impolite?—does a gentle and lovely lady of Quality wear the gown of a—er, rather less cultured person?"

Dimity uttered a little ripple of mirth, eased her foot from beneath Beast, who had fallen asleep on it, and began, insofar as was possible, to explain.

Emerging from his study following a lengthy discussion with his bailiff, Farrar was not greatly surprised to discover that the duke had left without talking with him. But Lady Helen was, he knew, very fond of Marbury, and he went rather anxiously in search of her. The footman and lackey of whom he enquired were unable to provide him with her whereabouts. He wandered down the steps and turned into the small dining room. The table was set for luncheon. He was staring rather blankly at those two neat and so meaningful covers when he was the object of a ferocious charge. From his own place at the head of the table (quite bare of cutlery) came a miniature tiger, all whiskers, flying paws, and perking tail, to hurl itself at his waistcoat, claw its way to his shoulder, and collapse across it, worn out.

Farrar's laughter died abruptly. The tiger's tracks were clear upon the snowy table linen. Blue, red, and yellow. "Oh—Gad!" he groaned, and looked down at himself. Small paw prints now decorated coat and waistcoat. Colourful, but decidedly unorthodox. "You furry imp," he said, "you've been in my palette!"

"Sir Anthony, I cannot find—" Hurrying into the room, Dimity paused and scanned the debacle. "Oh, dear!"

His heart leaping, Farrar came around the table to her. "Miss Mitten—how lovely you are."

She smiled up at his handsome, battered face, wondering how to tell him the whole truth. Once she did so, this idyll would be done. She had only these few days—hours, perhaps—with this man; this strange mixture of strength and cowardice of whom, against all common sense, she became more fond with each passing moment.

Farrar, watching her with the eyes of love, said gravely, "Yes. It is quite hopeless, my dear." She flinched and started to speak, but he put his fingers over her lips and said, his voice low and husky with emotion, "You will never—never know how unspeakably dark my life was, until you came. You can never begin to imagine what it meant to me to learn to laugh again. To see your disgust of me begin to fade into—I dare to think—a kinder feeling. Now," he lowered his hand, "what is it that you are unable to find?"

Fighting tears, she said quaveringly, "Yes, I think—I mean— Oh, I cannot find Carlton anywhere. I have searched and searched, but—"

"Sir . . . Uncle . . ."

They both turned in response to that desperate, gasping voice. Carlton, dishevelled and very red in the face, staggered across the hall and reached out to Farrar. "Nasty . . . Captain," he gulped. "Coming. Ran . . . miles . . ."

Holding the boy's hands strongly, Farrar sent a strained glance to Dimity.

"Tony!" she whispered, the colour draining from her cheeks, "Ah, no! My God, no!"

Horses were clattering along the drivepath. She heard Captain Holt's harsh voice and her heart shrank. Leonard and two footmen hastened to the front doors. Farrar lifted the somnolent kitten from his shoulder and handed it to the tearful child.

Carlton pleaded, "Go, sir! Run quick, and you—you might—"

"Thank you," said Farrar, "but—to run away does not seem to serve very well. If I should have to leave for a while, you take care of her for me, please."

The boy took the yawning kitten, but could not speak.

Farrar reached out and Dimity flew to take his hand. He pressed her fingers to his lips, turned his cheek against them for an instant, then walked swiftly into the hall.

Captain Holt marched through the front doors, waving aside Leonard's attempted intervention.

Aware that his aunt had come halfway down the spiral staircase and paused there, Farrar said quietly, "Captain, I am—"

Holt's cold eyes had widened when they saw the oddly decorated waistcoat and bruised features, but he now interposed, "You are the victim of a fraud, sir! This woman is not Mrs. Catherine Deene. Her name is Miss Dimity Clement."

For an instant, Farrar was weak with relief.

Dimity, on the other hand, felt quite sick.

"You will be so good, madam," the officer growled, "as to explain your reasons for the impersonation. And to produce your identification papers. At once!"

"I see no need for you to take that tone with the lady," frowned Farrar, recovering his wits.

"What you see is of no slightest interest to me, sir," snapped Holt. "Since you are obviously not startled by the news of her imposture, perhaps you are in this with her. Faith, but it'd not astound—"

Taken aback, Farrar demanded, "In—what?"

"A dangerous rebel was cornered six nights ago on the North Downs. He managed to give our men the slip, although he was known to be wounded. He last was seen riding near Basingstoke, and—"

"And you think that this lady might be your rebel? Jove, sir, but you've a fervid imagination!"

Holt flushed and said grittily, "I think she might well have given him aid. Why else would she hide by stealing the identity of another lady?" His chin jutting, he growled, "Have you a better explanation, Miss Clement? You would do well to tell the truth, else it will go hard on you *and* your accomplices!"

Her brothers and Tio must not come under suspicion. And there was the cypher—above all, that little document must be kept safe. It would mean more lies, but . . .

"Well, ma'am?" grated Holt. "Your papers?"

Lady Helen was coming to them, and the servants stood about, watching anxiously. There was not a doubt in her mind but that Farrar would fight to get her clear if it came down to that, and he had sufficient trouble. She gathered her courage. "I have no papers," she admitted. "I left my home in such a flame I brought only my horse and my purse."

"A likely story," sneered Holt. "A lady riding alone after dark and in the howling storm there was on that night!"

"I *had* to ride after dark. 'Twas the only way I could escape my brothers. They—they would never have let me come."

"Indeed? And where is this magical disappearing horse, pray tell?"

"A gypsy lad stabled him for me in Short Shrift."

"Describe the animal, if you please."

"He is a tall bay stallion named Odin."

The sergeant who had followed Holt volunteered, "The reb rode a big black, sir."

"I am aware of that," flared Holt testily. "Your tale makes little sense, madam. There remain the matters of the stolen child, the stolen identity, your masquerade here. For what reason save but to hide yourself?"

Her heart aching, she said, "I had meant to come here from the start. I just never dreamed to be given so golden an opportunity."

Farrar turned his head and stared at her.

"And may we be favoured with the real name of so designing a lady?" asked Holt, ironically.

She bit her lip. "I am Miss Dimity Cranford." From the corner of her eye she saw Farrar's right hand clench tight, and rushed on, "My twin brothers fought in Captain Farrar's battery at the Battle of Prestonpans. One of them was maimed for life because—''

''Oho . . . !'' said Holt, with a suddenly amused glance at the rigid and motionless Farrar. ''So you'd vengeance in mind, had you, ma'am? Commendable. What exactly had you hoped to accomplish, eventually?''

''You underestimate the lady. She *has* accomplished her objective.'' Farrar bowed cynically. ''You are a splendid actress, Miss Cranford.''

The grin faded from Holt's face. He eyed Dimity narrowly. ''Is she indeed?'' he murmured.

He was not convinced. Somehow, her tone harsher than she guessed, Dimity said, ''It is nigh to a year since Prestonpans, Captain Holt. We lost two dear friends there, and my brother was—was a splendid athlete. He will never walk easily again. That this—'' she gestured scornfully towards Farrar ''—this creature should be allowed to go free is a national disgrace!''

Confused and frightened, Carlton came to stand directly in front of her and tug at her hand. ''But—but Aunty Mitten—'' he pleaded.

''Be quiet. You do not understand,'' she said sharply, and squeezed his hand in a silent, desperate warning.

Holt looked from the tall hauteur of the girl to Farrar's set white face, and burst into a hearty laugh. ''By Jupiter, ma'am, but you've more than your share of gumption! I'll wager your brothers will have your ears for this, but were you *my* sister, I'd be dashed proud, I can tell you! As for you, sir,'' he turned to Farrar, ''the boy's aunt has recovered and will be here very soon, I've no doubt. And when *that* one descends on you, you will assuredly wish Miss Cranford had *really* been Mrs. Deene!''

Farrar looked at him without comment.

Not for the first time, something in those steady eyes made Holt uneasy. He bowed to Dimity. ''I offer you my escort, Miss Cranford. You'll have no wish to stay here.''

''I shall be quite safe with Lady Helen, thank you. I have sent off a letter to my brothers, you see, and expect them momentarily, so there is no need for me to delay you whilst I pack.''

As it chanced, Holt was most anxious to ride over to Fayre Hall to nose about a little. He was fond of Roland, but it did not pay to let that one have too long a rein. He hesitated.

Farrar, torn between rage and a bitter desolation, kept his eyes fixed on the stained-glass window. He knew that he had brought all this on himself, and it was as well it should end now and in just this fashion.

Lady Helen said, "I will vouch for Mrs.—Miss Cranford's safety, Captain. I cannot but be in sympathy with her, you know."

At this, Farrar's iron control faltered. He jerked his head away and walked swiftly from the room.

Holt said dubiously, "You are sure, ma'am? He would not . . . er . . . ?"

"Take out his anger on us? No. Whatever else, my nephew would never harm a woman."

"Very well, my lady, I'll take you at your word. As a matter of fact, there is another matter I've to attend to. Miss Cranford— my deepest respects."

"Thank you, Captain. Pray tell Mrs. Deene that I shall replace her wardrobe at my very first opportunity."

He glanced at Carlton. "What about the boy? I doubt Mrs. Deene is well enough to cope, but—"

Lady Helen said, "He may stay here until his aunt is able to claim him."

"You are very good, ma'am." Saluting, he bade them good day and marched outside, followed by his men.

Through a taut silence Dimity hurried to the window, watched them ride from sight, then ran up the steps. In the music hall the servants stood about in little knots, staring at her. She flew to where Cissie and Rodgers whispered together. "Where is the master?"

Rodgers said with frank hostility, "Ahem—reckon you've done about enough to him, miss. I'll say nought."

Dimity glanced up. Jordan stood on the stairs watching her with a troubled face. He hesitated, then jerked his head towards the back of the house. With a grateful smile she fled.

The chapel was empty. Nor was there any sign of his tall figure in the stableyard. She ran across the park for a short way, then turned into the rose gardens at the west side of the house.

Farrar stood gazing at the sundial, his shoulders very straight, his hands clasped loosely behind him.

With a flurry of skirts, Dimity flew to his side. "Anthony—you must have understood! *Please* say you understood!"

He turned to her, his eyes blank and expressionless. "Deceit on deceit. Lie on lie," he drawled. "Are you done now, Madame Vengeance? Did you plan to make me fall in love with you and then—deride me? Or is this just the first step in my chastisement?"

"No! No! Tony—please. You must listen!"

He beat away the frantic hands that sought to grasp his arm, and turned on her in a sudden blaze of fury. "*Listen* is it? Madam, I have listened till my ears ring with it! I'll give you credit for one thing—you wrapped me round your little finger easily enough. Like a—a blind fool, I thought I'd found—" The harsh words ceased. His mouth twisted into a bitter smile. "Which would have been most unfair, after all. You are to be congratulated, Miss Cranford. Your woman's wiles are—stronger than . . . than the whole damned army!"

He turned away, a dreary resignation replacing that searing wrath. And he looked so haggard, so lost that she ran in front of him and, desperate, begged, "Tony—my dearest, if you will just—"

Anguished by the form of endearment, he seized her arms and shook her savagely. "For the love of God, go *away* from here! Enjoy your triumph and *leave me be*!"

"No! I haven't—"

A wild thunder of hooves, shouts of wrath, and Dimity gave a shriek. "Piers! Perry! Oh, thank heaven!"

Piers was out of the saddle while his mare yet ran. He landed, staggering, and raced at Farrar, his face murderous. "Unhand my sister, damn your eyes!"

"No!" screamed Dimity, as Farrar thrust her clear.

Piers' fist whipped back. With another squeal, Dimity threw herself at Farrar and clung desperately.

"Get away . . . dammit!" grated Farrar, struggling.

"Let her go, you blackguard," roared Peregrine, scrambling erratically from the saddle, "or I'll—Blast and damn, my foot's gone again! Piers—grass the dirty villain!"

"Mitten," raged Piers, dancing about. "Can't you get out of the way?"

Lord Glendenning, very pale, rode up and more or less slid

from the saddle. "Mitten—thank heaven you're safe," he gasped, clinging to the stirrup. "Take your filthy hands—off her, Farrar!"

"I am—trying," groaned Farrar, tugging at Dimity's hands fast clasped behind his neck.

"What're you messing about at, Piers?" howled Peregrine, sitting on the lawn wrestling with a buckle. "Kill the bastard!"

"Well, curse it all, I will, can I just get Mitten away. He won't let her go!"

"Hiding behind . . . a girl . . ." gasped my lord, swaying and livid. He advanced, lifting one wavering fist. "I challenge you . . . Captain . . ." and he struck Piers in the eye and fainted.

"Ow!" yelled Piers.

"Tio!" sobbed Dimity.

"I accept your challenge," said Farrar, beginning to grin, despite himself.

"And mine, blast your eyes!" groaned Piers.

"And mine," raged Peregrine. "So soon as I get my foot on."

"Could we call a truce," suggested Farrar, "so that someone can help poor Glendenning?"

"All right, Perry?" called Piers, clutching his eye. "Tio's gone off again."

"Yes, of course. Mitten—did this libertine harm you?"

"No, no," said Dimity, running to kneel beside Glendenning. "I am so grateful that dear Tio is alive, but—oh, how ill he looks. You should never have brought him!"

"*Brought* him!" Piers crossed to blink down at Glendenning. "I'd like to have seen anyone keep him from coming. Silly idiot."

"Farrar," called Peregrine. "Give a hand here, will you?"

Farrar went over and knelt beside him. He stared at the mutilated leg for a minute, then looked up into the thin young face. "Charged to my account, I fancy," he said quietly. "I'm most terribly sorry, Cranford."

"I got off lucky, compared to some of my friends," Peregrine said rather brutally. "However, we can remedy that when I blow a hole through you." Farrar gave him a measuring look, and he added apologetically, "I know you have the choice of weapons, sir, but—I can't very well use a smallsword, you see."

"Of course," agreed Farrar politely. "Only I'm afraid you shall have to wait your turn."

"I claim first chance at you," said Peregrine. "My brother won't mind. Oh, that's very good. Thank you." He stood, and with Farrar's aid limped to where Dimity and Piers ministered to Glendenning. "Piers, old lad, you'll not object do I have first crack at—My God!"

They all stared at him.

"Mitten!" he gasped, scarlet. "What the *devil* are you wearing?"

Piers, who had been kneeling behind his sister, had his first full view as she turned to look up at Peregrine. "The deuce!" he exclaimed, flinging a shielding arm across the embarrassment. "Farrar! Turn your prying eyes away! Mitten, take that disgraceful thing off, at once!"

Glendenning, who had opened his eyes, said feebly, "Better not, Mitten." And with a faint grin murmured, "Matter of fact, I think it jolly—er, becoming."

"Becoming for a skirt," said Peregrine, taking off his coat and wrapping it primly around Dimity. "But where in the deuce is the top piece? By Jove, Farrar, but you'll pay for shaming my sister. How dare you put such a wicked frock on her?"

"What leads you to suppose I had a hand in what your sister wears?" asked Farrar in a rather unfortunate turn of phrase.

"By God, I'd best not find you had a hand in—" cried Peregrine, then broke off, turning an even deeper shade of red. "Ah, th-that is to say—"

"You've said too much already," interposed Glendenning faintly. "Mitten—forgive me for interrupting these tangled threads, but—did you deliver my—er, message?"

She tore her gaze from Farrar's fascinated expression. "What? Oh—yes, Tio. Never fret."

"Thank the good Lord," he sighed.

Farrar bent over him. "Shall I send for a hurdle, Tio? Or would you prefer we carry you?"

"I think I can manage, if you'll just help me up."

Farrar slipped an arm about him and lifted cautiously. Supporting Glendenning on the other side, Piers said, "I'm sorry, Perry. You asked me something, I think?"

Farrar said, "He wants to know if he can have first crack at fighting me. I'm afraid he cannot. I'm already booked for the morning.''

"Well, that's a fine state of affairs, I must say," grumbled Peregrine. "With whom?"

"Your sister's friend, Rafe. What happened to you, Tio?" And a sudden crazily logical explanation for all Dimity's false-hoods causing his heart to leap, he added, "Nothing to do with de Villars, I hope?"

" 'Fraid so," murmured his lordship, who had pushed himself too soon and too hard in the desperate search for Dimity. "Be safer if you . . . do not take me in your house."

"Take you *in* it?" snorted Peregrine. "I should rather think we shall *not* take you in it! I can scarce wait to know for how long my *sister* has been in it, and you may be sure I'll have a few words to say to you, Mitten, at which time, among other things, I shall require to know who is this 'Rafe' fella."

Farrar put in quickly, "He is a neighbour who meant to kill me, but killed my dog instead, which is why—"

The small party came to an abrupt halt at this, the twins staring in shocked disbelief.

"Killed your *dog*?" gasped Peregrine. "I should *hope* you mean to fight the beastly fellow! Sorry, Mitten, but whether or not he is a friend of yours, anyone who'd kill another man's dog ain't fit to go!"

"Of course he is not a friend, silly," she said. "He's Tio's friend, not mine. I never met him until I came here, and I must say, Tio dear, he is a *very* nasty man."

Lord Glendenning, whose dizzied head had sunk onto his chest, raised it and blinked at the blurred shape he rather sup-posed was Dimity. "Don't mean to—to contradict, m'dear," he faltered, "but—I'm not acquainted with anyone named Rafe, that . . . I can recall."

"Well, that's not his true name, of course," she said, with an uneasy glance to Farrar, "but—*you* know who I mean. He's the—er, gentleman you sent me to find. Mr. Green . . ."

"Oh—*damme*!" groaned Peregrine.

Glendenning's hand clamped hard onto Farrar's supporting arm. He gasped, "D-devil he . . . is! By God, Mitten—what have you done?"

Paling, she stammered, "Well, I-I . . . Oh Tio, you *said* 'Fayre' and 'Hall'—and D-Decimus Green, and—"

Vastly intrigued, Farrar interpolated, "But Green's name is not Decimus, ma'am."

Beginning to be really terrified, she blurted, "Only because he does not choose to use it. Your aunt told me he prefers to be called Rafe. Oh—*pray* do not frighten me so!"

"*Frighten* you!" sputtered Piers. "Do you realize—"

Farrar lifted an autocratic hand. "Miss Cranford, Green's given name is Oliver. Decimus Green is a nearby hamlet, not a man."

She gave a squeak of terror and clutched Peregrine's arm.

Appalled, Glendenning said threadily, "My fault, likely . . . I said 'fair'—meaning the colouring of the man to whom you were to give it, and if I said 'all,' Mitten, I—I must have been trying to tell you his name."

"Charles Albritton?" murmured Farrar, surprised. "The clergyman?"

"Mitten," groaned the viscount. "You—you didn't . . . ?"

Pressing clasped hands to her whitening lips, she whimpered, "Oh! My God, how can I have been such a widgeon? I tried. I really tried! But—I *did*, Tio! I gave the cypher to Mr. Rafe Green, and he is the most horrid man you could imagine!"

"Holy . . . Christ!" groaned Glendenning, and fainted again.

⍟ Chapter 13 ⍟

Lady Helen was upstairs fussing over Horatio Glendenning, who had been put to bed; Peregrine was stretched out on the sofa in the bookroom, looking broodingly at his foot; and Piers stood by the fireplace, glass in hand. Dimity, who at last had felt able to beg a fichu from Lady Helen and was thus considerably more at ease, sat in the great elbow chair, sipping at a glass of cowslip wine. Despite her preoccupation with this disastrous turn of events, she was also pondering the complete inconsistency of the male animal for, although both her brothers and Glendenning had called out Farrar, at the moment they appeared to find it perfectly convenable to accept his hospitality, drink his wine, and converse upon treasonable matters in his presence.

"What boggles me," said Piers, fixing Dimity with a darkling look, "is how you could have seized upon those four words—Fair, All, and Decimus Green—and managed to concoct such a farradiddle!"

"Could you not have taken one look at the varmint and seen he was no gentleman?" demanded Peregrine. "Any fellow who would train a dog to slaughter his enemy instead of coming slap up to him himself is merest scum, Mitten. Dashitall, have we taught you nothing?"

She blushed and said miserably, "I am very, very sorry. I have made wretched work of it!"

Farrar, who had been sitting on the reference table at the side of the pleasant room, stood, and said hotly, "No such thing! You did wonderfully well!"

"Well?" cried Piers, rounding on him. "Lord only knows

215

how many men have died for that damnable cypher, and what must my sister do but—''

"Risk her life to lead the dragoons away from Tio? Come into the home of a man she has every right to—to despise, and run all manner of risks only so as to try to complete a mission so deadly few men would dare tackle it? She is a true heroine and one you should be proud of, instead of—''

This defence won him a glowing look from Dimity, but Peregrine interpolated wrathfully, "We do not need *you*, Farrar, to be telling us of the value of our sister! Furthermore, *you* ain't in this mess, and come to that—By the bye, are you acquainted with Glendenning?''

Farrar said in a quieter voice, "Any time these ten years. He's a splendid fellow.''

"He don't hold the same opinion of you, sir,'' snapped Piers.

Farrar reddened painfully. He drew back, and his eyes fell. "No. Well—that is only to be expected.''

Dimity glared at her brother and with difficulty restrained an indignant comment.

Peregrine shifted and pointed out uncomfortably, "Not very sporting, old boy. After all, we *are* under his roof, and we *did* agree to a truce, y'know.''

His twin pursed up his lips. "So we did. Sorry, Farrar.''

"An I may venture an observation,'' said Farrar diffidently, "the most important thing now is to get the cypher back.''

"Hah!'' said Peregrine. "I wish I may see it! Your Green rascal is likely claiming the reward this very instant!''

"If he knows he has it, in the first place,'' Farrar qualified. "And if he knows *what* it is, in the second.'' They stared at him and he went on, "I don't mean to be interfering in your business, but—Green was at best half-conscious when Miss Cranford slipped the cypher into his pocket.''

"But—I whispered to him what I'd done,'' sighed Dimity mournfully.

"Still, Farrar's got a point,'' argued Piers. "If Green was halfway out of time, he might not have heard you—or understood what you said.''

Peregrine put in, "But surely his man would have found the curst thing by this time?''

"He might,'' acknowledged Farrar. "However, with all the

216

excitement, it is not beyond the bounds of possibility that the coat was either hung up, or set aside to be cleaned, or that, even if his man went through the pockets, so small a piece of parchment as you've described, may have gone unnoticed.''

"Jupiter! 'Tis a possibility!'' His blue eyes brightening, Piers asked, ''How can we get into the beastly place?''

"You might be admitted,'' Farrar said thoughtfully. ''Green is often in his cups, and if you're not known to him, you could claim a mutual friend. Unless—are you by chance acquainted with Roland Otton?''

Piers scowled. ''He was pointed out to me in Town once. And I've heard a few things. Bounty hunter, ain't he? Well-born but a regular scoundrel, and no longer received anywhere.''

"He is received at Rafe Green's,'' said Farrar dryly. ''Seconding him tomorrow.''

"Is he, by Jove,'' said Peregrine. ''Who's seconding you?''

Farrar hesitated. ''Chandler, I hope. Does he return in time.''

"Chandler?'' echoed Piers. ''Of Lac Brillant?'' He exchanged an incredulous glance with his brother.

Divining the cause of their surprise, Farrar flushed. ''Yes. Well, I hope he will.''

"Be damned!'' muttered Peregrine.

Shaking his head, Piers asked, ''What if he don't come back in time? Who else have you?''

Farrar stared at his glass and said awkwardly, ''I—er, can ask my butler, and—my doctor's agreed to be the surgeon—he might be willing to do double duty.''

"Good God! A fellow don't have his *butler* second him in a duel,'' exclaimed Peregrine, shocked.

Piers said severely, ''No, and surgeons make frightful seconds. Hate the business and don't have a gnat's notion of how to go on. Never met a doctor yet who knew one end of a sword from t'other. It won't serve, Farrar!''

Sighing, Peregrine said, ''I suppose we'll have to do it.''

Farrar, reeling, expostulated faintly, ''You cannot—second me! You're both *fighting* me as soon as my affair with Green is settled.''

"Not both at once,'' Peregrine pointed out, with obscure logic.

Piers grinned. ''There you are! Not both at once!''

Stunned, Farrar stared at them.

"Anthony," began Dimity, eagerly.

"Hey!" flared Piers.

"Oh. I mean—Sir Anthony. Piers is right! It might serve us very well!"

His eyes caressed her. He asked gently, "In what way, ma'am?"

"Well, Perry has been rather active in this duelling business, and I gather it is customary for seconds to meet *before* a duel and attempt to avert it. No?"

A smile hovering about his mouth, he murmured, "How very clever of you, Miss Cranford."

Leonard came in. "Mr. Gordon Chandler."

Greatly relieved, Farrar went with hand outstretched to greet his friend. "Gordie, how timely is your arrival! Thank you for coming."

Staring in astonishment at the Cranford twins, Chandler, quietly elegant in green and gold, said, "My pleasure, old fellow. Mrs. Deene—your humble, obedient. How are you, Perry?"

Peregrine reached up to shake his hand. "Splendid, thank you. Won't get up though, Chandler. Have to put my stupid foot on again, if I do. And m'sister's name is Miss Cranford—not Mrs. Deene."

Passing him, his brows lifting, Chandler bowed over Dimity's fingers. "I'll not pretend to understand, ma'am, but I am most pleased to find you still here."

"Glendenning's here, too," imparted Piers, in turn shaking hands, "so do not be getting overly pleased."

Farrar shot a quick glance at Dimity, who smiled at him demurely.

"Your business with Treve happily concluded?" enquired Farrar, passing a glass of sherry to Chandler, and proceeding to refill the glasses of the Cranfords.

"Concluded, but not happily," replied Chandler, looking grim.

"Not surprised," said Peregrine. "Treve's likely fretting for the same business that is giving us pepper at the moment."

Chandler assumed a commendably blank expression. "We shall have to chat about it." He set his glass down. "First though, I'd best have a word with Tio. Is he about?"

"About to expire by the look of him," muttered Peregrine.

"Perry!" exclaimed Dimity, distressed.

"What, is old Tio ill then?" asked Chandler anxiously.

"And upstairs," nodded Farrar.

"Tried to bounce a musket ball off his noggin," explained Peregrine.

"And is thus being pampered by Lady Helen," said his brother.

"Oh, Gad," said Chandler, in dismay. "When was he shot?"

"Last Saturday," answered Piers. "You—ah, know about the cypher, I take it?"

Chandler looked from one to the other and took the risk. "I do. Where is it?"

"Dimity had it off Tio," said Piers with a sigh.

"And mislaid it," said Peregrine.

Chandler lost all his colour and dropped his wineglass.

Tugging at the bell rope, Farrar said, "On a lighter note, Gordie, would you be so very good as to second me in a duel tomorrow morning?"

Dazedly, Chandler sat down.

Farrar drew Poli to a halt at the top of the hill, looked out across the sultry night to the far glimmer of Fayre Hall's windows, and reined around as the carriage lumbered up. The door was swung open, and Piers jumped out without letting down the steps and walked over to join him.

Dismounting, Farrar said, "Cranford, this is ridiculous. Your brother won't be able to move fast do we have to make a run for it."

"You tell him so," said Piers. "If truth be told, Farrar, you've sufficient trouble on your hands without sticking your nose into our tangle." He saw the immediate, almost shrinking withdrawal in the other man, so at odds with his remembered military demeanour, and appended hurriedly, "And if it comes to being fit, by what my sister tells me your arm ain't in just perfect condition to wield a sword tomorrow."

"Is my left arm. And as for tonight, I wish you will persuade your twin to stay with you and Chandler."

"Green would not be like to believe an invalid is to second

you, and you *must* have someone at your back. Use your brains, man! Do those hounds catch one whiff of Farrar, they'll finish the job they started! Perry has some notion his mixture will put them off, if you insist on this chancy business.''

Farrar said humbly, ''I know the house, and Green's room. I know which coat to seek. But—I'd not force you to accept my aid. If—if you are offended by my proximity, I will of course, stay clear.''

There was an instant of silence. Then, Piers said gruffly, ''Further, your slyness in keeping from Gordon the fact that Otton will be there, I heartily mislike. Is unfair to allow him to discover it at the last minute. Lord only knows how I shall keep him from the bastard's throat! Zounds, but had Otton visited his atrocities upon Perry, I know how *I'd* react upon meeting him face to face!''

'' 'Tis what I count on. There will be an uproar, to say the least of it, that will, I hope, draw attention to the front of the house while your brother and I creep in the back.''

Piers grunted and started towards Poli. ''What a murky stew this is! When I fought against Stuart, I little dreamed a year later I'd be risking my neck for his people!''

Farrar smiled faintly. ''Nor I.''

Halting again, Piers said, ''No. Well—I fancy—Ah, that is to say . . . Any silly fellow can let a gun carriage roll over his foot.'' Farrar tensed and was silent. With a small embarrassed cough, Piers went on, ''My twin and I were thinking before dinner of—of what m'sister *might* have—er, encountered. You've been pretty decent, considering the dance she led you.''

''Thank you.''

''Yes. And—ah, we wondered . . . I mean if there was any— Well, sometimes in battle, things can become—Mistakes happen. The—ah, wrong interpretations can be—er, placed on—If you thought . . . something of that nature . . . ?''

There was a brief pause, then Farrar said clearly, ''Regrettably, there was no mistake. But thank you for the chance.''

He walked to the carriage and swung up onto the box beside his coachman.

To lessen the risk of Farrar being recognized at the gatehouse, it had been decided he would take the guard's place on the coach, and in order to provide him a fast escape if that became necessary, Piers rode Poli as escort. When they approached the gates Farrar pulled collar high and tricorne low, but the precautions proved unnecessary. If there was a gatekeeper he was either sleeping or elsewhere. Piers dismounted and opened the gates wide, and the carriage passed through unchallenged.

They separated now. Piers rode into the trees and proceeded to the west side of Fayre Hall. The carriage rolled eastward at a very slow pace, stopping before it reached the front steps of the enormous mansion. Farrar swung down and assisted Peregrine to alight. The team was started up again, and the two men crept along on the off-side of the coach. Piers hissed at them from the bushes opposite the front steps, and they went to join him.

"All clear," he whispered breathlessly. "I tethered Poli under that acacia tree where the drive turns round to the rear of the west wing. No sign of man's best friend." He wrinkled his nose. "Egad, Perry, what the devil is in that jar you brought? Smells like rotten fish!"

"Just what it is, my pippin. Had it from Farrar's cook. Strongest smell I know, except bad eggs. Once we're in the rear court I'll simply sprinkle it about and, are the dogs on the prowl, they'll never detect Farrar. You'd best make haste!"

Piers made a dart for the carriage and scrambled inside just before the butler opened the great front door.

Farrar led Peregrine in amongst the shrubs along the west side of the mansion and around the darkened rooms to the rear. "They seldom use this part," he whispered. "Place is too large to keep heated, and it's full of dry rot, besides."

Their plans had been based on Farrar's knowledge that Green usually kept Town hours and that, with luck, he and his guests would now be in the dining room which faced east and was located towards the front of the ground floor. With a little more luck the rear court between the two wings would be darkened, enabling them to reach the court door unseen. When they arrived at the back of the mansion, however, they were dismayed to find that several of the east windows were lighted, throwing long bright rectangles across the court. "Damn!" muttered Farrar. "They must have dined early. That's the bookroom. Keep your pistol cocked, Cranford."

221

Peregrine, who had been leaning on his arm, relinquished it, and drew a pistol from his pocket. "All ready!" he whispered. "Be off with you! And good luck!"

Farrar trod soft-footed into the court. Below the bookroom windows it was quite dark. He edged nearer, dropped to his knees and started to crawl.

Peregrine tucked the pistol under his arm and watched Farrar anxiously while unscrewing the top of his jar. He took a whiff and clapped the top on again, gasping. After a few restoring gulps of air, he held his breath, opened the jar once more, and began to sprinkle the contents across the open end of the court.

Farrar, meanwhile, still on hands and knees, had paused and was listening to a burst of drunken laughter followed by Phillip Ellsworth's rich voice, blurred but understandable. "Who— Otton?" he cried, hilariously. "Lord, Rafe, that mercenary rascal'd be easy's the deuce t'buy off. Only jingle a purse of gold, my tulip, an' Rolan' Otton'll forget it if he sees you murder th'—th' king himself!"

"Ain't talking 'bout murder," argued Green, sounding offended. "Li'l slip in a duel ain't m—murder, Phillip."

"Even so, 'f it don't go quite as planned, y'might want to hire Otton to finish the job. Damned fine swordsman."

His grim face grimmer, Farrar yearned to stay and hear more of this fascinating conversation, but every minute counted so he crawled past the light area, then moved swiftly to the rear door. It was unlocked, but squeaked as he opened it. Holding his breath, he slipped into the long dark hall just as a wild uproar exploded at the front of the house.

Roland Otton was unimpressed with either Fayre Hall's stables or its grooms. He therefore excused himself directly after dinner and slipped out to check on the well-being of his horse. Returning by way of the east hall a short while later, he heard a thunderous assault on the front door and, curious, turned his steps in that direction.

The butler's small procession wound its ponderous way across the gloom of the Great Hall, and the lackeys opened the doors. Two men stepped inside. The first was a tall young fellow with a lean, finely cut face and an air of breeding. Otton wandered nearer. The second man, who had been partially screened from view by the butler's figure, was abruptly before him. The two locked glances and the result was electrifying. Two hands whipped to sword hilts, save that Otton had not carried arms this evening.

"*Otton . . . !*" hissed Gordon Chandler, and sprang forward, his pleasant features dark with hatred, his sword leaping into his hand.

Otton made a mad dash for the umbrella stand, tore a walking cane from it, and swung it to the guard position.

"Chandler!" shouted Piers at the top of his lungs. "No—you lamebrain!"

"Gentlemen! I beg you will refrain!" cried the butler, sprinting out of range.

Maddened by the sight of this man who two months earlier had helped brutalize his wounded brother, Chandler was deaf to their protests. Otton sprang nimbly aside, evading Chandler's enraged lunge, and waited, eyes bright, cane circling warily.

"Filth!" snarled Chandler, thrusting hard, his blade turned by Otton's deft parry. "Dirty, worthless . . . scum!"

"Temper . . . temper," Otton scolded, retreating, but contriving to either deflect or elude the fierce attacks of that deadly blade.

A footman with more spunk than the butler ran up behind Chandler and grasped his sword arm, whereupon Piers was obliged to seize his other arm. "Are you gone quite daft?" he roared.

Struggling furiously, Chandler shouted, "Let me *go*, damn you!"

"Otton has no weapon, you madman! Have done!"

At last, the words pierced Chandler's wrath. He ceased his efforts and stood trembling with passion, sweat gleaming on his flushed face and horror coming into his eyes at this unforgivable breach of the Code of Honour. "Oh . . . Gad!" he gasped.

"What the . . . *devil* . . . ?" Mr. Oliver Green came swiftly across the Great Hall, Phillip Ellsworth beside him. "Are you ripe for Bedlam, sir?"

Flushed with mortification, Chandler sheathed his sword and muttered, "My apologies. Unhappily, I have a prior acquaintance with this scoundrel."

Otton flourished the cane in salute. "Our paths have crossed—I'll own," he admitted, with his insolent half-smile and only a trace of breathlessness.

Chandler said harshly, "Our *steel* will cross tomorrow!"

"I do but second my principal, sir," Otton pointed out with saintly forbearance.

"We'll see that," rasped Chandler.

Cranford intervened, performing rapid introductions.

Conveniently forgetting his own recent lapse, Ellsworth said disdainfully, " 'Tis my opinion you owe the captain an apology, sir."

Chandler had a sudden picture of his illustrious father's inevitable reaction to the atrocious act he had just committed, and his eyes fell. Raising them, he looked into Otton's sardonic grin and somehow managed to say a more or less polite, "You have my—apologies, Captain Carrion."

Otton considered him reflectively.

This encounter had caused a surprising number of servants to recall business that drew them to the vicinity of the Great Hall. Praying it had also granted Farrar the diversion he needed, Cranford announced, "We are come as representatives of Captain Sir Anthony Farrar."

Green put up his brows. "Are you, indeed? You surprise me." And encountering the interested gaze of three maids and a brace of lackeys, he added, "Let us conduct our business where we are less in the public eye . . . This way, gentlemen, if you please."

Farrar searched with desperate haste through the second of Rafe Green's wardrobes. One branch of candles had been lit when he first crept into the room and, suspecting this indicated the early return of the valet, he had raced to the larger press and ransacked it without success. Now, he thrust aside coats of velvet, brocade, satin, and silk; green and pale blue and brown coats; mulberry, gold and puce . . . but not one of dark blue. Reaching the end of the rack, he spun about. Where else? The room was vast, having a great tester bed against the right-hand wall, chests of drawers and a dressing table between the windows, the presses on this side and, near the bed, a door that probably led to a dressing room. He sprinted over and flung it open, thus waking the man who had been softly snoring on a trundle bed.

Farrar's shock was augmented by instant action. He flipped up the blanket that covered the man's legs to enfold his head instead, and as the valet started up with a muffled cry, seized a heavy riding crop and brought the handle down, hard. The valet sank back without a sound. Breathing hard, Farrar scanned the small chamber. A clothes rack held garments doubtless intended for the morrow; a tall whatnot was littered with spurs, whip thongs, several ruffles, and a heavy dog collar studded with iron points. And draped over a nearby chair was a torn blue coat.

With a gasp of triumph, he snatched it up and rummaged through the pockets. Nothing in the left one. He groped feverishly and in the deepest corner of the right pocket his fingers detected a small object that rustled. He retrieved it and smoothing the scrap of parchment, carried it closer to the candle and read what had been written in a fine hand:

4

All is quiet in the city.
See the pigeons in the square,
Indignant. Waiting for their corn or bread.
Is it not strange, and dead?
Enthralling to see the streets so bare.
Our mansion and hovel drifts snow, so white.
One will bring food to the pigeons tonight.

"Good Lord!" he muttered. But however incomprehensible, this *must* be the cypher on which so much depended. He shoved it into his pocket and glanced sympathetically at the valet. Poor devil, he thought, remembering how his own head had felt after just such a blow, but suspecting he'd not struck as hard as had Green's butler. He put a couple of guineas under the man's limp hand, then raced to the door, opened it a crack, and jumped back. Two chambermaids were walking, giggling, along the hall.

"Only fancy," trilled one, "drawing steel on a unarmed gent!"

"Quality," said the other derogatorily. "My Willyum may

225

be just a gardener, duck, but he wouldn't never do such a nasty thing as that there!''

'Glory!' thought Farrar, 'Cranford properly let Gordie run amok!'

''And such a handsome chap,'' said the first maid as they went on past.

''Who? My Willyum?''

''Go on, Joannie! I meant that there Captain Otton. What a wicked devil though! Pinched me today . . . right on me . . .''

The voices faded and a door opened and closed again to the accompaniment of soft laughter.

Farrar peeped into the hall once more and found it clear. He ran lightly to the back stairs, sprinted down them, and was out of the rear door in a flash.

He beheld chaos. Peregrine sat against the wall, softly groaning and struggling with his foot. His efforts were impeded by approximately five cats. Several more cats were busily engaged in licking their way across the open end of the courtyard. At a conservative estimate, Farrar judged there were possibly as many as a dozen felines in all. Chuckling, he started across the court, quite forgetting the lighted windows. He came face to face with Roland Otton, reaching out to shut a casement. For an instant they stared at each other. Then, Otton closed the casement and turned back into the room. Farrar raced to Peregrine and shooed away some of his admirers. ''You and your concoction,'' he said.

''Did you get it?''

''Yes. Are you all right?''

''Devil I am! One of these blasted cats jumped on my back. Scared hell out of me and I dropped the pistol. It's gone slithering into that damnable drain, I think. While I was crawling about trying to find it, my stupid foot came loose again! Won't take me a minute to tighten things up.''

''Better not wait. Otton saw me just now.''

''Oh, damme! You go, then.''

''Not likely! Come on!'' He hauled Peregrine to his feet, pulled one arm across his shoulders, and started off, half carrying him.

They'd gone only a short way when a distant outburst of deep bays split the silence.

"Sniffed you out, by God!" gasped Peregrine. "Run for it, man!" And looking, horrified, at the two dark, oncoming shapes, he thought, 'My God! They're monsters!'

Farrar let him go and ran for his life. He found Poli tethered beside the house, stamping impatiently, and with a flying leap was in the saddle. Wrenching the stallion's head around, he drove home his spurs. Poli reared in resentment and was off like the wind. Peregrine, trying to stand and sweating with unreasoning panic, heard the thundering hooves and reached up gratefully. Two muscular shapes hurtled across the lawn, emitting slobbering snarls and a deep terrible growling that sent a bevy of cats streaking madly in all directions. The mastiffs ignored them and raced single-mindedly for the man they had been trained to hate.

Farrar reached down.

Still clutching his empty jar, Peregrine waved him off. "Can't . . ." he gasped. "Go!"

Farrar was out of the saddle in a wild leap. "Get your foot in the stirrup," he panted. "Lean back on me."

The mastiffs, ravening, were horribly close. Peregrine threw all his weight on Farrar, got his left foot in the stirrup, and was tossed to the saddle. With a supple leap, Farrar mounted behind him. A snarling brute launched itself at him. Farrar grabbed Peregrine's jar and flailed wildly at the gnashing jaws, dreading lest those great teeth again tear into his flesh. The jar connected solidly with the dog's muzzle, and the beast fell back dazedly. The second mastiff raced at them as Poli sprang into his great stretching gallop. Farrar hurled the redolent jar at the brute. To the accompaniment of a cacophony of barks, howls, shouts from the stableyard, and a sudden commotion from the mansion, they raced around the west wing, up the slope, and were away.

"Excelsior!" cried Peregrine, elated. "Oh, I say Farrar! Jolly well done!"

❦ *Chapter 14* ❧

Dimity put down her cards as Lady Helen came into the music hall. "Is Carlton asleep, ma'am?"

"They both are. Poor Glendenning is worn to a shade."

My lady crossed to look over Dimity's shoulder. "How goes your Patience?"

"Poorly, I'm afraid. I do not seem able to concentrate."

"Likely your mind is occupied with other matters. Come and sit with me, my dear."

They repaired to the beige velvet sofa and sat side by side. "Now," said my lady, "perhaps you will be so kind as to tell me where all the men have gone. And why."

Dimity hesitated. It was obvious that Farrar's main mission in life was to spare this gentle lady all possible distress. Her hesitation was brief. She said coolly, "To arrange the duel, ma'am."

Lady Helen gave a gasp. "B-between my—my nephew and Rafe? Oh, lud! Who is to second Anthony? Chandler?"

"And my brother Piers."

Astounded, Helen exclaimed, "But—I had thought—"

She was interrupted by a commotion in the lower hall. Voices rose in anger and both women came to their feet. Leonard, considerably dishevelled, ran up the steps, but was sent sprawling before he could speak. A sergeant and a grinning trooper followed the impressive officer who marched across the room to offer a brisk salute and drawl with a curl of the lip, "Ladies, your butler appears to suffer from a mental incapacity. He cannot recall where his master is gone. I feel sure you can do better."

228

Dimity's heart began to hammer with fright. This young captain was extremely handsome and his dark blue eyes flickered over her with obvious approval, but the arrogance of his manner appalled her.

Also very frightened, my lady said sharply, "How dare you force your way into my home and abuse my servants? Your name, if you please."

He laughed. "Ecod, but you terrify me, madam!" He waved a hand gracefully. "Present me, Sergeant."

The sergeant stepped forward and said without expression, "Captain Brooks Lambert, me lady."

"Who simply desires to know, ma'am," said the officer, "where is Farrar?"

Leonard had struggled to his knees. The trooper gave a sly shove, and the butler sprawled again. With an indignant cry, Dimity ran to help him. The captain's gloved hand shot out and caught her arm, swinging her around so that she almost fell. "I did not give you permission to leave us, pretty one," he jeered.

Lady Helen started forward with an outraged exclamation.

Furious, Dimity slapped the soldier's face hard. He swore, his grip tightening brutally.

"That will do!" The slightly nasal voice fairly cracked across the room. Dimity heard Lambert curse softly, but he released her at once, and she whirled about to see a tall, slim lieutenant colonel stalking briskly up the steps, one hand on his sabre, and his hard dark eyes fairly hurling anger. "You forget yourself, Captain! We are here to question Sir Anthony Farrar. Not to abuse a lady!"

"This woman, sir, refuses—"

"Not surprisingly." The colonel's gaze fixed on Leonard, still sitting on the step. "Be so good as to assist that gentleman to his feet."

The sergeant hurried forward, only to be stopped by a look that he later described as having frizzled his liver.

"Captain . . . ?" the colonel said silkily.

His jaw set and his handsome features very red, Captain Lambert crossed to the butler and hauled him up.

Turning to the silent women, the colonel said, "You have my profound apologies, ladies. These are hard times and our duty a thankless and often frustrating one. I am Mariner Fotheringay and regret the necessity to intrude on your privacy."

"To the contrary, Colonel Fotheringay," said Lady Helen, her usually serene manner a little strained. "We cannot but be grateful for your intervention."

Fotheringay slanted a glance at the silent but seething captain that boded ill for that individual. "Will you pray be seated, ladies?"

Dimity and Lady Helen sat down again, and the colonel drew up a chair, but Captain Lambert and the two other soldiers remained standing. Dimity's nerves were tight. She scanned the colonel's face; the proud tilt to the strong chin, the narrow swoop of the nose, the disdainful twist to the thin lips, and the coldness of the unreadable dark eyes, and her heart sank. Brooks Lambert was a dangerous and probably ruthless man whose inner cruelty was hidden beneath an elegant appearance and handsome features. But for all his charming manners and chivalry, she sensed that it was the colonel who was the more to be feared.

"I understand your nephew is from home, ma'am," said Fotheringay affably. "I trust Sir Anthony is fully recovered of his wound?"

"He is, I thank you."

"I'm glad to hear it. So many, alas, were less fortunate, and I cannot help but wonder, you know, why you should be reluctant to divulge his whereabouts."

Startled by the abrupt shift of emphasis, my lady said, "I—I am not, sir. It was the manner in which we were asked that was—unsettling. My nephew visits at a neighbouring estate. If you are eager to speak with him you'll likely find him there."

'With a treasonable cypher in his pocket,' thought Dimity, suddenly very cold.

"My thanks, ma'am. Are you all right, Miss Cranford? You are so pale."

His smile was, she thought, as warm as that of a spider. "You must forgive me, sir," she said, trying to be calm when her heart was thumping so loudly she was sure the colonel must hear it. "I fear I am rather tired."

"I quite understand. I've had a busy day myself. In fact, do you have no objection, my lady, I shall wait here for your nephew, rather than seeking him."

Lambert grinned broadly.

Terrified that Farrar might in some way be involved with this frightful Jacobite business, my lady sought desperately for a logical reason to deny her home to these military men.

Colonel Fotheringay did not wait for her response, however, but turned to Lambert and snapped out crisp orders. "Warn the house servants and the grooms and stableboys that anyone attempting to inform Sir Anthony Farrar or those in his party that there are soldiers here, will be arrested and charged with aiding the king's enemies. Get our fellows out of sight. I want not a thread of a uniform to be visible. Sergeant, you will watch the road, and report to me the instant any coach or rider approaches. Fast!"

Lambert and the sergeant ran out.

Lady Helen sprang up with a cry of shock. "Colonel! I demand—"

"To know what I am about," he interposed, coming to his feet politely. "We seek a traitor, my lady. And we seek the message he carried and which he may well have passed on to friends. Your nephew is known to have deplored the actions of the Duke of Cumberland. Additionally, he has friends whose loyalties are—questionable, at best."

Frozen, Dimity thought, 'I wonder if he knows Tio is asleep upstairs!'

"Whatever you have heard," said Lady Helen desperately, "Farrar is loyal to his king and country!"

He bowed, and said with his thin smile, "In that case, ma'am, he has absolutely nothing to fear. It will, however, be necessary that we search him upon his return. Until then, pray be at ease. We will sit here together, like friendly, civilized people, and—wait . . ."

"You've trained your people well, by Jove," said Peregrine, panting a little as he leaned on Farrar's arm and toiled up the front steps. "That lad must have been waiting for us."

"He did come promptly, didn't he," murmured Farrar, wondering if Aunt Helen had told the grooms to be on the lookout for his return. The boy had seemed rather stiff and unsmiling when he took Poli's reins. And his hands had been so cold,

231

although the night was mild . . . Peregrine stumbled. "Easy," he said. "You're likely rather pulled after that ride."

"Not too bad. But I'll own it would have been easier had we waited for the coach."

"Yes. Only a horse, you know, is less conspicuous than a coach and four, and I'd as soon get this cypher tucked away as soon as may be."

"You're perfectly right, and I'm a gudgeon," said Peregrine apologetically, pausing to catch his breath as they reached the terrace. "You have it safe, of course?"

"In my waistcoat pocket." Farrar bent and scooped up Swimmer as she charged in a fierce attack upon his boot. "Here's another welcoming committee." He straightened the wide scarlet ribbon Carlton had tied around the kitten's tiny neck, and glanced up with a smile as the front door was swung open. "Thank you, Leonard. Have the ladies retired?"

"No, sir," said the butler woodenly, following them across the lower hall. "May I be of assistance, Mr. Cranford?"

Irritated, Peregrine replied that he could manage perfectly well, and clung to the railing, dragging himself upward with weary determination and mentally consigning all stairs to perdition.

Farrar slowed his own steps and kept an eye on his companion. Cranford was pluck to the backbone, but he'd been pushed to the limit tonight.

"Good evening, gentlemen."

Little feathers of ice seemed to shiver down Farrar's spine. He heard Peregrine draw a hissing breath and, looking up, saw the tall, erect military figure, the cold disdainful face. He glanced swiftly to Leonard, who gave a wry shrug.

"You must not blame your butler, Farrar," said the colonel. "Your servants were instructed not to warn you that we were here."

Over the red-uniformed shoulder Farrar saw his aunt and Dimity standing watching, their faces pale and strained.

"Not another search, surely?" he drawled, allowing the squirming kitten to drop to the floor. "This becomes monotonous, Colonel."

Fotheringay shrugged. "I believe it was Euripides who said that a man is known by the company he keeps."

"Such as the crippled fellow," said Lambert, coming up the steps behind them, pistol in hand. "By an extraordinary coincidence, sir, we encountered him while we were searching the North Downs!"

Wondering how on earth they were to get out of this, Peregrine gave a snort of indignation and his eyes shot to Dimity. "Are you all right, Mitten? I've seen this fellow work before!"

"In which case we can forego introductions," said the colonel smoothly. "In view of the fact that you and your brother served with Sir Anthony in Scotland, Cranford, I suppose it is not remarkable that you should visit The Palfreys. I would be interested, however, in knowing why you both rode one horse."

It was odd, thought Farrar, that he could detect no hint of scorn in the demeanour of a man he'd have expected to hold him in abhorrence. He said, "Cranford experienced some slight misunderstanding with his mount, Colonel. Is it really necessary that we be held at gunpoint?"

Fotheringay's eyes flickered to Lambert's pistol. "Are either of you armed, Farrar?"

"No, sir."

"Then I think it unlikely that these two gentlemen pose a threat, Captain."

Lambert stared at the colonel with obvious incredulity. "You would take *his* word, sir?"

The colonel answered acidly, "It has been my experience—until now, at all events—that the word of an officer in His Majesty's service is to be trusted."

Lambert saw the grin that was swiftly erased from his sergeant's broad visage and knew this little episode would give the men a good laugh at his expense. He flushed and holstered his weapon, promising himself that someday he would repay Anthony Farrar for the amused twinkle he saw in the green eyes.

"I must now ask you," said Fotheringay, "where are the rest of your guests? I believe Piers Cranford stays with you, and Gordon Chandler also?"

Was it a guess, or did he know? And did he also know Glendenning was here? Farrar decided to risk it having been a guess. "I am involved in an *affaire-d'honneur*, and Cranford and Chandler are conferring with the other fellow's seconds."

"I see. Then you'd best not tell me whom you are to fight, or

I'll be obliged to put a stop to it. Meanwhile, you and Mr. Cranford here must be searched. I presume you have no objection, Farrar? Sergeant, take the gentlemen into another room. I feel sure Sir Anthony can find one that will answer the purpose.''

Farrar nodded, and as the sergeant crossed towards them, he turned away and hissed one soft word.

Seemingly unable to move or speak, so terrified was she, Dimity watched as her brother and Farrar were escorted across the lower hall by the sergeant and a trooper. If Sir Anthony had the cypher, he was sure to be arrested. And from the ashen pallor of dear Perry's thin face, she rather suspected he had. There was nothing to be done. Yet, how could they all be so calm, when those two fine young men were about to be dragged to torment and execution? She began to feel sick, and gave a cry of anxiety when Peregrine, who had been labouring along painfully, suddenly stumbled, fell headlong, and let out such an agonized wail as she'd never heard him utter even in those dreadful days when first he had been sent home. To her unspeakable horror, he lay doubled up and writhing on the floor. Every eye turned to him, even the colonel looking aghast. But despite her closeness to her brother, Dimity's shocked gaze flashed to Farrar.

He was the only person in the room not looking at the convulsed man on the floor. His piercing gaze instead was fixed on her. The moment their eyes met, he looked meaningfully to where Swimmer, curled into an agitated ball on the rug, pedalled furiously at the wide scarlet ribbon about her neck. Bewildered, Dimity followed his gaze, then looked back at him, but he was now bending over Peregrine.

Dimity started to her brother, crying a distraught, "My poor dear! Are you—"

"Stay back, ma'am!" snapped Fotheringay.

"My—my curst . . . foot . . . ." groaned Peregrine, clutching his leg.

Dimity, whose steps had carried her nearer to Swimmer, stooped and took up the kitten. Anthony had been trying to tell her something. He wanted her to do something with the kitten— but, what? "Is he all right? Oh, is he all right?" she cried, frantic.

Swimmer, still biting furiously at the abhorred ribbon, caught it between her sharp little teeth and gave a mighty tug.

"Sergeant, and you Trooper, assist Mr. Cranford," said Fotheringay, unrelenting. Something about this was worrying him. He knew the feeling and it seldom played him false. Cranford looked very bad, and certainly was not the type to make such a fuss for nothing. In point of fact, he looked the kind of high-couraged young fellow who would hide his pain behind tight-locked teeth and allow not a sound to escape him. It was this atypical behaviour that disturbed! The colonel frowned and thought shrewdly that if it *had* been a hoax, whatever they'd hoped to achieve had failed. He'd made damned sure that no one had come near them save for his own men. What such a display would have availed them if there was something fishy afoot, he could not think. Unless Farrar hoped to so play on his sympathy that Cranford would be spared from being searched, in which case, by heaven, he'd find he had chosen the wrong man!

He put Lambert in charge of the search, and then ushered the ladies back to their seats. "I feel sure that your brother will be quite all right in a minute, Miss Cranford," he assured the white-faced girl. "He likely has done too much, riding about like that. These amputations can be devilish tricky for a while. My goodness! Only look at this ferocious creature. May I?" He took the kitten from Dimity's reluctant hands. He was fond of cats and put Swimmer on his knee as he sat down.

Dimity's attention was diverted by a movement on the spiral staircase. Horatio Glendenning had started down. He glanced towards the little group, froze, backed up the steps silently, and disappeared from view. Dimity drew a breath of relief and returned her fearful gaze to the long fingers that caressed Swimmer.

Colonel Fotheringay tapped his whip against his gleaming top-boot and looked from Farrar to the drooping figure beside him. "You were very thorough, Lambert?" he asked, still unconvinced.

Fuming over the unnecessary roughness to which he and Peregrine had been subjected, Farrar adjusted his cravat and answered tersely. "The captain was so thorough I should be pleased to discuss his thoroughness with him at some time in the near future."

Lambert gave a mocking bow.

The colonel looked from one to the other. There could be little doubt but that they shared a mutual dislike. Lambert was by nature vindictive and would have been only too pleased to have discovered something to cause trouble for these men. Once again, thought Fotheringay, he had been given false information. He was irritated, for he did not enjoy frightening the innocent, especially a crippled ex-soldier, and poor Cranford looked totally spent. "My apologies, Sir Anthony," he said, making his mind up quickly as was his wont. "Mr. Cranford, you will do well to get to your bed." Stalking out of the library, he paused, one hand on the latch. "A word of advice, Farrar. Be very careful with whom you associate in future."

"Thank you, Colonel," said Farrar, yearning to plant his knuckles in Lambert's sneer.

Fotheringay lifted his whip in a gesture of salute and led his men out.

Peregrine straightened as the door closed. "Lord save us all! That was—"

"Hush!" Farrar hurried to listen intently, then open the door a crack.

In a minute or two the impatient dance of many hoofs could be heard on the drivepath.

Leonard hurried along the hall. Farrar said softly, "Make sure they are all gone, if you please."

The butler nodded and retraced his steps.

Farrar closed the door and turned back to Peregrine. "You were saying?"

"Strip and stap me, Tony! What the *devil* did you do with it? I *know* it was in your waistcoat pocket when we walked up the steps!"

"I think you do not appreciate that I have a magician's blood in my veins." Farrar chuckled. "Come. I'll tell you, but first let's set your wonderful sister's mind at ease. She was fairly beside herself with worry for her suffering brother. Will you fly into a rage an I offer my arm?"

Peregrine was too tired for pride and accepted the offered aid gratefully, but hobbled along, grumbling, because Farrar was so uncommunicative.

As they entered the music hall, Leonard hurried in to confirm that the soldiers were out of sight.

"Then I want the candles left burning and curtains open in the kitchens and library, but draw all the other downstairs curtains," said Farrar. "And lock all the doors and windows. We want no more uninvited guests tonight!"

Leonard hurried away. Dimity had run to Peregrine meanwhile, and now sat holding his hand solicitously as he sprawled on the sofa.

Farrar glanced at them, then went to his aunt. "Are you all right, ma'am?"

"Yes, but—"

"Are they gone?" Horatio Glendenning came hurrying down the stairs. "What the deuce has been—"

Lady Helen stood, holding up one hand. "No, no, I beg you! I have no least wish to know what is going on and am only grateful that we seem to have survived our unpleasant invasion. I must ask you all to excuse me, for I am very tired, and shall go to bed. Miss Cranford, do you care to come up?"

Dimity indicating that she would prefer to wait until Piers and Chandler came home, my lady bade them all good night, and Farrar ushered her to the stairs. She took the candle he lit for her but did not at once leave him, standing on the bottom step and staring sombrely at the small flame.

"I am sorry you were subjected to such an ordeal," he said gently. "Were you very much frightened when Colonel Fotheringay came?"

"Not at first. I was grateful, for that handsome young captain is a bullying creature—loud and violent. And violent people always frighten me. I dread to think what might have happened had the colonel *not* come when he did, for Miss Cranford had smacked the captain very hard, and—"

Farrar tensed. "*What?* Why? What did he do to her?"

She saw rage in his eyes and said thoughtfully, "He tried to prevent her going to poor Leonard, who had been tripped. He was rough and crude, but the colonel put a quick stop to it. Farrar, I do not ask any details, you understand, but—is poor Glendenning in terrible trouble?"

His blazing wrath cooled. "He is over the worst of it, I believe."

"Thanks to you."

"No, no. I did very little."

"I think that is not so, but I am glad you were able to help. He is a splendid young man."

"Yes."

"And deeply in love with Miss Cranford, I suspect."

His thick lashes lowered, concealing his eyes. "Yes."

"She is a delightful girl," my lady went on gravely. "It would be very sad if . . . grief were to spoil her life."

He looked up at that and said with his wry smile, "It will not come to her by any of my doing, I promise you."

She watched him steadily for another moment, then started up the stairs.

"Aunt."

"Yes?" she asked, over her shoulder.

"Do you still mean to leave me?"

She hesitated. "Not while Miss Cranford is here, certainly."

"Thank you. Why did you never *ask* me whether—whether I killed Harding."

She turned her head away and the hand holding the candle shook a little.

Not turning, she answered almost in a whisper, "I think because—because I was so very afraid of . . . of what would be your answer."

"And so judged me on hearsay." He reached up to clasp her arm and said wistfully, "Oh, my dear, how *could* you think it of me? Harding and I had our differences, but—"

"Differences!" She whirled at that. A flame lighting her eyes and her voice low and fierce, she said, "Do you take me for a blind fool, Farrar? Harding *hated* you! And to my sorrow I know you fully reciprocated his feelings!" And she turned before he could say another word and went swiftly up the stairs.

For a moment Farrar stared after her, then, rather heavily, he went back across the long room to join his guests.

Leonard had returned with a tray and was handing glasses around, wherefore conversation was restricted and Peregrine, looking ready to explode, was necessarily silent.

The butler assured his employer that his orders were being

carried out and that only one maid had succumbed to hysterics. Farrar thanked him, apologized for the rough handling he had received, and sent him off to bed.

When the man's footsteps had died away, Peregrine uttered an exasperated, "At last! Mitten won't say anything, and Glendenning don't *know* anything! For Lord's sake—"

Farrar stood, holding up his glass and looking at Dimity with an admiring smile. "Gentlemen, I give you a toast."

"Toast, is it," groaned Peregrine, struggling to his feet again. "Burn it, Farrar, if you ain't the most infuriating—"

"Two toasts," Farrar corrected, his smile broadening. "To a consummate actor!" He bowed to Peregrine.

"Too consummate," said Dimity, sipping her wine. "Though I might have known it was not like you to give way, dearest."

"I *was* good, wasn't I?" said Peregrine with schoolboy pride. "Always thought I'd like to have a crack at treading the boards."

"To Perry," said Glendenning, bewildered as he drank the toast. "What did he do?"

"Oh, that's right, you missed it, Tio. Well, Farrar whispered—'Diversion!'—so I went into a death scene would have made Garrick envious!"

"Why?" asked Glendenning.

Peregrine frowned. "You've a point. Why, Tony?"

"Which brings me to my second toast," said Farrar. "To a lady who is as brave as she is beautiful, and without whose quick wit, you and I, Cranford, would most assuredly be en route to our deaths tonight!"

Dimity blushed as all three men toasted her, but Peregrine said a disgruntled, "Mitten's a good girl, but be dashed if I can see what she'd to do with it."

"Your truly magnificent 'death scene' gave me the chance to get a message to her," said Farrar.

"What a rasper!" exclaimed Peregrine. "You were nowhere near her!"

"He looked at me," said Dimity.

Peregrine's jaw dropped. "He . . . *looked* at you? Oh, come now, Mitten! I've heard of speaking looks, but—"

" 'Twas a *very* speaking look," she said with a twinkle. "And then he looked at Swimmer in such a way that I knew he wanted me to do something with her, but I could not think—"

"Swimmer!" interpolated Peregrine excitedly. "You were holding her when we come in, Farrar! Did you shove the cypher down her little gullet, then?"

Farrar laughed. "No, you fiend!"

"Cypher?" Glendenning who had been looking downcast for several reasons, brightened and cried, "Never say you were able to *find* it?"

"By Jove, but we were," declared Peregrine. "Or at least, Farrar was. Though where the dratted thing is at this moment I've not the faintest notion."

Dimity turned away and reached into her bodice. "Here it is," she said, holding the cypher on the palm of her hand.

"Be damned!" Peregrine took the fateful piece of parchment. "It is! Then—where had you hid it, Farrar?"

"In Swimmer's riband."

"But—when? 'Twas in your pocket when we come up the steps. How could you possibly . . . ?"

Farrar chuckled. "You'll recollect you remarked on my stableboy's having been so prompt when we rid in? It struck me as odd, and he seemed stiff. He's usually a garrulous brat but he said not a word. When he took Poli's reins, his hands were like ice, though the night is not cold. I realized then that he was very afraid. And when Leonard let us in and was so solemn, I knew something was wrong. I think he has never opened that door to me without a smile. So I wound the cypher into the riband as we stepped inside."

"Jolly good," said Peregrine. "Thank God we have it safe again!"

"Amen!" said Dimity. "How I have worried! An it was lost, t'would have been my fault."

Ever loyal, Glendenning exclaimed, "Fiddlesticks! You have been wonderful, as always, Mitten, and I'm more obliged to you than I can say."

The tenderness in his face when he looked at Dimity was betraying. Farrar thought of his aunt's words, ". . . he is a splendid young man . . . and deeply in love with Miss Cranford . . ." There could be little doubt but that she had been right. He stifled a sigh. Tio, he told himself, heavy-hearted, would be a very good husband for her.

"For the life of me," muttered Peregrine, frowning over the

poem, "I do not see why this silly thing could not have been committed to memory. So much simpler."

"But quite impossible, apparently. Treve was adamant that it is to be destroyed only in the event of imminent death or arrest." Taking the parchment, Glendenning added, "Farrar must have thought very fast."

Farrar explained, "I daren't take the chance of waiting, you see—"

"I do see," cried an irate voice from the steps. Piers strode to join them, Chandler beside him. "A fine stew you left us in while you went jauntering off," he said, the twinkle in his eyes belying the indignant words.

"Oh, never mind about that, you block," said Peregrine with a grin. "Tony got it for us!"

When the excitement that followed that announcement had died down, the entire tale had to be told once more. At the finish, Piers muttered, "I remember that clod Lambert. Obnoxiousness personified."

"Well, we got rid of the beastly fellow," said Peregrine rather inaccurately. "Now you must tell us what happened after we debunked."

"Not much—but noisily," said Chandler. "You and your mixture, Perry! Those blasted dogs were quite berserk."

Farrar asked, "Did Green suspect we were outside?"

"No," said Piers. "He saw all the cats and assumed *they* had maddened his pets, and when he tried to whistle them in, they were both slobbering over Perry's revolting jar and had to be literally dragged away from it."

Peregrine laughed, delighted.

Watching him narrowly, Piers added, faintly irked, "What I cannot comprehend is why you subjected my twin to that long ride home. He'd have done a good deal better had you left him so he could come back with us in the carriage as we planned."

"I was going to leave him. Only—" Farrar stared rather fixedly at his glass. "Green's dogs killed my spaniel because she was always close by and I—stroked her sometimes, you know . . . And at the last minute it dawned on me that—well, you had leaned on my arm, Cranford. All the way to the rear court."

There were several gasps. Piers whitened and swore under his breath.

Also losing his colour, Peregrine whispered, "My dear Lord! They'd—If you'd rid off and left me . . . they'd have . . ." His hand went to his throat.

"You would have had no chance," Dimity whispered. "No chance at all! At this very moment—you might . . . Oh, Perry!"

Peregrine exchanged a grim glance with his twin.

Piers stood and crossed to face Farrar, who at once also came to his feet. Piers put out his hand. "You've my most grateful thanks, Farrar. He's a perfect dunce, but I've become accustomed to him. Dashed good of you."

Farrar retreated a step, eyeing the outstretched hand hesitantly. "It was—really, only a sudden thought, and—and not anything—"

"Oho, was it not," exclaimed Peregrine. "I wish you might have seen him, Piers, riding back for me right under the jaws of those monsters! And between my foot and his arm he couldn't pull me up, but had to dismount so as to get me into the saddle. Jove, but for a minute or two I feared you'd never get mounted in time, Tony! 'Tis *my* life you saved and I value it, so do not be saying it was really nothing!"

Piers snatched up Farrar's hand and wrung it firmly. It had been a long time since any man had done so and, scarlet and overwhelmed, he had to turn away.

The other men looked at each other and at once began an intense discussion regarding the final disposition of the cypher. Glendenning's assertion that he was the only Jacobite among them and that he would handle the matter was brushed aside. He was, Piers pointed out, already suspect and Holt or Lambert would only have to catch sight of him in the vicinity of Charles Albritton to come at the root of it. Dimity suggested that since Mr. Albritton was a clergyman they might simply go to church on Sunday and hide the cypher in a Bible and leave it in a pew.

"You'll go well escorted by military, I fancy," put in Farrar, having recovered himself.

"Besides which," said Peregrine glumly, "Bibles and the collection plate would be the first place they'd look, or so I'd think."

The discussion continued at some length, ideas being put forward and as speedily rejected, until Chandler glanced at his pocket watch and said, "Past one o'clock! Farrar, you should be in bed. The rest of us at least do not have to fight tomorrow."

Dimity thought 'Tomorrow!' and shivered. Standing, she said, "I shall bid you good-night, gentlemen."

They all rose and started toward the stairs, Dimity walking between her brothers.

In a low voice Farrar said, "Tio, I've an idea—of sorts. But I'm afraid it would mean that you—er, entrust the cypher to me."

Glendenning looked at him searchingly, then handed him the precious little document. "I can scarce refuse, when had it not been for you, Fotheringay would have it at this very minute."

Peregrine was near exhaustion as was evidenced when he asked Piers for his arm. His brother at once supporting him, they went slowly up the stairs, Chandler lighting their way.

Farrar lit a candle for Dimity. She rested her hand on his wrist. "Thank you for my brother's life, Sir Anthony."

He put his hand over hers, his fingers trembling, and rather thought he said that it had been his honour. They stood gazing at each other through a suspended moment of perfect understanding. Then, Dimity came back to earth, blushed rosily, and turned away. Farrar gazed after her, enchanted by the grace of her every movement as she went up the stairs.

"Er . . ." said Glendenning, hesitantly.

Shocked out of his trance, Farrar jumped, realized that he was smiling like an idiot, and felt his face burn, which made him feel even more idiotic.

"You'd best tell me what you have in mind," said the viscount quietly, "Just in case."

"Oh—er, of course," stammered Farrar. "Matter of fact, I'll show you, if you'll come with me. But I'd as soon keep the hiding place from Miss Cranford."

"The less she knows, the safer she will be. Quite." Glendenning spoke evenly, but he looked troubled.

The bubble burst, and Farrar was back in the harsh present. Despising himself, he thought bitterly, 'Where the devil were my wits gone?' "You—you must surely be aware," he stammered, "that I am not—could never be—a rival, for her hand, Tio?"

Glendenning sighed. "I've really no wish, you know, to win her by default."

> *She cannot have her sweets,*
> *So she huddles 'twixt the sheets,*
> *Listening to the tears*
> *Dripping in her ears.*

The memory of the small poem which Peregrine had made up long ago brought a watery smile to Dimity. She'd been seven years old, stricken with mumps, and denied even one of the bonbons a sympathetic but uninformed cousin had sent. Her brother, home from school for the summer, and watching her misery from a bedside chair, had thrown the teasing little verse at her. It had made her laugh then. It helped restore her spirits now, and she sat up in bed and dried her eyes.

There was not the least good to be obtained from weeping the night away. Nor was there any point in refusing to admit that she had been so unwise as to give her heart to a gentleman who was barred from her by a wall that was invisible, intangible, and unbreachable. Sir Anthony Farrar had deserted in the face of the enemy, a heinous crime which he not only admitted, but for which he offered no defence. In a very different action he had saved her brother's life, despite the terrible risk to himself, wherefore she was very sure that neither the twins nor Horatio Glendenning would fight him. But in a few hours he would face a man who hated him and had already sought to kill him. She trembled to the knowledge of the escape the duel offered; how much less painful for his family were he slain by the Code of the Duello rather than by the Code of Military Justice. He could be buried as an unfortunate who had fallen on the field of honour, or as a deserter, executed by his own countrymen and condemned to an unmarked grave of shame. And how like him to take the path that offered the least pain to his aunt. She closed her eyes and gripped her icy cold hands together and prayed.

Five minutes later, wrapper clasped over nightgown and candlestick in hand, she crept along the hall and went down to the kitchen in search of the British remedy for war, flood, famine, pestilence, and other sundry ills—a cup of tea. She was surprised to see a glow of light from the partly open kitchen door. Upon pushing it open, she was further surprised to see Carlton in nightshirt and slippers wrestling with a coffeepot while Swimmer crouched in the middle of the table lapping a saucer of milk. "Hello, dear," she said. "What are you doing?"

He gave her a tolerant smile. "I knew you'd say that, Aunty. I 'spect you can't help it, being a grown-up. I'm making coffee. I'm helping."

He could not be helping Anthony, for Anthony would be sleeping at this hour. Duels, she knew, were usually conducted between sun-up and eight o'clock, so he would have a few hours of rest, at least. She crossed to take down a tray the boy was vainly endeavouring to dislodge from its hook. "Whom are you helping?"

"My uncle."

She stared at him, the tray arrested in mid-air. "Sir Anthony is still up? Could he not sleep?"

"He don't want to. He's got 'portant things to do. May I have the tray, please?"

Dimity handed it over and began to assemble mugs, sugar, and a jug for the hot milk. 'He's got things to do . . .' What things? Her heart contracted. A farewell letter? His Last Will and Testament, perhaps? She cringed, and asked, "And why are you not in your bed, nephew?"

Carlton poured the milk into the jug, concentration causing his tongue to curl over his upper lip. "I was worried 'bout his cat. I'm looking after her for him, y'know. She wasn't on my bed when I waked up, so I went looking for her. She was with him, an' I told him he looked tired, so he said he wanted some coffee but he didn't want to bother the servants, so I came down an' made him some. I know how, so don't worry 'bout that. I learnt it in the Home. 'Sides, he told me to earn my keep, so I said if I made his coffee it would be a shilling please, only—"

"Carlton! You never did!"

"Yes. But I din't get it, 'cause Sir Uncle said soldiers don't earn that much money for fighting all day. I said I'd do it for nothing only he'd told me to barter my services an' I din't want him to think I'd forgot, an' he laughed an' said I'm a rascally halfling, so I only got sixpence." He grinned, obviously far from dismayed by this cut in pay.

"May I help, too?" asked Dimity.

He considered her. This was *his* help and, just like a girl, she had to come trying to get into it. Still, she had been kind and she was very pretty considering she was so old. "All right," he said generously.

And so they eventually set forth on their small mission, Carlton bearing the tray with the cups, saucers, sugar, biscuits, and currant cake, and Dimity conveying the pots of coffee and hot milk and the candlestick. It was a long way, but at last they were traversing the upstairs hall leading to Farrar's quarters, Swimmer charging madly back and forth as she escorted them.

Carlton led the way to the studio, and Dimity was considerably taken aback to discover Farrar, a disreputable smock over his shirt, the laces at his wrists rolled back, working busily at a canvas.

Her gasped, "Good heavens!" brought him swinging around in mingled delight and dismay.

"We bringed coffee and all sorts of things," announced Carlton proudly.

"*Whatever* are you doing?" cried Dimity, edging her tray onto a crowded bench.

"He's painting," Carlton explained with a pitying look.

"Well, he should be asleep. In only a few hours—" And she paused, unwilling to alarm the child.

"Thank you, Carlton." Farrar took the tray and peered about for a place to put it.

With typical male efficiency, Carlton cleared a space by sweeping papers, some books, and several periodicals to the floor, and Farrar set the tray down. "Never worry, Miss Mitten," he said. "I can go on well with very little sleep, and—"

"But not *tonight*! You must be at your best in the morning."

"I knew she'd grumble," said Carlton darkly. "I shouldn't have let her help. Jermyn said ladies can always find something wrong when a fellow's having a bit of fun."

"And let that be a lesson to you, ma'am," said Farrar, his eyes twinkling. "On the other hand, my lad, ladies wield a coffeepot much better than we men do, so perhaps we *should* allow your aunt to help." He extracted Swimmer from the dish of biscuits and retrieved the few she had knocked to the floor upon her precipitous arrival. "Although," he added *sotto voce* as Carlton went to clear a place in the window seat, "you should not be here, Miss Mitten."

"No more should you, sir. And if you drink much coffee, you'll never get to sleep." She added the hot milk and sugar he requested and handed him the cup.

Carlton commandeered a cup of hot milk and a goodly supply of cake and retired to the windowseat, and Dimity followed Farrar to his easel.

He had painted a small church having a look of great antiquity, its high narrow spire overhung by dark clouds so thickly massed they stood out from the canvas. The trees bowed to the wind and the air was full of flying leaves and twigs, but distantly the skies were clearing to a bright blue. It was unfinished, of course, and far from the quality of the work in The Village Green, but she said an astonished, "However did you manage to get so much done?"

"I'd started it some time ago. Not very good, is it?" He sipped his coffee and surveyed the painting critically. "I used a palette knife for those clouds. I want to get as much done tonight as I can."

Her apprehensive gaze flashed to him. Why? Did he think he would never have another chance to finish it? She knew her cheeks had whitened, and she begged, "Anthony—do not give up. *Please*—do not."

He had told himself very firmly that he must not touch her, but at this he put down his cup and took both her hands, saying gravely, "You are very good to worry so. It would certainly be an easier—exit, I allow. But—rather a cowardly one."

Her throat choked with strangled sobs, she could not reply.

Farrar read anguish in her tear-wet eyes. With all his heart he longed to kiss her. And why shouldn't he? The promise in her lovely face was unmistakable. They could run away together, escape the dark fate that menaced him, start life anew somewhere else. What a glory that would be! Life, love, and a bright future with this beautiful creature at his side. Yet if he seized his happiness—what of her? Could he be so selfish, so cruel as to condemn her to exile from the land she loved? To a sharing of his shame? For wherever they went, they would be shunned by their own kind. She would never again see the brothers to whom she was so obviously devoted; or any of the rest of her family. There was, he knew, a general somewhere in that family. *His* reaction was quite predictable! Dimity would be cut off forever. A fine future to offer this peerless girl—this lovely, warm, delightful human being who rated the very best life had to offer! For how long would the cheerful optimism continue to shine in her eyes under those circumstances? For how long would her joyous little gurgle of laughter continue to be heard? How long would it be before he knew that she was crushed and grieving . . . ?

Exerting every ounce of his willpower, he released her abruptly. ''I really must get this done. You shall have to excuse me, Miss Mitten.'' His smile very bright, his eyes empty, he pulled up a stool and sat down at the easel with his back to her.

Dimity blinked away tears and looked at the rumpled fair hair, the broad shoulders, the long sensitive hand that was savagely daubing vermillion paint into the centre of a white cloud. She whispered, ''God keep you . . . my very dear.''

With a small, brittle sound, the brush snapped in his hand. That one act told her more than any words could have done. Her heart swelled with love for him and with a reluctant admiration for the strength of character that forbade him to speak of his own feelings. She slipped a hand onto his shoulder. His head was bowed, but he reached up as if to touch her hand, then stood and strode rapidly to gaze out of the window. He heard a smothered sob, the rustle of draperies, soft footsteps running down the hall, and closed his eyes.

Carlton yawned and asked drowsily, ''Are you finished, Sir Uncle?''

For a moment there was no answer.

Then Farrar said in what the boy thought a very odd sort of voice, ''Yes. I'm quite finished, Carlton.''

✐ Chapter 15 ✐

Gordon Chandler awoke with a start as Peregrine dug an elbow in his ribs. "What—are we there?" he asked, peering out of the carriage window.

"No, you dolt," Peregrine nodded to their companion. "Only look at him!"

Farrar was fast asleep, his head lolling against the side of the coach, his long body relaxed on the jolting seat.

"Glad to see it," said Chandler, keeping his voice low. "Poor fellow was up most of the night working on that confounded painting."

They exchanged a meaningful glance. Peregrine asked, "D'ye think it will do the thing?"

"I think it the best chance we have, and if 'tis packed off to the church bazaar with the rest of the stuff, the military might not make anything of it. Rather clever of him to stick the cypher under that bit of oilcloth and paint over it, I thought."

"Hmmnn," grunted Peregrine, scowling. He sighed and added, "What a beast of a mess it is."

Chandler had no doubt of what he meant. "I know. And I know *him*. I still find it so damnably hard to believe he'd run—from anything!"

"Oh, he ran all right."

"You—*saw* him?"

Peregrine said reluctantly, "You may believe I did. Never saw a man run so fast in my life. A good pair of legs has Farrar."

Chandler swore under his breath.

"I know," sighed Peregrine. "It's the very devil."

The carriage lurched to a halt. Chandler let down the window and peered through the misty dawn. "No redcoats about. Your brother must've led them off, all right. If he don't get here in time are you sure you can manage?"

" 'Course I can. Be surprised how I can hop about. Is Green here?"

"He is. But the surgeon—Oh, here he comes." He leaned forward and shook Farrar. "Wake up, old fellow."

Farrar blinked at them, then sat up, stretching.

The footman opened the door and let down the steps. Chandler climbed out and looked without favour on the misty morning. Peregrine's descent from the coach was awkward and Chandler watched him worriedly.

Peregrine saw the look and said with airy nonchalance, "Don't be in a pucker, my tulip. I'm quite able to second till Piers comes."

They started across the dew-spangled grass to where Green, Ellsworth, and Otton waited with cloaks drawn close against the chill air. Farrar darted an uneasy glance at Chandler. His friend's pleasant face was grim, the usually calm grey eyes narrowed and glinting. "Gordie," he murmured, "you will remember that you're here to second me, I trust."

"This time—yes. But, by God, that filthy hound won't escape without my gloves across his face!"

Struggling along in the rear, Peregrine was startled to be asked—

"Could I interest ye in a broom, sir?"

A gypsy youth was beside him, all gaunt features and great pleading dark eyes. "The devil," he exclaimed. "I'll tell you flat out I can't think of nothing *less* interesting! Why would you ask such a tomfool question?"

Farrar cast an amused glance at the boy, but his concern was with Chandler and he stepped out to keep up with him.

Pursuing the little group with the zeal of desperation, the youth cried, "A gold cameo brooch for your lady wife, milor'? A—a fine horse . . . ?"

He had said the magic words. Peregrine halted, eyeing him suspiciously. "With a certificate of sale, no doubt?"

"Yes, sir! Oh, yes sir!"

"Come *on*, Cranford!" shouted Green irritably.

"Tell me about this horse," invited Peregrine, but starting

off again, caught his foot in a long-trailing clump of grasses, stumbled, and would have fallen had not the gypsy leapt to steady him. For just an instant Peregrine's face convulsed, and the boy asked wonderingly, "Are ye hurt, sir? I can help, maybe. Florian knows herbs and simples, wondrous remedies for—"

Fighting back a groan, Peregrine gasped, "For—that?" and stuck out his leg, the artificial foot hanging at an impossible angle.

A horrified stream of words in the Romany tongue, then the soft voice said, "Ah, poor Gorgio gentleman. Florian will help you to sit down and put it on."

Farrar called, "You all right, Cranford?"

"What's he resting for?" bellowed Green. "Dammitall, I'd as soon get this over today, an you've no objection!"

"Coming!" called Peregrine. "Hurry, lad."

Working with gentle hands, the gypsy boy looked up, shocked. "Sir—you cannot walk on *that*! It's—"

"Never mind, and keep your voice down. I've to second my friend."

"But—sir—it's *raw*!"

"Well, I have no other to spare. A shilling can you get it back on so I can stand."

The nimble fingers flew. "It will not help, sir. I could carve you a wooden leg would fit better."

"What, and thump about like a cripple? Be damned if I will!" Peregrine stood, caught his breath, and reached for his purse.

Florian drew back. "I do not take money for helping a— cripple," he said brutally.

Peregrine glared at him. "Now—damn your eyes!"

"There is an old Romany saying, Gorgio rye: 'He who would know himself must look in the mirror with a clean eyeglass.' "

"Is there! Well, there's an old Berkshire saying—'He who would sell fine horse, not tell Gorgio rye he is a cripple!' " With which, Peregrine stalked off, head high and teeth clenched, anger sustaining him.

"You shall have to keep an eye on him, Cranford," murmured Farrar, watching Chandler obliquely. "He looks ready to scrag Otton."

Peregrine nodded and went off to join the other seconds, thinking that he'd have all he could do to keep an eye on the duel, let alone on the belligerent Chandler. Limping about, checking the site, he prayed that his brother would come soon.

It was Ellsworth who delivered the solemn instructions to the protagonists. He was clad in shades of puce, his hair well powdered and curled, his manner grave. Only when his eyes rested on his cousin did his hatred peep through. Farrar had discarded coat and waistcoat and was rolling back his lace ruffles, his manner cool and impassive. Green required Otton's help to remove his tight-fitting olive coat. A dark bruise marred the right side of his jaw, his mouth was puffy, and when his high cravat shifted, purple bruises could be seen on his throat. His light hazel eyes were fixed on Farrar with a baleful, unblinking glare.

The seconds took their places, swords ready, and the antagonists swung up their weapons in salute. Both men had chosen Colichemardes, the lightweight triangular blades, tapering to a flattened foible, being especially suited to the dangerous business of duelling. Before Farrar had lowered his weapon, Green sprang to an attack in *carte* so swift and fierce that the duel was almost ended in the instant it began. Chandler uttered a shout of indignation, but in a lightning reaction, Farrar parried and as swiftly thrust within the sword and returned to his guard. Thwarted, Green recovered and circled warily. In that first encounter, each had the measure of the other and knew he faced a formidable swordsman. Pacing himself, Farrar attacked in *tierce* with less fire than Green, and Green parried deftly. They fought more carefully now, blades ringing softly in the cool hush of the early morning, boots stamping forward in the advance, moving lightly back in the retire. The seconds, ever watchful, circled, their keen eyes on the protagonists, except that Chandler's gaze slipped often to the handsome features of Roland Otton who, like the duellists, had shed his coat and moved about with easy grace, his full attention on the deadly struggle.

Farrar had forgotten everything but the thirst for revenge on this murderous enemy who, in trying to kill him, had brought about his beloved Shuffle's death. His fury was not at the searing heat it had been when he'd first ridden to Fayre Hall, but it was intense. He had not the slightest doubt but that Green had meant it when Ellsworth had enquired mockingly, "First blood, gentlemen?'' and Green had snarled, ''To the death!'' That unsportsmanlike opening thrust had been a sure indication of the way the man meant to fight, and the hatred in the hazel eyes left no room for doubt that this was a killing matter.

He sprang suddenly to the attack. Green, having barely parried in time, thrust in low *carte*. Farrar essayed a parade in *seconde* with an ease that brought a scowl to Green's face as he feinted in a large shift of his body. Farrar refused to be drawn, keeping his sword close. Green leapt to the attack again, and there was a furious flurry of thrust, parry, and riposte. Green's point flashed, *carte* over the arm, straight for Farrar's throat and in that instant a rock, hidden by the grass, turned under Farrar's boot and he stumbled. With a shout of triumph Green thrust hard. His razor sharp steel ploughed across Farrar's shoulder and crimson splashed, vivid, on the white shirt.

Chandler ran in to strike up the blades, but Green plunged forward, his face flushed and eager, his slightly protuberant eyes gleaming with the lust to kill.

''Hey!'' shouted Peregrine angrily, limping up.

''Let be, Green,'' raged Chandler. ''A blooding!''

''Blooding, hell!'' Green roared. ''I said to the death, damn you! Stand clear!''

Amused, Otton put in, ''You really must stay back, Chandler.''

The half smile, the mockery in the dark eyes, the lazy drawl, were irresistible goads to Chandler. Memory jerked him back to the brutal night when he had found his younger brother, wounded and tortured, a helpless prisoner of this man and his merciless employer. With Quentin's agonized face in his mind's eye, he hissed, ''You stinking bastard! I've waited for this!'' and fairly leapt to the attack.

His attention diverted, Farrar had to jump for his life as Green came at him without the *''En garde!''* that was *de rigeur*.

''Be damned!'' cried Peregrine, but even as he ran in again to strike up Green's blade, Ellsworth was before him, shouting, ''Keep off, blast your eyes!''

''What d'you mean—'keep off'?'' raged Peregrine. ''That was a dirty foul! You saw it as well as I!''

Ellsworth grinned. ''I saw no such thing.''

''Are you blind, man? Or do you perhaps call me a liar?''

"Whichever you wish, *mon ami*."

"You'll answer for that, by God!" gasped Peregrine, and they also were engaged, the blades flying.

Retreating before a whirlwind attack, Farrar saw the secondary battles from the corner of his eye, but for a space was powerless to do anything but defend himself. Then Green came at him, his sword held in a level glittering line. It was the opportunity Farrar had waited for; he engaged in *carte*, swung his blade a little to the left, turned his wrist in *tierce* and in a blurring crossover, thrust hard. Green's weapon flew into the air and he fell back, panting, both hands held out at his sides in a gesture of helplessness.

Farrar advanced, stamped down on Green's sword and glanced to Chandler. "Gordie!" he shouted angrily. "You're supposed to be *seconding*!"

Chandler, his steel whirling in a desperate attempt to counter Otton's brilliant swordplay, heard, but was powerless to stop.

His gaze flashing to Peregrine, Farrar saw him stagger awkwardly. Grinning and bold against his handicapped opponent, Ellsworth stamped forward. Farrar sprinted, his blade barely in time to block Ellsworth's lunge, and Ellsworth retired from distance to stand glaring at Farrar, but with his weapon held point down.

"Dammitall, Tony!" gasped Peregrine. "I almost spitted you!"

Leaping out of distance himself, Otton shouted, *"Farrar!"*

Reacting to the note of warning in the voice, Farrar flung himself aside in the nick of time as Green came at him in murderous violation of the code of the duello. The sword sliced through the side of his shirt, but did not touch the flesh this time. Leaping back, Farrar returned to the guard position and then was countering a ferocious assault. Half mad with rage and frustration, Green fought with an utter disregard for convention, his blade darting in one furious attack after another. Farrar contrived to defend himself, but seldom attacked, luring on his impassioned adversary with deliberate openings. It was dangerous work and three times death missed him by a whisper. Peregrine, who had abandoned his own fight, watched intently. Convinced that by one means or another Green meant Farrar's murder, he was determined to prevent such a deed.

Chandler and Otton were again desperately engaged, but Ellsworth also was concentrating on the initial duel. He glanced to the side suddenly, and muttered, "Troopers, damme!" Dismayed, Peregrine turned to the new threat. Ellsworth struck hard with the hilt of the sword, and Peregrine went down without a sound. Ellsworth ran to join the attack on Farrar, and Green gave a crow of triumph.

Hard-pressed now, and tiring rapidly, Farrar's blade darted and flashed in a brilliant but desperate defence.

With a hard beat on Chandler's blade, Otton disarmed him, snatched the fallen sword, and flung it far off into some shrubs. Cursing him savagely, Chandler tore away in search of his weapon. Otton gave an enigmatic grin, whirled about, and ran to the uneven attack on Farrar.

Exultant, Green cried, "Finish the swine!" But his grin faded. Instead of adding what must have been the *coup de grace* for Farrar, Otton engaged Ellsworth.

"Damn you!" Ellsworth retreated hurriedly. "What're you about?"

"Don't like . . . your way," panted Otton, "of conducting . . . a duel."

Farrar, who had expected death at any second, took heart, but the stain on his shirt was wider now, his movements were less agile, and he was visibly weaker.

Red in the face with excitement, Green shouted in triumph to see his enemy's blade faltering at last. Farrar retired slightly. Pressing in, merciless, Green lunged. In a blur of speed, not seeking to counter Green's blade, Farrar's right foot stamped forward, his body leaning gracefully over his bent knee as he thrust in low *carte* hard and true. Green's weapon scraped across his ear, but his own sword had gone home. Green uttered a gasping shriek, raised a greying and convulsed face, and sank to the grass as Farrar disengaged.

Retreating frantically, Ellsworth jumped out of distance and flung down his sword.

Otton raised his blade in salute to Farrar, his dark eyes glowing. "A time thrust, by Jove! And damned neat, Tony!"

Too short of breath to respond, Farrar grinned at him.

Chandler, who had recovered his weapon but stayed clear of the wild battle, let out the breath he had held these last perilous seconds, and ran to Peregrine. A gypsy boy was pressing a handkerchief to a gash beside the unconscious man's temple.

"I'll look after him, sir," said the boy. "It's just a cut. The big gent hit when he wasn't looking."

Chandler swore under his breath, and started back to the other men.

Replacing his sword in its scabbard, Otton strolled over to look down at Green and enquired with a marked lack of interest, "Is he dead?"

Ellsworth glared at him as the doctor cut away Green's wet and crimson shirt. "Small thanks to you if he ain't, you dirty turncoat."

Otton shrugged.

Chandler came up, said grittily, "Your pardon, sir," and backhanded Otton across the mouth.

Otton rocked on his heels.

"Your reason for helping Farrar, I do not pretend to understand," Chandler continued. "But I take leave to tell you that you are a dishonourable, conscienceless, money-grubbing scoundrel!"

Otton dabbed a handkerchief at his mouth. "A fair summation," he drawled, and with a slight bow walked away, leaving Chandler staring after him in stupefaction.

Breathing hard still, Farrar caught Otton's arm. "You may believe I don't like being obliged . . . to you. But I'll own I am. My thanks."

Roland Otton seldom allowed himself the luxury of anger. He indulged it now and turned on Farrar, his black eyes glittering wrath. "Do not delude yourself! I found I liked Green and his methods less than I like you, is all. You're a damned fine swordsman, but you're a fool, and I've neither time nor use for fools." Warming to his theme, he shook one slim finger under Farrar's nose and declared, "I shall be blasted well glad when this whole confounded business is over, one way or the other! I have *never* encountered such an infuriating set of dimwits in my life! You're cut of the same cloth as that chawbacon Delavale, may he rot! And Merry Carruthers! Could I but afford it, Farrar, I'd wash my hands of the lot of you here and now! From start to finish you consistently interfere with my plans and turn me aside from my objective. Well, you'll not succeed, and so I warn you! I shall win! In spite of the whole miserable and misguided lot of you!'' He turned on his heel, fuming.

"I have struck you!'' raged Chandler. "I have challenged you to a duel! A gentleman cannot walk away from a challenge!''

Otton checked. "Then you may be grateful that I am no gentleman,'' he sneered, "for I could cut you to ribbons without half trying.'' As Chandler, infuriated, opened his mouth to respond, he raised one hand in an oddly compelling gesture. "Besides,'' he went on, "you know perfectly well I cannot fight you. I am most fond of your sister-in-law, which forbids I should bring grief on the sweet lady.''

"Bring . . . *grief?*'' gasped Chandler. "Wh-why, you devious mountebank, you nigh killed her husband!''

Otton said reasonably, "Well, there you are, then,'' and wandered over to where Rumpelstiltskin grazed among the trees.

Glancing up, Dr. Steel murmured, "You've some strange friends, Anthony.''

"He is no friend of mine.''

"Hum. Would that I had such enemies. Why is he so enraged with you?''

"Do you know, I rather think he is not. Are you all right, Gordie? I thought he had you for a minute.''

"He could have, easily enough, but—'' Chandler tore his baffled gaze from Otton's retreating figure. "Ecod, Tony, you're the one was almost spitted! Be dashed if I ever saw such a fight!''

Farrar said dryly, "You saw very little of it, I'd have thought.''

Flushing, Chandler admitted, "Let you down, didn't I? Quite unforgivable, I know.''

"Oh, go to the devil!''

Chandler grinned. "Yes, but how is that shoulder?''

"A scrape, no more. What about Cranford?''

"His head is cut. Not too bad, I think. Our noble Ellsworth knocked him down and came to help Green put a period to you.''

"Not the upstanding, all-around sportsman, are you, cousin?'' drawled Farrar, contempt in his voice. "How much lower would you stoop to be rid of me?''

Ellsworth glared at him sullenly. "You can prove nothing! We *did* nothing.''

"To the contrary,'' said Dr. Steel, winding a bandage about

Green's chest, as Chandler obligingly lifted the injured man, "I was witness to an attempt at deliberate and cowardly murder." Over his sagging spectacles he threw a grim glance at Ellsworth. "And I shall so testify. Besides the three other witnesses. That young fire-eater who goes snarling off yonder might well testify also, for I seldom saw a man look more disgusted."

Chandler observed judicially, "You've put yourself outside Society, Ellsworth."

Paling to the awareness that he was ruined, Ellsworth snarled, "We'd have done Society a favour! Do not pretend Farrar's death would have been mourned."

"You'll find the road of the dishonoured a grim one," said Farrar. "Will Green live, Roger?"

Tightening his bandage, Steel answered, "If he does, you'll do well to have an investigation of this whole business. You never think all these dark doings and desperations sprang purely from a loyal desire to avenge Harding's death?"

"He's perfectly right!" exclaimed Chandler. "Ellsworth—"

But Phillip Ellsworth had slipped away.

"A fine thing when both a man's seconds desert him," said Steel irritably. "And he's taking Green's carriage, the cur! Give a hand here, will you, Chandler? We'll put him in my coach."

The young gypsy, meanwhile, was bending over Peregrine. "What a fight!" he exclaimed, his big dark eyes glowing. "Sir, is your head feeling very poorly?"

"Head?" groaned Peregrine. "Is it still on the end of my neck, then?" Clutching it, he swore. "That black-hearted rogue! What did he hit me with?"

"The hilt of his sword, milor'. And tried to murder the tall, fair gentleman."

Starting up, Peregrine gasped and sat down again. "Oh, burn it! Who's dead?"

"The fine Gorgio in the olive coat, maybe. Sir—you wish to see the horse?"

"Not . . . right at this minute," sighed Peregrine, content to sit and wait until his head fell off and rolled past the foot Florian was tightening.

"He is a very fine horse, milor'. There, I've done. We could—"

258

"Devil we could. Help me up." Florian obliging, Peregrine muttered curses but began his painful hobble to join his friends.

Supporting him, the gypsy boy persisted, "This is not comfortable for you, sir. Only give me a shilling and I will buy a piece of oak and carve you a wooden peg you will go along with much nicer."

Very far from comfortable, Peregrine halted. "Oh, all right, blast it. Reach my purse from that pocket and find your confounded shilling. How long will it take you to make me a peg leg?"

The thin face brightened. "An hour, milor'. Two, perhaps. But I would have to fit it properly." He saw Peregrine's hesitation and said eagerly, "I could stay outside, sir. I wouldn't prig nothing, I swear!"

"Oh, stow your clack," said Peregrine.

Having endured one of the most miserable nights of her life, Dimity rose early, dressed herself, and crept into the hall. Lady Helen's door opened as she approached it, and my lady came out and waited for her.

"Have you breakfasted, my dear?" she asked gently.

"I think I could not eat a bite, ma'am."

"Nor I. But I have ordered some coffee." She took Dimity's arm and they went down to the breakfast room, not speaking.

Because of the chill in the air a fire had been lit and the room was pleasantly warm. Lackeys hurried to pull out chairs and the two ladies sat down, saying little until coffee was steaming fragrantly in their cups and the servants had departed.

Helen searched the wan face opposite, and murmured, "Is pushing, I know, to ask but—you have become fond of my nephew, I think."

Dimity flushed but answered proudly, "Extreme fond, ma'am."

"He is a handsome young fellow and can be very charming, but," Lady Helen sighed, "I do hope he has not attempted to fix his interest with you."

"I only wish he had."

Dismayed, my lady took Dimity's cold hand. "My dear, you must realize—he cannot."

259

"I own that—that his future is—"

Helen interpolated with heartfelt sympathy, "Miss Cranford—he *has* no future."

"Good morning, ladies." Horatio Glendenning, fully dressed and looking much more his customary blithe self, came to join them and, immediately noting Dimity's stricken expression, kept up a steady flow of small talk while the servants came hurrying to bring him slices of cold pork, mustard pickles, and hot muffins. When they were alone again, he said, stirring his coffee, "D'you know, I'd never realized what this waiting is like. You poor creatures have the worst of it at such moments, be dashed if you don't. Though I suppose—" He was interrupted by the sound of carriage wheels and Carlton's voice upraised in excitement.

Dimity had managed to regain her composure, but now her heart gave a great jump of fear. She was scarcely aware she had moved but found herself standing at the top of the steps leading to the lower hall, clinging to the rail with hands clammy and icy cold, her breath fluttering in shallow, nervous little gasps.

Chandler's voice, angered, said, ". . . may believe that between Dr. Steel and Cranford and me, the whole *ton* will hear what those murderous varmints attempted!"

Two men were entering the house, but Dimity saw only Farrar. He looked tired, but his eyes lit up when he saw her, and he halted, the very special smile that she now knew was hers alone, softening his mouth. "All present and correct," he said lightly.

Relief was making her feel dizzied. She tried to be sensible. "Thank heaven! Where is Peregrine? Was he able to second you?"

"Very ably, ma'am."

Chandler grunted a shamefaced, "Compared to some. Your brother went off with a gypsy lad, Miss Cranford, who offered to sell him a horse."

She stared at him. "At a *duel*?"

"This was not your polite, well-conducted affair of honour," he remarked dryly.

She turned to Farrar. "And—you are quite all right, sir?"

He had determined to be calm, but when his eyes met hers he

found there such a tender look of concern that words failed him, and he could not tear his gaze away.

A small hush fell and deepened. Glendenning had to turn from that silent embrace, the knife in his breast the sharper because the lady he had loved for so long could find only heartbreak with the man to whom she had so obviously given her heart.

Lady Helen had come to the top of the steps, and Farrar drew a deep breath and forced himself to go to his aunt.

"Is Rafe killed?" she asked.

"No, ma'am."

She nodded gravely. "And you are not hurt at all?"

"He'll tell you no," said Chandler. "But the truth is—"

"That I took a small scrape," Farrar interrupted. "So if you will excuse me, I'll let my man maudle over me for a minute or two." He bowed and left them, studiously avoiding Dimity's eyes.

My lady said that now all the male dramatics were done with, perhaps they might return to normality, and that she must consult with her housekeeper about items to be donated to the bazaar for the restoration of the church. "Farrar will bear the lion's share of the costs, of course, Miss Cranford, but the people like to think they help, and it is good that they should do so. An I know men, they will have much to discuss that cannot be said in front of ladies, so perhaps you would care to join me?"

Longing to find out more about what had transpired at the duel, Dimity knew she could not properly refuse, and accompanied my lady to the kitchens.

❧ *Chapter 16* ❧

A dressing taped over the cut across his shoulder, and wearing a clean shirt, Farrar hurried downstairs. He was turning towards the breakfast room when he heard a woman's shrill voice speak his name in anger. With an uneasy premonition of her identity, he walked to the front doors.

Leonard's quiet but frigid tones were drowned by the strident response. "No least use for you to deny him! I know he's here, and you may tell him that the hussy who is passing herself off as me—"

Farrar intervened coolly, "Is there some difficulty, Leonard?"

The butler turned a troubled face. "Sir—this person—"

"So you are my poor sister's brother-in-law!" A handsome dark lady, wearing a gown that might more properly have been donned for an afternoon social event, elbowed her way past Leonard and the footmen. The butler exclaimed angrily, but at a nod from Farrar led his minions away, the ears of all three straining to hear what transpired.

"No matter what you may have been told, I am Mrs. Catherine Deene," announced the new arrival, her rather hard brown eyes sparking. "And fine Turkish treatment I have had from you, sir! I wonder you are not ashamed to stand there and look me in the eye, with all that has been going on in this house."

"Indeed?" Farrar bowed her to the music hall. "Perhaps you would care to enlighten me. Although," he went on, following as she flounced past, "to the best of my knowledge I have no sister-in-law. Nor can I perceive why the running of my household need concern any but myself."

Mrs. Deene's eyes narrowed. A regular top-lofty article was this noble deserter, but he'd soon find he'd not come it over her! "Hoity-toity, aren't we?" she sneered, settling herself into the chair he indicated. "You may be sure I am concerned as to the morals of a house into which my sweet nephew has been kidnapped!"

Farrar infuriated her by laughing softly. "You are talking nonsense, Mrs. Deene, as you are perfectly aware. However, I am glad that you have found the time to come and take the boy away."

"Why should I take Carlton from what is rightfully his?" she riposted, the picture of abused innocence. "Do you think to bully a poor defenseless widow, Captain Farrar, I must say 'tis conduct unbecoming an officer and—" she paused and finished with a faint sneer, ". . . a gentleman."

Silent, Farrar looked at her. She flushed, fidgeted, and her eyes fell before that steady gaze. To be disconcerted was an unfamiliar emotion, and she said plaintively, "I'd think you would be kinder to a lady who has been very ill."

He went over to tug on the bell pull. Leonard appeared almost at once, and was instructed to send in a glass of ratafia for the lady. "And find Master Carlton so he may accompany his aunt."

"Accompany me where, pray?" she demanded, mustering her forces once more. "You have given house room to that scheming trollop who kidnapped my nephew and impersonated me, and I—" She paused, drawing back a little in her chair, alarmed by the sudden steely glint in the green eyes.

At his most cynical, Farrar drawled, "My dear ma'am, do you say *you* desire to accept the hospitality of a craven deserter?"

Her high colour deepened and once more her gaze flickered and fell. "If Miss Clement told you I said that—"

"In view of the confusion as to her identity, Miss—er, Clement felt obliged to act as your emissary and has handed me the documents you brought to prove your claim, so—"

"That wicked little slut!" she shrilled, springing up with remarkable agility in view of her infirmity and rather belatedly clinging to the chair. "I warn you, Captain! I'll have the law on you if you've tampered with them papers!"

"But of course we shall have the law in this, madam. My

solicitor has your proofs and is in the process of conducting enquiries to prove—or more probably disprove—your claim.''

"If only *one* of them papers is missing, Captain Sharp," she flared, her accent slipping disastrously, "you'll be sorry, I promise you! And as for that baggage what you've had in keeping here—"

"Miss Clement has been in the care of my aunt, Lady Gilbert Farrar. As soon as she was able to tell us her true identity, her brothers and her betrothed were notified, and came to conduct her back to her home."

"A likely story," she sneered, but sat down again as Leonard returned with a tray on which was a single glass. He tendered it, his manner so icily disdainful that Farrar had to repress a grin. Her eyebrows and little finger elevated, Mrs. Deene took up the glass, and when the butler had withdrawn, she said with less force, "Where is my dear nephew? If one hair of his sweet head has been harmed, I warn you—"

"How odd," Farrar interposed, "that I had fancied you would thank me for having cared for him during your absence. Indeed, I have wondered why the boy would have been so willing to accompany a lady he certainly knew was not his aunt."

Her eyes narrowed vengefully. "I suppose the little ingrate claimed I was harsh with him!" She saw Farrar's lips tighten into a thin hard line and, recognizing her error, cooed, "But of course he did not. The poor baby was likely terrified of being left all alone in the world with his dear aunty dead—as he was deliberately misinformed—and so fell in with the Clement woman's plans! You may be sure I have informed the authorities of *her* wickedness, and she will be hauled into court when the time comes!"

Farrar thought, 'Hell! We must get Mitten out of this!'

Mrs. Deene said a triumphant, "Don't like that, do you, your mightiness? Formed an attachment for the little doxy, have you? It don't surprise me, considering as—"

"Farrar," Lady Helen made her graceful way from the rear hall, "I wonder if—"

"I shall attend you in a moment, ma'am, an you will wait in your parlour," he interposed swiftly.

"What he means," Mrs. Deene explained with an angry titter, "is that he don't choose to introduce me. I am Mrs. Catherine Deene, whose sister was cruelly abandoned by Mr. Walter Farrar, and I—''

"Have come to take back the child?" enquired Lady Helen, advancing with a relieved smile. "Oh, I am so glad. I am Lady Farrar, and although I sympathize with your predicament, it has really been most inconvenient to have the boy here. Farrar, do pray have the goodness to desire one of the maids to pack his things at once."

Farrar, who suspected that his aunt had become very fond of Carlton, hid his surprise and crossed to the bell pull. Reaching it, his hand was arrested as a piercing shriek rang out.

Carlton came into the room, a mottled red and white, and looking utterly miserable.

Mrs. Deene, who had sprung up, spilling her wine, retreated behind her chair. "Carlton! My God! What have they done to you?"

"Hello, Aunty Cathy," the boy said feebly. "I'm not very ill, you know. The gardener says it's only measles, and—"

"*Measles!* Oh, you stupid boy, of all times—" and then, with a crocodilian smile, "Not that it is your fault, dearest." She turned to my lady. "Small wonder you were so eager to be rid of him! For shame, to throw a sick child into the gutter!"

Inwardly amazed by this unexpected development, Farrar pointed out that measles was no longer considered a very severe ailment, "For not nearly so many die of it as were used to do. Caught as an adult, of course, it can be extreme dangerous, but as you have already had the disease, chances are you'd not contract it again."

"Well, I have *not* had it!" Mrs. Deene cried, horrified. "And only *look* at him!"

Carlton trod closer. Farrar, a certain quick-witted young lady in mind, had half-suspected that horrid rash to have been applied with his own paint brushes, but he now saw that the boy was indeed sadly afflicted, his arms and legs full of the angry spots that adorned his cheeks.

"You *have* come to take me with you, haven't you, Aunty?" Carlton sighed pathetically. "They don't like me here, and now Miss Clement's gone—"

"Oh, she *has*, has she?" Controlling her frustrated wrath with an effort, Mrs. Deene added a cajoling, "Stay back, dear little fellow, but tell your aunty why you went off with—with that person.''

"They said you was dead," he explained, his trusting gaze fixed upon her. "And Miss Clement was coming here 'cause she hated Sir Anth'ny, so—"

"*Sir* Anthony . . . ?" she echoed, with a sort of gasp, her widening eyes darting to Farrar.

"A windfall, ma'am?" he drawled sardonically.

"So she said she'd help me if it would dis'blige him," Carlton finished. "But I'd like to go with you, please."

"Of course you will go with her," promised Farrar. "The lady is, after all, your own flesh and blood and will want to care for you."

"Have you the least vestige of human kindness," cried Mrs. Deene, wringing her hands and assuming a martyred air, "you will allow me to stay *here* and care for the sweet baby."

"What? While you attempt to steal my home and estates? You give me credit not for human kindness, but for the disposition of a saint!" He saw her mouth opening for a predictable response and continued hurriedly, "We'd no choice with Miss Clement for she was carried into this house."

"Very clever of the hussy," said Mrs. Deene waspishly.

"Furthermore," my lady interposed with a hauteur she seldom employed, "the young lady left as soon as she was able. I will thank you to do the same, ma'am. Ah, here you are, Leonard. Pray tell one of the maids to pack Master Carlton's valise at once."

"No!" snapped Mrs. Deene, red with anger.

Ignoring this unseemly interruption, Leonard said smoothly, "Is already done, ma'am. When this lady announced herself I instructed Rodgers to pack the young gentleman's belongings. Shall I have his valise put into Mrs. Deene's vehicle?"

"You will do no such thing!" shouted Mrs. Deene. "I came here to fetch a well child—not one infected with a deadly disease! My solicitor means to bring you to court very shortly, after which the boy will have *your* valise packed, Sir Anthony Farrar! What *you* may do, my good man, is to have my stolen belongings made ready."

"That was done before Miss Clement left, madam," said Leonard, who had received some advance instruction from his employer, and was also very much on his dignity at having been addressed as a "good man." "Miss Clement also left a sum of money to recompense you for their use."

"And only proper she should do so," said Mrs. Deene, betraying not the least appearance of gratitude. "For I shall be obliged to burn every stick and stitch of it sooner than use objects worn by a woman little better than a—"

"An it would suit you better, we can simply burn your trunks and so spare you the task," interjected Farrar, blandly.

She threw him a venomous glance. "I shall leave this depraved house at once. Carlton, come outside with me. I'll have a word or two with you, my lad. Not too close, mind!" Her look of blazing contempt was wasted on my lady, and equally wasted on Farrar, who offered a deep bow as Leonard ushered her out.

The instant the front door had closed, Lady Helen murmured, "Oh, what a dreadful woman! And I fear she means mischief! Thank heaven Miss Cranford is still in the barn making a list of our bazaar donations!"

"Holt has evidently not divulged her true name nor did we— for which I thank you—so can we get her away quickly, she may be safe." For just an instant a bleak look came into his face, then he said," Now—tell me, ma'am, have you really had measles?"

Any demonstration of his devotion never failed to wring her heart. She turned her head from him slightly. "Yes. When I was eight, I think. And when you were ten you contrived to bring it home from school and pass it on to three of the maids and—and Harding."

He heard the break in her voice and said bracingly, "We must hope Carlton's case is not as lurid and lengthy as was mine. Though, if it has rescued him from that harpy . . ."

She raised anxious eyes to his. "An her claims prove false, whatever is to become of the boy? He is terrified of her."

He asked, smiling, "What would you, ma'am? If he truly is her nephew, we cannot very well wrest him away."

"Nor abandon the poor child to her tender mercies!" She frowned worriedly. "How I wish poor Major Rhodes yet lived. He would know just what to do. But perhaps Dr. Steel may have some suggestions."

"*Roger* Steel? Why, he is so in awe of you he fairly trembles do you wish him good day!"

"I have scarce done so since your recovery, but I believe he has a fine understanding and is a most shrewd gentleman. We must have him out to look at the boy at all events, if he has measles."

"I don't, Lady He'n," a small voice sighed.

Carlton was coming up the steps holding Swimmer. He was very pale and looked scared, the spots more lurid than ever. He said wryly, "It is—stinging nettles."

"Good God!" exclaimed Farrar. "You never did!"

The fair curls nodded. "I saw her coming. She don't like it when I'm sick, and if I just brush past a nettle I get spots all over, so I ran through that patch down by the woodshed."

"Why, you Trojan," said Farrar, touched.

Lady Helen said kindly, "Poor little fellow. You must feel dreadful. Come—" she stretched forth her hand, and with considerably less than his usual vigour, Carlton went to her. "You shall be bathed in salts, which will make you feel very much better," she promised.

"You'd best not take Swimmer," advised Farrar. "She's not fond of tubs."

Carlton looked back at him with a quivering grin.

Farrar's smile faded as they climbed the stairs, and he walked across the hall, his steps as slow as his heart was heavy.

He entered the breakfast room to find that Piers had come back and that he and Glendenning were bemoaning the fact that they had not witnessed the duel, and marvelling at the part Roland Otton had played.

Chandler said grudgingly, "That mercenary hound was born a gentleman. I suppose once in a great while some vestige of chivalry surfaces. Of a certainty, his defection played hob with Green's plans for you, Tony."

"What I cannot fathom," said Glendenning, "is why they should be willing to take such risks. The gudgeons surely—"

"You spoke of gudgeons?" Peregrine limped into the room, leaning on his cane. He was pale, the lump on his forehead dark and angry looking, but a spark lit his blue eyes. "I arrive prompt to my call."

Piers hid his concern and said, "Well, don't you look horrid.

I take my eyes off you for five minutes and you get your brains knocked out! You were likely fair game for that thieving gypsy.''

Peregrine essayed a bow, thought better of it, and occupied the chair a lackey pulled out for him. ''Much you know of it, twin. Fact is, that young varmint showed me one of the finest stallions I ever saw.''

At once, they were all attention, and in response to a battery of eager questions, Peregrine imparted that it was a sixteen-hand bay with good straight legs, a deep barrel, and splendid hindquarters. ''A goer, if ever I saw one!''

''You lucky dog,'' exclaimed Piers, envious. ''How much?''

''Twenty pounds.''

There was a stunned silence.

''You *did* buy him?'' asked Glendenning, awed.

''Certainly not! There was a—er, feature I could not like.''

''The deuce,'' snorted Piers. ''What feature?''

''The price was too high,'' said Peregrine and, laughter dancing into his blue eyes as he viewed their stupefaction, he added, ''since I already own him! That wicked young reprobate tried to sell me Odin!''

After an uproarious few minutes, Piers wiped tears from his eyes and gasped, ''I hope you had him clapped up!''

''Ah—er, well . . .'' mumbled Peregrine.

Piers shook his head. ''Where is he, you great block?''

''I was ready to floor the sly little reprobate, let me tell you. But—blest if he didn't go and faint dead away. It seems he'd scarce eaten for two days. So I—er, took him to a hedge tavern and bought him breakfast. I—well, I began to think—if *I* was nigh starved and living in a cart . . .'' He shrugged.

'' 'But for the grace of God, there go I,' '' nodded Farrar. ''Have you brought him back with you, then?''

''Yes, as a matter of fact.'' Rather red in the face, Peregrine added defiantly, ''And you may all cease to sneer. I've set him to carving me a peg leg. Does it fit better than this confounded foot, I shall feel well justified.''

The laughter and the teasing quieted. Farrar gripped his hands tightly under the table and thought, 'Now!' and as if from a distance heard himself speak the words he had so dreaded to utter. ''I am sorry to have to tell you this.'' He saw Glendenning catch his breath and the Cranford twins exchange dismayed

269

glances and, knowing what they feared he was about to say, his mouth twisted cynically. "I have very much enjoyed having you as my guests," he went on, "but you must leave here at once."

Dimity's list of the many items that had been collected for the bazaar was lengthy, but at last it was completed and she started back toward the house, eager to see if Farrar had come downstairs yet. A lackey passed on his way to the stables and bowed respectfully. She smiled at him, but had gone only a little way when she halted, alarmed by a strident shout from the barn.

"Sir Anthony's beige coach with the blue trim! Get the bay team poled up, lads! Look lively!"

She swung around and looked back. The head groom's authoritative commands transformed the quiet stableyard into a maelstrom of hurry and bustle. Stableboys and grooms came running, a sleek, gleaming carriage was wheeled out, four splendid horses were led from the paddock, men called to each other, wheels grated on the cobbles, hoofs stamped, and harness rattled. Another voice was raised to order my Lord Glendenning's black mare and the mounts of the Cranfords.

A cold and terrible fear gripped Dimity and she ran to the house.

In the side hall, Piers, already wearing cloak and sword, walked beside Farrar, deep in low-voiced converse. Farrar saw her and halted abruptly.

Piers said with forced jollity, "Must get home, you know, Mitten. Time to go, m'dear."

Go? Now? She could not. Not *now*! Her eyes, frantic, were on Farrar.

Looking unhappily from his sister's white-faced shock to Farrar's haggard attempt at nonchalance, Piers scarcely dared breathe.

"Aunt Jane will be worried," he gulped, thinking bitterly that he'd never really known how compelling a force was love and that it could be a devilish thing. "And we've—er, much to do about the place. Hurry up, there's a good girl. I'll go and see how things are coming along in the stables." With which he all but ran to the side door, leaving them alone together in the quiet serenity of the music hall.

Dimity stared numbly at the averted face of this man she had tried desperately to hate, but who had become the centre of her universe. She'd known that the time for good-byes would come, but had refused to admit that its dark shadow grew ever nearer. She had only just surmounted the terror of the duel. Surely, *surely* they could be allowed a brief respite? Just a little space in their lives for love and for being together? It was too cruel that now, so mercilessly soon, so stunning in its impact, the moment of parting was upon her.

With an enormous effort, Farrar smiled at her. "I fancy," he drawled, "it will be good to see your home again, Miss Mitten."

Ignoring this foolishness, she stepped very close to him. "What about the cypher?"

"Oh, all arranged, never fear. There is—"

"It has not been delivered. *You* are going to do that."

He shrugged. "You did your part, Mitten. Allow me to do mine."

"Your part! You should not have been involved at all! It is my fault that you are at risk!" But as terrible as was that risk, neither of them were at this poignant moment really conscious of it, or of anything but their own personal tragedy. Desperately searching his fixed and enigmatic smile, Dimity whispered, "Anthony—oh my dear, are we saying good-bye?"

It *was* good-bye, God help him! And he had no right, absolutely no right to have dared dream of any other ending than this. But—he *had* dared to dream . . . "Good-bye," he said huskily, "means—God be with you. And—saying that to you from the bottom of my heart, I am also saying—thank you." He had to look away from the anguish in her eyes and, staring at a vase of roses that might have been turnips for all he saw of them, he went on, "To have known you has—has meant more to me than you—than you can ever imagine."

Speechless, she reached out. With a muffled exclamation he jerked back, gasping, "No! Mitten—do not make it harder for—for both of us."

She felt as if she was drowning in tears, but managed to say brokenly, "Your aunt says—we all cling to hope. Anthony, I will be . . . praying for you."

He must not—he *dare* not look at her. But he found that he

could not let her go without just one last look. Her face was before him; pale and uplifted, and with the diamonds of grief glistening on her lashes, a grief he had brought her, when he loved her so and wanted only to bring her joy. Recklessly, he took her face between the palms of his hands and drank in every beloved feature. She was so lovely, so brave and tender and altogether perfect. And so hopelessly forbidden. She had come too late into his life; this brief little episode was all that had been granted him. He must not even tell her how much he loved her, for she was beautiful and would not want for suitors. Eventually she would marry some fine gentleman like Glendenning and as time went by she would forget the shamed man to whom she had so generously given her affection. Which was . . . as it should be. But her face blurred before his eyes, and the ache of loss was so intense it was almost beyond bearing. He thought, 'Mitten, oh my dearest love . . . if only I had not wrecked my life . . . If only—' His control broke. He turned and strode swiftly away, and into the empty desolation that was life without her.

❧ *Chapter 17* ❧

Decimus Green lay some eleven miles to the east of The Palfreys and, being situated within a half mile of the London Road, had benefitted when a fine posting house was built on its outskirts. With the carriage trade came custom; new shops sprang up, new families moved in, and the village now had a second street and was in a fair way to becoming a small town. On this bright Sunday afternoon, the streets were in even more of a bustle than usual, for this was the day of the bazaar in aid of the restoration of the poor old church in Palfrey Poplars. Entertainments were few and far between, especially entertainments for a good cause. The Quality had turned out full force, a sure sign there would be plenty of pretty plates and dishes and kitchenware, ells of cotton and cloth, and near new garments and shoes, all to be had at bargain prices. Thus, the crowd swelled; luxurious chariots and finely mounted aristocrats threaded their way among villagers, farmhands, merchants and pedlars, bakers, chimney sweeps, blacksmiths, and the servants of the gentry—all in their Sunday best, all heading towards the tall spire of old St. Michael's Church, and the bright awnings of the many booths already fluttering on the village green before it.

Conspicuous among the throng were many red uniforms, and on the green itself a cluster of soldiers ignored the protests of Sir Anthony Farrar's servants and, much to the amusement of the onlookers, minutely inspected the contents of the wagon that had been sent over from The Palfreys. Sir Anthony's tall figure loomed up, and the crowd broke before him. A large, well-built man, one sleeve pinned to his shabby coat, did not move, however, but stood squarely in his path. For a moment the two faced each other, eye to eye. Sir Anthony regarded the flushed and hostile features gravely. Someone giggled. An angry voice muttered, "Quiet, dang ye!" The large ex-soldier, who had suffered a great deal and had determined to at the very least confront this coward and tell him what kind of scum he was, found himself as if struck mute by those steady green eyes. His own gaze fell and he stepped aside. Furious with himself, he spat deliberately as the young baronet passed, and laughter rang out.

Ignoring it, Farrar said, "My contributions have already been searched, Corporal."

"And will be searched again, I do not doubt," declared a mocking voice behind him.

He recognized the arrogant drawl and, without turning, added, "Have a care, man! Those articles are to be sold to help rebuild the church."

"Much they'll bring," jeered the corporal, taking his cue from his officer and the grinning faces around him. He unearthed a framed picture from the tumbled piles of goods and, holding it upside-down, peered at it. "Lookit this horrid thing. Who'd want to buy that? Why, me four-year-old could do better!"

Farrar had expected humiliation but, despite himself, he flushed. His penchant for art was well known, and the resultant hilarity attracted more individuals to the growing crowd.

Not far off, the low-spreading branches of an oak had attracted two rustics and the buxom object of their affections. With much coarse wit and loud guffaws that had offended several bystanders they had hoisted the girl onto a limb. Now, sitting one on each side of her in their leafy bower, they viewed the distant confrontation with taut anxiety. The taller of the pair nudged the girl, laughed boisterously, and leaned to her. "I warned you," he murmured in a soft, cultured voice.

His lass, her cheeks and mouth too bright, her eyebrows too dark, her cheap wig looking considerably the worse for wear, replied as softly, "What I cannot understand, Piers, is why Farrar came! That horrid captain will do anything in his power to humiliate him."

"Aye," murmured the "yokel" to her left, gesturing with a half-eaten apple. "He's a natural-born bully is the handsome

Lambert. But you might have known Farrar wouldn't send his people into danger without he shared it."

"My coward," said Dimity bitterly.

Piers sent a swift glance over her head, but Glendenning's face was deeply shadowed by a most disreputable hat and the straggles of greasy hair that hung over his brow.

"By God!" exclaimed his lordship. "Lambert's got the picture!"

With a muffled oath Piers jerked his head around.

"Here comes Ellsworth," Glendenning went on. "He looks like the fox that ate the lion!"

"And only see how Lambert examines the painting! Lord save us all!"

Frightened, Dimity whispered a soundless, "Anthony . . . !"

"If they take him," said her brother grimly, "there had best not be a sound out of you, my girl! Even with these disguises we might be recognized and then we'd all be properly in the frying pan!"

The crowd was pressing in closer around Farrar. Jostled, his head lifted higher.

Captain Lambert, having contributed his share of disparaging remarks about the painting, made a show of inspecting the frame, turned it in his hands, and ruthlessly ripped off the backing.

Farrar's voice lifted in protest. "I presume you have bought that, Lambert."

"You presume too much," drawled the captain.

Over his shoulder, Farrar encountered a pair of smiling blue eyes. He slanted his own meaningfully at the painting Lambert held, and Father Charles Albritton lifted his brows in acknowledgment.

"I'd not hang such an atrocity in my outhouse!" declared Lambert. "Here," he thrust out the abused painting but as Farrar reached for it, deliberately let it fall.

A howl of laughter went up, but the one-armed soldier frowned and looked troubled.

Fists clenched, Farrar managed to ignore the contempt in Lambert's eyes, and moved forward to take up the painting. Someone shoved him, and he staggered. A hard-eyed man wearing a scratch wig, shouted, "There's enough on us ter give the dirty deserter wot 'e shoulda got long since. He ain't got his men ter pertect him now!'' He grasped Farrar's arm roughly and the crowd surged forward. Farrar winced and struck away the brutal grip.

The ex-soldier pushed the hard-eyed man back. ''Fight fair, my cove,'' he said grittily.

''Wot—like he done?'' The man gave a derisive howl, and two big farmhands moved closer, growling their agreement.

Piers muttered, ''I don't like this, Tio.''

''It looks very contrived to me,'' said Glendenning. ''But—aha!''

A tall, ragged individual gave a hee-haw of a laugh, and brayed, ''Don't spoil our fun, me boys! 'Sides, fifty ter one ain't sporting odds—not in England it ain't!''

Dimity held her breath, and held Piers' hand tightly.

The intervention of the ex-soldier and the ragged individual's mention of sportsmanship had taken effect, however, and the mood of the crowd had changed.

An elegantly clad gentleman cried, ''By Jove, but Farrar ain't been tried nor formally accused! We're not here to do murder! Let be!''

Irked, Lambert recognized the voice of the majority and yielded to it. ''By all means,'' he drawled. ''Allow the noble deserter his painting, Corporal.'' Turning away, he collided with the young priest who had wandered up behind him. ''My apologies, Father,'' he said, sketching a salute.

Charles Albritton lowered his blond head beneficently. ''We must make allowances, my son,'' he murmured.

Glancing scornfully to Farrar, who had added the painting to the growing pile of goods on a booth, Lambert said, ''Would that I had your tolerance, sir.''

The priest blinked. ''Do you refer to the man? Or to his artistic—er, endeavours?''

Lambert chuckled. ''I doubt his work of art will sell, Father.''

''Oh, I don't know. If no one else buys it, Captain, I rather think I might.''

''Good—Er, I mean—you *like* it?''

Albritton pursed up his well shaped lips. ''As to that . . . let us just say—'' a twinkle brightened the blue eyes, ''I'm only a temporary man here, you know, but—there's a hole in the wall by my bed makes a dreadful cold draught . . .''

Lambert gave a hoot of mirth, turned back to the booth and snatched up the painting. "I'll buy this!"

On hearing that raucous declaration, Piers Cranford came near to tumbling from his perch, my Lord Glendenning swore under his breath, and Dimity uttered a faint squeak of fright.

Captain Lambert tossed a florin into the cash box on the booth, tendered the painting to Father Albritton and, with an exaggerated bow, said loudly, "A work of art, it ain't, sir. But if it keeps out your draughts, 'tis money well spent."

There was much laughter at this.

Farrar, who had held his breath for a moment, managed to look affronted, although he was hard put to it to keep from joining in the hilarious mirth emanating from a nearby oak.

Father Albritton accepted his gift with grateful humility and, bearing it off, was approached by the ragged individual who had spoken of fair play. "It's a good thing you warned me that Farrar would deliver the—message," murmured the young priest. "Even so, for a moment I thought we'd lose that one."

The Honourable Trevelyan de Villars cringed and extended one grubby palm fawningly. "They came for a happy occasion," he said, low-voiced, "not a lynching. But did you notice the bloody-minded individual had a London accent? Odd, eh?" And in a loud whine, "A penny, your Eminence? A groat, only . . . ?"

Albritton thrust a hand into his pocket and dropped a farthing into de Villars' slim hand. "At all events, we've got it, by Jupiter!" he whispered, exultantly.

"Do not be counting your chickens, Saint Nipcheese," cautioned his irreverent friend. "Only see where Lambert treads now."

Albritton turned his fair head and caught a glimpse of the captain deep in conversation with Phillip Ellsworth.

"I'd give something to know what that sly duo is about!" muttered de Villars. "And were I you, dear Charles, I'd make off with that work of art before someone as astute as Mariner Fotheringay graces the scene."

"He's hot after our courier who carries the list."

"Haiwell?"

The priest nodded and murmured apprehensively. "Poor fellow, what a chase he's led them. If he's to reckon with Fother-

277

ingay now—may God help him!'' A church deacon was approaching, and he added kindly, ''Now be off with you, my son, and strive to live to better purpose!''

De Villars crouched, mumbled, and as the priest walked on, made a derogatory gesture but pocketed the farthing nonetheless before slouching off.

Meanwhile, Leonard had arrived and, assisting Farrar to add a small chest to the booth, scolded, ''Sir, you should not have come here! You do but ask for trouble!''

His butler, thought Farrar, had no suspicion of just how deadly was that trouble. He said, '' 'Tis *my* church we hope to restore. The least I can do is—'' He caught his breath suddenly, and was still.

Glancing at him, Leonard turned to see what had brought about that arrested expression and stifled a groan of apprehension.

My Lord Hibbard Green approached, one hand bandaged. Catching sight of Farrar, he paused and stood motionless, his little eyes glinting hatred.

Word of the duel had gone out, and those standing nearby waited expectantly, their eyes flashing from his lordship to the younger man who, despite his height and the proudly erect set of his head, looked slight and vulnerable by contrast with the great bulk of the baron. After a moment of rigid immobility, however, the peer moved on, the disappointed crowd dispersed, and the danger was averted, much to the relief of the three who had watched tensely from their leafy vantage point.

The afternoon grew warmer and more people came. Soon, all the booths were well stocked and business was brisk, the food stands, as always, being heavily patronized.

Lady Helen arrived, a picture in ecru muslin with lace scallops, and took her place at the stand where lemonade and jam and custard tarts were offered.

Wrenching her yearning gaze from her beloved, Dimity turned to find Piers watching her, a worried look in his blue eyes. ''Dearest,'' she pleaded, ''could I not, just for a moment—''

Aching for her, and for poor Glendenning, Piers said gruffly, ''By all means—do you wish to betray him, and all of us!''

Dimity sighed and bowed her head, helpless.

278

With typical gallantry, Glendenning murmured, "No call to be so harsh, old fellow. She—loves him."

Dimity's hand went out to clasp his own. "Dear Tio. I—truly, I wish—"

"Yes," he interrupted, patting her hand gently. "I know, Mitten.

By four o'clock it was apparent that the bazaar was going to be a huge success. Charles Albritton, carrying his painting into the vicar's study in the old church, was assured by a beaming deacon that they were bound to reach the goal that had been set for the event. "Apart from that, Reverend," said the old gentleman, "there's a poor fellow waiting in the choir loft. He says you spoke to him earlier and so convinced him of his need to repent that he is eager to confess his sins and learn how to become a better Christian."

"Praise heaven," said Albritton, mentally asking his Heavenly Father's forgiveness for such duplicity.

He went at once to the hushed sanctuary and climbed the winding stair to the choir loft. De Villars sprawled on the time-darkened wood of the rear pew, and greeted him with a sober look. "I thought you'd never come! I must be off, Charles."

Knowing this man, Albritton sat down and asked, "What's amiss?"

"Hibbard Green has come. He'd spot me in an instant, and my life—our lives—would be worth not a groat. He has not the mercy of a cat with a cricket! You've found the cypher?"

"I've not had time. It's concealed somewhere in that painting, I gather."

"Is it so? Well, have a care, friend, and be very secret with your search. Now," de Villars stretched, "fare thee well."

"A moment, I beg you. Treve—the man who will decipher the messages—do you know when he will come?"

"No."

"Or—his identity?"

The sardonic sneer that often characterized this brave man was very pronounced. "Oh, yes. And—no, Charles, I'll not tell you."

Albritton said with a slow smile, "You've no liking for my

involvement, have you? When I was your hapless slave at Eton I'd not have dreamed you ever could be so solicitous of my welfare!''

"No,'' retaliated de Villars with a grin, "because you were the laziest new boy ever passed through those hallowed portals, and had I not exercised my rights as a senior to bring you into line—'' He broke off with an impatient gesture, and regarded the younger man worriedly. The truth was that Albritton had been one of Eton's most brilliant scholars, but because he was as shy and frail as he was quick to win the admiration of the faculty, he had become the target of a jealous bully. De Villars, in all the glory of his senior year, had intervened to protect Albritton, his well-meant effort resulting in the new boy's having been brutally beaten. Furious, de Villars had dealt with the bully and undertaken the instruction of his protégé in the art of fisticuffs. By the time de Villars had left the school a fast friendship existed between the two, but they had drifted apart in the intervening years, and only recently learned that they both worked to aid the persecuted Jacobite fugitives. The discovery that his old friend had become a man of the cloth had shocked the cynical and worldly de Villars, and he made no secret of his wish that Albritton get out of so dangerous a game as treason.

Now he said slowly, "Charles—I wish to God you'd let be. Jacob Holt is liable to put two and two together does he lay eyes on you, and—''

"Your risk is greater than mine. You and your uncle Boudreaux are known Jacobite sympathizers, and now that you have found your lady and are soon to be wed, one might think—''

"Have done! Have done!'' De Villars lifted his hands resignedly. "You'll no more convince me, than I you.'' He stood. "You know where to reach me at need.''

"Yes.'' Standing also, the young priest said, "Tell me this, at least. Do I know this fifth courier, Treve? The man who will decipher the messages, I mean.''

De Villars hesitated, then nodded. "You do. And I'll tell you this, Charles, I think they must all have run mad in Scotland, for 'tis the most damn ridiculous piece of folly imaginable. Oh, your pardon! I forget you're a priest and I in a house of God. But—only wait. When you meet the courier, you'll be as disgusted as I!''

Farrar had stayed close to the booth in case trouble should threaten his people, although it appeared the cypher was safely delivered at last. He knew better than to help as he had done in happier times and stood alone a short distance away. All about him was talk and laughter, prospective purchasers chatting pleasantly enough with his servants but, save for when Roger Steel wandered over, or one of his own villagers shyly greeted him, he remained shunned and silent, a pariah who watched the colourful, carefree throng expressionlessly and with seeming indifference, but who inwardly longed to be a part of it. His thoughts turned often and wistfully to the love he had so nearly won and to the what-might-have-been, but as the slow moments slid past, he never dreamed that a few short yards away the girl he had enshrined in his heart watched him, grieving to see him so ostracised, yet proud also, because he bore his punishment so well.

Piers, who had stayed on for his sister's sake, now murmured, "Come, Mitten. It's done, thank heaven."

"Thanks to Farrar," put in Glendenning.

"Thanks to Farrar," Piers acknowledged. "But we've far to go and I fancy Perry is pacing the floor, worrying."

Dimity dreaded to leave, but Piers had been deeply opposed to her coming at all, and every minute they stayed was an added risk, for Tio especially. Gathering her courage, therefore, she took one long look at the man she loved, then allowed herself to be lifted from her perch. Piers had been afraid they might attract attention, but no one paid the least heed to the three, and they started to move casually in the direction of the lane.

There was some small disturbance ahead now, people halting and craning their necks, then hurriedly moving clear.

Piers glanced uneasily to Glendenning, only to find that his lordship had wandered off and was inspecting some pasties a village belle offered for sale from a much depleted tray.

Dimity whispered, "Oh, God!" and clung to his arm.

He spun around.

Captain Brooks Lambert, six troopers following, marched purposefully towards them.

Praying, Piers slipped his arm around his sister and drew her back.

He felt positively weak when the soldiers went on past, not so much as deigning them a look. "So that's why Tio left us," he muttered. "The silly chawbacon thought they'd come for him and feared to jeopardize us. How typical that—Oh, the devil!"

Dimity was already running, pushing her way frenziedly through the excited and converging crowd. Sprinting in pursuit, Piers caught her and gripped her elbow hard.

"Ain't no call to shove, young no-manners," complained a wizened elderly man in a spotless smock.

"Sorry," gasped Piers. "Women! They've more curiosity than the cat!"

The old man sniffed and grumbled on, but Dimity heard not a word, her attention fixed on Farrar.

He had been talking with his aunt when the troopers started through the crowd. He glanced at them, saw Lambert's gloating smile, and knew. His face became paper white. He stepped a pace away from Lady Helen, but he said nothing.

The troopers closed in behind and beside him. As he was pushed roughly away from the booth, he saw a girl in the forefront of the crowd; a shabbily dressed country lass with great hazel eyes having a slight and fascinating slant to them. He thought, '*Mitten*! Lord, no!'

The crowd hushed, the only sound the distant wailing of an infant.

"Captain Sir Anthony Farrar," barked Lambert, eyes glistening, "I arrest you in the name of the king, on charges of cowardice in battle, deserting your command in the face of the enemy with resultant heavy loss of life, and suspicion of the murder of Lieutenant Sir Harding Farrar."

This recital of infamy drew a chorus of shocked cries and exclamations of horror from the onlookers.

Wishing he had died at Prestonpans, Farrar thought of Helen and turned to see her weeping in Roger Steel's arms. Instinctively, he tried to go to her.

"Chain him!" snapped Lambert.

Indignant, Steel protested, "There's no need for that, surely!"

Lambert gestured to his sergeant. Iron manacles connected by a heavy chain were locked around Farrar's wrists. He stared down at them disbelievingly. Then he was being marched through the crowd, the chains clanking their message of shame and disgrace. The word spread and was embellished, and the rage of these simple, God-fearing people mounted. Flanked by his escort, Farrar looked neither to right nor left, but tried to shut out the faces distorted with anger and disgust, the shouts of condemnation of the murdering aristocrat's wickedness, the derisive catcalls, the fists that were shaken, the contemptuous women's voices shrilling "Shame!" and the many less polite epithets hurled his way.

Egged on by judiciously placed rabble-rousers, several men broke the military line. Fists flew, and, powerless to defend himself, Farrar sank under them.

Dimity saw his head disappear in the maelstrom, and it was fortunate that the uproar drowned her shriek of terror. Frantic with despair, tears streaking her face, she fought wildly to get clear as Piers and Glendenning stepped in front of her, shutting off her view. Piers grasped her wrists hard. "Mitten!" he hissed. "I know how you must feel. But there's Tio here, besides you and me! If we're recognized, we're as good as dead! For the love of God, compose yourself!"

"They'll kill him!" she sobbed out distractedly. "Oh, Lord! I must go to him! I must—"

"You must control yourself," he grated through his teeth. "For Tony's sake! We can do nothing if we're *all* in the Tower!"

The words penetrated her terror. With a tremendous effort, she choked back the sobs and wiped away her tears. "You're right, of . . . course," she gulped. "I—I'm sorry. But—what can we *do*? How can we help him?"

Piers met Glendenning's gaze and his heart sank as he saw the faint, regretful shake of the head. He bit his lip, but said jauntily, "Something, love—just you wait and see!"

Farrar was up again, for despite a lucrative agreement to assist certain gentlemen in any way possible, Captain Lambert had only recently suffered a stern reprimand and he was not yet ready to risk another. Therefore, although taking his time, he rallied his men, the crowd was beaten back, and the prisoner, somewhat the worse for wear, was restored to his feet.

Stumbling blindly through the chilling sights and sounds of contempt and loathing, Farrar scarcely felt the pain of his mauled

283

arm, or of the many bruises angry men had put on him. His hurt went deeper, for the nightmare was much worse than he had expected. In his darkest moments he had envisioned himself at The Palfreys, hearing the troop ride up, and being torn from his home. He had never imagined he would be arrested in the middle of a hostile mob and dragged away in shameful chains before the tearful eyes of the lady he worshipped.

The cell was cold and dank, moisture seeping down the ancient stone walls. There were no windows, for Captain Lambert had decreed that this prisoner was in considerable danger from the outraged populace, and must be kept isolated. Sitting on the floor, his back propped against a wall, wrists balanced on his updrawn knees, Farrar frowned at the chain that looped between the manacles and tried to remember details. He could see the anguish in Mitten's dear face; and then fists raining at him. Everything that followed seemed blurred and unreal.

He was in gaol, of course. But whether he had been carried to the Horse Guards, or whether he was in the Tower, he had no notion. It seemed that he had been pushed into a coach of some kind . . . Yes, for he remembered the wheels rattling over cobblestones. Perhaps he'd fallen asleep. He smiled faintly; how very blasé, to have dozed off on one's way to Death . . . .

He wondered where the trial was to be held—and whether he would be allowed to name the officers who would judge him. When he was permitted to speak, he would plead for a firing squad rather than to be hanged. He shuddered. To be denied a soldier's death and instead hanged as a common thief was beyond bearing. They would allow him some small vestige of an honourable dying, surely . . . ? His tired mind began to turn over names . . . Thaddeus Briley had been discharged as a result of wounds sustained in the Low Countries, but he would still hold the rank of major, and he was a good fellow; however revolted he might be by the charges, Thad would probably consent to serve. He frowned, remembering that someone— Gordon, he thought—had mentioned that Briley had hurt his foot, or was it his knee? and was away somewhere . . .

He had not heard the approaching footsteps and was startled when the door was swung open. The glare of the lantern dazzled him, and when he instinctively made to fling up a hand to shield his eyes, the heavy chain dragged bruisingly on his wrists. He sat back against the wall, blinking, waiting for his eyes to adjust to the brightness.

"Dear me," said Brooks Lambert. " 'How are the mighty fallen,' to be sure." Farrar remaining silent, he strolled into the tiny cell and went on, "My poor fellow, you do look dreadful. Have you been brought your supper?"

"I am sure you are aware I have not."

"You misjudge me, Farrar. Really, you misjudge me. The cook here is quite competent. I know, for I just dined. I will order a tray sent in at once. Is there anything else I may do to oblige you? Only name it."

"Some water, if you please."

"But of course."

Farrar could see the young captain now. Beyond his scarlet splendour, a rough-looking civilian held up a lantern whose light revealed flagged floors, and walls of stone blocks. Puzzled, he asked, "Which barracks is this?"

Lambert raised his brows innocently. "Barracks? You are not in a barracks. You are held in a keep, no less. A most—er, distinguished gaol for your kind, assure you."

A cold fear beginning to gibber at the edges of his mind, Farrar said, "I have a right to be tried as—"

"But, of course you will be tried. Speaking of which, my dear fellow, since you do not dispute the charges, a confession has been drawn up for you to sign. It will shorten the whole beastly procedure." He stepped closer, smiling genially, and holding out several sheets of paper.

Farrar tilted them to the light, and scanned them quickly. Looking up, he said contemptuously, "What poppycock! I'll not confess the murder of my cousin."

Lambert shook his handsome head. "Unwise, Farrar. Most unwise. You know how these country magistrates are. Any unnecessary delay irritates 'em beyond—"

"*Magistrates?* What have magistrates to do with it? I will be court-martialled, not—"

"Ah. You are confused, I see. No, friend, your trial will be civil."

Farrar dragged himself to his feet—a far from graceful procedure during which he was unpleasantly reminded of his bruises. "I am a soldier! I—"

"You—*were* a soldier," corrected Lambert softly.

"And I've a right to a military court-martial, which—"

"Which certain—ah, people feel has been delayed—much too long, I regret to say. Therefore, the Magistrate of this district felt the time had come to—er, expedite matters."

"What in hell does it matter what he feels?" raged Farrar. "A civil magistrate has no jurisdiction in a mili—"

"You may well be right," Lambert agreed musingly. "The point is, my dear fellow, that I am a servant of the people, and if a peer of this realm, who is also a magistrate, asks for my assistance in quelling a riot in a public place, I can scarce—"

"By God!" Farrar grated, his eyes narrowing. "This begins to have an odour! Name this magistrate who dares flout military authority!"

Lambert made a graceful gesture towards the open cell door.

Faintly, through his shocked incredulity, Farrar had been aware that the light was not quite as bright as before. Now he saw why. Much of the aperture was blocked by the great bulk of the man who stood there.

Lord Hibbard Green gave a soft, gloating chuckle. "All these months, dear Anthony, you have escaped the consequences of your craven cowardice; the families whose dear ones died, or were maimed because of you, stand unavenged. But you are in my jurisdiction now!" He touched his bandaged hand, smiling. "Tomorrow morning you will be tried, judged, and hanged for the shivering poltroon you are!"

It was ridiculous; impossible that this should be happening. Norris would soon intervene. But, knowing that his lordship could very easily see to it that his solicitor was kept from any intervention until it was too late, Farrar felt so cold that it was as if the finger of death had already touched him. He tossed his head higher, and said scornfully, "You would not dare! Decimus Green is outside your jurisdiction. You'd be called to account before—"

"Before we could hang you? Oh, but no, I assure you! I am a legally appointed magistrate. I was present when you caused a riot, and if I was so outraged by your infamy that I carried you off for immediate trial . . . ." he shrugged. "Who would really

286

care? It would, at most, be a case of shutting the barn door when the horse has fled. Why, how pale you are become! Frightened again? Perhaps—a glass of cognac . . . ? Have you fed the poor lad, Lambert? I'd not have anyone accuse us of—unkindness.''

They grinned at each other.

With a snarled oath, Farrar leapt forward. Using his chain as a weapon, he swung it with all his might. Lambert uttered a muffled shout as the chain smashed across his arm, sending him reeling back and the papers flying. Lord Green was very eager to jump clear but, impeded by blubber, his movements were too slow and the heavy chain flailed into his stomach. He uttered a most ungenteel belch and sat down with solidity if not grace. The gaoler, knowing better than to laugh at the embarrassments of the Quality, threw one hand over his mouth and backed away, then gave a gasp as Farrar leapt Green's bulk and came at him.

My lord uttered a wheezing howl.

Cursing, Brooks Lambert sprang after Farrar, gripped his shoulder and spun him around. Farrar, slowed by the manacles and by the beating he had taken at the bazaar, raised his chained hands to defend himself, but Lambert's fist was already whizzing at him. It struck home, hard and true. Farrar was slammed back, and fell down and down into an echoing half-world.

Lambert went at once to assist the profane peer to his feet. Raging, Green staggered to Farrar and kicked him viciously. His oaths and the smell of him, caused the soldier's lip to curl. ''Not too much, my lord,'' he murmured. ''We must— ah, restrain our enthusiasm for, most assuredly, there will be an investigation.''

''All the more . . . reason . . .'' gasped his lordship, holding his middle painfully, ''that he must . . . sign that confession . . . Did he?''

''No. He balks at the admission of his cousin's murder.''

''Damned carrion! Unbalk him, then.''

Lambert looked at him steadily. ''It will be—expensive, sir. The risk is not inconsiderable . . .''

Green thrust his empurpled face under the captain's slim nose. ''Blast your eyes! Do not speak to me of risk! My son will lie abed a month and more by reason of this clod!'' He glanced at the discreetly distant gaoler and lowered his voice. ''I want that confession *signed*," he hissed. "By morning! You'll be well paid."

"Double?"

My lord swore. "Oh—very well. Double. Damn you!"

Captain Brooks Lambert bowed.

Fate, reflected Roland Otton, standing before his mirror, could only be directed by the mind of a female, it was so capricious. For instance: his steadfast pursuit of wealth had led him not to the legendary pot of gold, but to a lady who would have suited him very well as a wife—had she not for some inexplicable reason rejected him (even when he'd offered marriage!), choosing instead to share the perils and eventual enforced exile of a wretched Jacobite. Twice since his Penelope had run away with Quentin Chandler, he had come close to laying his hands on the key to the location of the vast and elusive Jacobite treasure, having been thwarted once by Fate, and once, devil take it, by his weakness in coming to the aid of a friend. 'Which should teach you, my good fool,' he informed his reflection, 'that friendship is a luxury not to be indulged in by a dedicated villain.'

He glanced up as his man-of-all-work came, soft-footed, into the room. "Sorri," he said, "I look frightful. I think we must powder my hair before I venture down to dine. In the morning we shall leave this miserable place."

Sorenson, regarding his handsome employer's tall, elegant figure with amused affection, enquired, "Have we not prospered here, Mr. Roland?"

Otton grinned whimsically. "Do you know, I can scarce recall when last we prospered."

"There was the matter of the Alderman's lady . . ." murmured the valet, reaching for the powder box.

"Ah, yes . . . the delectable Mrs. Hancroft's mislaid pomander . . ." Otton chuckled. "Thank you for reminding me." He seated himself before the dressing table. "We do sometimes triumph—eh?"

Sorenson, who would have died for this careless young soldier of fortune, but had his own ideas of the "triumphs" they enjoyed, unfolded the powder wrapper, hesitated, and said blandly, "Perhaps I should first ask the lady to wait, sir?"

Otton's dark head jerked up. "Lady? You scoundrel! Where? Who is she?"

"She says her name is Mrs. Catherine Deene, but she has no card, sir. She is downstairs."

Catherine Deene. Now why was she come? Not the type of lady to have a card, certainly, nor the type he would have hoped to entertain on a sultry August night, but—The White Dragon was becoming a bore, and one should never overlook an opportunity. "Show her into the parlour," said Otton, waving away the wrapper. "We'll manage without powder after all."

He brushed back his thick hair, retied the riband, placed a large ruby pin in his lace cravat, and slid the heavy and ancient gold signet ring onto his finger. From the press, he selected a coat of dull maroon satin and, having donned it, returned to survey himself in the standing mirror. He would have had to be a blind fool not to realize he was an extremely well-favoured man, and he grinned at his reflection. "You dashing devil," he murmured. "Where were Penny's wits gone begging that she could have preferred Chandler over you?" And staying only to hang a gold-chased quizzing glass about his neck, he opened the door to his private parlour.

The lady who waited there stood at the window looking into the dusk. She wore a fine French shawl and a gown of pale pink silk over moderate hoops. Her hair was simply dressed and powdered, and she seemed taller than he remembered. "Good evening, ma'am," he began, advancing towards her.

She turned quickly and as quickly he halted, his amused dark eyes narrowing. So it was *this* Mrs. Deene! He bowed gracefully. "But how different you look. Now, this is a great piece of luck, because I was hideously afflicted with *ennui* and—" A frown came into his eyes. The lady had been weeping and her hands wrung and wrung at the dainty handkerchief she clutched. Stepping forward, he bowed her to a chair. "You are troubled, Mrs.—but it is not 'Mrs. Deene,' I hear."

"No." Dimity fought for control, but her voice was unsteady as she said, "I am Miss Cranford." He smiled and bowed again, and she wondered how much he knew. It was ironic that this wicked and notorious gentleman should be her only hope. Piers

289

and Peregrine, and Tio, bless him, were doing the best they knew. Any one of the three would have been horrified to see her—alone, at this hour of the evening, in the private apartments of a rascal and a libertine. It was outrageous conduct, but she had not dared wait. The life of her beloved was measured by hours; no stone must be left unturned in the battle to help him. "I would not presume to—to trouble you," she went on, "but—there is so little time. And I—I do not know where—to turn."

The last thing Otton had needed, he thought glumly, was to be visited by a watering pot, especially one related to so volatile a pair as the Cranford twins. Still, she was very lovely, and she was waging such a desperate fight to keep her pretty lips from trembling. He drew her to the rather drooping sofa, sat beside her, and took up one cold and shaking hand. "Now, surely," he said, stroking that hand soothingly, "it must be very bad if you are come to me. You'd best explain, ma'am."

And so, trying to ignore the fact that he sat much too close, that his knee touched hers, that his hand showed no inclination to release her own, she told him. She began to take heart when she saw the twinkle fade from his dark eyes to be replaced by a frown, and she was further heartened when she described Anthony's brutal arrest and felt the sudden tightening of his long fingers.

His classic features for once lacking all traces of the amused cynicism with which he viewed the world, Otton stood and gazed silently at the quizzing glass he swung gently to and fro. His eyes drifted to the pale face of the distraught girl. "I must be honest, Miss Cranford," he said gravely, "and tell you that you've made a poor choice in coming to me. Surely your brothers have other resources. I'd think—"

"They are doing their best. One of my brothers is racing to beg the help of Sir Brian Chandler at Lac Brillant; the other is gone to the army post in Salisbury. Lord Glendenning is driving Farrar's swiftest team in search of his father, the Earl of Bowers-Malden."

"Well then, ma'am, I fancy you've done all that can be done. When such formidable allies arrive, they will—"

"Find Sir Anthony has been hanged," she whispered brokenly.

"No, no, ma'am. Scarcely that. He will be held at the barracks until—"

"He has not been taken to the barracks," she interrupted once more. "It was what we had surmised also, but—but he is imprisoned in Buckler Castle." The lazy swing of his hand arrested, Otton stared at her in mute astonishment. Desperate, she stood and faced him. "The priest in Decimus Green accompanied us there. Sir Anthony is denied all visitors. They would tell us nothing, but my brother has taken a gypsy boy to be his page, and Florian knows a scullery maid in the castle. He was able to learn that Anthony is held without food or . . . water." Her eyes filled with tears. She blinked them away and went on threadily, "He has been—cruelly beaten, sir, and—and is to be tried early in the morning, on charges of desertion and . . . of murdering his cousin, which is a wicked lie! Everyone in the castle knows he will be found guilty. They are—already preparing the—the gibbet!" Her voice broke. She wiped frantically at her eyes.

"Be damned!" gasped Otton, shocked out of his customary imperturbability. "They must be demented! What bucolic fool would perpetrate such a gross miscarriage of justice?"

"Lord H-Hibbard Green!"

He tensed and stood very still and silent for a moment, then quoted half to himself, " 'A beast that wants discourse of reason . . .' So that's it!"

"Are you acquaint with the gentleman?" asked Dimity anxiously.

"Lord forbid, ma'am. I've met him, and leave his vicinity so soon as may be. But I'll tell you this, you'll find no man hereabouts will dare oppose him. I guarantee that when your brother reaches the army post and reveals his errand, he will find the Commandant mysteriously unavailable. Sir Brian Chandler would challenge Green, but lacks the rank to prevail against him. As for Glendenning's formidable sire—" he pursed his lips judicially. "The earl's a crusty old devil, who would delight in such a contest, but if what you tell me is indeed so, Bowers-Malden can never hope to reach here in time." He shook his head as tears slid silently down Dimity's white cheeks, and drew her into his arms. "No, no, my pretty. Never weep over spilt milk. I'll kiss away those—"

Enraged, she pushed him back. "Horrid creature! I come to

beg your help, and you try to make love to me! What manner of gentleman are you?"

"No manner, m'dear." He grinned unrepentantly. "I deny such an appellation most vehemently. I am a wanderer—a fighting man whose sword, wit, or loyalty are to be had for a price. No, never curl your lip—I do but tell you the pure truth of this marvel that is me."

She frowned into his laughing eyes. "You were Anthony's friend once! Do you care nothing that, even as we speak, they are trying to force him to sign a confession to a murder he never committed?"

A muscle rippled in his jaw, but he said easily, "Farrar denied me. Ran me out of his house, by Jupiter! You heard him. Besides, even did I want to help him—which, mark you, is at odds with my principles—there's nought I could do against Hibbard Green. He's a very bad man, even I will admit that, but in his own district he is all-powerful. And old Tony, poor fellow, has been living on borrowed time since Prestonpans." He shrugged his broad shoulders. "My regrets, but—"

Dimity sprang forward and seized the edges of his coat. "You are the grandson of the Duke of Marbury! *He* could help! And he likes Tony!" She caught a rare glimpse of anger, and before he could speak, she put her hand over his lips. "No, no! Do not refuse. For the love of God, *help* me!"

He removed her hands from his coat and anxiously smoothed away the wrinkles she had made. "You are—something fond of our—er, deserter, I think?"

She wept openly now, racked by the terrible pain of hopelessness. "I love him with—with all my heart . . . all my soul. And I know . . . he must—must die, but Florian said . . . Anthony had pleaded for a firing s—squad. That monster taunts him with—with public . . . *h–hanging*! No matter what they say of him, sir, he is a—a brave man, and not afraid of d-death. But the shame of—of being *hanged* will break his dear heart! Oh, God—have pity on him!" She bowed her face into her hands and sobbed.

Otton scowled, then a thoughtful expression came into his eyes. Not one to miss an opportunity, he said slowly, "There is, perhaps . . . one way in which you could—er, buy my services . . ."

Dimity lifted a pathetic, tear-streaked face. If this man could prevail upon his grandfather to come, the duke might be able to influence the court to grant Anthony's plea for a less shameful death. For that, she would do anything. No sacrifice was too great. "N-name it . . ." she gulped resolutely, having a very fair idea of what he meant to ask.

She had reckoned without the driving ambition of Roland Otton. "I am most interested," he murmured, "in a certain . . . cypher . . ."

❦ *Chapter 18* ❧

In some respects Buckler Castle resembled its owner. Certainly, it had seen better days and, crouched like some vast and malignant menace some distance from the market town of Greenlow, it lacked both grace and dignity, inspiring travellers not with a desire to investigate the ancient structure, but rather to depart its vicinity without delay.

On this cloudy morning, however, many people had braved the rather chill wind and toiled up the hill to where Lord Hibbard Green presided in the vast chamber that had once been the hall of audience and was now converted (at no little expense to the ratepayers) to a court of justice for the district. The crowd was in a holiday mood; many had known and admired handsome young Sir Harding Farrar and were eager to see his heartless murderer brought to justice. Others, including several groups carried in by special coaches, were the grieving relatives of men who had died in the Battle of Prestonpans and who were equally eager to see justice done.

In the study adjacent to the courtroom, the local representative of the King's Justice preened before the mirror, adjusted the flowing wig that was so at odds with his bloated features, straightened his robes, and barked, "Well?"

Brooks Lambert closed the door behind him and strolled closer to my lord's bulk. "He would not sign, sir."

"*What?*" His face mottled with rage, Green jerked around. "You had all night, damn you! Do you mean that the three of you were unable to break one man? By God, but I should have done the thing myself!"

"In which case, my lord," said Lambert dryly, "you'd likely

have killed him. It seemed to me desirable that Farrar be able to walk to the dock. As to whether he signed the confession, I fail to see it as vital. You can very easily prevent his denying the charges. *You* have appointed his Counsel, and your men are already in place to stir up the yokels. With luck he'll be dragged out and lynched before the trial is concluded, and I and my fellows quite unable to hold back such a mob."

"Humph," growled his lordship begrudgingly. "It might serve, at that. You're no fool, Lambert."

"I've to give you credit, sir," murmured Lambert. "You've planned it very well. How did you manage to bring in all the grieving kinfolk?"

The baron chuckled. "Sent my men searching for them days ago. I was fairly sure Farrar would attend the bazaar since 'tis his church that is to benefit. Not that it's necessary they be here, but it adds a touch of pathos to the scene which don't hurt."

"I only hope the boy appreciates the service you render him," said Lambert idly.

My lord frowned. "Boy? What boy?"

"Why—the young, er, Pretender, sir. Carlton Farrar. The child who will inherit The Palfreys and the fortune."

Hibbard Green's laughter could be heard all the way down the stairs.

Dimity clung very tightly to Peregrine's hand and stared with red-rimmed eyes at the monstrous figure of the man who would, she was sure, pass sentence of death on her beloved. How pleased and smug he looked, seated at the lofty bench. Even as she watched him, he directed a confident smile to someone seated in the front row. She craned her neck and caught sight of Phillip Ellsworth's handsome profile. With a pang, she thought of him stepping into Anthony's shoes as master of The Palfreys. But there was always the chance that young Carlton's claim was a true one. 'In which case,' she thought dully, 'the child had better be closely guarded!'

Roland Otton had been all too correct in his prediction of Peregrine's reception at the army post. Having stated his mission, he was left to cool his heels for an hour, then advised that it was most regrettable, but the Commandant was in London, and he was the only person able to intervene in such a matter. Word would be sent to him "at once." Well aware of how slowly grind the wheels of the military administration, Peregrine had returned, raging, and now sat beside his sister, tight-lipped and seething with frustration.

Dimity felt him start, heard a muffled exclamation from Lady Helen seated to her left, and jerked her head around as a ripple of talk swept the large room. The prisoner was being brought into the dock.

Peregrine whispered, "Hang on, Mitten! Courage!"

His words seemed very far away. She saw only the beloved figure, bowed now and moving weavingly between his guards, the fair head hanging low. She heard the clank of chains as one of the guards lifted his arm and guided the manacled hand to grip the edge of the dock. Someone was reading the indictment in a singsong voice. Somehow, Dimity fought away the ache of grief and sympathy, and made herself attend.

My lord said irritably, "The prisoner does not raise his hand. Does he understand? We quite appreciate his shame and his unwillingness to meet the eyes of those who will judge him, but it must be ascertained that he is aware of the gravity of the charges against him."

The words found their way through the haze of pain and thirst that tormented Farrar. He dragged his throbbing head up. There was an instant of stunned silence, broken by Lady Helen's horrified cry. One side of his face was almost covered by dark bruises; his mouth was swollen, and there was a deep gash above his right eye. Scarcely able to comprehend what was going forward, he swayed drunkenly as he peered about the great room, but the instinct for self-preservation was strong and he managed to croak, "Not . . . guilty—murder . . ."

However the spectators might lust to watch a villain hang, that the accused had been badly treated before a verdict was brought in did not suit their ideas of fair play, and a small ripple of protest spread and grew louder.

The shock to Dimity was less than it had been for Helen, for when Florian had brought word that Sir Anthony was being "persuaded" to sign a confession, her imagination had supplied a picture of the means of that persuasion. But although she was to an extent prepared, to see him in such a condition was so painful that she could not keep back a sob. Peregrine's hand tightened crushingly on her fingers, and she heard him swear savagely. Then, my lord was pounding with his gavel and gradually silence was achieved.

"Another demonstration of this nature, and the bailiff will clear the court," he roared. "Captain Lambert, what is the meaning of this outrage? Sir Anthony Farrar is a prisoner in my district, and as such is under my protection. That he has been most roughly handled is all too evident, and I tell you plainly, sir, that I do not tolerate such abominations. I may be a stern man, sir, but I am an humanitarian, and as such, I demand an explanation!"

There were murmurs of gratification and support for these proper sentiments, and all eyes were on the tall young soldier as he stepped before the bench.

"I take full responsibility, my lord," he said clearly. "When we arrested Sir Anthony yesterday, the crowd became enraged, and my men were unable to hold the line. Regrettably, the prisoner was rather mauled about before we were able to prevent such an atrocity. However, I assure you he has received continuous attention throughout the night."

"That's very obvious, you damned nail," growled Peregrine, *sotto voce.*

The captain's forthright answer appeared to have pacified his lordship, however, and the crowd raised no further demur when he ordered that, the indictment having been read, Mr. Eccles, the Counsel for the Prisoner, might now address the jury.

Mr. Eccles, a round-faced man of middle age with a perpetual smile, folded his hands upon his ample paunch and faced the jury. This was composed of three men who whispered together and giggled throughout, a fourth who looked around with the vacuous leer of the mentally deranged, while another appeared to be slightly intoxicated, since he hiccuped repeatedly. Two older gentlemen cupped their hands about their ears and nodded at the wrong moments. Of the five remaining, one kept nodding off to sleep, one was surreptitiously sketching on a pad of paper, much to the amusement of his neighbour, and the foreman was busily engaged in flirting with a buxom damsel in the front row of the spectators.

The prisoner, Mr. Eccles pointed out to these sterling jurymen, had been taken into the home of Sir Gilbert Farrar as an orphaned little lad. He had been well treated, nay, treated with a love as deep as his own parents might have given him. From having been cast adrift upon the sea of adversity, he found himself in the most luxurious surroundings imaginable and grew up enjoying such an environment. What more natural than that he be touched by the wicked spirit of covetousness? Surely, the jury were compassionate human beings who could appreciate the temptations such a background might provoke?

"Good God!" snorted Peregrine, incensed. "The man is convicting his own client!"

The ample farmer's wife next to him, hissed a loud "Sssshh!" and fixed him with a beady-eyed glare, and he subsided.

In an apparent attempt to extenuate the subsequent dastardly behaviour of the prisoner, the Counsel discoursed at length upon Farrar's life, coming eventually to his military career and thence to the Battle of Prestonpans itself. "Although many soldiers saw Captain Farrar abandon his men and run to the rear," he concluded solemnly, "you must consider that no one could *definitely* say he deserted for reasons of cowardice."

Again, Peregrine was moved to exclaim, groaning aloud and gripping his forehead in his rage. Fortunately, the magistrate, for all his brutish and unprincipled rascality, was not without a sense of humour, and this ridiculous exposition caused him to utter a roar of laughter which, being promptly joined by half the spectators, drowned out Peregrine's reaction.

The uproar woke up the somnolent juror, and startled Farrar, who had lapsed into a kind of stupor.

Peregrine leaned to Dimity's ear. "Is a farce!" he groaned. "They mean to hang him and are scarce bothering to stage a proper trial! That ugly old toad will rush it through, mark my words. I hope to God Piers or Tio come soon!"

On the other side of her, Lady Helen murmured a distracted, "This is *ghastly*! I think poor Anthony is barely conscious! How will he ever be able to defend himself?"

The equally distracted girl managed to squeeze my lady's hand and tell her that if it was at all possible, Piers or Glendenning might return in time. She did not add that she personally believed either possibility so slight as to be negligible. Lac Brillant, the great estate of the Chandlers, was situated near Dover;

it would be a miracle if Piers had reached there before midnight; another miracle if he'd found Sir Brian at home. Even had they set out at first light, driving a racing coach and four horses at the gallop, they could not arrive until late afternoon. Her best hope, and that a very slim one, was Roland Otton. She had refused to name the gentlemen involved in the delivery of the cypher, but, half distracted with grief, had written out the verse, as closely as she was able to remember it, and handed it to him. What Anthony, her beloved brothers, or dear Tio would make of such treachery, she dared not think. She would confess her sin when this nightmare was done, and then life would have no more meaning and she had as soon enter a nunnery at all events. At the moment it mattered only that Otton, seemingly not much pleased with the extent of her betrayal, had said grudgingly that he would try to find his grandfather, although the chances of his doing so, or of being attended to if he succeeded, were slight.

His lordship's gavel having restored order, Mr. Eccles droned on with his address, creating another sensation when he blandly asserted that Captain Sir Anthony Farrar was cognizant of the heinous nature of his crimes, that he deeply repented his cowardice on the field, and that even if it should be proved he had murdered his cousin, Lieutenant Sir Harding Farrar, it might be reasoned that the deed had likely been perpetrated while the prisoner, at a moment of extreme personal danger, was in a state of shock.

Through the resultant wave of exclamation and excitement, Dimity heard her brother's gritty profanity and Lady Helen's shocked little whimper.

My lord pounded with his gavel but did not look displeased. The clerk, an easily upset little man, was most agitated, and ran about shouting, "Order! Order!"

When silence fell, Farrar, who had been bowed against the rail of the dock, straightened, and in a hoarse croak of a voice, cried defiantly, "*Filthy lies!* This man is not my Counsel! I—" The protest was shut off as the surprised guard sprang forward and dragged him back, clapping a hand over his mouth.

The diminutive clerk, who had just sat down and was mopping his brow, jumped up again. "*Silence!*" he screamed. "Silence in the court!"

Lord Green leaned across the bench and levelled his gavel at the feebly struggling Farrar. "You will have your moment to speak when all the depositions have been heard," he said harshly. "Another such outburst, sir, and I shall have you gagged—to protect the ladies against your profanities!" He turned to the jury. "Gentlemen, you will ignore the ravings of the prisoner. Counsel, we will now hear the depositions."

"God grant they're all long-winded," muttered Peregrine.

Dimity glanced to the clock on the wall that relentlessly ticked the minutes away. It was half past ten.

The first deposition was given by a short, square man named Dodd, who asserted that he had been employed for some years as second gardener at The Palfreys. He had known both Sir Harding and Sir Anthony Farrar and, to his sorrow, was aware of the extreme jealousy existing between the two young gentlemen. He had on frequent occasions seen Sir Anthony—or Mr. Farrar as he was then known—strike his gentle cousin in a fit of rage. Further—and here he paused, blinking his round eyes solemnly as he looked one by one at the jurors—much as it went against the grain to report such evil, he had once overheard Sir Harding say with great sadness that Anthony Farrar would one day make an end of him.

Farrar, now listening intently, gave an exclamation of disgust and leaned forward to speak, only to be jerked back by the guard. Dimity saw his battered face twist with pain and she closed her eyes and prayed that he would not further provoke his tormentors.

Flushed with wrath, Peregrine bent forward and whispered to Lady Helen, "*Was* that fellow employed by you, ma'am?"

For a moment she could not reply. Then, in a voice choked with emotion, she said that she did seem to remember the man and that he had left The Palfreys to enter the service of Mr. Ellsworth.

"Huh!" snorted Peregrine.

Mr. Dodd was followed by a groom and then by a housemaid, both of whom corroborated Dodd's statements and reaffirmed the mutual dislike of the cousins, a dislike that deteriorated to violence only in the case of Mr. Anthony Farrar, and that was never displayed when his aunt or Sir Gilbert were nearby.

The next man called was a soldier. A stir of anticipation went through the courtroom, but Farrar shrank and his head bowed.

It was the moment he had dreaded for almost a year, the moment when his shame would be dragged into public view, when his honour must be trampled into the mud and his proud name disgraced forever. Mitten was watching and Helen . . . they would hear it all. Or almost all. His very soul seemed seared by the horror of it. He heard soft, scornful laughter and some jeering comments. He knew that he should be standing proudly to face what was to come. But this charge he could not defend. He was sickeningly ashamed that he had let his men down. Their faces passed before his mind's eye as they did so often in the awful silence of the night—one after another of the fine young men who had died—because he had not been there to hold them together . . . Because he had run, and so the gunners had run . . .

". . . and it looked bad fer us," Corporal Goodwin was saying. "The men was droppin' like flies, and the Scots was breakin' through all along our lines, wi' their perishin' great claymores what could nip orf a cove's head like a scythe goin' through grass. I hears Captin Farrar yellin' at a man ter stand his ground and fight like a Englishman, an' I says ter me mate, 'it's a good thing we got the captin left 'cause it needs a orficer like him ter keep us tergether!' And no sooner has I says it than orf he goes. Running like a perishin' deer orf the field! Strike me dead if I could b'leeve me perishin' eyes! That done it, a'course. Wasn't nothin' to hold them perishin' gunners we got from orf the navy, and they run like rabbits—almost as fast as what he done!"

Farrar forced his head up and stood very straight, looking blindly in front of him. He wondered what Dimity thought of him now. What her brother must think, sitting there, knowing he'd never walk properly again.

The Counsel for the Prosecution was saying in his high-pitched, clipped voice, "And—let us be sure we have it correctly—the prisoner you see before you is the *same* officer who deserted at the very height of the action? This is an extreme serious charge, Corporal. Are you perfectly sure?"

"Yussir."

"And this most reprehensible cowardice occurred shortly after the death of your commanding officer, Major Horace Rhodes?"

"Yussir. 'Bout five minutes arter the major had it."

"So at that point, Captain Farrar was in command of the battery, correct?"

"Yussir."

Mr. Eccles stood once more. "I understand you have spent many years in the army, Corporal Goodwin. You must have served under many commanders. Prior to this incident, what was your impression of Captain Farrar? Was he a good officer?"

The corporal hesitated. "I 'spose he was orl right, sir. 'Cept fer . . ."

My lord smiled genially from the bench. "Do not be intimidated, Corporal. You will not be penalized for answering the question."

"Ar—well beggin' y'r lordship's pardin, but I be a rank an' file, an' he's a orficer, an' Quality—"

From the side, a pale-faced man with a furtive manner, hooted, "What Quality?" and there was a burst of derisive laughter that did not appear to offend his lordship.

Peregrine thought, 'They're whipping 'em up!' and glanced around for the nearest door in case he must get his ladies out in a hurry.

"I permit of no discrimination between a working man and an aristocrat in my court," declared Lord Green magnanimously. "Answer the question."

"Well," said the corporal reluctantly, "it was only—he's got a proper temper has the captin, and him an' his cousin used ter go at it hot and heavy. They had a proper turn-up, just 'fore the battle. Me mate said as he heard Captin Ferrar say to his cousin, "I'll make damned sure you don't never get The Ponies, or The Hosses, or something like that."

There was a concerted gasp from the spectators.

In the dock, Farrar stiffened and stared frowningly at Goodwin.

Counsel for the Prosecution interjected smoothly, "Is it in fact possible, Corporal, that what Captain Farrar said was, 'I'll make—er, sure, that you never get—*The Palfreys*?' "

"Ar! By cripes, you got it, sir! That's just what he said. The Palfreys!"

"That's a lie!" raged Farrar, leaning over the dock. "And

302

what's more, I never saw your face! Who was your sergeant? What—"

"Gag him!" roared Lord Green.

"And during the battle," shouted Counsel, jabbing a finger at Farrar who was again struggling with the guard, "during the battle, Lieutenant Sir Harding Farrar fell! Supposedly to an enemy musket ball! But I put it to you, gentlemen, is it not far more likely that the ball came from the pistol of the prisoner? That this fine young soldier fell not to an enemy of England, but to the mortal enemy that was his own avaricious, unprincipled, and dastardly cousin?"

Many men were on their feet. Howls of rage sounded, knotted fists were brandished at the prisoner. Someone shouted, "He was murdered, poor chap!" and another voice contributed, "While fighting for his country!" to which a third voice howled, "Hanging's too good for him as done it!"

"Proof!" roared Peregrine, inflamed. "It's all hearsay! You have no proof, dashitall!"

Lady Helen was weeping softly. Dimity, white and stricken, jumped up, trying to see Farrar but unable to do so over the ravening crowd.

The little clerk was hopping up and down like a man demented, his shrieks for quiet and order adding to the din.

Half suffocated by the grubby rag knotted tightly across his mouth, parched with thirst, Farrar reeled under the rough hands of the guard and sank, consciousness fading.

"His own cousin!" howled a man in city clothing.

"We all knew Sir Harding, hereabouts!" roared another man—also in city clothing—"And I fancy we know how to deal with a deserting murderer!"

Pounding his gavel, Green raged, "*Quiet!* or I will clear this court!"

The perspiring clerk ran frantically about, shrieking his demands for silence, and to an extent the uproar lessened.

"Thank . . . heaven, the judge stopped it!" whispered Dimity, pale and shaking with fright.

"Best not be too grateful," her brother grunted, slipping his arm about her. "If Justice Toad has stopped a lynching, it's for some slippery purpose of his own."

A husky one-armed individual who had somehow insinuated

himself between Peregrine and the farmer's wife, muttered, "If I knows Lord Hibbard Green, sir, he means to pertect hisself as best he can. Just you wait and see."

Peregrine eyed him narrowly. "I think I've seen you before . . . Oh yes, you was at the bazaar. I'd the impression you'd no love for Captain Farrar."

The big man gestured to his missing arm. "Blamed him fer this. Not at first, y'understand. At first I didn't so much as think of it. Wasn't till the man come and told us what had really happened, I started to holding it agin the captain. I come here to face him with it. But—Lord alive, sir, I don't like the smell o' this lot! There's been rank lies told, what—"

"ORDER IN THE COURT!" screamed the clerk, both arms in the air.

Much to Peregrine's regret, silence was restored.

My lord thanked Corporal Goodwin for his testimony and asked the Counsel for the Prisoner if he had any questions. Mr. Eccles said that he did indeed have some questions, and proceeded to ask the good corporal why he feared Captain Farrar.

"A man what would murder his cousin, sir," said the corporal, "wouldn't think twice on havin' a common soldier done away with!"

Waiting for the learned Counsel's protest, Peregrine waited in vain, and whispered to the ceiling that he could not believe this farce was in fact taking place in civilized Britain!

Mr. Eccles, satisfied that he had done his duty, sat down while the next person to make a deposition, a Sergeant Shortbridge, was called. He was a tall, well set-up man, but was so unfortunate as to suffer a slight speech impediment, in addition to which he dropped his "h's" and his words were very rapid, so that it was necessary for his lordship to interrupt from time to time and ask that he repeat his remarks. He stated without bombast that he had been in the army for seventeen years, had been mentioned for bravery while fighting in the Low Countries, and had later served under the command of Major Horace Rhodes at the Battle of Prestonpans. He praised the conduct of Captain Farrar during the night before the battle and went on to describe the death of Major Rhodes in such vivid terms that the judge was again moved to intervene.

"Such sad events are heart-rending," Green declared solemnly. "A man of Major Rhodes' stamp is a true hero and a credit to the England we all love and reverence. For whom," he directed a stern glance at the sagging prisoner, "*most* decent men, I thank the Lord, would die without hesitation!"

Peregrine muffled a hoot of disgust, and Dimity leaned to him and whispered, "Is this one telling the truth, Perry?"

"So far," he answered. "I didn't see Rhodes go—Hey! Poor Farrar is up again! He'll fight them to the finish, be damned if he won't!"

Her gaze flew back to her beloved. He had indeed managed to straighten up and now leaned against the rail, watching the sergeant who was sombrely recounting the dramatic moments following the death of their commanding officer.

"Captain Farrar instructed me to keep the men at their guns sir," he said with his odd, half-swallowed enunciation. "I did the best I could but then I 'eard 'em all 'owling and raving and there was the captain one minute and gone like a flash the next me-lord."

His lordship leaned forward, his small eyes glinting craftily. "It astounds me, Sergeant, that no effort was made to—ah, halt so reprehensible and dishonourable a performance."

"There was a effort made your worship," asserted the sergeant, his manner as grim as his lordship's was kindly. "I shouted to the captain to stop—I knew we'd never 'old the men without 'im for the enemy was slaughtering at such a rate and yelling their war cries what you wouldn't believe if 'ad you not of 'eard 'em wherefore our lads was fair knocky kneed. Captain Farrar made no sign of stopping and Lieutenant Sir 'arding Farrar says to me 'Sergeant' 'e says 'that gentleman is my kinsman and I cannot allow as 'e shall throw mud on the family name I am going after 'im.' So off 'e went poor gentleman though it did no manner of good 'cept 'e died young."

"Did you personally see Sir Harding remonstrate with his cousin?" asked Counsel.

"No sir but poor young Private Slate done—er, did so."

Hibbard Green said heartily, "Then by all means, let us call the private and hear what he has to say of it."

The sergeant pursed his lips. "Cannot be done melord since 'e died a few minutes arterwards but 'e told me what a 'orrid sight

305

it was to see such a fine young gent cut down in the flower of 'is youth as you might say.''

"And," purred his lordship, folding his fat hands and smiling benevolently, "did the poor private chance to describe the manner of Sir Harding Farrar's death?"

There was a tense silence.

Aware that every eye in that hushed room was upon him, the sergeant drew himself up. "Yes 'e did. 'E says as Lieutenant Sir 'Arding Farrar was shot through the 'eart melord by 'is cousin Captain Anthony—"

The rest of his words were drowned by the din.

✑ *Chapter 19* ✑

For several moments, pandemonium reigned. Farrar, who had been unable to defend himself on the charge of cowardice, would dispute with his last breath the horrendous charge of murder. It seemed for a short space as though his last breath was imminent, but although the military made only a token effort to restore quiet, the mob did not attempt to drag the prisoner out and lynch him. That calm was restored was due in part to the efforts of Peregrine, Roger Steel, many of the staff of The Palfreys, some villagers from Palfrey Poplars, and the one-armed ex-soldier, but the failure of the hoped-for mob scene to materialize was also due to the fact that my Lord Hibbard Green's hatred for Anthony Farrar had clouded his judgement. Had he treated the young aristocrat with deference and kindliness, the bereaved relatives and the majority of the simple villagers, egged on by the rabble-rousers, would have been willing to take matters into their own hands, judging that Farrar was being pampered because he was of the Quality. As it was, not all the vociferous proddings of Green's hired bullies could provoke the crowd to do more than shout and threaten before eventually quieting down again.

Restrained by the powerful guard from tearing the gag from his mouth, Farrar sought desperately through the sea of up-turned and hostile faces for a glimpse of Mitten or his aunt. He located the girl at last, ministering to Lady Helen, who appeared to be in a swooning condition. His anxiety was cut short when the guard shoved him violently, and he became aware that Green was speaking.

"... blame these good people for such a display! What we

have heard here this morning has been enough to appall the most callous of men, and the effect on the ladies must be such that I will allow any gentle creature who feels overcome to leave the courtroom." No gentle creature availing herself of this offer, my lord went on, "What a sad pass we have come to in this modern age, that a well-born man, bred up with every opportunity for the improvement of the mind and the shaping of strength of character, instead descends to such dastardly behaviour as to revolt every sense of honour and decency. I put it to you, Anthony Farrar, that, for the sake of your immortal soul, you will be well advised to confess your guilt and throw yourself upon the mercy of this Court!"

Farrar again striving to remove the gag from his mouth, my lord lifted a hand to restrain the guard's immediate and harsh reprisal. "So you wish to confess, do you, poor wretch? Very well, but I warn you—attempt another vile outcry and you will discover you stand before one who will not hesitate to take drastic measures." He nodded to the guard, and the gag was removed.

Farrar's attempt to speak was foiled by his parched throat, however, and his faint croaks were almost inaudible.

"Speak up," snapped my lord. "If you are unable, we shall ask Counsel to speak for you."

With all his strength, Farrar strove to make himself heard. "If I might—have some water . . . please."

My lord cupped a hand about one ear. "What does he say, guard?"

"He asks for a drink, your worship."

"Good God! The audacity of it! Sir, you are here to stand trial on what may well be a capital offence, not to indulge in a bacchanalian orgy!" At this, many of the spectators who were beginning to be uneasy about this trial, eyed each other askance, and a low and faintly resentful murmur arose from the crowded benches. My lord heard, and knew he had suffered a reverse. Irritated, he went on swiftly, "Since you find it difficult to be coherent, Farrar, I shall ask questions, and you may answer. You heard the charge made by Sergeant Shortbridge?"

"Yes . . . but I—"

"What have you to say for yourself?"

Farrar gripped the dock and leaned forward. "All—lies! I did not—"

"Did not—what? Run? I had understood you admitted that disgusting act."

"Yes, but—"

"Why? Why did you run, Captain Sir Anthony Farrar? Was it because you were paralyzed with fear of the Scots?"

"No, I—"

"When you address the Court, you will say, 'No, *my lord*.' You are in sufficient trouble, do not add contempt to your charge list! You ran then, because," he grinned at the crowded benches, "you were *not* afraid?"

"No. That is—yes! I—"

"You change your testimony, sir! You must make up your mind! Is your answer yes, or no?"

Farrar blinked at him and wished he would not shout so. Every syllable came like a blow at his pounding head; he was so tired he could scarcely see, and the heavy manacle dragged agonizingly on his hurt arm. It was so hard to think and even harder to try to talk with this raging thirst turning his mouth into sand. "I—I am sorry, but—I forget the question," he stumbled.

"Forget the question, indeed! Jove, but you will not make mock of this trial, sir! Nor of these patient and long-suffering jurors! You have *admitted* desertion. But you claim you were not afraid." His lordship leaned back, smiling. "Well, well. I wonder you ran at all, in that case. Unless—" He jerked forward suddenly, his eyes narrowing. "Can it be possible, Farrar, that you were not running from fear of the enemy, but from fear of being apprehended for the disgraceful act you had just committed? The murder most foul of your innocent cousin!"

"No!"

"Is it not a fact that you coveted the great estate your cousin was to inherit, and meant to have it whatever the cost?"

"No!"

"Is it not a fact," thundered his lordship, "that you saw the battlefield as a perfect place to commit so heinous a crime, seized your opportunity, and then panicked and fled? Do you dare deny it?"

"Yes."

"Yes—what?"

"Yes—my lord . . ."

"To which question? Are you confirming, or denying?"

Swaying and bewildered by the barked out rapid-fire questions, Farrar lifted a manacled hand to his brow. "I—"

"Why will you not give an honest answer? Admit the truth! You shot your cousin and—"

"No! It is—"

His lordship gave a roar of rage. "Do not *dare* to interrupt a King's Magistrate when he speaks! By the rood, Farrar, I am well justified to have you hanged here and now!"

"I did—did not m—"

"Lies and more lies! Are you incapable of speaking truth, sir? You have heard the sworn testimony of a fine soldier. A man at point of death accused you of the murder of your cousin! Own the truth and the Court might be disposed to be merciful!"

What he was saying was that to admit Harding's murder would buy a less shameful death than the gibbet . . . Farrar gripped hard at the bar. He was going to die anyway. What difference to give in, and at least not suffer the nightmare shame of public hanging . . . ?

His weary gaze turned to the benches. He blinked his eyes into focus and saw Helen, pale and shaking, a handkerchief pressed to her lips, watching him in horror. She half believed it, at all events . . . And then he saw another face; a white, lovely face, the great eyes full of anguish, the hands tight gripped, the mouth trembling. Mitten, his beautiful dream wife, was suffering torment down there—because she loved and trusted in him.

"Speak up, man! I've another case to try today!"

Farrar dragged his head around and saw yet a third face. His cousin Phillip, a sly, gloating grin on the handsome features. Phillip would inherit The Palfreys, and had apparently run out of patience, waiting for a military tribunal to despatch the man who stood in his way. That was why they had tried to kill him during the duel. That was why Hibbard Green was fighting now to have him executed with even deeper dishonour.

"I will hear your confession," barked my lord, angrily, "within sixty seconds—or instruct the jury as to their decision."

Farrar's chin came up. He met that hate-filled glare and managed the travesty of a smile. "You," he said clearly, "may go to hell!"

"And despite the shameful and depraved nature of these heinous crimes," expounded his lordship, enjoying himself as he instructed the jurymen, "you have seen this man consistently refuse to answer questions put to him in a fair and impartial Court of Law. In defiance of your authority, and indeed of your intelligence, he has uttered blatant falsehoods, used foul language to a King's Magistrate, abused the ears of the gentle ladies present, many of whom are bereaved as a result of his infamy, and in general behaved in a manner contrary to every concept of the oath he swore upon entering the service of the king.

"You have heard him accused of murder most foul—nay, you have heard a stalwart fighting man recount under oath the statement of a doomed comrade—and what, I ask you, could carry more weight of honesty than the word of a man about to meet his Maker?—who was eye-witness to the cruel killing. Had it not been that cowardice under enemy fire got the best of him, Sir Anthony Farrar might well have achieved his despicable object with no least suspicion falling upon him. He would have continued to use a title to which his very guilt denies him; his bloodstained hands would greedily have clutched the fortune he wrested unto himself, and there is no doubt in my mind but that he would have proven loath to allow any more than a pittance to the trusting lady who took him in as an orphan, who nurtured and loved him down through the years, and whom he repaid with the brutal murder of her only and beloved child!"

Gagged once more, Farrar watched Green with a weary disgust. The man's rascality was beyond belief. He ascribed to his victim the very crimes he himself had committed—and intended to commit. But his eloquence was succeeding with the jury, and the intoxicated member went so far as to wipe a tear from his eye.

Encouraged, my lord said sadly, "I need not tell you how it grieves my very soul to have to sit in judgement on one of my own station in life. An aristocrat, who has sunk to deeds that an honest working man would abhor! None the less, duty must be served, and I think you know the verdict you must in all good conscience bring in; the only verdict that men sworn before God to serve king and country, could deliver, or that would be acceptable to this Court." He paused, fixing them one by one with a stern and meaningful stare. "Shall you find it necessary, foreman, to withdraw?"

The foreman of the jury, happily convinced that he would enjoy a pleasant dalliance with the buxom lass in the front row of the spectator section, leaned forward and whispered to the jurors, one of whom had to be woken up so as to respond.

Dimity closed her eyes and leaned her cheek against her brother's shoulder. Her betrayal had been for nought; Otton had likely never had the least intention of trying to help. And her beloved, there could be no possible doubt, was to be taken out and hanged by the neck until dead . . . Her grief was so intense that it was a sharp pain within her. She knew vaguely that Dr. Steel was comforting Lady Helen. She was aware of her brother's ragefully whispered promise that they would rush an appeal to the king, that this farce was a disgrace to every concept of British jurisprudence. And she knew that Perry was as without hope as she; that the gallows waited outside for its helpless victim; that Anthony would hang because of the evil and greed of a man who misused his power. But, prepared as she was, her heart felt as though rent apart when the foreman coughed and said that he had now conferred with his fellow jurymen. She jerked erect, her fingers tightening convulsively on Peregrine's hand, her face so deathly pale that her brother felt hot tears of sympathy sting his own eyes and turned a blurred but rageful gaze on the magistrate.

Triumphant, and therefore expansive, his lordship said smilingly, "I want it understood that you are quite free to take all the time you need to reach a decision. Are you perfectly sure you do not desire to withdraw?"

"Ain't no need for it, melord," said the foreman with a careless shrug.

"Oh, but you know, I really think there is."

The voice came from the rear of the great room. It was not a loud voice, and yet it seemed to ring through the quiet and all heads turned to see who had spoken.

A gentleman strolled gracefully up the aisle. A figure not overly tall, but of impressive elegance, with a splendid French wig upon his head, and a silver-laced tricorne tucked under one arm. His cloak was thrown back carelessly to reveal a coat of dark blue velvet richly embellished with silver thread, and a waistcoat of lighter blue whereon delicate bluebirds were depicted. His small clothes were blue-grey satin, his shoes sported chased silver buckles and the high heels made a firm clicking sound as he proceeded towards the bench.

Scarcely a figure to alarm, yet a certain Captain of Dragoon Guards stationed at the side of the room whistled soundlessly and stepped back into the shadows; the prisoner, trapped in an unending nightmare of thirst, pain, and despair, stiffened, stood straighter, and a gleam of hope dawned in his dulled eyes; Mr. Peregrine Cranford gasped an exultant, "Now, by Jupiter, only look who's come, Mitten!" and his sister, half blinded by tears, whispered a heartfelt, "Thank God!"

The King's Magistrate did not appear to share such sentiments. Indeed, a dark scowl had descended on his brow and a slow flush warmed his unfortunate features. "Your Grace honours us with his presence," he snarled, "but you will forgive an we respectfully request silence. The prisoner is about to hear his sentence."

"Oh, by all means, my lord," murmured the Duke of Marbury, glancing with a twinkle at the awed faces of those about him. "I would not be here at all, you know, save that the king has charged me with the onerous duty of ensuring that justice, as he—ah, perceives it, is being enacted in his courts." He moved in his casual fashion to where the clerk sat, and smiled upon him until that gaping individual recovered sufficiently to relinquish his chair and back away.

My lord, about to respond, was obliged to wait until the dolorous howl of a large dog somewhere outside the courtroom had ceased. It was well known that Marbury had the ear of His Majesty, wherefore his lordship rephrased the irate and perhaps unwise remark he had been about to utter. "I was not aware," he said, "that your Grace had been appointed to such a post."

"You surprise me," said the duke mildly. "A notice was, I am sure, sent to all magistrates. Perhaps you have not kept abreast of your correspondence, my lord?"

Green, who very seldom read anything that his overburdened secretary could deal with, blew out his cheeks and replied in rather resentful fashion that his calendar was very full and there were not enough hours in the day to read every scrap of paper that crossed his desk.

" 'Tis precisely because you are so overworked, my lord," Marbury said earnestly, "that I am come. To help you."

"You are too kind. As soon as this case is disposed of, I—"

"*With* this case," Marbury interpolated. "You see—there are certain facts relating to the accused, of which I think you may be una—" Here, having for the first time looked squarely at the dock, his Grace checked. For a taut moment he sat very still and many of those present found themselves holding their breath. "I see," he resumed, his voice having a slight edge now, "that you have been extreme conscientious in your handling of the prisoner."

"We do not coddle traitors, sir, if—"

"Might one enquire," went on his Grace, as though Green had not spoken, "why Sir Anthony is gagged?"

"Because he has a foul mouth," said his lordship awfully. "And I will not have ladies offended in my courtroom."

"Untrue!" shouted a voice from the crowd.

His Grace, having a fair notion of who had dared such an accusation, did not turn towards Peregrine, but nodded to the guard. "Remove the gag, if you please," he said politely.

The guard glanced to the suppressed fury that was the King's Magistrate. This dandified shrimp might be a duke, but my lord Green would make mincemeat of him if he thought to come it over—At this point, having had no instructions from the judge, he turned his gaze again to the duke and, meeting the light blue eyes, received the horrifying impression that he had been pierced by a lance levelled from the back of a fast galloping warhorse. His fingers shaking in their eagerness, he untied the gag.

Farrar drew in a grateful breath, coughed, and staggered. Chains clanked. The duke's eyes opened a shade wider and he turned to the bench, eyeglass levelled, incredulity in every line of him.

"I think you do not apprehend, my lord Duke," rasped Green, "that this is a most desperate and despicable rogue who not only betrayed his country, but has done bloody murder upon his own kinsman!"

314

Marbury pursed his lips. "Despicable, indeed," he agreed. "How say you, Farrar?"

Striving desperately to defend himself now that hope was reborn, Farrar could no longer find the strength. His voice rasped incoherently. Lifting a feeble hand to his throat, he tried in vain to make himself heard.

"I think . . ." said the duke, very softly, "the prisoner does not constitute a major threat in his present . . . condition. Perhaps you will be so good as to remove the chains."

"I presume you are aware, your Grace, that this is *my* Court, and that you are impeding the execution of the king's justice!"

Marbury said nothing, but the fingers of one hand snapped like a pistol shot in the quiet room. The guard was not a man of powerful understanding, but he had detected a shift in the balance of power; he fairly jumped to unlock and remove the manacles, and when the prisoner sagged weakly, his was the strong arm that supported him.

"Is there," enquired that cool, resonant voice, "a doctor or apothecary present?"

Steel sprang up. "Here, your Grace! And if I dare remark it, the prisoner has been most cruelly treated and—"

Up went that slender hand again. "My dear sir, you may remark whatever you wish. Later. For the present we must not impede his lordship's justice any longer than is necessary. Do you be so good as to tend to Sir Anthony's immediate needs, and we will proceed."

"He has asked for water, your Grace, but was denied. Indeed, I think he has been denied all night."

"Then by all means give him some," said the duke, still smiling although the smile no longer reached his eyes, which seemed to Hibbard Green to glitter most unpleasantly. "A little brandy would not come amiss, doctor, are we to hear from him today."

"Now, by God!" snorted the magistrate, rising.

The Counsel rose.

The Court rose.

The duke did not. "I do apologize, my dear Green," he said in his amiable way. "You were about to pronounce sentence, I believe you said."

"I was." Green, Counsel, and Court sat down again. "If you have no objection," he added with heavy irony.

"But, my dear, none in the world."

"Thank you. Foreman, you were saying that—"

"Only—I think you have forgot a witness," put in the duke meekly.

"All the witnesses have been heard, your Grace," said Mr. Eccles with an expression of sad resignation. "To no avail, alas."

"Well, of course not. For you have left out the most important one."

A flurry of excitement stirred the onlookers, who were having the time of their lives.

Lord Hibbard, who was not, opened his mouth to protest.

"And I am assured you are the most just of men," murmured the duke, "and would not ever wish that a helpless prisoner be deprived of his rights . . ."

Green glared, chewed his lip, and said nothing.

The duke took a folded paper from his pocket and offered it to the clerk.

Hurrying to take and open it, the clerk stared, gasped, and turned terrified eyes to the bench.

"You *can*—read . . . ?" asked the duke, curious.

For a moment it seemed that the clerk could not, for on his first attempt his voice was as faint as that of the prisoner. He cleared his throat and said failingly, "Call . . . Major Horace Rhodes!"

Farrar, who was beginning to feel less dazed now that his terrible thirst was eased and the brandy was burning through him, choked on a mouthful, dropped the glass, and reeled up from the chair Steel had dragged in for him. Gripping the bar, he gasped, "Oh . . . my God!" and stared, his face between the bruises, white with shock.

Amid a flurry of neck-craning and excited comment, a tall man in regimentals limped in, leaning heavily on a cane.

Almost as pale as her love, Dimity sat very still, her mind spinning.

"He's—*dead*!" a woman shrieked, crossing herself.

"Burn it, but he's not!" Peregrine exclaimed joyously.

316

Lady Helen, a flush lighting her cheeks, uttered an odd little cry, and sat up very straight.

"My lord," enquired the duke with gentle deference, "is it your wish that Major Rhodes be sworn?"

The magistrate's wishes at that moment had very little to do with Major Rhodes, but he bowed to the inevitable and the major was duly sworn.

Mr. Eccles jumped up and asked shrilly for some proof of the gentleman's identity. Major Rhodes handed Counsel several documents and his calling card. My lord Duke commended the prosecutor for his astuteness.

"I am Counsel for the Prisoner, your Grace," gulped Mr. Eccles, scarlet.

The duke lifted his eyeglass and surveyed the learned gentleman. "Dear me," he murmured. "Perhaps we may hear your deposition, Major."

Horace Rhodes, keen of eye and ramrod stiff of back, was a career officer who had been in the army for twenty-eight years, having purchased a cornetcy at the age of twenty-two, but exchanging to the artillery five years later, intrigued by the big guns. He had not been acquainted with Captain Anthony Farrar prior to his appointment to the Battery and had been pleasantly surprised to find him a steady and reliable officer with a good head on his shoulders and a nice touch with the men.

"Surprised . . . ?" murmured his Grace.

Major Rhodes looked at him levelly. "I was unacquainted with Anthony Farrar. I had, however, met Lieutenant Sir Harding Farrar," he hesitated briefly, "and his mother."

"And you expected the cousins to be of similar temperament?"

The major shrugged. "I've known cousins be as close as twins. These two weren't. Fortunately."

Lord Green said bitingly, "If his Grace is done with cross-examining the witness, perhaps we may continue with the deposition!"

With an apologetic smile Marbury sketched a bow, and the major resumed. "I do not propose to bore your lordship and this Court with a recapitulation of the Battle of Prestonpans. Nor of the trials that beset us from the very start. Suffice to say it was a disaster. My own personal disasters were many. I was

317

extreme fortunate to have so splendid a second-in-command as Captain Farrar. I relied on him heavily.''

''How shocked you must have been when he deserted,'' sneered Lord Green.

''*After* you were killed, my dear Rhodes,'' inserted his Grace sweetly.

''Neither of which happened,'' said the major, with a faint grin.

Farrar reeled and through a wave of blinding dizziness clutched the rail convulsively.

Dimity's heart gave a great leap, and her breath was snatched away.

''*Aha!*'' whispered Peregrine.

''In that event,'' cried Lord Green, purpling, ''one might expect Captain Sir Anthony Farrar to have protested his innocence!''

''One might indeed, my lord,'' said his Grace. ''But, pray continue, Major.''

''We were under heavy attack,'' the major went on, ''when one of my officers lost his nerve and ran. You may suppose this to be a common occurrence. I assure you it is not, especially in the case of a well bred-up young gentleman instructed from childhood in the Code of Honour. I have seldom been more shocked, but—if there was a second crime involved, it was— alas, my own.'' His eyes fell. He hesitated and said in a less crisp voice, ''I knew the boy's mother, and what it would mean to her to have her son desert under fire, so I—I took a risk I'd no right to take.'' He turned to where Farrar watched him with bewildered intensity. ''I sent you after him, Captain—don't you recall?''

''You . . . *sent* me?'' gasped Farrar. ''I—no, I . . . seem to have lost—so much after I was hit. I thought it was . . . because I just didn't want to—to remember. I thought I'd run after him because—''

''Of your love for your aunt,'' put in his Grace.

Another buzz of comment shook the spectators. Farrar peered at Lady Helen. She was staring at him wide-eyed. Dimity turned and slipped an arm about her.

The gentleman in the front row who had defended Farrar

earlier, said a hushed but audible, "Then—it was *Harding* who ran!"

"This is all very dramatic," rasped Green with a curl of the lip, "but makes no sense whatsoever. Farrar would have us believe that although his mind was clouded from shock he remembers that he ran not for his own safety, but to bring back his fleeing cousin! And all these months he has said not one word about this, but nobly took all the blame to himself? Now come, your Grace! If you mean to imply that he would be willing to carry filial loyalty to the extent of suffering shameful execution rather than upset a relation, I say pshaw, sir! I say rubbish!"

"I agree," said the duke. "Can you explain it for us, Captain? Tell the Court what you do recall."

"I remember seeing Harding run," Farrar said slowly, groping his way back through the misted memory. "I went after him. I was hit. Afterwards, nothing is very clear. While I was in hospital . . . I was told people came to see me, but—I cannot seem to recall that period. When I was sent home, I began trying to—to put it all together. I thought I'd gone after Harding because I wanted to spare my aunt from being hurt. The colonel who came from Whitehall told me Major Rhodes had been killed just before I deserted and—"

Major Rhodes flung up a hand imperatively. His voice harsh and brittle, he snapped, "One moment! Do I understand you to claim, Captain Farrar, that you were *officially* advised I had been killed? Some while *after* the battle?"

"Yes, sir." Farrar blinked at him. "By letter, and—and by the colonel's visit to my home."

Puzzled, Marbury intervened, "But why should they have said you were slain, Major?"

Rhodes shrugged. "Not so remarkable on the field, Duke. I'm told I was a mess. I was hit in several places, one being a head wound that could very well have appeared to have been fatal. Not until after the battle was it found that I yet lived. No, I've no difficulty understanding that part of it. What baffles me is that I wrote to Farrar and—" his eyes flickered to the spectators, "—to Lady Farrar, telling them I had survived. It is very obvious now that my letters were intercepted by someone— *someone*," he glared at Phillip Ellsworth, "with a strong motive for mischief. At the time, when I received no answer I simply thought—Well, never mind that. Tell us more about this official visit, Captain Farrar. What further gems of wisdom had this—er, colonel to impart?''

''He warned me to hold myself ready for court martial,'' said Farrar, numbly. ''I—I knew that regardless of why I ran . . . I should never have left my post. I had abandoned my men for personal reasons. There was no excusing that, nor any escaping the punishment. I—I could see no least reason to further distress my aunt by revealing Harding's conduct.''

His face a thundercloud, the major growled, ''The predictable reaction of a man of honour. However, I know of no officer having been sent to see you, Farrar. Certainly his errand was either erroneous or—a deliberate and vicious misrepresentation of the facts! Do you remember his name?''

Farrar put a hand to his temple. ''Knight, I think . . . No! It was Light! Colonel Light!''

Rhodes said grimly, ''I think we shall require a full description of the gentleman.''

''Though I doubt he will ever be found, or Whitehall have any knowledge of him,'' the duke murmured.

It was beginning to dawn on Farrar now, and the possibilities were so awesome, the ray of hope so unnerving, that the courage which had sustained him through this long ordeal ebbed away. He found that he was shaking and asked in a thread of a voice, ''Sir—am I . . . are you saying I am—am innocent? That—that this whole hideous thing is—over?''

''Not by any means!'' barked Green angrily. ''You have admitted you ran after your cousin, but not how he died. Did you catch him?''

''Yes, my lord. I was trying to make him return to his post when I was hit. But, as God is my judge, I swear I did not kill him.''

Major Rhodes looked at the duke. The duke sighed, and shook his head.

Lord Hibbard brightened. The day might yet be saved. ''The murder charge against you stands, Farrar. The testimony of the earlier witnesses cannot be ignored.''

''Athough their identities are subject to question,'' said the duke dryly.

Once again, shock ran riot in the courtroom. Pounding his

gavel angrily, Lord Green roared, "I would give a deal to come at your meaning, your Grace!"

"I make no charge for revealing my meaning," said the duke. He stood and seemed suddenly very tall and formidable. "I put it to you, my lord, that Captain Sir Anthony Farrar has been the victim of a cruel plot. That those who conspired against him knew how highly he regarded his personal honour and, trading on that commendable trait, did all they might to destroy him. He was never held in anything but the highest esteem in Whitehall. I have, in point of fact, discovered that a letter was sent to him at The Palfreys, commending him for his gallantry on the battlefield. And that this letter also was delivered into the hands of a near relative who was staying there at the time," he sent a glance of scalding contempt at the white and twitching face of Phillip Ellsworth, "but obviously never received by Captain Farrar!" He held up his hand to quiet the burst of indignant comment. "Am I correct, Sir Anthony?"

His head swimming and his knees like water, Farrar leant heavily on the guard. "Quite . . . correct, your G-Grace," he stammered. "But—but I still don't understand. *Everyone* thought . . ."

"Not everyone, Captain," interpolated Major Rhodes, his strong face stern as he regarded the battered wreck in the dock. Tony, he thought, fuming, had been put through a year of hell that would have driven many a man into madness. God send this last ordeal did not push him over the edge! "Whoever was behind this despicable affair," he said raspingly, "despatched messengers to the families of many of our people who fell at Prestonpans. Under the guise of exposing your 'guilt,' these paid agitators, who'd probably never been near a military barracks, much less fought a battle, stirred up hatred and animosity against you. Rumour, once let loose, is the very devil to silence! Your enemies knew that you had no clear recollection of what had actually happened. It was their hope, Captain, that you would become so crushed by despair, so weary of contempt and villification, that you would oblige 'em and put an end to yourself, thus effecting a perfect murder!"

The room was in a turmoil, the spectators coming belatedly to the awareness that they, too, had been used in this infamous plot.

Over the uproar Lord Green, pale now and having a hunted look, bellowed, "And are we asked to believe that every previous witness has lied? Can you explain, your Grace, why a soldier would swear to have seen the prisoner brutally shoot down his cousin, if that were untrue? Bailiff! Let us have Goodwin and Shortbridge in here again!"

The bailiff was absent for a very few moments, and returned in a state of great agitation with the word that both corporal and sergeant seemed to have slipped away.

"Scarce to be wondered at," said the duke scornfully, "since both were paid impostors!"

"I shall require proof of that, sir," raged my lord, becoming ever more pale.

"It most certainly shall be proven," said Major Rhodes. "And those responsible will be brought to justice!" Again his cold gaze turned with deliberation to Phillip Ellsworth, who shrank, sick and terrified, before that condemning glare. "However," Rhodes added, "we must first, I think, verify Captain Farrar's actions that day. He did indeed catch his cousin. Harding refused to return to duty and fought to escape. When Anthony tried to detain him, in his terror, he turned on him. It was *Harding* shot you down, Farrar! I saw that much before I was hit myself!"

The babble of excitement that greeted this shocking revelation came only very dimly to Farrar's ears. The courtroom was a blur, and the effort to hold his head up now quite beyond him. He thought he heard Peregrine shout and Mitten's dear voice scream his name, but his tired mind was unable to cope with any more. He was possessed by a terrible fear that this might only be a dream and that he would waken to find Lambert still attempting to force a confession from him. His frantic prayer that it was not so was smothered by an overwhelming exhaustion that swiftly and inexorably dragged him down and down into a stifling emptiness.

The last thing he heard was what sounded like the distant and distressful howling of a large dog . . .

↞ *Chapter 20* ↠

His Grace, the Duke of Marbury, leaned back in the satin brocade chair in the luxurious cream saloon of Dominer, his favourite house, and gazed over loosely interlocked hands at the handsome bastard who was his grandson.

Impressive in blue and black, Roland Fairleigh Mathieson (who for various reasons went by the name of Otton) shifted uncomfortably in his chair. The silence was becoming nerveracking; he still did not know why he had been summoned to an estate that usually closed its doors against him, and, perhaps because his conscience was never entirely easy when in the presence of his formidable grandfather, he said with strained lightness, "A penny for your thoughts, sir."

"I was wondering," murmured his Grace, "whether your nature might have been—different, had you been born on the right side of the blanket."

Otton flinched inwardly, flushed, and answered with a shrug, "I fancy not, your Grace. My traits are all inbred, I suspect."

For just an instant the duke's fine hand clenched. *"Touché."*

Otton's flush deepened, but he met the duke's gaze with a certain arrogant defiance.

"Despite those—ah, inbred traits," his Grace resumed, "I must confess I was rather taken aback by Farrar's attitude when he ousted you from his home. You did, after all, see service together. One might think—"

Otton gestured with faint impatience. "Much I care what he thinks of me."

"Hmmn. And yet, Roland, I could wish you had remained in the army. Farrar is a most gallant young fellow and—"

"Is paid a pittance," his grandson again interrupted, misliking this topic. "In return for which his life was near forfeited and his only reward was a letter of commendation that he never received." He gave a scornful bark of laughter. "When I venture my life, your Grace, it is only after having been well paid! I do not consider Farrar to have the best of that bargain!"

The duke sighed. "Do you—ever—bestir yourself for other than gold? Is not surprising that you have not a friend in the world."

This was not perfectly true, but Otton chose not to dispute it. "Only a fool works without pay, sir," he said disdainfully. "And friends are a questionable asset, at best."

"So you prefer your horse."

The sneer in the dark eyes was replaced by a softer expression. "Rump is one in a million. A far better conversationalist and more loyal friend than most men."

"One cannot but wonder," murmured the duke, "that you pushed him so hard the night you rode to enlist my aid in Farrar's behalf."

Otton tensed, catching his breath. He had blundered into yet another of the traps this man was so adept at constructing.

"Or," went on the duke silkily, "why you would have bothered at all, considering that you care so little for him, or his treatment of you." His grandson maintaining an enigmatic silence, he went on, "I fancy you have heard about the poor fellow?"

"If you refer to his having been exonerated of all guilt—"

"I refer to the fact that he is gravely ill. He has never regained consciousness, you know. Steel is a good man, and says that from Farrar's delirium it appears he is unable to accept his sudden vindication; that his mind fears the trial was no more than a dream and shrinks from returning to a reality in which he is as deep sunk in guilt and disgrace as before." He frowned at one cuticle and pushed it back carefully. "It would help, I fancy, were his lady at his side. He calls for her, but she will not come. Odd, is it not? She appeared so devoted." His eyes lifted then, and Otton saw the glare in them and nerved himself.

"Most odd," he said, his voice a little strained. "But I quite fail to see—"

"Do not fence with me, sir!" Marbury stood, frowning down

324

at this regrettable kinsman. "You will find me no mean swordsman, I do assure you, for I am not near so old and decrepit as
you suppose!"

The voice was a whiplash that brought Otton to his feet with
somewhat less than his customary grace. "Indeed, Duke, I—"

"Should by this time know that I have spies everywhere! I
have learned, for example, that Miss Cranford visited your rooms
the night Farrar was arrested. Why?"

"To—er, to beg that I find you, and—"

"And help a man for whom you cared nothing? 'Only a fool
works for no pay,' remember?"

Otton moistened his lips. "There—there are, circumstances,
your Grace, that must change any man's mind, even—"

"Even such a heartless, soulless, mercenary rake and oppor-
tunist as Roland Fairleigh Mathieson? Oh, I think not!" The
duke stepped closer. "How pale you are become, dear boy!
Guilt, perchance?"

Otton fought to collect his shredding nerves. "Not—at all.
I—"

Marbury took another pace, and his grandson, retreating, collided with a table and stopped of necessity.

"What did you have of that poor, terrified child, my most
unvaliant soldier? Her virtue, perhaps? Is that why she will not
go to the man she loves, even though he lies ill and crying out
for her?"

"No!" gasped Otton. "Sir—I swear—"

Marbury's lip curled. "*You?* Upon what would you swear?
Your honour? You have none! Your God? Hah!"

Very white, Otton said, "Upon the thing I hold most dear—
my mother's memory! I swear I did not violate the girl, nor
force her in any way—"

"To do—what?" The duke stood very close now, and Otton,
unable to escape, faced him in silence, but he could not meet
that piercing gaze and his eyes fell.

"I know what you are about, you greedy money grubber!"
said Marbury with icy contempt. "As always, you seek an easy
path to riches. Miss Cranford must have had something you
wanted—something perhaps that she was sworn not to reveal, is
that it? 'Sdeath, but you are even lower than I suspected! That
any kin of mine should stoop to terrorize a loving, grief-stricken

lady!" He stepped back, pale with wrath. "The very sight of you offends! Go! Take your only friend, and go!"

Otton's bowed head lifted. "Sir—I—I did not terrorize the lady. I beg—"

"Oh, I believe that last! You would beg and crawl to be named one of my beneficiaries, would you not?" Marbury shook a white finger under his grandson's aquiline nose. "Now hear me, Roland. If you—*ever*—expect anything from my estate, you will undo whatever mischief you have done! If that fine boy dies— or that gentle girl is denied the happiness she so richly deserves . . . Heaven, help you—you'll get not a penny! Now—out!"

Otton did indeed want something from Marbury, but not even to himself would he admit how desperately he longed for his grandfather's affection and respect. Even so, his hand went out pleadingly. "Sir, I promise—"

"Pah! Out!"

Otton bowed and left him.

Riding through a glory of sunset, he told Rumpelstiltskin all about it. "Wicked old devil," he said, without much heat. "Did you ever, Rump, hear of a man stooping so low as to set spies— *spies*—on his own grandson?" He stroked the chestnut's silken neck. "You may be thankful that I am your only relative," he added bitterly.

Rumpelstiltskin, feeling that something was expected of him, tossed his head.

His master was silent for a little while. Then, "Damn and blast!" he muttered. And at the crossroad, turned to the east.

The afternoon was still, and Muse Manor drowsed peacefully under the hot August sunshine, the curtains at the open lattices billowing occasionally to the touch of a warm and fitful breeze. The smell of baking bread drifted tantalizingly from the kitchen, and Dimity smiled as she heard Peregrine's new peg leg tapping along the hall. She selected a snowy white rose, snipped it neatly just above the seventh leaf-cluster, and held it for a moment, admiring the perfection of the softly furled petals and the sweet fragrance of the bloom.

Peregrine was much more at ease with the "foot" Florian had carved for him. At first professing indignation because he "clumped about like a one-legged pirate," he had come, she suspected, to be rather proud of his new leg. It had also become something of an indicator of his mood, for when he was in a pet his stamps were rapid and loud, whereas when he was content his steps were lighter.

It was becoming quite hot in the sun. She took up her basket of blossoms, moved into the shade, and sat down for a minute on the old bench by the Mimosa tree. She sighed, staring blindly at the roses. How was he today? Better, surely. It was, after all, nigh two weeks since the trial. Lady Helen had sent word asking that she come—had said he was calling for her—but that had been a week ago. A terrible week, during which she had been all but driven out of her senses, longing to go to him, and knowing she dare not. When she went to The Palfreys it must be to confess her betrayal. And that was news he should not hear—not yet. She would have to go, eventually, when he was more fully recovered. She bit her lip. Whatever would he say to her? How would he feel? Conscience whispered, "Whatever he says, you know how he will feel. He will know you did it for his sake. He has just been given back his honour, and now he will surely think his good name tarnished again by the terrible thing you did. He will never forgive you. Never want to see you again!" She closed her eyes. It was done. And he was alive. But in saving him, she had lost him. There could be no doubt, for she knew him so well and, understanding the relentless Code by which he lived, adored him the more because of his stern adherence to it.

Peregrine and Piers had obviously put another interpretation on her refusal to return to The Palfreys. They believed that she feared to implicate Farrar in the Jacobite business. She had made no attempt to enlighten them, striving to appear content, and they had been so careful to avoid all mention of the matter. But she had caught Peregrine sometimes watching her anxiously, or Piers would give her one of his searching looks, and she would know that they were worrying. Perhaps they were watching her now. A fine picture she must present!

She looked up swiftly and saw at once that she was no longer alone for the westering sun painted a shadow onto the lawn beside her. A tall shadow. A slim gentleman with a sword at his side and a tricorne in one hand. Her heart began to pound wildly. She closed her eyes for a second, trying not to tremble and to quiet the hurrying of her breath. Standing then, she turned and gave a gasp.

Instead of the beloved features, the green eyes and fair hair she had been sure she would see, she encountered a breathtakingly handsome dark face, black, curling hair, twinkling eyes of jet, and a shapely mouth that trembled on a smile.

Her hand fluttered to her throat. "You!"

Otton swept her a low bow. "Neither flattering nor original," he said scoldingly. "I had expected a warmer welcome."

"Oh! I am so sorry! Of—of course you are welcome." Apprehensive, she tried not to show it, and waved him to the bench. He waited respectfully until she was seated, then sat beside her. 'Too close, wretched man,' she thought and, edging as far away as was possible, went on, "I have wanted so to be able to thank you. It is—it is only due to you that Sir Anthony was not—did not die that dreadful day! How you ever managed to find your grandpapa and bring him to us in time—"

"With the very greatest difficulty," he interrupted, managing in some incredible fashion to have both halved the distance between them and acquired possession of her hand. "I have, dear Mistress Mitten," he lifted and kissed her fingers, "a superb horse. The fastest in all the Southland, I do believe." Dimity rather hurriedly reclaiming her hand, he looked at her soulfully and appended with a sigh, "But—my grandsire is not—er, enamoured of me, as you know. It took all my powers of persuasion to win my way into his august presence."

"Oh," said Dimity, feeling the most ungrateful wretch alive. "Then—I must be doubly thankful for your invaluable assistance. He was—he is—superb!"

"He is. And you should."

She blushed before his really very naughty eyes and looked away.

"But you are not," he observed, moving even closer.

Dimity drew a deep breath. "Captain Otton—"

"Roland," he murmured, twining a glossy ringlet about one finger.

"You and I struck a—a business arrangement," she went on, removing the ringlet.

"Of which you are deeply ashamed," he said with sudden gravity.

328

She winced and shrank a little.

Otton lifted her chin. "Poor gentle child," he said in a tone she would not have believed him capable of. "How innocent you are. Is a rare quality. I vow I quite envy Farrar. You—mean to tell him, of course."

She looked at him steadily, wondering at the compassion she read in his eyes. "I have no choice. I—I can only pray, he will forgive me."

"Confession is good for the soul," he agreed musingly. "Of the confessor."

Her eyes, which had fallen again, shot up at this and scanned him anxiously.

"But it can play hob with the one hearing the confession," he finished. "Besides, there is no need for you to so immolate yourself at poor Tony's expense, and—"

"Immolate!" she gasped, indignant. "At *his* expense? But I must—"

"Destroy the happiness he has only just found?" He shook his head. "I am not the man to be much concerned with the troubles of others, and your beloved was far from kind to me. However, I will admit he has had more than his share of misery. If you insist upon piously relieving your conscience, ma'am, you will break his heart, plunge him back into despair, and ruin your every chance for a rich and joyful life together."

Dimity's eyes filled with tears. She said in a low voice, "Do you think I do not know that?"

"Besides which," said Otton, "there is not the need for such nobility. No, be still and listen to me. I have already learned a good deal of what I wish to know about the treasure, but your cypher was, alas, quite worthless. There were, as you know, four such messages sent out. Even could I discover the key to the one you gave me, I would have only a small part of an apparently long message. As it is, I have wasted some very expensive candles during the hours of darkness, trying to make head or tail of it, to no avail. So, to all intents and purposes you have done nothing."

She lifted tragic, despairing eyes to his, and he went on, "I mean the rebs no harm, I promise you. I am out only for the gold. I would never betray them to the military, for I—"

Why his arms were about her, or how it had occurred, seemed

329

very unimportant. On a sob, Dimity faltered, "B-But—I betrayed them! I cannot be silent. I *cannot* let him go on thinking me pure and—and worthy to be his wife when—"

"Then you shall have to confess." He drew her closer and said earnestly, "Unless you are willing to bear the greater burden and remain silent. And it *will* be the greater burden, my sweet Miss Cranford. Besides, consider poor Farrar's alternatives. Would he call me out? No doubt of that. I am no braggart, m'dear, and will confess to you that I have been bested with the sword. Once. I have seen Farrar fence, and he is excellent. Only—not in *my* class. And—in despite everything, I really have no desire to kill him."

She was briefly silent, huddled in his arms, torn by doubt and longing with all her heart to accept his solution. Still clinging to his cravat, she looked up. "Is it true? Is it really true? Will you give me your word of honour as a gentleman that you did not decode it and that you will never repeat what you know? That you will never betray any of them?"

He stared at her with an odd expression. "Would it set your mind at ease if I did so swear, pretty one? My grandpapa does not place much value on my word, nor fancy me a gentleman, you know."

"Perhaps not. But I do."

"Do you, by God!" He flushed darkly. "Then—you have my word, ma'am. On both counts."

"Thank you. Oh, thank you! If you but *knew* the weight you have lifted from my shoulders!"

He gave her that same odd look, then swooped down and kissed her on the forehead.

"Rogue," she said, smiling, but pulling away. "I might have known your humility would not last long!"

He threw a hand to his heart. "Gad! Why must I always show my true colours? And here comes your fine brother to defend your honour. In truth, I cannot bear it! Adieu, sweet maid. Go to your fine beau. He needs you."

"Hey!" roared Peregrine, stamping rapidly along the path. "Otton! What the devil are you about?"

Otton gave a whoop, and ran. A few minutes later, riding at a leisurely pace along a sun-dappled lane, he chuckled to himself. He had not been entirely truthful with the delectable Miss

Cranford. Less than a month since he had been involved in an interesting little business that had come near to costing him one of his few friends. Fortunately, he had managed to not only retain his friend, but to come away from the affair with something almost as valuable—a copy of the third cypher. It was true that he had failed to break the code, but to his way of thinking that was unimportant. He knew now the man he must watch. And with luck, young Father Charles Albritton would lead him to the pot of gold at the end of his rainbow—the treasure of Charles Stuart and his ill-fated Jacobites.

"Do you know, Rump," he confided, "I think I have contrived to satisfy my curmudgeonly tyrant of a grandfather. And additionally, if I could look into the future, I believe I would see vast riches for me, and a happy and contented retirement for you, old friend. A pleasant prospect, is it not?"

Rumpelstiltskin offering a companionable snort, Roland Fairleigh Mathieson chuckled again. He seldom permitted himself to be downcast, but today his inherent optimism soared to new heights, for he sensed that he was at last within reach of his goal. He began to sing a naughty little French song as he rode on through the glory of the summer afternoon.

It was perhaps as well that he was not able to look into the future.

"Anthony," whispered Dimity, bending over the bed. "Wake up, my darling."

Her starches rustling, the nurse sniffed. "He cannot hear you, miss," she said huffily. "We have tried that these two weeks— to no avail."

Dimity stroked back the fair, dishevelled hair. "Anthony, wretched creature," she murmured, "how dare you hide from me? Wake up!"

Folding her arms, the nurse cast an exasperated glance at the ceiling. Such terms as those were enough to drive the poor soul even deeper into his coma! "Dr. Steel has been here daily," she imparted, "and also a fine London surgeon by name of James Knight, and if they wasn't able to—" She paused, outraged, as Dimity knelt and lifted a hand to silence her. "Well!" she exclaimed, but then, because she was really a very fine nurse, she checked and stood motionless.

The fair head tossed restlessly against the pillows.

"Beloved," said Dimity yearningly. "Oh, my love—come back to me."

The long lashes fluttered and parted to reveal a pair of intensely green eyes that frowned at the ceiling in a bewildered fashion.

"Anthony," Dimity murmured again.

Very slowly, the thin white face turned to her. The green eyes lit with a radiance that awed the starchy nurse. Sir Anthony Farrar lifted one hand a quivering inch from the coverlet and smiled at the girl he worshipped.

With a muffled sob, Dimity took up his hand and pressed it to her cheek.

"Well, I never!" whispered the nurse, blinking as she tiptoed away.

Farrar, thought Norris, was beginning to look halfway alive, thank the Lord! "Wasn't no need for a hearing," he said, pulling his chair a little closer to the pomona brocade sofa in the morning room. "Why d'ye think I asked you for your mama's diary, eh?"

A blanket over his knees, and his love perched on a footstool at his feet, Farrar dragged his attention from the sheen the sunlight awoke on her curls, and asked apologetically, "Asked for—what, Norrie?"

"Oh, a pox on the boy!" exclaimed the solicitor, casting an irked glance at the ceiling.

"Poor Mr. Norris has been trying to tell you," said Lady Helen, looking with amusement from her nephew's adoring eyes to Dimity's blushes. "You really must try to pay him a *little* heed, Anthony."

How splendid it was, thought Farrar, to hear her speak his name again. "Yes. Well, I am," he said, directing a contrite grin at the solicitor. "You must try to bear with me, Norrie. It is taking me a little while to get used to," he gave a rather shy gesture, "to—all this."

Norris looked at him soberly and reflected on the changes the

332

past three weeks had effected in this house; on the once deserted drivepath, for instance, that was now seldom quiet for long without some coach came rattling up it, full of people eager to make amends to this man they had despised and shunned. For Lady Helen, unfortunately, her nephew's vindication had brought pain as well as joy, and her loveliness was marred by a sorrow that persisted despite all Anthony's efforts to dispell it. There were rumours, however, that Major Rhodes had called at The Palfreys several times while Sir Anthony lay ill, and had twice taken my lady for a short drive to get her out of the sickroom. Nor could one fail to note that when his name was mentioned sorrow fell away from Lady Helen, and a glow came into her eyes that augured well for her future happiness. Most noticeable by its absence was the quiet despair that had haunted Farrar and that awful guilt-ridden humility that had been so painful to witness. Only look at the boy now! Be curst if it didn't make one wonder if there wasn't something to all this "love" business, after all . . .

He realized with a start that they were all waiting. "Ar—rumph!" he said gruffly. "Where was I? Oh, yes—about Walter. You'll likely not recall it, Tony, but when you were both quite small, Walter contracted a childhood ailment. Your papa chanced to mention it to me. He was quite cast down, because it—er," he glanced uneasily at Dimity, "it resulted in Walter's being—ah, unable to ever—um, sire any children."

Farrar asked, "And are we able to prove that, sir?"

"As I was saying, that is why I needed your mama's diary. It was in there, sure enough, together with the name of the attending physician."

"Norrie sent for us all," said Lady Helen. "Mrs. Deene, and her man of business, and myself, and Norrie read the deposition from the physician who had taken care of Walter all those years ago."

"As you might imagine," grunted Norris, "the Deene woman ranted and raved and screamed, and then went off on another—er, tack, so that I had to threaten her with a charge of attempted fraud to get rid of her."

"And then," my lady put in, "if you can believe it, Anthony, she went rushing out, and when the poor child made to follow her, she turned on him like a fishwife, berating and slapping him and saying he was a viper and an ingrate, and that he could march straight back into the Foundling Home for all she cared!''

"Wretched creature," said Dimity, indignant. "He will certainly not be placed in a Foundling Home, will he, Anthony?''

"No, he will not," declared a deep voice from the doorway, "Helen and I mean to adopt him—with your permission, Farrar."

Dimity jumped up, and Farrar stood also, leaning on her arm a little unsteadily as he turned to the tall soldier who watched him hopefully.

"Major!" he said, beaming as Rhodes came gladly to shake hands. "I've wondered why you did not claim my lovely aunt long since."

The major, having made his bow to Dimity, crossed to kiss his lady's hand, then draw a chair close beside her. "As I've told you," he explained, "I was rather badly mauled during the battle. For a while they," he cleared his throat, embarrassed, "well, they er, thought I might not walk again, so when you did not answer my first letter, I thought it best to—er . . . well, there you are."

"Yes. I see. Well, I'm jolly glad you're to be part of the family, sir."

"And I shall be jolly glad when you are sitting down again, Captain Farrar," said Dimity, tugging firmly at his hand until he grinned and allowed her to settle him on the sofa once more. She occupied the footstool, then turned to the major and Lady Helen and exclaimed, "Good gracious! I neglected to offer you my congratulations!"

They looked at her uneasily.

Farrar chuckled. "You are quite sure, Miss Mitten?" he asked. "You seem more dismayed than pleased."

"Oh dear. I *am* sorry. Truly, I wish you both happy, but—I'll own myself just a little disappointed. I had rather hoped Carlton would come to—er, *me*." She glanced from under her lashes at Farrar's suddenly grave countenance. "If—of course, he proved to be unrelated to you, Anthony."

Farrar was silent.

Lady Helen said gently, "But you see, my dear, Carlton *is* related to Anthony."

Dimity's pretty lower lip sagged. "But—Mr. Norris said—I mean—Anthony . . . ? I do not understand."

The major said, "Farrar don't either, m'dear."

Lady Helen smiled sadly. "We decided to tell you both at once. I wish it were not necessary for it is an unpleasant tale, and a shameful one."

Dimity twisted around to again scan her love's face. "Perhaps we should wait for another time, ma'am. I think Anthony is getting tired."

"Thank you, but I am quite all right," said Farrar, his fingers resting briefly upon her soft hair, his eyes ineffably tender. "And in my experience, Mitten, 'tis best to get unpleasant matters over and done with as quickly as possible. Pray go on, Aunt."

My lady began: "From the start I marvelled that Carlton bore so marked a resemblance to the Farrar children. We suspected, of course, that Mrs. Deene had sought for a boy with the same colouring, but I found it difficult to believe that she had managed to find one who not only had such a strong family resemblance, but who had obviously been properly bred up. I asked Norrie to look into Carlton's background. This was not an easy task, but Norrie has a man he sometimes employs in such investigations, and he discovered that . . . " she bit her lip and hesitated.

"We discovered," said Mr. Norris, taking up the story in his dry, rasping voice, "that Mr. Walter Farrar and Sir Harding Farrar had more in common than the fact that they were cousins." He cleared his throat, and peered over his spectacles at the circle of intent faces, his expression somewhat apprehensive. "Your pardon, but I must be blunt. Miss Mary Arnold was an excessively beautiful but not very well-bred young woman. Still, she was shrewd and had learned how to behave and how to dress, and because of her beauty she acquired admirers who took her into Society. She met Walter Farrar at a party in '39, and he fell deeply in love with her. One evening, he took her to Drury Lane. They encountered his cousin. I scarcely need remind any of you that Harding Farrar was an exceeding handsome and dashing young man, besides which he was very wealthy." Again, he paused, glancing at my lady, but she avoided his eyes, looking down instead at Major Rhodes' strong hand firmly clasping her own.

"Miss Arnold," the solicitor went on, "saw in Harding a

much better prospect than Walter, and Harding was captivated by her. He did not offer marriage, but he showered her with gifts. Within the month she became his—ahem—*chere amie*, shall we say. She was determined, however, to become Lady Harding Farrar and evidently she was so foolish as to think he would marry her if she bore him a child. She had misread her man. Harding was not one to accept responsibility and when he learned she was increasing, he was furious.''

Lady Helen turned her face away at this point, and Farrar murmured, ''Easy, Norrie.''

The solicitor pursed his lips. ''Your pardon, my lady, but—truth is truth. At all events, Harding paid Miss Arnold a small sum of money and cut her off completely. I suspect that she had every intention of coming here and attempting to obtain help, but evidently Harding managed to so frighten her that she turned instead to Walter. He, poor fellow, was still lost in love for her. He was an honourable man and it may be that he felt partially responsible for his cousin's behaviour, although I suspect that he was so besotted over the woman that he would have done anything in his power to help her, even if it had not been his cousin who'd ruined her. He bought her a nice little house and provided her with an allowance. Her ambitions soared far beyond Walter, but he suited her for the time, so she took him for her lover, but refused his dearest wish, which was that she become his wife. His uncle, Lord Elsingham, was enraged when he learned of their liaison and told Walter he would cut him off without a penny if he married her. Walter knew that Miss Arnold wanted riches and, desperate, he went out to Jamaica, promising her that he would come home a wealthy man. Each quarter, without fail, he sent funds for her support. He made only one stipulation: that she have young Carlton reared and instructed as became the son of a gentleman.''

Lady Helen said, ''Miss Arnold had no room in her head or her life for an active little boy. She had other admirers now, I suppose. She put Carlton in the care of her maid's parents, but there was always the chance that Walter really would make a fortune, so she complied with his wishes, and the child was taught proper speech and manners. And then, Mary suddenly became ill and died.''

Much shocked, Dimity cried, ''But—Carlton told me he had

no mother or father! Did she never go to see her own child, Mr. Norris?''

"Never. She paid for his care and ensured his proper guidance, is all. Mrs. Deene knew the whole story, of course, and she lost no time in writing to tell Walter of her sister's demise. She was, she told him, newly widowed and would be willing to care for the child if he could continue to provide funds. Otherwise, she would have no alternative but to place Carlton in a Foundling Home. Walter was not in any way bound to continue his financial support, but he did so. From that time until his own death, the monies were sent regularly to Mrs. Deene.'' Again, his eyes glinted at them over his spectacles. "I might add that on the day she received the first payment, Mrs. Deene took the boy from the couple who had been paid to care for him and abandoned him at the Foundling Home.''

"Where he'd likely have stayed, poor little fellow," put in Farrar, grimly, "had Mrs. Deene not learned that before he died Walter had amassed a sizeable fortune.''

"Exactly so," said my lady. "She saw her opportunity at once. Carlton *was* a Farrar. She must have been sure that between the family likeness and the papers she'd had forged, she could pass him off as *Walter's* legal heir. After all, no one knew he was Harding's child.''

"So she used him," muttered Dimity, "to bring her to the fortune! Oh, what a horrid woman she is, to be sure! But—when she realized she could not pass off Carlton as Walter's heir, did she not try to capitalize on his being Harding's natural son?''

"She would have caught cold at that," said Norris, "and she knew it. Her sister had left Harding and moved in with Walter, who had supported her and the boy for some years. Legally, Carlton has no claim to any inheritance, although Lady Helen has now made very generous provision for him.''

Dimity looked at Helen's anxious face and exclaimed, "So— you have a grandson, ma'am! Of course you want him with you. How splendid for you! And for him! I am *so* glad!''

"Thank you, you are very good." My lady was watching Farrar. "Are you very disappointed, dearest? I know how fond you have become of the child.''

"I'll own that," he said, smiling at her. "But I think he will go on very well in a household where he is a loved grandson.

337

Rather better, perhaps, than were he the eldest child in a growing family but not the—er, heir apparent, as it were.'' He tugged one of Dimity's ringlets, and she blushed furiously.

They all laughed. The major said, ''If you are wondering about my feelings, Tony, you may be sure I am delighted. I have been blessed to win my lady, at last, but we are not of an age to have children of our own. Now, I shall have a fine young fellow to guide and care for. You may be sure you will see plenty of him. But—I think none of this came as a great surprise to you, did it?''

Helen's head jerked to her nephew. ''You—*knew* that Carlton was Harding's boy?'' she gasped.

Embarrassed, Farrar shrugged. ''I rather suspected he was. When Norrie was so anxious to obtain Mama's diary for 1720 I puzzled at it and remembered a remark Uncle Gilbert had once made about my brother's health. After that, it was relatively simple. The family resemblance and the fact that I was so drawn to Carlton could not be denied. Certainly, he was not my son. Nor, it seemed, was he Walter's. There was only one other answer.''

My lady shook her head at him. ''Yet you said nothing. Protecting me again?''

He flushed. ''I—er, was just waiting for Norrie to prove his case.''

''Well, I have proved another, Farrar,'' said the solicitor, closing his bag. ''I'd expected you'd have been asking me about it.''

Farrar said, ''I think there was little of mystery there, sir. Rafe Green and I had long been at daggers drawn. He and Ellsworth were always after Harding to play cards. I objected because the stakes were much too high.''

''Did you know,'' barked Mr. Norris, ''that Hibbard Green gave his son a great sum of money that was to be used to refurbish Fayre Hall?''

Farrar looked at him, mystified.

''Rafe lost much of the money to Harding,'' Norris went on, ''and, while in his cups, entrusted the rest to Phillip Ellsworth, who knew of a horse that 'couldn't lose.' Needless to say, it lost. Rafe was terrified lest his father discover the truth, and he begged Harding to lend back the cash he'd won. Harding said he would gladly do so, save that you had warned him that if he squandered any more of the estate funds, you would make it known to your uncle Elsingham who, as head of your house, would have him declared incompetent.''

Farrar smiled mirthlessly. "That piece of news must have really endeared me to Phillip and Rafe."

"Very true," said Norris. "You and Harding went off to Scotland, and while you were gone, Lord Green learned how matters stood. He was enraged and told Rafe in no uncertain terms that he was to replace the monies entrusted to him or be disowned. Rafe was frantic. Your cousin Ellsworth has long coveted The Palfreys and all that goes with it. When Harding was killed, you were the only obstacle to his inheriting. The two rogues put their heads together. Rafe promised to help Ellsworth by getting rid of you—which he hoped his dogs would manage for him. In return, as soon as Ellsworth inherited the fortune, he was to repay Rafe's losses, Fayre Hall would be restored, and everyone would be happy."

Lady Helen shook her head sadly. "I would never have dreamed Phillip could be so wicked, or so cunning."

"Well, he wasn't, ma'am," said Norris. "Old Hibbard soon wormed the plot out of his son. He approved it, but probably guessed those two nincompoops lacked the brains to murder Tony without being caught, so *he* decided to mastermind the scheme."

Beginning to look worn and very grim, Farrar said slowly, "I'm not really surprised. I might have known neither Ellsworth nor Rafe was capable of concocting such a devious plot. The impostor who came from Whitehall to tell me of my—disgrace; the rumour mongering; the families who were visited and told I was to blame for their bereavements . . . So much trouble; so many details to be handled."

Norris said, "And well worth the effort if they'd managed to drive you to self-destruction, or so paved the way that you could be disposed of without suspicion falling on them! Shall you press charges, Farrar? If we can find 'em, that is."

Farrar looked at him sharply. Norris shrugged. "There was quite a commotion in the courtroom when you collapsed, my boy. By the time the smoke cleared, our Grand Inquisitor and Phillip Ellsworth were least in sight. Word is that because of his

339

son's serious injuries at your hands, my lord has taken Rafe to Spain to recuperate. I rather doubt they will dare show their noses in England for some considerable time to come.''

"And I rather think,'' said Dimity, who had been watching Farrar closely, "that our invalid must rest now, ladies and gentlemen . . .''

When the door closed behind them, she returned to her footstool. Farrar was leaning back with his eyes closed, but another visitor had slipped in. Swimmer had taken possession of his lap and was purring grittily into the curve of his hand.

Dimity sat very still, watching him lovingly. His eyes opened and he returned her gaze, not speaking.

After a quiet moment, she said, "You look very sombre for a man who has won his battles, sir. Of what are you thinking?''

"I was wondering,'' he answered gravely, "whatever would have become of me if a madcap girl had not taken it upon herself to confound a troop of dragoons and descend upon my home like—like—''

"A hurricane?'' she asked, with the soft little chuckle he so loved.

"God send I am never again becalmed,'' he murmured, and reached down to touch her hair.

She nestled her cheek against his hand. "Anthony . . . I have often wondered . . .''

He put the protesting kitten down and drew Dimity to sit beside him on the sofa. "Yes, Mrs. Deene?''

"All those long terrible months, when your aunt thought—I mean when she suspected—''

"That I had killed Harding?'' He kissed her temple lingeringly.

"Yes,'' she said with a happy shiver. "Did you not ever . . . that is—how could you have gone on—loving her?''

He ran the tip of his finger around her cheekbone. "I told you how very kind she was when I was a child. You don't stop loving someone because they are not always as you would wish—and besides, Helen stayed here when her every instinct must have been to go far away from me. She loved Harding very deeply, you know.'' He glanced up when she did not answer, and flushed a little. "Now, why do you look at me like that?''

340

Her heart very full, Dimity murmured one of her favourite quotations,

> *" 'Love alters not with his brief hours and weeks,*
> *But bears it out even to the edge of doom.'*

"And—my very dear, you truly were—at the very edge of doom . . . Oh, Tony—how splendid you are . . . And how very much I—"

It was really remarkable, she thought in a remote way, that a man who had been so very ill could yet be so strong . . .

"Good . . . gracious . . . !" she gasped, when he at last released her lips and she lay weakly in his arms. "Have you spoken to my brothers, sir?"

"About—what?" he asked innocently.

"Anthony . . . Farrar . . ."

"Oh. Do you mean that you expect me to ask for your hand in marriage? Well, I would you know, but—I will confess—my heart was given some time ago. Beyond recall . . ."

Dimity eyed him narrowly. He looked so bland, but the side of his mouth was quivering suspiciously. She reached up and slipped her hand around the back of his neck.

"To a fascinating creature," he continued, as his head was slowly pulled down, "who was fond of ashes and . . ."

After a long, ecstatic pause, with wanton if rather breathless provocation he went on, "And who had a most delicious collection of gowns. They were a trifle short, and somewhat lacking in the way of bodices, but . . ."

Another pause, then Dimity whispered, "Are you quite finished, evil one?"

"But it has been my hope," gasped Farrar, "to ask her to wear the blue one again, on . . ."

Some minutes later, Dimity opened her eyes. "On—what . . . ?" she asked faintly.

"What . . . ?" echoed Farrar, dazed, delighted, and quite distracted with love. "Oh . . ." He smiled down into her flushed and beautiful face. "On," he murmured, bending until their lips were just a breath apart, "our . . . wedding day . . . my most adored . . . Mistress Mitten . . ."

It was very difficult, Swimmer discovered, to find a suitable lap. She jumped about without much success and at length clawed her way up the master's sleeve to his shoulder. En route, she thought to hear a muffled protest, but settled herself contentedly. She thought she heard another, equally muffled, protest when she began the necessary business of kneading his coat, but he was evidently too occupied to put a stop to her activities, so she continued until, purring loudly, she went to sleep.

⌒ *About the Author* ⌒

Patricia Veryan was born in London, England, and moved to the United States after World War II. She now lives in Riverside, California. Ms. Veryan is the recipient of the first Barbara Cartland Silver Cup for Idealizing Romance and the *Romantic Times* has said of her "... if Georgette Heyer is considered the Queen of Regency Romance, then Patricia Veryan must surely be declared a Princess."

ROMANCING ADVENTURE...

by Patricia Veryan

Allow at least 4 weeks for delivery.